'Fast

Victoria Selman

'I couldn't put it down ... A compulsive and complex
tale of the toxic effects of revenge'
Mary-Jane Riley

'Mind blown! The end was a triumph, absolutely brilliant!'
Rona Halsall

'A compulsive story that oozes such a sense of injustice you
can't stop turning the page to find out if revenge is taken ...
An addictive page-turner'
Samantha Tonge

'Gripping and powerful! The tension in the novel was cranked
up notch by notch until I was gasping as the story unravelled'
Lauren North

'School run revenge at its best'
Jacqueline Ward

'Hard to put down! ... the ending is as dramatic and
surprising as Zoe Lea's clever writing promises'
Marianne Holmes

'So clever. Reading it as a mother, you can't help but question
yourself throughout: Would I do that? Would I go that far?'
Laura Pearson

'[A] page turner'
Barbara Copperthwaite

Zoe Lea lives in the Lake District, UK with her husband, two children, dogs and peregrine falcons. As well as writing, she helps manage an animal tracking company used for raptors and other wildlife. She's previously worked as a teacher, photographer and in the television industry, but writing has always been her passion. She is currently working on her next novel, *The Influencer*.

To find out more about Zoe, visit her website www.zoelea.com or follow her on social media:

@zoeleawriter
/zoeleawriter
/zoeleawriter

the Secretary

ZOE LEA

PIATKUS

PIATKUS

First published in Great Britain in 2019 by Piatkus
This paperback edition published in 2020 by Piatkus

1 3 5 7 9 10 8 6 4 2

A CIP catalogue record for this book
is available from the British Library.

ISBN 978-0-349-42268-8

Typeset in Garamond by M Rules
Printed and bound in Great Britain by
Clays Ltd, Elcograf S.p.A.

Papers used by Piatkus are from well-managed forests
and other responsible sources.

Piatkus
An imprint of
Little, Brown Book Group
Carmelite House
50 Victoria Embankment
London EC4Y 0DZ

An Hachette UK Company
www.hachette.co.uk

www.littlebrown.co.uk

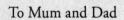

To Mum and Dad

ONE

You're getting these letters, aren't you?

I thought the prison was stopping them, they confiscate stuff in here for no reason sometimes and I thought that might be it. But it's been six months and I've been writing every few weeks since I began my sentence. That's seventeen letters and not one reply. Not one. That's cruel. I knew you could be bitter, but this is a bit much, even for you.

You want me to beg? OK, I'm begging. Please, for Christ's sake, please write me a bloody letter. Anything. A postcard, a scrawl on the back of an envelope, even you can do that. Before I came in here, you promised to visit, to write. I'm not asking for a visit, I know you won't come and see me, but I need a letter.

I need to be able to write to someone who was there when it happened. I only had the light from my mobile phone, I didn't

1

have a torch. I could only see shadows and it happened so fast. I can still see the expression of that woman police officer. She was so young; do you remember her? You said you wouldn't trust her to write out a parking ticket, never mind sort out what happened that night. And her face! It went white when she saw and she put her hand over her mouth. Was she sick? I remember the screams, or am I imagining the screams? That's why I need you to write, because it's blurring around the edges. I've thought about it too much. I'm not certain how it happened any more and I feel like I'm going mad.

I keep thinking of the Border Reivers, those raiders who invaded the border and were put in the castle as a prison. We went there on a day trip, about six years ago. You were wearing those sunglasses, the ones you thought made you look like you were in an eighties movie and you lost them in the café. We went to Queen Mary's Tower, she was held captive there for a while. You didn't like the prisoner's carvings on the second floor of the keep because some were so detailed, so finely engraved and labour intensive, you thought it was depressing, but that's exactly how I feel.

Like I want to carve the memory of that night into stone, solidify it. I want to spend hours going over and over the same line, just to get it out of my head and somewhere else. Did you know that Kinmont Willie was one of the prisoners in there? He was a notorious raider and a large group of his friends broke into the castle to free him. I keep thinking that you'll free me.

Write me a letter. Anything. Tell me you were there when it happened. It's been long enough, and I'm so very, very sorry. Please, I can't stand the company of my own mind any longer.

TWO

Seven months earlier

I've often thought there's a secret pact between mothers. A pact so unspoken and private, most don't realise they're in it. *You* don't realise you're in it until you hear yourself telling someone who isn't a medical professional just how unreliable your pelvic floor muscles are. A person who, under regular circumstance, you would never speak to, never mind tell them that you can no longer go on a trampoline without peeing a little, and yet here you are.

You listen to their confessions about how they lost their child in the park for a minute, or how they ate three chocolate bars in the car without taking breath, and you can't stop yourself. You join in, admit your faults and enter into the pact that makes it all right to have these conversations with virtual strangers.

You give unwanted advice, make judgements, discuss

intimate details with people you have nothing in common with, other than you are both mothers, and it's fine. It's all fine. And then the kids stop playing, the soft play shuts, the party ends and it's time to go home and everyone goes back to their normal lives, forgetting that they've shared something private, showed their underbelly.

But again, it's fine. And that's because of the other thing that ties parents together in this secret pact: the unspoken understanding of love.

The love we have for our kids: it cuts through all the bullshit and allows this kind of behaviour to take place. We are all agreed that we'd do anything for our kids, and this understanding is a great leveller. It's also what led me to be waiting in an empty car park at six-thirty in the morning that September.

It was the third week of a new term, a fresh school year. The leaves had not yet turned, jackets were not yet needed and the sky was as clear and bright as if it were still late July. I wound down the window, breathed in the hot air and looked at the tarmac as it sparkled in the sunlight.

'Thanks, Mum.' Sam, my eight-year-old son, was in the passenger seat beside me. I turned to him, his face still puffy from sleep, the curve of his cheek particularly round and full, his hands clenched in a tight ball on his lap, and felt a rush of love, a familiar clench.

We were waiting for Gary, the school caretaker. I reached over and smoothed down the back of Sam's hair. It was sticking up from where he'd been sleeping.

'You don't need to thank me.' I gave his hand a squeeze. 'I'll speak to Miss Gleason this morning, before school starts. Promise.'

He nodded, keeping his eyes on the building in front of us. It was a squat thing, late seventies in style, and the interior, although covered by children's artwork, was much the same as the exterior, badly in need of refurbishment. It was a relatively small school but it had a great Ofsted report and a reputation for being very nurturing. It was why we were here and why I was overjoyed when Sam got a place.

'Miss Hooden was good,' Sam said quietly. 'Why couldn't I stay with Miss Hooden? I liked Miss Hooden.'

'Because Miss Hooden teaches year three and you're in year four now.' I smiled, but his eyes were fixed on the empty car park. 'Miss Gleason teaches year four.'

He nodded. 'I liked Miss Hooden,' he said. 'She isn't nasty like Miss Gleason.'

'Miss Gleason isn't nasty,' I told him. 'She's just trying to get you to do your best work.'

I followed his gaze. I'd been working at the school for nine months; three more and I'd be made permanent. It'd been such a triumph to get the job of school secretary. I hardly dared believe it when I got the call, but they were desperate as the last secretary had left abruptly and it helped that I knew one of the teachers, Becca, and that Sam was a pupil there so I knew some of the staff, but still, it was a surprise.

And it had been wonderful, it meant I was there for Sam and that I could talk to his teachers about how best to handle his needs. It meant I could tell Sam confidently that I could sort this little episode he'd had, that I'd see his class teacher, Miss Gleason, and would be able to talk to her as a colleague as well as a parent. She'd been supportive so far, but there was more she could do. She was new, I didn't know her as well as the others, but I would, I'd make a friend of her.

5

'Will I have to live with my dad now?' he suddenly asked, and I felt myself contract.

'What? No, of course not, where did that come from?'

He paused. 'Last time I was with Dad he said that if I got into trouble again, he'd make me live with him.'

I did my best to contain the shot of anger that swooped up inside of me.

'And now I've done this –' his bottom lip stuck out, trembling '– so does this mean that I'll have to go live with him?'

'Listen to me.' I leaned over so I was close to his face and took both of his hands in mine. Warm little things, chubby fingers. 'You are never going to live with anyone else other than me, understand?'

He gave a small nod, but his eyes told me he was unsure.

'No matter what your dad says, you are with me for ever. I won't let anyone take you away, not even your dad. OK?'

A fat tear plopped down his cheek, and not for the first time I wanted to strangle Will, my ex-husband. I leaned over and wrapped my arms around Sam and swallowed down the anger. It was something I was used to, pushing down the rage at my ex-husband. I know most divorced women will tell you that their ex is a wanker and an idiot but mine really was. First rate. And with each passing day and new stupid thing he did, he grew into his wanker persona even more. But threatening to make Sam live with him? This was new. He'd made noises about visitation rights and custody before, but saying it outright to Sam was new. It seemed we were on another level of prize wanker-dom. Oh joy.

'Here we go,' I said, as a familiar Renault swung into the car park. 'You OK, sweetie?'

He nodded, wiping his face, hands scraping over his soft

cheek, trying to get it together. 'Thanks, Mum,' he said, but it was barely above a whisper and there was that inner clench again, the grasping of my love for him tugging at my heart. I'd deal with Will later.

'Stop thanking me,' I told him. 'I'm your mum, this is what I do.' I kissed him, smiled and waited for him to smile back at me before we got out of the car.

'Bit keen, aren't you?' Gary looked at his watch. 'It's not yet seven.'

I smiled, warmly I hoped. Sam's hand in mine as we followed Gary up the driveway to the school. 'I needed to get on with some paperwork,' I lied, 'before the rush starts with the parents.'

He rolled his eyes. 'Oh, don't get me started about the bloody parents,' he said, unlocking the gates, although that's exactly what I wanted to do. 'Only three weeks in and the stuff I'm having to deal with.'

'I'm chasing up money for the residential,' I told him. 'Should have been paid in full before the summer holidays, they go away at half term and most parents have still only paid the deposit, and don't get me started on the consent forms. Be thankful you've not got a morning ringing around asking for cash and allergy information.'

This got a shake of the head and a *pfft* sound, as I knew it would. Gary was from a time when parents had little say in anything to do with their children's school.

'Allergy information!' he scoffed. 'Bloody kids are allergic to everything these days.' He unlocked doors and switched off alarms as he spoke, me and Sam following him. 'Even fresh air! You heard about what's going on in year one? What they've got me doing now?'

7

'No, what's that?'

I did, in fact, know all about the year one parents and how they'd demanded the windows in there only open from the top. It had all happened within the first few days of term when a slightly fussy woman, on kissing her son goodbye, had observed a teaching assistant opening a window. Even though they had safety catches on, she deemed them unsafe, claiming that any adventurous five-year-old could, if they had the mind to, escape.

I had typed up the reports, the complaints, logged the minutes of the meetings. Been in contact with the governors and the PTA, the health and safety officers at the LEA. I knew more about it than Gary but I let him tell me. Kept him talking while he switched on lights and brought the school to life. I got to my office and put down my bag, Sam's tense small body at the side of me. I had to unpick his hand so I could take off my jacket.

'So,' Gary went on, 'it'll cost a fortune, all have to be done in half term, and by the time it's sorted it'll be winter and no bugger will want to open the windows anyway.'

I pointed to a chair in the corner and Sam slowly went to it.

'Well then,' I said, and switched on the computer. Gary loitered in the doorway.

'Actually, Ruth, I'm glad I've caught you early. You couldn't do us a favour, could you?' He pulled out a piece of A4 from his pocket and handed it to me. 'I wouldn't ask, only it's for charity and there's a few local businesses donating stuff. I just thought . . .'

I unfolded the paper to see a poster advertising a bring and buy that was to be held in the church hall.

'When is it?'

Gary pointed to the bottom of the poster. 'Saturday. We've a few cakes already, from the Mothers' Union, but –' he shook his head '– one of yours would really set it off.'

Next Saturday, less than a week to bake and decorate a cake for no payment. I had thirty fairy cakes to bake for one of the dinner staff by Friday and hoped to get some things together for the farmers' market on Sunday. I didn't have any time to bake for no profit.

'It's good exposure,' Gary said, 'and it's for charity. Sue said you were doing her some cakes for her fiftieth and I thought you could just . . .' He gestured to the advert.

This was the problem with trying to run a small business on the side: everyone thought you could do it for free. It had taken me almost six months to get Custom Cakes up and running, and the most requests I seemed to get were people asking for freebies.

'I can give you a dozen cupcakes,' I said, thinking that I'd increase the batch I had planned for Sue. 'Swirl topping in rainbow icing with a neon case, how's that?'

'Brilliant,' Gary said. 'How about I get you a coffee as a thank you?'

'Lovely,' I told him, and managed to stay smiling until he left.

I turned to Sam. 'Right,' I said brightly, 'shall I do it now?'

His eyes went wide.

'I won't be long, and if he comes back while I'm gone just tell him I've gone to the loo.' I glanced at the clock on the wall, 'I'll have to do it now, sweetheart, before people start arriving, or I won't be able to do it at all.'

Sam stared at me a moment before giving a little nod.

'Ask him about football,' I said. 'Just say, "Blue Army" – that'll keep him going.'

I went to my bag and took out what Sam had shown me last night, his yellow exercise book and the accompanying maths one. The words 'school property' stamped on the front which had got Sam all in a state and kept us both up half the night.

'Won't be a second.' I gave his worried face a small kiss and went down the corridor past the hall.

It was silly really, but Sam insisted we do it this way. He didn't want the rest of his class to know that he couldn't do the work. He was having serious trouble with one boy and was terrified of adding 'stupid' to his list of taunts. In his anxious state, he'd stolen the books from school and brought them home to me so I could explain it to him. And, as I was the school secretary, he knew we could put the books back before anyone found out, or rather, *I* could put the books back.

I had tried to persuade him that we tell Miss Gleason together, that she wasn't doing her job very well if Sam had to steal his books and bring them home, but Sam had gone hysterical at the suggestion. The thought of needing yet more special attention was mortifying and I could understand that. There were several things the school were doing to accommodate his anxieties, small things like letting him have the clothes peg next to the door, allowing him always to sit in the same chair and never making him line up with the others. They were only silly things, but they singled Sam out, made him a bit of a target to the less understanding children in his class, and he couldn't bear the thought of getting more unwanted attention by not understanding school work.

I was seeing Miss Gleason to deal with Toby, the boy who was bullying Sam, and as he was currently going through a cycle of struggling with PE and all that entailed, I'd relented. I'd agreed to help him with his division and then return the books before anyone found out, on the basis that he let me speak to Miss Gleason alone about the maths situation, so we could discuss how best to support him with no fuss and without his classmates being made aware.

I went into the classroom and switched on the lights. Sam had told me where his tray was, over by the back wall, but for a moment I stood where I was. In front of the whiteboard, all the chairs and tables facing me. I'd wanted to be a teacher. Back when I was at college. I'd even gone so far as to get the application forms, but then something happened, a boy or an offer of employment in town, and I'd been too impatient to start earning. Teacher training had seemed such a long process when I was eighteen. I thought about it again when Sam was born, those school holidays, the hours, but it wasn't feasible then. Will had dismissed the idea, telling me that teaching wasn't a job in the 'real world', that I'd be bored talking to kids all day, and at the time I believed the wanker so I didn't pursue it. Fool that I was.

I went over to the desk at the front. Miss Gleason had some kind of reward chart on the wall behind it and a pile of gold stickers in the shape of stars were on her desk. I picked one of them up. Sam had told me about the gold stars. They were big news. I looked at his name on the chart, how many stars he had compared to his classmates. He was woefully behind.

She had a mug with 'best teacher' written on and a file full of what looked like lesson plans and teaching notes. At the side of it was a red pen with a silly cluster of feathers on the top. This was the pen she used to mark the work. I'd seen it in Sam's maths book, all that ticking and crossing. The underlining she'd done over his poor working out, the numbers that he sometimes still put down back to front. Those snippy little

11

comments: 'Must try harder Sam!' I put my finger to the nib and drew a red dot on my finger tip.

And taped to the desk, she had a list of everyone in the class and their birthday, so she'd know when to make the class sing. When to give what child attention. I'd typed that up for her. I did it for all the teachers so they'd look good to the kids. I took a moment before going to the back of the classroom where the trays were.

I found Sam's tray and had a quick look through the stuff inside. There were some drawings – animals, roller coasters, the usual. A couple of test papers in which he'd done OK, those annoying big red underlines and another snippy comment, 'Good try'. Some spelling work, handwriting practice and I took a moment over his spidery letters. His carefully drawn words, I knew he'd have done them with his tongue sticking out, his fingers tightly wound around the pencil, and then I placed the stolen books on top and closed his tray.

I'd see Miss Gleason, Lisa, when Sam was in breakfast club, before the day started. I'd catch her as soon as she arrived. I'd tell her about it all, confess that he'd brought the books home, tell her how worried he was. I'd ask her to give him a gold star, not for bringing his work home but for caring about it so much. He was so anxious to do well. If Lisa spoke to him, reassured him and told him to come to her if he needed any help rather than stuffing his maths book up his jumper, then gave him a gold star because he was trying so hard, it might just work towards him feeling secure in the class. It might help with all the other stuff.

I switched off the lights and could make out distant voices as I walked back to my office. People were arriving already.

'It's all to do with the strategy,' I could hear Gary telling

Sam. 'Carlisle United have a long, firm reputation and you can't just—'

'Blue Army!' I sang as I went in and Gary smiled.

'Your mum gets it,' he said, 'she knows.'

'Thanks for the coffee.' I went over to my desk. 'OK if I bring those cakes into school on the Friday, give them to you then?'

'Perfect.' Gary smiled broadly. 'I could kiss your mother sometimes,' he told Sam, ruffling his hair. 'She's the best thing about this godforsaken school.'

'Flattery will get you everywhere,' I told him. 'Now I think it's time we got you,' I said, turning to Sam, 'into breakfast club, so I can get on with my work.'

Before we got to the hall I crouched down to Sam so I was level with his face.

'All done,' I told him, 'back in your tray. No one knows.'

He took a moment and I nodded. Reassuring him. He smiled hesitantly, a small dimple showing in his left cheek, and I could see him tentatively relax, his shoulders drop a little. 'Love you, Mum,' he whispered, and I hugged him tightly. Squeezed his shoulders, breathed in the scent of him and held his small body against mine.

'By the end of today,' I said into his hair, 'it will all be sorted. Promise.'

'Promise?'

I cupped his cheeks in my hands and kissed his forehead.

'Promise,' I told him. I watched him walk along the hall, find a space at one of the tables and pick up a book. I stayed a moment, making sure he was settled, then waved to Kim, the breakfast club supervisor. I turned to go back to my office, putting my hands in my pockets as I went. I felt something sharp suddenly stab me and grabbed the offending object.

13

It was the red feather pen from Miss Gleason's classroom. I'd taken it without realising. The silly feathers sticking up, the bright red barrel in my hand, a streak of ink along my finger. I took a step towards her classroom, then stopped.

The thought of her without it made me pause. I put it back in my pocket. She'd have to do all her crossing and snippy comments in another colour for today.

THREE

You wouldn't think a primary school reception area would be so busy, but that morning they were queuing out the door. Two were waiting for me when I got back from dropping Sam off at breakfast club, and in the three quarters of an hour I had before my job officially began I hadn't been able to leave once. There had been a steady stream of parents and grandparents.

My office directly faces the entrance to the school, and there's a small area in front where people (mostly parents) congregate. Mr Cartwright, John, the head of the school and my boss, has his office to the right, hidden away behind a small seating area and a large Swiss cheese plant. He'd raised his eyebrows as he entered, shuffled his large body through the throng of people with heavy breaths, then shut his door and that was it. He wouldn't come out again until he had to, wouldn't see a single parent without an appointment. Unlike me, he wasn't trapped behind a glass partition that's never closed and constantly available.

There's a slight chip in the glass of that partition, right at my eyeline, and a small silver bell is fixed to the desk beside the signing in book. Whoever fitted that bell has a sadistic sense of humour. It's a silver one, the type mostly seen in hotels, and people tended to ring it, repeatedly, even when they could see me. It was worse if a child got hold of it.

Once, an elderly man rang it and shouted, 'Two fish and chips, one with gravy', and since then I've never been able to shrug off the feeling of my office being like a kitchen. Like I'm taking orders, peeking out of the cubby hole and everyone's crowding in, waiting to be fed.

'The thing is,' the woman in front of me went on, 'that the supermarket ones don't have the school emblem on, and that should be a priority.' She was a fat little thing and sounded slightly asthmatic, the grandparent of some child in reception, and this was her third time blocking the reception area that week.

The man queuing behind her waved an envelope at me, coins rattled inside and I reached out. He passed it over the top of her head, me reaching awkwardly so as not to knock off her glasses, but she didn't pause for breath.

'What should be a priority is the fit,' she announced, 'and the durability.'

'Thanks,' he mouthed and went to leave. I glanced at the envelope, it was blank, no child's name, no class.

'Wait ... ' I called after him, but it was too late, he'd gone.

'And,' the woman went on, 'parents deserve the best for their children. And children deserve to be comfortable.'

It was at this point that I remembered I'd not yet eaten breakfast. My stomach churned, a familiar pang of hunger, and I looked to my bag where I'd optimistically packed a banana.

For the second time that week I wished I'd eaten the cereal I'd bought for Sam instead of thinking I could manage on fruit.

'Ruth?' It was Linda, the year six teacher. She'd entered the office from the door behind me that led directly into the school. She saw the grandparent at the hatch and almost about turned.

'Letters for the library system are just there,' I pointed to the shelf and she took them gratefully.

'You're a star,' she said before leaving. 'I owe you a drink.'

'You owe me more than one,' I said, but she'd already gone and the grandparent was still talking at me. She was rummaging in her bag now and I knew what was coming.

'Please,' I began but it was no good, she was pulling out the polo top, the school emblem sewed on the left breast.

'See?' she said thrusting it towards the glass partition, 'expertly done and not much more expensive than those in the supermarket.'

I took a moment.

'They're four times as expensive as those in the supermarket,' I told her gently, 'but I have shown it to Mr Cartwright, and if we think you can go on the official list he'll be in touch.'

I'd told her as much yesterday. She looked down at the polo shirt and ran her finger across the purple emblem. I got an image of her sitting by her sewing machine, attaching the school logo to countless white polo shirts, the idea of setting herself up as a uniform supplier. It was a ridiculous idea; the school could only recommend establishments that were approved by the governors and Lord knows who else. Something I'd told her the first time she visited but she seemed to have forgotten that information, thinking that if she showed me or someone her work, we'd change our minds.

There were two uniform suppliers currently on the school website and both were professional companies, reasonably priced and able to deal with a large demand. Not a lone grandparent with a sewing machine and few extra hours in the evening.

'Oh, give it here,' I told her quickly, and she looked up. 'I'll take this one into him and see if he can't show it to the governors, or whoever decides these things. Maybe they'll put you on the list as an independent set-up.'

Her face lit up, she went to say something but was stopped by a loud ring. We all froze, mid-pose. The school bell had that effect.

It was the first ring, five minutes and lessons would start. This was the cue for the children to line up in the playground, for the saying goodbye to parents, for the gathering of books and bags and lunch boxes, and it meant I only had five minutes in which to grab Miss Gleason. To tell her about the stolen homework, about how Sam was feeling, about her giving him a few of those gold stars.

'I'm so sorry,' I said, 'but I have to go. Just leave it there.' The grandparent nodded and began pushing the polo shirt through the glass partition.

'Thank you,' she was saying, 'you won't regret it, I work far better than any of those big companies.'

The woman behind went to protest and waved an envelope. I felt for her, she'd been waiting patiently for ten minutes.

'Just leave it there,' I told her and pointed to the area beside the bell. 'Please,' I told the rest of them, 'any payments just leave them on my desk and if there's anything urgent . . . ' I waved in the general area, 'I won't be long.'

I ducked out of the door ready to head down the corridor but was stopped by the breakfast club. They were filing down past the hallway, dropping off children into the classrooms as they went, Sam among them. If he saw me he'd realise that I'd not spoken to his teacher yet and that couldn't happen. My only chance was to go outside and get to Miss Gleason's classroom by way of the infant playground, through the main entrance. I could catch her before the majority of the children came in, it would only take a moment.

I hurried past the queue of parents and children who were all now trying to get out themselves and went onto the street, the quickest way to get to the lower end of the school. The sun was bright, just at that place where it's blinding, reflecting off the pavement and putting a white sheen over everything. I put my hand up to shade my eyes. There was a slight panic in the air, children running into school, parents shouting instructions and as I went past his car, I didn't think much of it, my mind too full of Sam, Miss Gleason and the gold stars.

It was parked on the double yellows outside the junior entrance, forcing parents and children to walk in the gutter. I went to scurry around it when the door opened and there he was. No more than a few yards in front of me, blocking my way and the sunlight from my eyes.

I felt my jaw slacken.

I imagine I must have looked like a cartoon character, chin hitting the floor, eyes on stalks, because that's exactly how I felt. I was aware of people rushing past me, of my heart beating wildly, but I couldn't move. He was helping a young girl out of the back seat. I watched as a pretty little thing came out, curly long hair, deep brown eyes, must've been about nine, and then another one came scrambling out behind her. Younger, maybe seven or so.

'Bye, Daddy!' she shouted to him, and a hot flush of adrenalin shot up through my torso.

He turned to a well-dressed woman who'd got out of the passenger seat and was handing out school bags and lunch boxes. She was older than me, early forties, with a face full of make-up and expensive jewellery. She looked familiar, like I should know her.

She raised her head to him and he kissed her on the lips. My hand went to my throat as he did so, my breath catching.

'See you later,' he said, pulling away from her.

'Don't be late.' There was a warning in her voice. 'Book club's at six.'

He gave a distracted nod. 'Be good!' he shouted to the girls as they walked away from him. 'Be good for your mum until I get home.' And then, with his car door open, as his wife and children disappeared into the playground, he sensed me.

Our eyes met.

It was definitely him.

He was wearing a grey suit, well-tailored, expensive looking, and his hair, which had been short when I last saw him, was longer, a floppy fringe against his forehead. My heart pounded, a flush went up through my body. The last time I'd seen him, I'd been naked. I'd been sweating and I'd been drunk.

He tilted his head. I could see his mind working as he remembered who I was. Who I was *to him*. I slowly went forward, my hand nervously fiddling at my collar. I didn't know how to behave; I felt as if the world had tilted on its axis.

'Hello,' I said, and he gave me a vague smile. 'Ruth,' I prompted, 'it's Ruth.' I waited a moment, and then, 'Quibeck Gym? Valentine's dinner?'

20

There was a moment before a look of complete horror passed over his features.

His eyes went round as his brain registered who I was and slotted me back into his past. I saw his body recoil a little, his eyes flick towards where his wife and children had just gone. A fleeting moment of terror.

'Oh,' he said, and gave a little laugh, '*it's you.*' He shifted nervously, moving his weight from one foot to the other until he was hiding behind his car door. 'Hello.'

There was a moment's silence.

'You're married?' I asked him.

He held up his hands, palms facing me. Car keys dangling from his thumb.

'You've got children?'

He waved his hands and there was a jangle of the keys. His eyes flitted from me to the school gates and then back again.

'February, wasn't it?' he asked with a small laugh, empty of humour. He rubbed his hand along his chin. 'God, I was hammered that night.'

'You told me you were single –' I was close enough now to see the fear in his eyes '– but you've got children here? Two girls? You said those things to me, we did those things, but you had children and a wife at home?'

For a second, he looked ashamed. He opened his mouth to say something, then thought better of it.

'Does she know?' I asked him, glancing towards the junior entrance. 'Were you on a break, was that it? Tell me you were separated when we met.'

He followed my stare, swallowed. I saw every muscle in his throat work. 'I wasn't even meant to be at that dinner,' he said, not meeting my eye. 'Bloody hell, I was drunk that night.' He ran his hand through his floppy fringe and looked at me. 'We were both drunk, weren't we?'

He smiled then. It was the smile he'd used on me the last time we'd met. A dip of his head, a look of mischief in his eyes, and I felt sick. 'Both out of it. Both of us completely hammered, what did we have – two? Three bottles of champagne?' he asked conspiratorially. 'We had a good time though, didn't we? You enjoyed it. Don't beat yourself up about it, you were drunk. What we did was nothing, it was just a bit of fun. Best forgotten.'

A familiar rush of mortification coursed along my body. 'A bit of fun? That night was a *bit of fun*?'

He winced at the sound of my voice.

'I tried calling you, but I thought I'd typed in the wrong number. I waited months for you to ring me.'

'Listen –' his voice was low '– that night, we were out of it. That dinner, it was terrible, full of sad desperate types on Valentine's.' He paused. 'As I remember you enjoyed it quite a lot. We both had a good time. Let's leave it at that, shall we?' He gave a curt nod, as if the matter were over.

'But you lied to me,' I said. 'You told me you never did that kind of thing either, you said you were single and you promised to call.'

A woman was watching us. I was aware of her in my peripheral vision, but I was too preoccupied with him. How to tell him how he made me feel all those months ago? How low I'd felt that night, how confused I was when I met him. How embarrassed I was the next morning and how desperately I wanted to explain to him who I really was, to tell him that I never behaved like that, that I was a different woman to the drunk one he met that night, but he never gave me a chance.

'I didn't even like you –' I shook my head '– that's the ironic part. I didn't even like you and yet you humiliated me.'

He bristled slightly. 'Have you followed me here?' he suddenly asked. 'Is that it? Is this some kind of *Fatal Attraction* shit?'

His words hit me like a slap.

'I work here,' I hissed back at him. 'I thought you were in Edinburgh, you told me—'

He waved his hands, stopping me and looked back to the school. 'It was what you wanted to hear.'

'What do you mean, what I wanted to hear? You came over to me, you got me drunk, you said—'

'Oh please.' He checked his watch, suddenly overcome with a business-like attitude. 'You're all the same. Sad, lonely divorcees. All up for it after a few glasses of prosecco and then clingy and desperate again the next morning. You knew the score that night, so don't give me all this "promising to call" shit. Now be a good girl and piss off.'

Rage roared in my ears. I heard a shocked gasp and realised it was me. 'You're unbelievable,' I whispered, 'what you did, those lies you told me. You're a complete monster.'

'Yeah? Well you wanted it that night, love, don't pretend you didn't, so if that makes me a monster then it makes you a slag.'

He slammed his car door.

I was rooted to the spot, unable to catch up with what had just happened. He reversed his car angrily and then screeched off, swerving around me.

The air was still. I stood frozen, watching the back of his car.

'Can I help?'

I turned and she was suddenly at the side of me. His wife.

Stood next to me, a confused smile playing on her lips, that familiar look about her, like we'd met before.

'It's Miss Clarkson, isn't it? You're the school secretary here.' She nodded. 'I'm so sorry we parked there, we were late. I know it's strictly forbidden but ...' Her words trailed off as she looked at my face. 'He didn't shout at you, did he?' She put her hand to my sleeve, a light touch of her fingers on my elbow. I could smell her perfume, flowery and strong. 'He's late for work, we were all late this morning and he can be irritable, insensitive. If he raised his voice—'

'He called her a slag.'

We all turned at the words; they came from a small boy with a pale face.

'He said she wanted it and called her a slag.'

'Ryan!' It was the woman who had been stood at the side of us, there throughout the whole thing. She put her hand over her son's mouth, as if to make him swallow his words back up. 'Stop that.'

I looked to his wife, who was staring at the woman and her boy, her face quizzical as she took in what the boy had said and then she turned back to me. I wasn't sure what expression my features were holding, what my face told her, but something in her eyes grasped the situation.

'I'm so sorry,' I found myself whispering to her. 'I didn't know he was married.'

The school bell rang. Slicing through the air.

It was the second ring, the one that meant the doors are closing, and it was only then that I got the first sense of what I'd just done by saying that to her, what I'd admitted to.

My arms went goosefleshy, a prickling panic crept up my body. There was silence. And for a moment it was just me and her. Her eyes locked on mine. And she was me, four years ago, learning it from one of Will's friends. He'd been poking fun about my love of fish and then realised he was talking to the wrong woman and a canyon of horror opened up before me. I could see her canyon open up before her, her life sliding into it, tumbling down.

'He's ill,' the woman with the boy said. 'I'm taking him back home, we only came to drop off his sister. I'm just waiting for my mother, she's taken Zara in. Ryan here's got a fever.' She put her hand on the boy's head. 'I thought some fresh air might do him good, but he doesn't know what he's saying.'

I recognised her. Eve, was it? She was chubby, fat cheeks, the kind that are always red. Her boy with the pale face was in the same class as Sam, I was sure. Ryan Trebank. A nice kid, I wanted Sam to make friends with him. I silently pleaded with her, tried to convey that I needed help here, that our boys were in the same class, and please, please, take the heat out of this situation.

'He doesn't know what he heard,' she offered, but it was useless. His wife had taken hold of my arm, her fingers tight around it.

'What do you mean, you didn't know he was married?'

There were two women a little way up the street, near the railings leading off from the main entrance, car keys in hands, laughing, but they'd stopped at her voice and were watching us.

A woman dressed in gym gear with a high ponytail came out of the school gates and joined us.

'Janine?' she asked, taking in the situation. 'What's going on?'

I realised that within minutes, all the other parents would soon be leaving. This moment of quiet would be over, the street would be full of people going back to their cars, back to their days. I needed to be in my office and off the street. I needed to speak to Sam's teacher and tell her of the gold stars. I went to pull away but his wife held me tight.

'Janine?' The woman in gym gear prompted. I thought she was one of those that didn't work, but I would later learn her name was Ashley, and she was a solicitor.

'What did you *mean*?' his wife asked me again.

'I didn't know ...' I began, but she dug her nails in, stopping me.

'You didn't know *what*?'

'I'm sorry.' I was stuttering now, my words tripping over themselves.

'You're sorry for *what*?'

I swallowed, my throat dry. Everything I said was making it worse, I couldn't find words that wouldn't incriminate me further.

'Why would he call you a slag?' she asked.

'He called her a slag?'

Janine nodded at Ashley and then they both turned to me.

'I'm very sorry,' I said, pulling my arm free and trying to move past them. 'It wasn't who I thought it was. Wrong person. He got the wrong person. I don't even know Rob.'

'You know his name,' Ashley said, and I flinched.

No one moved.

I stepped out into the road. Like the parents earlier who'd been forced to walk around his illegally parked car, I was forced to walk around his wife.

And then I paused, right beside her, so only she could hear. 'He lied,' I said. 'I didn't know who he was. I'm so, so sorry.'

My legs were unstable as I walked back up to the main building. I felt weak, like I'd just sprinted up a steep hill. Why did

I even talk to him? So I could tell him what a prick he was? Why talk to her? Why apologise?

Stupid. Stupid. Stupid.

My heart was racing. The two ladies by the main entrance had started to walk over to Janine and Ashley, to hear the gossip. They'd been watching the whole episode but now they needed details. I could hear them ask what was going on as they reached them.

And then it hit me.

My head snapped forward as a sharp pain shot down my neck.

I felt at my collar and then looked at my fingers. They were covered in blood.

Something had been thrown at me. I looked down and realised it was a mobile phone. The screen shattered from where it had hit my head. I turned around, and there Janine was. Crying, her face distorted into an angry, wet mess. Her mouth open in anguish, her arm still outstretched from where she had launched her phone.

The two women had joined Janine and Ashley, and they stood in a huddle. Arms going around Janine's shoulders, reassuring words spoken and shocked faces looking at her thrown mobile phone, at my fingers covered in blood.

Ryan, the boy who had heard it all, who told it like it was, looked at me from his mother's side, his pale face shining out at me like a moon.

'Ruth?' It was Becca, she was by the school entrance, holding open the main door and I almost ran to her.

I went inside the building and into my office, grabbing a tissue and holding it to my head. I was shaking. My head was pounding.

27

'Bloody hell,' Becca said, as I shut the door and closed the blinds to the office window, and for the first time since working there, the glass partition.

'Did I see Janine Walker just throw her phone at you?'

I looked at the tissue – it was bright red. 'It's fine,' I told her. 'It's nothing.'

'Let me see.' I tried to move away but Becca held me tight. 'Ruth, let me see.' She breathed in sharply. 'That might need a stitch.'

I put the tissue back over it, sitting down on the chair.

'Walker.' My words came out thinly. 'Sally Walker's mum from year five?'

'Orla Walker in year two,' Becca agreed. 'Head of the PTA and runs that private tutoring company, Top Marks.'

How could I have not placed her? Of course, that's who she was. Janine Walker. Always sending in emails, asking for appointments, teachers nodding in recognition at her name. That was *his wife*? Head of the PTA? I closed my eyes.

'What happened?' Becca almost whispered. 'What happened out there?'

I looked up slowly. 'You remember the Valentine's dinner at your gym?'

Becca thought for a moment. 'The one with the terrible DJ?'

'That man –' I swallowed, my throat tight '– Rob. The one who was sending drinks over to us all night?'

She nodded again. 'The bastard who never called?'

'That's her husband,' I told her, and Becca opened her mouth in disbelief.

'He's Janine Walker's husband? That slimy bastard who never called, is her *husband*?'

I nodded. 'And Janine just found out what I did with him.'

28

FOUR

It was Becca's idea. She'd fallen prey to one of those daft adverts that the gyms put out every January involving reduced membership fees and vague aspirational slogans. *Discover yourself. Join now and be the best you can be!* And Becca, in her post-Christmas slump, had signed up. I thought it was a massive waste of money, but three weeks in she'd been proving me wrong, she was loving it. A new sense of purpose, she'd said, which really meant a new group of men. She told me I needed to go, and I started getting the monologue in earnest of how I should be meeting someone new, and wasn't three years long enough being single.

I was used to that, used to smiling and shaking my head. Used to explaining that, after what happened with Will, I was steering well clear of men. Used to saying that Sam was enough, that I was still raw, but then she'd done the unthinkable. She got my mother involved.

They'd bumped into each other at Tesco, Becca told her of

the Valentine's dance, the fresh group of suitable men, and dates were swapped. Babysitting was agreed and an impossible situation arose.

My mother said it would be good for my mental health, Becca said it would be good for her so she didn't have to go alone, and after two days of a losing argument I found myself sat at a round table with seven other women eating carrot soup and wondering what the hell I was doing there.

It was in a function room at one of the big hotels in town that was more suited to holding wedding events than it was intimate dinners. The chairs were backed in white linen, a chiffon red bow tied around each one. Small glittery love hearts were strewn across the table, a menu with overly sentimental prose was displayed on each setting as well as a small tube of Love Hearts sweets.

'Be mine,' Becca had said, showing me hers before popping it in her mouth, and I was overcome with a great feeling of dread before the night had even properly begun. Because what Becca omitted to tell me before we got there, what she failed to say in all the pleading and cajoling, was that the Valentine's dinner at her new gym was a strictly 'singles' event. Meaning that there were no couples, no people companionably sat together without an agenda, and so the whole event had the air of a school disco. And even worse, there were 'games' to be played of writing notes of who you liked on a whiteboard, sending drinks to people by waiter service and, worst of all, a name badge should you want to wear one.

Giddy anticipation filled the air and, ridiculously, all the men seemed to be at one end of the room while all the women were at the other. Whole tables of single sexes, me and Becca sat among a pottery group who debated endlessly whether certain celebrities were homosexual.

After the meal, a DJ set up playing a series of annoying songs and it was at this point that I decided to go home.

'I'm done,' I remember saying to Becca as the introduction to 'It's Raining Men' blared out and the ladies at our table started singing along at top volume. 'My feet are killing me and I want my bed and I need to get home to Sam.'

Becca's eyes worked the room as I talked.

'You don't need me here,' I told her, 'you know everyone. I don't. And I'm tired, Sam'll be up early and I need my sleep.'

She grabbed hold of my hand. 'One drink,' she said, 'just have one more drink and then you can go.'

I was already slightly fuzzy. I'd had too much of the wine at the meal. I yawned and nodded; one more drink wouldn't hurt. I got out my phone and started dialling a cab while she was at the bar. I hadn't finished punching in the numbers when she came back carrying a bottle of champagne.

'Becca . . .' I began, but she shook her head.

'I didn't buy it,' she told me. 'They did!'

I followed her gaze and saw two men by the bar. They were slightly older than us and looked out of place. Most of the men were wearing ill-fitting suits, bellies hanging out, shirts pulling, buttons gaping. But the two men Becca was pointing to were dressed casually and expensively. Smart shirts, open at the collar, no tie. They had an air of confidence, looked like they were at an elite function, not in a room full of sweaty individuals, faces filled with desperate hope. They looked out of place because they were. They raised their glasses as I looked, toasting us, and Becca giggled.

'Mark and Rob,' she said, pouring our drinks, 'they seem ever so nice.' She held up the champagne bottle for me to look at before putting it back in the ice bucket. It was expensive.

'Becca, I'm going home,' I told her. 'I don't want champagne, it gives me a headache.'

'Don't be so miserable.' She handed me a full glass. 'Get that down you and you'll perk right up. Besides –' she flicked her hair, picked up the ice bucket and gave a wide smile to the men at the bar '– you need to come and say thank you.'

It was apparent when we got to the bar that Becca had her eye on Mark, leaving me with Rob. I wasn't interested. I told him I wasn't staying as he poured me a second drink. He smiled, he was charming, told me to leave whenever I wanted to, no pressure.

He asked me the right questions to get me talking, told a few jokes and we finished the champagne and ordered another.

Halfway into the second bottle, I found myself telling him about Will, about how he'd been having an affair. He confided that he'd had the same thing done to him, he hadn't been married but they'd been together seven years. I remember getting hold of his hand when I heard that. I was drunk by that stage and had that deceptive feeling of connection that too much alcohol induces. I gave him my sympathy, I asked about his girlfriend and how he found out about her infidelity. We swapped sob stories. I think I may have been crying a little.

'You're not going, are you?' he asked when I got my jacket. Becca was nowhere to be found and I was very drunk. I stumbled. 'Here.' He helped me get my coat on, I swayed and found it funny. 'I've a room,' he said, 'come and get a coffee and sober up a little before you go home.' He held up his hands. 'Just coffee,' he insisted. 'No funny business.'

It was the oldest trick in the book. I genuinely went to his room thinking that coffee would be good, that I could sober up before facing my mother. That she would be waiting for me, and I needed to be a little more in control before I told her how dire the night was and how she was never to force me out again. A hot cup of coffee and a moment away from the DJ and his overbearing music sounded ideal.

I didn't even like him that much. I remember thinking that as I followed him into the lift and then down the corridor to his room. I was safe because I didn't even fancy him. He wasn't my type, too thick set, too much muscle and girth. He wore slip-on shoes and his hair was too neat, his clothes too pristine.

I did not go up to his room to have sex. But after kicking off my shoes, lying on the bed, hearing more about his break-up and seeing how sensitive he was, thinking we'd made that connection, when he kissed me I didn't push him away. When he unzipped my dress and held me, I didn't say no. I didn't fancy him but, after three years of nothing, it felt good to be close to someone. It felt nice to have flesh on flesh and that bodily warmth and, as I let him undress me, as I surrendered to the sensations, I believed I was doing it with a man who was single. Who had recently undergone a serious break-up, a man who was a kindred spirit. Someone just like me.

It was over quickly. I dressed laughing at what had taken place. It was so out of character, so unusual. I cried a little, too much alcohol mixed with old sensations and the fact that it was the first man I'd slept with since Will. He held me, reassured and comforted me, told me he felt the same way, that we were two lonely souls who had comforted each other. I gave him my number, watched him add it to his contacts. He gave me his and we made brief arrangements to meet the following weekend.

It was justified in my head that night, but in the morning,

33

hungover and slightly ashamed at my behaviour, I couldn't get on with myself. I'm not the kind of woman who meets a man in a bar and lets him have intercourse with her after an evening of light flirting. And so, I rang him. Now I was sober, I wanted to let him know who I really was. I wanted to apologise for all that talk about Will, about my divorce. I wanted to tell him that I never cry about it, that I'd been far too maudlin and it was the combination of the Valentine's dinner, too much champagne and his sympathy. I wanted to thank him for listening to me, for his company. I wanted to introduce myself properly.

Number not recognised.

I don't think I've ever felt like a bigger idiot than I did that morning. I waited for him to call me, convincing myself that I'd got one of his numbers wrong, that he was sincere. That what we'd talked about hadn't all been hot air, but when his call never came, slow realisation and humiliation dawned. He'd said it all, done it all, just to get me into bed, and I'd let him. He must've thought I was the biggest, saddest pushover going, and what was worse was that I didn't even fancy him.

I wished I was one of those women who could chalk it up to experience, who could say that I used him as much as he used me, but I'm not. Never have been. It's not what I do. I've only ever slept with a handful of men and every one of them I'd been in a relationship with. He was my first one-night stand, my first stranger in a bar. So to see him like that, in such a domestic setting, to see him with a family after hearing his hopes for 'children of his own', well, it shook me up.

'The one that bought all that champagne?' Becca asked, and I nodded. 'That's . . . he's . . . ' She shook her head, trying to catch up with herself. 'He's Janine Walker's *husband*?'

'I didn't know it was him,' I said, 'obviously. He told me he'd just come out of a seven-year relationship. He told me he was single. Did you . . . ?'

'I only saw Mark a few times after that night and we never talked about him. He said Rob was an old schoolfriend, someone he rarely saw.'

I nodded; we both remembered how she'd gone on several dates with Mark before declaring him boring, while I waited in vain to hear from Rob.

We stared at each other.

'Bastard,' Becca said in a low voice.

Sounds of children's voices carried from the corridors. They were lining up, ready to file into the main hall.

'Shit, is it that time already?' Becca glanced at her watch. 'You need to tell John that Janine assaulted you,' she said. 'But leave out what you did with her husband.'

'I don't think—'

'Ruth, listen to me, you need to report this. Do it now, before she does anything else.'

'Anything else?' I pressed the tissue to my head and looked at it. The bleeding was coming to a stop.

'Ruth,' Becca leaned forward, touched my shoulder and made sure I was looking at her, 'this is Janine Walker, not some random parent, but Janine Walker, head of the Parent Teacher Association. You realise what that means?'

I looked at her blankly and Becca shook her head slightly.

'It means she's not going to let this go. She was the one who made all that fuss about the kids eating with a knife and fork,' she reminded me. 'That stupid "eat-right" campaign?'

My face blanched.

'That was Janine,' Becca said.

I remembered that. The stupid PTA campaign that was concerned not with what the kids were eating, but *how* they were eating it. There were endless complaints from the dinner staff who suddenly had the extra burden of teaching the children to use cutlery properly. At the time I was at a total loss as to why it was happening, and why the school was supporting her.

'That was *her*?'

Becca nodded. 'She takes her role very seriously, always fundraising and making donations to the school. Half the teachers are friends of hers, they work for her on the side in the holidays.'

I stared at her.

'Tutoring. Cash in hand.' Becca rubbed her finger and thumb together, the universal sign for money.

'Is that allowed?'

'It doesn't matter what's allowed,' Becca said, gathering her things together. 'The point is you need to tell John now, before she . . .'

There was a tap at the glass, and then the *ping* of the bell that was outside my office window. Someone was there and wanted my attention. I looked at Becca in alarm; I wasn't ready for round two.

'Wait there,' Becca whispered and opened the door. I heard muffled words, and then Eve, the woman with the boy, the woman who'd heard it all, appeared at the door.

'I'm so sorry,' she said, 'about Ryan. What he said out there. What happened.'

There was a shout from a child in the hall as the children went in for assembly. It was loud and close. Any minute the school bell would go and the time for talking would be over.

'I've sent Ryan home with my mother, and I was going to

keep out of it,' she went on, oblivious to the ticking clock, 'but then, when they started talking about your dismissal, and then Amy and Caroline came over, and then Janine and Ashley went in to see Mr Cartwright—'

'They went in to see John?' I interrupted, and Eve nodded.

'Janine and Ashley. Amy and Caroline are waiting outside.' She glanced over her shoulder as if to see the other two women, and I stared at Becca in horror, my heart pounding.

'They were talking about what you said to Janine and how it wasn't right with you being the secretary here, but I saw her throw her phone. And I know what she's like, so I thought I should come in.' She straightened her shoulders. 'And if you want me to see Mr Cartwright, to tell him my side, then I will. I'm not afraid of Janine. I'm not afraid of any of them.'

'Sorry?' I couldn't keep up. 'You're not afraid of who?'

Eve opened her mouth to answer but was stopped by the sound of John's office door opening.

Suddenly there they were, facing us in the small area between our offices.

Janine's eyes red and puffy, Ashley behind her, talking. She stopped mid-sentence as she saw us. Janine's body went rigid, her arms stiff at her sides, and I felt myself go hot under their scrutiny. Eve took a step back, cowering slightly. Despite what she'd claimed, she did look afraid.

Ashley turned to John, her eyebrows raised, but said nothing. No one moved. I pressed the tissue to the back of my head; it had started to pound again.

'Ruth,' John began after a moment.

The school bell rang and I jumped, my free hand going to my throat. Janine stared at me as it rang out, her eyes boring into mine, unblinking.

'Thank you, ladies,' John said as it finished ringing. He ushered them towards the main exit. 'I'll be in touch.'

'You'll have a formal letter this afternoon,' Ashley said, still staring at me. She put a hand on the small of Janine's back, leading her out of the building as if she were elderly. 'Your immediate action is appreciated,' she said to John as they went, 'considering how serious the situation is.'

He nodded to them and, once they were out of the building, signalled for me to go into his office.

'Misconduct,' he said, as he closed the door, 'you want to tell me what went on out there because Ashley Simmons, a solicitor, and Janine Walker, chair of the PTA and our biggest financial donor, I might add, are demanding your immediate suspension due to gross misconduct.'

'Gross misconduct?' I heard myself say. 'They can't.'

'They barged in here,' he said, going to his chair, 'no appointment, no knock, just straight in demanding I suspend you on the spot. There's a group of them out there apparently –' he waved in the general direction of the door '– all parents, all heard what you said and all shocked at your behaviour.'

I went to answer but he held his palm out, stopping me.

'And they have a point,' he went on. 'You know I don't care what you get up to in your own time, but from eight-thirty to four you are a school secretary and it matters what you do. You should have been in here –' he rapped his knuckles on his desk '– not out there, provoking parents, shouting accusations and slanderous rumours. It's the last thing you should have been doing. What were you thinking?'

I felt like one of the children, hauled into his office for a ticking off. I was hot, sweating suddenly.

'She threw her phone at me!' I sounded like a child, petulant and whiny. 'She attacked me.' I showed him the tissue I'd been using, dotted with red, then turned and lifted my hair at the back, matted from where the blood had begun to dry. 'She did this and I have witnesses to prove it. Eve. She wants to speak to you, she saw it all. How I was assaulted.'

I heard him shift in his chair. When I turned back around, he'd taken off his glasses and was rubbing at the space between his eyes.

'Unbelievable,' he said, before lifting the phone. 'Is Teresa there?' He was on the internal line, asking for the year one teaching assistant and dedicated first aider.

'No,' I said, 'I don't want to make a fuss.'

He held up his hand. 'Send her up to my office, would you? Bit of an incident. Thanks.'

He breathed out heavily through his nose and looked at me.

'John,' I leaned forward, 'what I did was perhaps unprofessional, but it's got no bearing on my abilities in here. It's got nothing to do with my job. It was a misunderstanding.' I paused, debating if I should go on. 'I met Janine's husband last February,' I began, 'but I had no idea who he was, no idea at all. I didn't know he was her husband. I didn't know he was married. So this morning, when I saw him . . . ' I faltered a little. John's eyebrows had shot up near his hairline. 'None of it was my fault,' I said. 'Really, John, I didn't know who he was. I apologised to Janine. I tried to explain, to tell her that he'd lied, that he'd told me he wasn't married, but—'

'Ruth,' John interrupted, 'stop. Stop. You're making it worse.' He shook his head. 'What you did with Janine's husband, who you thought he was or what you told her is something I don't need to know. This incriminates you in all kinds of areas of unprofessionalism.'

'Please, John.' I leaned forward. 'You can see how it could've happened. How it wasn't my fault. She attacked me out there. Threw her phone at me. A parent assaulted me, surely that matters?'

He stayed silent.

'You can't suspend me,' I went on, 'there's too much to do. I've a temp to hire for year five and the half-term residential to sort out.'

He didn't speak.

'And there's the window situation in year one,' I went on. 'I've already talked to Gary about it, and he's coming in later to discuss the fittings and suppliers. Who else will you get at such short notice?'

We stared at each other.

'If anything, I should be asking that Janine be restricted on school property. I should be asking that you—'

'All right, all right,' he said, and rubbed his temples. 'This is all I need.' He stared at his desk. 'They did omit the fact that she attacked you.'

'Assaulted me,' I agreed.

'And that changes things, changes them quite a lot.' He looked at me. 'You understand what this means? There'll be an investigation, which is the last thing you need. You'll need to speak with your union rep. I imagine I'll have the formal complaint in writing by this afternoon . . . '

There was a tap at the door. 'First aider!' Teresa called in a sing-song voice.

'Janine Walker and Ashley Simmons.' He shook his head. 'I'll give you this, Ruth, you know how to pick a fight.'

FIVE

I once read somewhere that the suicide rate for primary school teachers is nearly double the national average. Surprising that, isn't it? Apparently, statistics were collected over a four-year period and the conclusion was that if you work in primary school you've a higher chance of taking your own life. And approximately ninety per cent of this work force is female.

The staff at our school was almost entirely female. John, the headteacher, Gary, the caretaker, and one other teaching assistant being the only men. So when I finally braved the staffroom, when I plucked up the courage and walked into it that lunchtime, I was acutely aware of a gossipy, bitchy undercurrent. From a pack of women who, according to the statistics, were depressed and slightly suicidal. And all of them directing their judgemental thoughts at me.

In hindsight, I can see I was a welcome distraction. Something to take their mind off their own stressed lives, but as I walked in, I couldn't find any perspective other than a room filled with vindictive women. Women who I now knew were secretly working for Janine.

Several conversations stopped. A teaching assistant stared at me openly, someone sniggered from the far corner. Lucy and Denise from reception were talking to Teresa. They all turned and gawped as I walked in, and I instinctively put my hand up to the plaster on the back of my head.

I suddenly realised that every woman in there knew what I had done and had made a very definite decision about it. A formal letter of complaint had been delivered to the office just a couple of hours earlier. It was from Ashley, written on Janine's behalf, asking for my suspension. They were going for gross misconduct. It was so unfair, so outrageous and unjust. I couldn't quite believe that it was being taken seriously.

John had told me that, as the complaint was not of a child protection or safeguarding issue but one of my professional conduct, it was up to the governors and the head teacher to make a decision. An investigation was pending, but because I wasn't putting any of the children at risk my suspension was not immediate, and John had told me he was happy to have me continue at work.

So if John, the head of the school, was happy for me to stay, then why were the staff being so hostile?

'Hello,' my voice cracked. I should've said it louder, with more confidence. Teresa gave me a small smile and looked away, the rest of them didn't even bother with a smile. They all ignored me. No one said anything. Not a word.

I straightened my shoulders and looked around for Lisa, Sam's teacher. His bullying was more important than what had happened to me. I needed to find Lisa and tell her what was going on. I saw her over by the sink and headed towards her, aware that I was being covertly watched by the entire room. She was opening a Pot Noodle, reaching up into the cupboard for the communal ketchup.

'Lisa,' I smiled warmly. She looked at me and blanched. Lisa was young, still completing her NQT year. She still thought teaching was a vocation and not a job, and – I realised as she swallowed and looked past me – still a little unsure of herself. She was searching for help, for someone else.

'Ruth,' she said, and went back to her Pot Noodle.

'I won't keep you long,' I said. 'I know how busy you are, but I really, really need to talk to you.'

She kept stabbing her fork into the dried noodles, her head down.

'I meant to see you first thing,' I said. 'I need to talk to you about Sam, about something –' I paused '– well, it's delicate.' I gave a slight laugh. 'I could really do with having a chat about—'

'I know what happened,' she interrupted and looked at me. She took her glasses off and gave them a wipe as the kettle switched off to the side of us. In the silence I was aware of everyone listening. There were a few low murmurs in the room but it seemed eerily quiet. Two had come forward, towards the sink under the ruse of returning their cups, and Lisa cast a glance at them. Her eyes registered the situation and she raised her chin slightly at me. 'I know what you did to Janine Walker this morning,' she said firmly.

I didn't think I'd heard her correctly. *What I did?*

The two teaching assistants loitered around the sink, making a meal over rinsing their mugs. I side-stepped towards the fridge, turning my back on them, trying to lure Lisa away, but she actively stepped out, so they could see and hear her. She was enjoying the attention.

'The thing is,' Lisa went on, 'Janine's been wonderful since I've started here. I don't want to take sides, so I'd rather not be involved.'

I took a moment. I couldn't understand.

'But I'm talking about Sam,' I said slowly, 'my son. He's in your class and he's being bullied . . .'

'Janine is happily married,' Lisa interrupted, stretching out the words and I went hot. A flush of adrenalin rushing up through my chest. 'An urgent staff meeting has been called after school. I've had to cancel a doctor's appointment.' She shook her head. 'So I don't think we should discuss it until I've taken advice.'

'Advice?'

'And I think it would be more professional if we spoke about Sam outside of school hours,' she said. 'I think we're in danger of blurring the boundaries and I think it's confusing for Sam. I'm aware he's a challenging student—'

'*Challenging?*'

'I'd prefer it if you made an appointment in future to talk to me rather than ambushing me in my lunch hour.' She lifted her chin again and I wanted to slap her face. 'I also think it would be best practice if there was a chaperone. For protection.' A small patch of pink had developed on each cheek, her eyes flicking to the other women for approval.

'A *chaperone*?' I gave a hollow laugh, aware that I was repeating her every last word with an air of disbelief. 'Lisa, is this a joke?'

'In light of recent events –' her voice was shrill '– I think it's best practice. Thursday next week, after school would be OK. I'll see if Julia can be present and get back to you.'

'Next week?' I asked. 'But I need to talk to you today, Sam is—'

'That's the best I can do,' she said, and left me open mouthed by the sink.

It was only after she'd gone that I realised that by saying nothing I'd more or less agreed to her demands. A chaperone. As if I was the one to be feared.

I was erratic and twitchy for the rest of the day. I got on with my job, made the calls, wrote the letters, but the events of the morning hung over me like a dark cloud. I'd left John's office that morning and wanted to slam the registers against the wall, overturn the computer and smash the chair into the monitor. It had taken me almost three years to get a permanent position – after how it had ended at the car dealership – and the thought of having another vague 'reason for leaving' on my CV made my stomach lurch. I couldn't do it. My fledgling cake business was only just starting to make a minor profit. It wasn't yet providing a regular income. And I couldn't leave Sam at that school alone. I couldn't let Will accuse me of unemployment again and I couldn't stand the thought of job searching.

All those interviews with awkward questions and lack of references. I was behind on the rent as it was. I *would not* lose this job. I could not lose this job. So I didn't slam the registers or overturn the computer at how stupid I'd allowed myself to be. Apart from my horrendous trip to the staffroom, I hid instead. Blinds drawn, hatch closed, and didn't see a soul until Becca popped her head in at afternoon break. She looked at me trying to eat my forgotten sandwich from lunch and shook her head in pity.

'Oh Ruth.' She closed the door gently behind her.

'They've put in an official complaint,' I told her. 'I'll lose this job.'

Becca stared at me wide eyed.

'Ashley Simmons.' I put my uneaten sandwich back in its bag. I was close to tears. 'On her formal solicitor paper. John showed me. They have to do an investigation and I have to find a union rep. And I didn't do anything except apologise. I tried to be kind to Janine.'

She put her hand on my shoulder. 'Bitches.'

'I can understand she's upset,' I said. 'Janine probably thinks I did it on purpose, slept with her husband and told her about it in front of her friends, but this –' my stomach churned '– putting in a formal complaint. Getting all the staff against me.'

'The staff?'

'You should've seen them at lunchtime in the staffroom.' I shook my head. 'I could practically feel the venom coming off them. All thinking I'm some kind of homewrecker and Janine is the victim.'

Becca was quiet.

'You going to the staff meeting?'

She nodded. 'Urgent. Everyone has to, no exceptions.'

John had called a meeting about it, of course he had. The head of the PTA had attacked a member of staff, everyone needed to be made aware. And then there had been the phone calls, several parents who wanted to speak directly with John, concerned over the 'incident' outside school.

I knew who they were. Janine's friends, the two women who ran to her side after she'd launched her phone at me, Amy and Caroline. I could see their faces as they put their arms around her, Ashley the solicitor and the two others. Janine Walker's very own band of Hench Mummies.

'She has this cliquey group,' Becca told me, 'all of them doing stuff for the school in one way or another. Fundraising, that kind of thing.'

'I don't know any of them.'

'Why would you? They're the mums from year five, been together since reception.'

'So not only is she best friends with half the staff in school,' I asked, 'but she's some kind of "alpha mum" with the other parents? I didn't even know they were a thing. I thought they only existed in books and sitcoms.'

Becca gave a nod. 'Oh they exist, but only if you're in their orbit. She's one of those types. In everybody's business all the time.' She took a moment. 'Actually, she's quite nice.'

'Don't!' I said in a high voice. 'I feel bad enough about it all as it is, please don't tell me Janine is nice.'

'Sorry,' Becca said, 'but she kind of is. If she knows it's been a busy week for us, she sends biscuits and stuff in with her daughter for the staffroom; she's quite thoughtful like that. And she organises all the rotas with the parents for the end of term discos so we don't have to do it ourselves. She's –' Becca gave a sigh '– nice. Thoughtful.'

I screwed my eyes closed. I felt wretched.

'But she did throw her phone at you,' Becca offered, 'and now she wants you sacked, so –' she held up her hands '– she can't be that nice, can she?'

'I should be there,' I said, 'to explain my side. To say what really happened, that it was an accident how she found out, that I wasn't being malicious. If there was ever a time where I should be in a staff meeting, it's tonight.'

Becca crinkled up her nose. We'd had this discussion before. I strongly believed that as school secretary I should be involved in all staff meetings, but it seemed the teaching staff thought not. Even though they depended on me to send through forms, letters and general admin, even though I was the one responsible for passing on urgent messages, payments and parent correspondence that made their jobs go smoothly, I still wasn't considered worthy to attend the meetings. The reason given was that they were solely for 'teaching matters'. I only found out what had been discussed if there were notes to be typed up.

'I'll suggest it to John,' I said. 'I was the one who was assaulted after all. I should be there.'

'I wouldn't,' Becca said carefully. 'John's made it clear to everyone that it's a confidential matter, and if he almost suspended you this morning –' she crinkled her nose again '– you don't want to aggravate the situation.'

I stared at her.

'Besides, it might make it worse if John allows you in,' she said. 'They might resent it.'

I took in a sharp breath, ready to argue, but she had a point.

'Leave it this time.' She smiled. 'You might need their support, and gate-crashing a staff meeting might not be the best approach. And besides –' she put her hand on my shoulder '– I'll be there to stick up for you. Tell your side of the story. Make sure they know exactly what happened. I'll call later or fill you in tomorrow.' The bell rang signalling the end of break time. 'Try not to worry.'

I nodded, let her go back to her class. I could understand the need for a staff meeting: it was John's job to make his team aware of what was going on, but I hated the thought of being discussed. Judged without being there to defend myself. Even though I knew I could rely on Becca to support me, it wasn't the same as doing it myself. I hid in my office for the rest of the afternoon and, when the last bell rang and it was home time, I left early for fear of Janine or Ashley, or some other fan of Janine's, coming in for round two. John agreed, obviously fearing the same, and I collected Sam from the after-school club that had not yet started and then suddenly froze.

The street was still full of lingering parents, gossiping and chattering. Teachers were still in classrooms, awaiting the parents that were late for pick up. It had been a mistake. I hadn't thought that far, I couldn't walk out into them, not certain of who knew what. Not knowing who were friends of Janine, who knew Rob and had got wind of what I done. I felt the plaster at the back of my head and decided to hide in the one place I was certain would be free of parents and teachers at that time: the staffroom.

I closed the door gently and we perched on the fat, cushioned chairs to wait it out. Sam was wide eyed at being in there. The sounds from the street filtered in, children shouted and screamed outside, parents chattered. It would be a good ten minutes until all of the children had been collected and the streets were empty. Until the teachers would be piling into the staffroom, eyes alight at the thought of gossiping about what I'd done. How I'd slept with a parent, how I'd been assaulted. My stomach churned at the thought, at how Becca might be the only one to support me.

'Mum?' Sam looked at me.

'Just five minutes,' I told him with a smile. 'I just needed a sit down before we go to Nanna's.'

He nodded, slightly unsure, and went back to his reading book. His bag and lunch box on his knee, my handbag at our feet. We were ready to go as soon as I deemed it safe, and it was then that I saw my uneaten sandwich. I'd managed to eat the fruit and biscuit I'd brought in, but had only had one bite of my sandwich before Becca had told me about the urgent meeting and put me off my food.

I brought it out; it was warm. It had been left on my desk by the window, basking in the afternoon sunshine. As I lifted the lid of the box, the smell of stale egg hit the air.

'Mum!' Sam comically held his nose. 'That stinks.' He got up and went to the far side of the room, turning his back on me and the offending smell.

I was about to tell him not to be silly and throw the sandwich away when something stopped me. It was limp in my hand, the filling bulging out of the sides. I stared at it a moment. I'd made egg as they needed using up and it would save on buying anything else, but it had been a mistake. It was far from appetising and the smell was pungent. It needed to be put back in the box, sealed tightly until I was able to throw it out, but the thought of the impending meeting made me pause.

The teachers would shortly be coming in, discussing my private life. It shouldn't be allowed. I should be at the meeting and given a chance to explain. *I* was the injured party and, more to the point, as secretary, it was ridiculous that I wasn't invited. Who were these teachers who deemed me below them? There was no chance of them supporting me, Becca was wrong about that. Whoever thought I shouldn't be attending staff meetings were going to have a field day about me sleeping with a parent.

Without thinking too much about it, I bent down and pushed the sandwich as far as I could under my chair. I hid it right at the back, near the radiator, felt the egg smearing the carpet tiles as it went. The staff meeting would take place in about fifteen minutes, and by the time they'd all got themselves a coffee and sat down the smell would have permeated the whole room. *It* would become the discussion. They could talk about the smell instead of talking about me.

I turned to check that Sam hadn't seen, his back still facing me, and then I felt my face colour.

What was I doing? Leaving a rotten egg sandwich in the hopes it would defer the attention from me? I was being stupid. Feeling intimidated by Janine's popularity and my best retaliation was to hide a rancid egg butty? I'd lost my mind. I bent forward to retrieve the sandwich when Sam was suddenly at my side.

'Mum,' he said, 'is it time to leave yet?' He was holding his nose and his voice was high pitched and comical.

A sudden image of all the teachers doing the same – holding their noses between smelling the air as if taking part in an odorous treasure hunt – popped into my mind, and a childish laugh escaped me. Sam laughed back and I was shocked, shocked suddenly at how good it felt to laugh, even if it was at something completely ridiculous. It was relief. I did it again, Sam laughing with me. It was the best I'd felt all day.

'It's time,' I said, and kissed his cheek. The sounds of the parents outside had lessened, the streets seemed quiet. It was only a sandwich after all, a stupid attempt at interrupting the precious staff meeting and causing a delay. It wasn't anything serious. 'Let's go,' I told him and we left the staffroom and the smell behind us.

SIX

Carlisle, known as the Border City, is England's biggest city by area although its population is just over one hundred thousand. It's the capital of Cumbria and the last city before Scotland. But when the Romans established their settlement here in the first century AD, serving the forts on Hadrian's Wall, and then when it was subsequently developed with the building of the castle and then the cathedral, they didn't realise that they'd be doing me a massive favour hundreds of years later. While the size of a large town, Carlisle is sprawling and easy to get lost in.

With the addition of holidaymakers and day-trippers, it's relatively easy for me to hide. I can go for weeks, months even, without bumping into someone from my old life. I stayed away from the centre, did all my shopping online, rarely went out. And perhaps if I'd been one of those people that regularly wanders through the city I would've seen Rob before now. If I'd been frequenting the clubs and bars at the weekend I'd have been able to have my outburst with him then. A drunken shouting match conducted in the safe environment of public anonymity. But I wasn't, it didn't. It happened outside the school gates, on a busy morning, and it may have cost me my job.

My mother's house lies on the outskirts of the city, over near the Solway Coast on the course of Hadrian's Wall, right on the border. The small Burgh by Sands is her nearest village, but her house was, apart from that, set on its own, among farmers' fields. To get there I had to travel through the city traffic, past the castle and alongside the River Eden. It's a tedious journey, full of stops and starts, and it was made no better by the bright sun.

It was hot, and although I had the car windows down full, my blouse was sticking to my skin. I pulled it away from me in a wafting motion as I drove, trying to get some air in. Sweat was trickling at the back of my neck and the plaster that Teresa had stuck on the back of my head was itching.

I glanced over to Sam, who was leaning out of the open window, his back to me, his brown hair whipping about his face.

'Not too far,' I warned, 'it's dangerous.'

'But I can still smell that egg,' he complained, as I used the main controls to lift his window. He sat back, a resigned look on his face, staring down at his hands.

When we'd started the journey, I'd had to tell him that I hadn't talked to his teacher. That I didn't tell her he was struggling, that I hadn't had a chance to make things better for him and the guilt was heavy.

'Hey,' I said, reaching over and ruffling his hair, 'I've said I'm sorry, and I mean it. I'm really, really sorry, Sammy. Really.'

He gave a slight shrug. 'S'OK, Mum.'

'It's not OK.' I glanced over at him. 'I promised you this

morning that it would be sorted, but something happened. Something happened and I wasn't able to speak to Lisa, Miss Gleason, like I said I would.'

He nodded and looked out of the window. He seemed unusually small. Sam was a big lad, one of the biggest in his class, but he looked like he'd shrunk, as if he was folding in on himself on the seat beside me.

'Is that why we had to wait in the staffroom? Because of what happened?'

I took a deep breath. 'Kind of.'

'What was it? What happened?'

I took a deep breath. 'Nothing, sweetie, nothing at all for you to worry about. Work was busy today, really busy, and that's why I didn't get to speak to your teacher. That's why I needed a rest before we started the drive.' I glanced over at him. 'I'm really, really sorry, Sam. I'll try to talk to her tomorrow, promise. So –' I changed the tone in my voice, made it brighter '– how did the maths work go?' I asked. 'Did you get a gold star?'

He shook his head. 'I got a smiley face,' he said, and I felt a flash of anger at Lisa. That work was perfect. No mistakes, not one digit wrong. I knew because I'd done it with him, explained it to him, done her job. It was more than worthy of a gold star.

'And Toby?' I asked. 'How was he today?'

Sam looked out of the window. 'Don't want to talk about it.'

My stomach contracted. We were coming up to a roundabout and I kept my eyes on the road, my voice in the same neutral tone. 'What did he do?'

'Nothing.'

'Sam?'

He remained tight lipped.

'Sam, if you don't tell me, I can't help.'

'You don't need to tell Miss Gleason, Mum. I think if I ignore him, he'll stop.'

'Stop what?'

'Spitting.'

We both lurched as I got the change in gear wrong, my shock reflected in my bad driving. I fiddled with the gear stick, slotting it into fourth.

'Spitting?' I tried to keep my voice steady.

'He doesn't do it much,' Sam said, 'just a bit. Sometimes at lunch, in my sandwiches, and some of the others do it with him.'

'Did you tell someone?' My hand was sweaty on the wheel. We were on a dual carriageway and I glanced across at him. His face was blank, devoid of any emotion, and it made it worse that he was just accepting it. 'Did you tell Miss Gleason?' I pressed. 'Mrs Ruby? The teaching assistant?'

He shook his head. 'I didn't tell anyone.'

'Why not?'

He shrugged again and continued to stare out of the window. I felt my anger rise as I imagined these boys spitting at Sam, *spitting in my son's food*, and I tried to rein it in. It would do no good for Sam to see my rage. I pressed down hard on the indicator instead, taking out my fury by swerving us off the busy carriageway and onto the single lane leading towards my mother's faster than was necessary.

'Sam, you have to tell someone when he does this stuff,' I said, trying to keep my emotions out of my voice. 'You need to let the teachers know.' I kept my eyes on the road. 'Spitting is serious. It's not something you can ignore.'

He didn't move.

'I know you think it'll get worse if you tell, that Toby will get worse, but if you don't tell someone, it can't get better.'

He was silent.

We both knew the situation: he'd already tried that. He'd already told someone. Told several people, in fact, when the bullying started, and nothing had been done and it did seem to be getting worse. I'd already spoken to Lisa about Toby, I'd spoken to John, so they all knew what was going on, but nobody seemed to be doing anything about it.

'I'll speak to John, Mr Cartwright, tomorrow—' I began but Sam turned suddenly, a look of horror on his face.

'No!'

'Sam, we need to—'

'Mum, if you tell Mr Cartwright and Toby gets in trouble again then the whole class will know it was me. And last time I did what you said, last time I told on him, he blew his nose on my jumper and started writing "fat" on my books.'

'But Sam,' I said, straining to keep my anger at bay, 'you can't just let him spit on your food!'

'He won't,' Sam said. 'He told me he won't do it tomorrow so long as I give him my crisps. He says I need to go on a diet.'

'*A diet?*' My voice was shrill. 'He said you need—'

'Please, Mum –' Sam wiped his face roughly, tears brimming '– you're already speaking to Miss Gleason about how I'm stupid . . .'

'You're not stupid . . .'

I reached out to him as I was driving, trying to give some comfort, but he pulled away. I wanted to wrap my arms around him. I wanted to get this boy, this Toby, and do whatever I had to.

'I'm fat and stupid—'

'You are *not* fat and you are *not* stupid,' I almost shouted. 'I'll sort Toby tomorrow, you leave this to me, I'll—'

'STOP!'

There was a loud bang and Sam screamed as I slammed on the brake. We both lurched forward as I came to a stop. I was breathing hard. I turned quickly.

'You OK?'

He nodded. His eyes were very round.

I ran my hand over his head, along the back of his neck.

'Here, does it hurt here? Does it hurt anywhere?'

He shook his head, looked out of the window as I continued to check him over, to make sure he was OK.

'You're sure?' I pressed. 'I didn't mean to slam on the brakes, I just panicked when—'

'You hit it,' Sam told me. 'I heard it against the car.'

I stared at him, unsure what to do, and then we heard it. A high-pitched cry filling the air, piercing. Like the wail of a small child, of a baby in turmoil. The kind that makes you stop what you're doing and search for the cause of such a noise.

'Where is it?' Sam asked in a small voice. 'Where's the rabbit, Mum?'

A large hare had darted in front of the car, forcing me to come to an emergency stop. But the bang we'd both heard, the feel of it against the car, told me I'd not been quick enough. And now its damaged cries were filling the air.

'Stay here,' I told him as I undid my seatbelt. 'Don't get out of the car, OK?'

Sam nodded.

It was at the rear of the car. There was a bright red smear on the road leading up to it from the back tyre. I walked slowly towards it and felt a wave of nausea wash over me as I saw the full extent of what I'd done. I had to turn away a moment, take in a lungful of fresh air.

It was a large, beautiful creature. Its fur the deepest brown, its ears unbelievably long and its eyes wide and fearful. And it was screaming in agony. Its back legs, both of them, were completely flattened. The lower half of its belly open and gushing with blood, organs and other unrecognisable matter on display. It was screaming from the pain.

'Hey,' I said quietly as I went towards it. 'Hey, it's OK. Shh, it's OK.'

But it was very far from OK. The hare's front legs were moving, trying in vain to drag its destroyed body away.

My hand went to my mouth and I took a step back. I'd never seen anything so gruesome, never been in a position like this before. I looked up the empty road. I didn't know what to do. And the sound it was making, the horrendous cry. It was all I could do not to put my fingers in my ears.

'We need to take it to the vet.' Sam was staring down at it, his face motionless.

'I told you to stay in the car!' I went to put my hand over his eyes but he pushed them away. 'You should've stayed in the car!' I shouted at him. 'I told you to stay in the car.'

Sam ignored me. He went forward as if to lift the hare up.

'NO!' I screamed and pulled him back. Unsure if the frightened creature would bite him if he went to touch it. It was in so much pain, panting and screaming, blood coming away from its mangled legs. I wasn't sure how it would behave if we got too close.

'It's dying,' Sam said, and I nodded, my throat going tight.

'I tried to miss it,' I told him. 'It just jumped out. I was too late. Oh honey, I didn't want you to see this, I thought I'd missed it.'

'The vet will help . . .'

'Sam, we can't take it to the vet,' I told him. 'Look at it, what vet can help that?'

The hare was gasping now, in between the screams.

'And how would we get it in the car? It's frightened and in agony. If we go near it, it'll attack, it'll bite us.' I bit my lip. Tears were pricking my eyes.

'We can't just leave it like that,' Sam said, looking up at me. 'Mum, you have to do something.'

I stared down at the creature, the small pathetic movements it was making as if it could crawl away from death.

Over by the grass verge were rocks, large rocks. One sharp knock and it would be over. The screaming would stop. The pain would stop.

'Back in the car, Sam,' I ordered.

'What are you going to do?'

'Now,' I told him, 'back in the car now.'

Sam stared at me a moment and then went back to the car. He slowly climbed in. 'What are you going to do, Mum?'

'Close the door, Sam,' I ordered, 'and don't look out of the window.'

I waited a moment, making sure he was doing as he was told, and then I picked up the largest rock I could find. I went back to the hare, back to the mangled body lying in the road, the screaming. I lifted the rock high in the air.

'I'm so sorry,' I whispered, before letting it fall, and in an instant it was over. The screaming stopped. Silence.

'You killed it.'

'SAM!' I stumbled back. 'I told you to stay in the car!'

He looked down at the hare, now under the rock. 'It's dead.'

I wiped my face, went over to him and put my arm around his shoulders. He didn't respond.

'It's kinder,' I told him. 'No vet would've been able to save it. It was dying. It was in pain. It was kinder to kill it and put it out of its misery.'

He stared at it a moment. 'How do you know?'

'What?'

'How do you know it was kinder?' He looked up at me. 'Maybe it wanted to die on its own. Maybe we should've left it. Or taken it to someone for help.'

'Sam –' I leaned down so my face was level with his '– it was the humane thing to do, you can't just leave an animal in so much pain. It was better to kill it quickly rather than leave it to have a long, painful death. And where would we have taken it to? I'm not even sure the vet would look at a wild animal. It's not a pet,' I told him gently, 'and it was in a lot of pain. Too much pain.'

He nodded but I could see my words weren't hitting home. In Sam's mind he probably thought we should've done something else.

Maybe we should've done something else. Would a vet have done anything? The RSPCA? I swallowed, my throat dry. Too late now.

'Get back in the car,' I told him, trying to be matter of fact. 'I mean it this time, Sam.' He looked at me for a moment, then slowly went to the car.

We drove the rest of the way to my mother's in silence, the dead hare wrapped in a Co-op bag in the boot. I was shaking and trying not to show it. My heart wouldn't slow its beating, even though I kept repeating to myself that it was only a hare, only a stupid hare that ran in front of the car and there was nothing else I could've done.

When we arrived, Sam got out of the car without saying a word. I felt like a murderer, like a killer. I couldn't protect him from the bullies at school and now I'd killed a beautiful innocent creature right in front of him. I was still shaking slightly, upset and jittery from what I'd had to do.

'Sam!' I called after him, but my words were lost. He went straight up to my mother's house. I watched him go. He was well built for his age. Looking at him you'd have thought his size and shape would've been a barrier to bullying, but it turned out to be the cause of it. They called him the 'big fat giant' and shouted out 'BFG' whenever he walked past, and now they were spitting on him.

'Sam, it was an accident!' I called again.

He yanked open the front door. My mother never locked it and he went inside, leaving it swinging behind him. I took a moment, blinking away the tears.

Why did everything have to be so bloody hard?

There was a high-pitched *ping* from my bag, a text notification.

I reached over for it quickly, thinking it was from Becca. I'd tell her what had happened, get some reassurance that I'd done the right thing in killing the hare, and then the thought that she'd found my hidden egg sandwich hit me. Perhaps she'd made the connection. Or the staff meeting had resulted in a different outcome for my job? They'd all complained and I was being suspended after all.

I fiddled with the locked screen, putting in my password as the thoughts raced around my head. When the text screen opened I saw it wasn't from Becca at all, but from an unknown caller.

One word.

SLAG

SEVEN

To a stranger, it looked like the cover of a chocolate box, my mother's house. Think of those old oil paintings done of a cottage in the English countryside, wild flowers around a door. Add a couple of my mother's large hanging baskets and decorative bird table out front and there you have it. What you wouldn't know is that, once inside, the charm ends.

When my parents moved here ten years ago, it was advertised as needing 'quite a bit of TLC', and my dad had major plans. He was going to renovate. Update the place, modernise it without losing its charm. He was going to spend his retirement and savings doing it up, installing central heating and double glazing. He wanted to expose the beams, knock through the pantry into the kitchen making it all open plan, put skylights in the back rooms to lighten the place up. He wanted to clear out the garden. I think he'd had ideas of a vegetable patch – there was talk of farmers' markets and perhaps bee keeping eventually – but then he got ill. And the renovations happened sporadically or not at all.

It was like they grew into each other, my parents and the house. They got new carpets and some oil-fired radiators, but the windows stayed single pane and insufficient, so the log fire was on more than not. They never did knock through the pantry and kitchen, so my mother used it as was originally intended, as a kind of semi-fridge. I'd often wander in and find a bit of cake that she planned to finish later, or half a banana.

As my father's condition got worse, my mother took to collecting miniature china animals and they decorated every available surface. It was a common pursuit for them in his final months, scouring the internet for these small woodland ornaments, and my mother lined them up along the window-sills so they hid the mould. They adorned the mantelpiece that my father had originally declared monstrously old fashioned, added to the overall clutter, and, in short, my parents became the exact kind of people that would live in a run-down cottage. Slight hoarders, generally living in a couple of rooms and who, no matter what the weather, always lit a fire.

The ceilings are low, it's quite often dark and the walls are full of faded photographs. But there is a certain cosiness to it, despite the slight smell of damp and ill-fitting doors.

'Back's still bad,' she said, as I switched on the kettle to boil. 'Ibuprofen not touching the sides.'

I heard her groan, purely for my benefit, as she shifted herself into the wooden chair at the kitchen table.

'I wish you'd get teabags,' I said, as I scooped out the tea; it smelt dry. 'You're the only person I know who insists on loose tea.'

She made a clicking sound with her teeth. 'Tea without a teapot is not done proper. And don't give me that builders mug, I want mine in a cup. With a saucer.'

The teapot was stained from use, the lid chipped. I made a mental note to get her one for Christmas. I would've liked to get her a new kitchen entirely, or sort out the damp in the dining room, or at the very least replace the leaking tap in the bathroom, but a teapot was about all I could manage at the moment.

Sam was in the lounge, sat on the sofa with Trixie, my mother's old Yorkshire Terrier, on his knee. The pair of them were watching my dad's old DVDs of *On the Buses*. It had been his favourite sitcom from the seventies and was now Sam's failsafe. I heard Blakey's laugh and then Sam's quiet titter in response and knew he was some way towards calming down.

'He's fine,' my mother said, as if reading my thoughts. 'The hymns and singing that animal got was better than your dad's.'

We'd buried the dead hare in the field behind my mother's. I want to say garden, but that doesn't really go far enough to describe the space at the back of her cottage. Mostly because the partitions between my mother's property and that of the farmers have long since worn away, meaning that behind my mother's house is a large expanse of fields. Fields and fields, going on for ever.

I'd dug a hole near some shrubbery and we'd put the Co-op bag containing the dead hare inside. Then my mother, who isn't remotely religious, did a kind of service for Sam's benefit. Even making us all sing some half-remembered version of 'Jerusalem'. It worked. Sam seemed placated and was now watching his favourite show.

I took the brewing teapot, the china cups and saucers, to the pine kitchen table where my mother was sitting.

'It's just here,' she was saying, 'right at the base. I think it's something serious, has to be for it to be so painful.'

'Mother –' I heard her shuffling '– please.' I looked up and inwardly groaned. 'Pull your jumper down.'

'At the base.' She rubbed at the small of her back that she'd turned towards me. 'See? Is there anything there?'

I shook my head. 'Mum, please, not today.'

'I've checked in the mirror but can't see anything.'

'What d'you expect to see?'

She shrugged. 'Slipped disc? Lump or something?'

I closed my eyes again.

She paused a moment. I heard her sigh and then move, her heels clicking as she got up. She was going for the biscuit tin.

'That's your problem,' I told her, looking down.

She paused, her face innocent, then looked at her feet.

'These?' She lifted her foot and rotated it at the ankle to show off her shoes, black velvet, stiletto heel.

'You wearing those around the house? Cleaning in them? No wonder your back's hurting.'

'Nonsense,' she said, and I noticed how her back didn't make her wince once as she reached up for the biscuit tin. 'They're practically slippers.'

I watched as she brought the tin over to the table, then, as she remembered, did a kind of limp, her hand going to her back, before sitting down. It was comical really. Since my father, it was one thing after another, and always something madly dramatic.

A bad back was a slipped disc, a headache was a brain tumour, any slight cough was lung cancer. After weeks of discussing ailments and symptoms, of suggesting medicine and appointments that were all ignored, I'd come to the conclusion that she didn't really want my help, or the help of any medical professional. She just wanted sympathy and to be listened to, and any other day I would have indulged her. Let her carry on while I zoned out a little, barely listening until she'd got it all out of her system. But not today. Not when I had Janine and Rob's faces looming in my mind. Not when the words 'gross misconduct' were circling at the forefront, not when I'd just slaughtered a wild animal in front of my son, who was now sitting in the next room, comforting himself after another excruciating day at a school with classmates who were now *spitting on him*.

'You OK?' my mother asked. 'How's the cake business going?'

I made a face as I thought. 'Not bad. Got an order for a birthday party this week, one of the dinner ladies at school. Turning fifty so it's a lot of cupcakes, all with fancy toppers and icing.'

My mother made an agreeable sound.

'And I'm hoping to do the farmers' market on Sunday –' I went on nodding '– so I've a lot to do.'

'Want me to have Sammy?' she asked quickly and I shook my head.

'Will's got him this weekend,' I told her and felt the familiar clench of anxiety in my stomach. I hated Sam going to his father's, and after hearing Will's threat of making him live with him, I didn't want him to go at all. Impossible, as the agreement was every other weekend, but at the moment I was finding that too much. I'd have preferred it if Sam never saw Will again.

'So,' she said after a moment, 'what's happened to the back of your head?'

I went to tell her and then checked myself. I couldn't tell her part of the story without telling it all, and there are some things – no, there are lots of things – that I can't talk to my mother about.

'It's nothing,' I said.

'Is it to do with Sam?' she asked, biting into a custard cream, and I snapped.

'Why does it have to be Sam?'

'I'm just asking because last time, when you hurt your hand, it was one of Sam's tantrums that—'

'It was not Sam,' I said carefully. 'And last time was my fault, he didn't know my hand was in the doorway.'

We were both quiet as she picked up the strainer and placed it over one of the tea cups.

'Sam's doing great,' I said after a moment. 'Sam's not a problem, but there's this one boy in his class . . . '

She nodded and waited for me to go on. It was an ingrained memory from childhood, my mother sat at a table, making tea as things were discussed. She did it for her friends. For my father. I felt a waft of sadness as I thought of her doing this alone.

'I didn't mean to snap,' I said, taking the cup, 'but Sam's being bullied by this awful boy in his class and he doesn't want me to tell the teacher. And his teacher isn't doing much about it. I should've said something today, but I didn't get a chance and now I'm not sure what to do.'

My mother took a moment.

'He's spitting on him,' I told her, and her eyes went wide.

'In my day,' she said, 'bullies got the same treatment they dished out.'

I shook my head. 'I can't tell Sam to spit back.'

'A good smack,' she said, and I snorted on my tea. 'One sharp shock instead of all this namby-pamby talking and meetings and whatever else they do. If a jumped-up little whipper-snapper thinks it's funny to spit at people, then he needs to know there's consequences to his actions.'

'I don't think smacking is . . .'

'It was the back of a shoe for us. We were sent to the headmaster and he got the back of our legs with the underside of a rubber sole.'

'Mum . . .'

'Was there bullying back then? Of course there was. But did it carry on like today? It did not! And don't get me started on all that ADHD . . .'

'Mother, you can't just—'

'I can! And I'm only saying this to you, in here, but I don't think it exists. ADHD –' she took a sip of her tea '– or OCD. All those kids need are less stimulants, less TV, less screens and a proper diet.'

I closed my eyes.

'Too much protein!' she declared. 'I read it in a magazine at the doctor's waiting room. It's all the animal protein, sugar and food colourings that do it. All these problems with kids today could be sorted if they changed what they eat.'

I took a deep breath. 'It's not just a case of diet, Mum. ADHD is a complex issue, it's not like there's one cause and solution. And it does exist, just listen to the parents of any child who's been diagnosed.'

She stared at me over the brim of her cup. I could've told her how many children are diagnosed with the condition each year, how it's, in fact, a neurobiological disorder that's defined at a behavioural level and how challenging it can be for all involved. How schools were struggling to cope, how parents can find it draining, how getting the right treatment can be a minefield. I'd seen it in my job often enough but telling my mother any of this would be a complete waste of time.

'I think diet could make a huge difference is all I'm saying,' she said quietly. 'You are what you eat and all that. You should consider it.'

And I suddenly realised she wasn't talking about children in general any more and she wasn't talking specifically about ADHD. She was talking about Sam.

I was quiet.

'If you're referring to what Sam—'

'I'm not saying anything!' She put her hands up, as if I was holding a gun to her. 'I love that boy.'

'I know you love him, Mum, that's not what I said.'

We were both silent.

'I really love him. I'd do anything for Sammy. You know that.'

I studied my mother. I felt like she'd accused me of something but I wasn't sure what. The theme tune to *On the Buses* played out in the living room and then started up again. Sam was watching them back to back.

'How's he sleeping?' my mother asked after a while, and I put my cup down.

'Fine.'

'Ruth, you just told me he's being bullied. Has there been any more of . . . ?'

'He's fine, Mum. Fine. Can we drop it?'

'He's sleeping through? In his own bed?'

I gave her a look and she held up her hands again, the imaginary gun pointed right at her. I wiped my palms on my trousers. It was stifling in the kitchen and my head was beginning to thump.

'Mum, I've had a rough day, can we just . . . ?'

'I thought you working at that school would change things,' my mother went on. 'You. In that school. Where he is. And now kids are spitting at him?'

I closed my eyes.

'He's too sensitive.' She was warming to her theme. 'No wonder he's still tantruming and wetting the bed if his class-mates are doing that. And all this about his weight, a boy of his age should be—'

'Right!' I stood up. I couldn't listen. The visit had been a mistake. I sometimes still thought of my mum as she was fifteen years ago, like she had all the answers and the ability to make everything better. I'd come expecting a different reception. A large part of me wanted to be able to tell her all of what had happened and for her to listen.

I wanted her to hold me while I cried and felt sorry for myself, for her to tell me everything was going to be OK and what I should do about the whole mess. But the only answers my mother had were bigoted rants and judgemental ideas about what I should be doing with my son.

I heard the familiar long drawn out laugh of Blakey filter through from the lounge, Sam's small giggle in response. I picked up my handbag from the back of the chair.

'You're going?' She looked up at me. 'You only just got here!'

'Stuff to do,' I said, rinsing out my cup. 'Just came to check up on you.'

'Why not stay for supper?' she asked quickly. 'We've enough for a shepherd's pie. I could whip one up in half an hour.'

'You know Sam won't eat that.'

'Pizza then. I've a pizza in the freezer, one of those rubbish ones full of cheese that Sam likes, and I'll do you and me some chicken.'

I considered it, the thought of someone else preparing our food was tempting, but eating in the dark kitchen with my mother was not.

My thoughts were interrupted by the *Jurassic Park* theme tune. It was my ringtone. My heart quickened; it might be whoever had sent the text. One of Janine's clique who had got my number and was about to give me an earful. My mobile was on the table, vibrating against the wood as it rang. I leaned closer to see who was calling, and saw it was Will, my ex-husband.

'Will,' I breathed.

My mother looked at my face. 'Want me to answer?' she asked. 'I don't mind.'

I snatched the phone up off the table and held it as it rang. It finally stopped. I put it down and we both stared at the 'missed call' notification in silence for a while. Speaking to Will after the day I'd just had would've been the worst. I felt like I'd dodged a bullet.

'Is he being an idiot again?' my mother finally asked, and I nodded.

'No more than usual,' I said, and was about to explain what he'd said to Sam when the phone beeped. A voicemail had been left.

'He left a message?' my mother asked as I picked the phone up. 'What's he said?'

She came closer but I held up my hand. I went out of the kitchen, into the hallway and my mother followed me with the energy and mobility of a teenager, all thoughts of her bad back gone.

'Keep Sam in there,' I told her, and she registered mild disappointment that she wouldn't be listening to the message with me, before nodding and going into the lounge, shutting the door behind her.

'Ruth.'

The pain never went away. Hearing him say my name felt like a small dagger was slicing through my chest. When we first separated, I considered asking him to call me by my middle name, Ann, just to avoid the feeling. It was one of the main reasons I couldn't talk to him. It was stupid but after four years, hearing him say my name still sparked up such anger. It made me furious, even now. I recently spoke to someone at school, a teaching assistant who'd got divorced and remarried within two years, and she spoke of her separation fondly, as if it was something fortunate. I wondered at her courage at the time before realising she was barking mad.

'I just got off the phone,' Will went on, 'with Rob.'

My heart jumped, making a bid for my throat. I made an involuntary sound that was close to a cry. Listened to him pause, take a sharp breath.

'*What were you thinking?*' he hissed. 'With Rob? Knowing he was married? And telling Janine like that, in front of everyone at the school gates. Humiliating her.' He paused again and I felt sick. A physical urge to vomit, saliva filling my mouth.

'Rob's chairman of the rugby club,' he said. 'I see him and Janine at training, he helps out with Little League, for Christ's sake. Janine went to his office. *To. His. Office.* After you'd screamed obscenities in her face, and they put two and two together. Worked out that it's you, my crazy ex-wife, that's shouting in front of all the kids and parents, and then he gets on the phone to *me*. I didn't even know he had my number,

73

he's the *bloody chairman*, Ruth. I'm seeing them tonight and I just ...' he trailed off, as if lost for words. 'So anyway, you've had it. This is the final straw. I'm not letting you do this to me any more, to my son. Enough is enough. Sam needs to be with me. Last time I had him he was a nightmare, the checking things, staying inside, those tantrums and the sleeping ... and now I see why. He needs someone sane in his life, not someone who's ranting at the school gates and can't keep her legs closed.

'This alternate weekend bullshit has gone on long enough. I'm entitled to see Sam for fifty per cent of the time, you know this. It's the law. I'll be collecting him on Friday. You don't need to leave him at my mother's, that's stopping as well. I'll come to you. And we'll talk about –' he paused '– all of it. I'm taking early leave, so I'll be with you at about five. And Ruth?' I heard him draw his breath in. 'Don't be a bitch.'

EIGHT

2 MAY

It was murder. Whatever way you look at it, however you justify it, someone is dead. Someone is no longer on this planet because of what happened. You are to blame just as much as I am.

I understand why you behaved like you did after we realised this person was dead. Have I told you that? I realise that you were out of options, that you were backed in a corner, up against a wall. I know that. Me, of all people, knows that. It doesn't excuse what you did, or how you're behaving now, but I can empathise with the situation.

I've been over and over the events, and I can't say I wouldn't have acted in exactly the same way as you. But it was murder.

Do you think about it? Do you believe in an afterlife? I do. I often wonder, when it's late at night, after lights out and I'm in the dark, staring into the blackness, if the victim can understand. If there is forgiveness wherever they are. Do they look back to that night, that autumn night that was to be their last ever on this earth, and sympathise? Have pity on us? And do they see me now, locked up in here, and you, out there.

It's funny how things spiral out of our control without us realising; that's something I've time to comprehend here. I didn't mean to lie to you. I took advantage and that was wrong of me, I didn't mean for it to end that way. I've had time to think it over. I've got time. All the time. I can look back on those events last autumn and see where I went wrong. But you've had enough time now. It's my turn. You need to come forward, admit your part. It was the deal we made, remember? I know you haven't forgotten. Someone is dead. Come forward and admit it, like you promised before you put me in here.

NINE

The next morning, I awoke to a text from Becca. She had meant to call, but only got away from the staff meeting late. It was postponed due to a smell. One of the TAs thought it might be a gas leak. Another teacher thought a dead mouse, and it took Gary the best part of an hour to find a half-eaten sandwich that someone had dropped down the side of a chair. The upshot being that the meeting didn't start until late, so it finished late and she was freezing. They'd had to have the meeting with all the windows and doors open, and once the heat of the day had gone it had got cold.

Her text only referred to the meeting as being 'the usual rubbish', telling me 'not to worry'. Reading that, and how my sandwich had made an impact, gave me a small moment of pleasure before the reality of the day dawned on me. What lay ahead, what might happen.

Last night, when I got home from my mother's, there was a part of me that wanted to call Janine. To apologise again and explain how her husband had lied to me and tell her it wasn't my fault, but I didn't.

For one thing, the text could've been from anyone and I didn't have her number, and for another, me responding would probably make everything worse. Rob, her husband, knew Will. They both did. And the thoughts of them all together, all talking about me, was horrendous. So I'd deleted Will's voice-mail and switched off my phone. I didn't want to be contacted. I decided I didn't want to hear about the staff meeting, I didn't want to listen to Becca after hearing Will's outpouring of hate. All I wanted to do was pretend it hadn't happened. Any of it. I'd wanted to hide and lick my wounds and that's exactly what I did. I'd let Sam climb into my bed and we'd watched some kids' film that I can't remember. He'd fallen asleep at around eight, and at about nine-thirty I'd put him in his own bed and taken a sleeping pill from an old prescription I had years ago when Will had first left me.

I probably shouldn't have taken it, but it was either that or replay out the scene with Janine and see all those women staring at me, or relive the humiliation in the staffroom with Lisa and wonder what was said about me when the staff meeting finally got underway. Hear Will's words going around in my head all night and imagine the scene of Rob calling Will. And what would Rob have told him in that conversation? That he'd got his ex-wife drunk and lied to her for a quick shag?

I kept imagining the scene where Janine walked into Rob's office. In my imagination, it was an open plan office. I had no idea what Rob did for a living – he'd told me that he was a sales rep, living in Edinburgh and travelling through Carlisle on a job, which was obviously a lie, so I knew nothing about him. Or her.

Will had said she went straight into his office after throwing her phone at me. Did she tell him that? While asking him if he'd had sex with me? And what would've been his reply? Did he tell her how he'd lied?

If I hadn't taken one of the old sleeping pills I kept for emergencies, the questions would've buzzed around my head all night.

The next morning my mind was groggy and I desperately wanted to stay in bed. To pull the soft duvet up over my head and hide, but then there was Sam.

He needed to get to school, needed to be shown how to deal with bullies, and seeing his mother hide under the duvet wasn't the way. So I dragged myself up and, as I was telling Sam how to deal with Toby, I realised what I was saying could be applied to how I should deal with my own situation.

'Stand up for yourself,' I said, as we made the journey in. 'Keep calm and don't let him call you names or steal your food. And if it gets too bad, tell an adult. Tell a teacher.' I thought of Lisa, her screwed up face when she spoke to me in the staffroom, how she'd said that Sam was the one with challenging behaviour. 'And if that teacher doesn't do anything,' I went on, 'tell a different teacher. Keep telling someone until they do something about it. But whatever you do –' I turned to him as we reached the school '– don't ignore it and hope it'll go away. Bullies never go away, you have to make them.'

Sam looked back at me.

'But what if you're scared?' he asked, and I nodded, looking to the squat school building with my heart thumping, thinking what the day might contain for me.

'And what if something happens,' he went on, 'when there're no teachers around to see it and they might not believe you later?'

I turned back to him and took his hand. 'I know,' I told him, 'it can be frightening to stand up for yourself. So, if something happens . . .' I paused, unsure of what to suggest.

Sam was bigger than Toby, but I couldn't tell him to lash out. As a parent, it wouldn't be good to advise violence and, besides, although Sam was twice the size of Toby, he'd be useless in any fight. He would cower and most probably burst into tears at the slightest touch. If Toby did decide to fight Sam, Sam would inevitably get beaten up. Hurt. No, recommending that Sam confront Toby wasn't the way forward.

'If something happens,' I went on, 'and a teacher isn't there, keep calm and . . .' I took a moment.

What could I tell him? Apart from punching the child, or telling a teacher, what else was there? Lisa was proving useless and I didn't want Sam in a fight. I was at a loss.

'Mum?'

I looked at him a moment.

'Mum, what should I do?' he asked again.

'OK,' I said, an idea slowly forming. 'When Toby picks on you today, don't do anything . . .'

'But Mum, you said . . .'

'I know, I know what I said. But you won't be ignoring him. This is what you do.' I picked up my bag and took out the red pen that I'd taken from Lisa's classroom. The ridiculous red pen with the feathers on top that she used for marking.

'That's Miss Gleason's . . .'

'I know,' I said, and handed it to Sam.

He took it and stared at me, his eyes wide. 'This is Miss

Gleason's pen. She was looking for it, she asked us all, said that whoever had taken it was in trouble, that they—'

'Listen,' I interrupted. 'I took it for you.'

He blinked rapidly.

'If Toby spits at you today, or calls you names, or does anything, then you can say that . . .'

'Toby took it,' Sam finished, and we stared at each other.

His fingers were tight around the barrel of the pen. I could see him tremble a little. I reached out and put my hand on his. I wasn't completely sure if what I was doing was right, but Sam got the idea. He finished my sentence for me, he knew that this was the only way to defend himself. Blame Toby for something he hadn't done, put him in trouble with the teacher so he wouldn't cause further trouble for Sam. I looked at the pen in Sam's hands. I almost took it back and then I remembered that they were spitting at my son. *Spitting at him.*

'Put it in his drawer,' I said after a moment. 'Without anyone seeing you do it.'

Sam looked down at the pen in his hand.

'Then, when it's in his drawer,' I said gently, 'that's when you tell the teacher what Toby did.' I looked at his small fingers wrapped around the pen, thought of him lying to Lisa, his class teacher. The words he'd use to blame Toby and how his small innocent face would look as he lied.

What was I telling my son now? To frame a fellow pupil for stealing the teacher's pen? That's what it had come to? That was better than him getting beaten up? Than being spat at?

'Actually, Sam,' I began, 'on second thoughts, perhaps you should . . .'

'I'll do it when she's taking the register,' he said. 'Everyone's sitting at their desks then, doing silent reading. I'll do it when I get my book. No one will see.'

I took a deep breath as he looked up at me. Sam's face had taken on a different expression. Hope. I saw hope in his eyes and something eased a little in my chest. It was only a pen, after all. And it was only a small lie. I wasn't asking him to steal anything, just put something back.

'Make sure no one sees you,' I said, 'and don't tell anyone what you've done. *No one*. You hear? Not a soul.'

He nodded.

'All we're doing is showing Miss Gleason what Toby is really like. She doesn't believe that he's being mean to you, but if he's mean to her, then she'll have to do something. And besides, it's only a pen. Just a pen. It's not like it's anything really valuable.'

We both looked at it, the ridiculous red feathers.

'If Miss Gleason finds you with it,' I added, 'tell her you found it on the floor.'

He was quiet. Then after a moment, he hid it in his pocket. I leaned over and gave him a cuddle.

'You can do it,' I told him, as we got out of the car. 'And once everyone realises what Toby is like, they'll do something and it will all get better. Promise.'

So there I was, dealing with the queue of parents, taking in money, residential slips and letters, all the while my heart pounding should Janine or Ashley walk in. Should Lisa march in brandishing her red pen.

They didn't.

Despite me being ready for battle, nothing happened apart from the usual barrage of parents and grandparents. John hid in his office, teachers came and went, and the morning ran along with nothing unexpected happening. It passed like any other.

I avoided the staffroom at lunchtime; I didn't want another episode like yesterday. Later, I was trying to find out who my union rep would be, if I was even in the union. I was trying to work out how to contact Eve, Ryan's mum, and see if her offer of being a witness still held, when there was the sharp *ping* of the bell.

'Bloody hell, that must annoy you.'

I looked up.

'Glen Harrow,' he said, and held out his hand, 'supply.'

His hand was large, it engulfed my small one. 'I'm taking over Mrs Kirkold's class, year five,' he smiled. He had dimples. A grown man with dimples. For a moment I was at a loss.

'I'm not due in till tomorrow,' he went on, 'but I like to prepare. Thought I'd see how much planning there is to do. The agency said a couple of TAs have been holding the fort?'

'Of course,' I said, it coming back to me in a rush. I'd booked a teacher with the temp agency yesterday afternoon, when I was still reeling from the events of the morning. 'I just didn't think you'd be . . .'

I was still holding his hand.

'Right,' I said rather too brightly, 'there's a few forms, some admin stuff to go over. Then you can see the class if you like? Pop down there and have a chat with the teaching assistants. They can tell you where they're up to.'

I went to the filing cabinet, collecting together the pack of forms that was needed, aware of him watching me. It was unusual to have a man in the office that wasn't John or Gary; I felt ridiculously self-conscious. I noticed I was doing this strange thing with my hair, tucking it behind my ear and smoothing it around my forehead and I found myself blushing.

He started to whistle, a low tune I didn't recognise, and he emitted an air of composure that you rarely saw in a primary school. Most of the people in education were all nervous energy, always hurtling themselves against some deadline. It was the same with the parents; the clock-watching was infectious in a primary school. I saw it when they came in for a visit – be it an assembly or parents' evening, they couldn't help but watch the time. All the clocks and bells forced you into it, but Glen Harrow had time.

He was totally at ease and I got the impression it had nothing to do with the fact that he didn't have a class to teach that afternoon. I got the feeling that Glen Harrow was easy-going.

And as I passed him the school policy forms and explained about the fire procedure and the alarm system, I found myself watching him unashamedly. There was something fascinating about how he handled himself after all the drama and hysterics I'd been dealing with.

'So, what happened there?'

I was still wearing the large plaster. I'd figured reminding John that I was the victim would work in my favour and had reapplied Teresa's dressing. He reached up and briefly touched the back of my neck. A completely innocent gesture but it took me a second before I could reply.

'Yesterday –' I let my fingers touch where he just had '– there was a . . .' I paused '. . . bit of something with one of the parents.'

He raised his eyebrows and no, I wasn't imagining it. There was a current in the air between us. 'One of the parents here –' I shook my head '– it was a minor thing.'

'Doesn't look minor,' he said, suddenly amused. 'With one of the parents?' He smiled. 'What happened?'

I took a deep breath, shook my head. 'I think you've got everything now, when you arrive tomorrow—' I began, but he interrupted.

'Oh no. No, no, no.' He put his hand to his chest in a mock horror pose. 'I didn't think this was the bad end of Carlisle, but now, parents attacking the staff at the primary school? Should I be afraid to work here?'

There was something so playful about him, so unguarded. I found myself smiling back, found myself talking about the last thing I wanted to. I was even recalling it as an anecdote, my words hiding a slight laugh.

'It was my fault –' I heard myself saying '– a misunderstanding. And I don't think I'm allowed to talk about it. There's an investigation ongoing, but basically, one of the parents took something I said out of context and there was a small incident. Nothing at all to worry about, it'll all blow over soon I'm sure.'

Glen narrowed his eyes as I spoke. 'You're not talking about Janine Walker, are you?' he asked, and all humour disappeared from me.

'You know her?'

'I know something happened with her, it was on Facebook—'

'Facebook!'

'Didn't mention that she'd attacked someone though.'

'You're friends with her?'

He let out a huff. 'Hardly. I'm on that group she runs. Top Marks? I keep meaning to leave the page, or unlike it, or whatever you have to do, but I forget. Someone left a post up asking if she was OK after the incident with her husband at school.' He looked at me. 'Sounded juicy. I thought it was a bump in her car but I guess not, I guess they were talking about you. You're the incident.'

'It's on Facebook,' I said quietly. I was gossip on- and offline.

We stared at each other for a moment before he let out a raucous laugh.

'You're famous!' He smiled at me and then, when he saw I was no longer sharing the joke, put his hand out. I was suddenly in danger of crying. 'You OK?' he asked, and I nodded, swallowing down the lump in my throat. I went to say how I was fine and then realised he was the first person to ask. The first person to care about me in this whole sorry situation.

'So she has a Facebook group for her tutoring page,' I said, 'and I'm being discussed on there?' I looked up at him. 'And you work for her along with everyone else around here?'

He grimaced. 'Hardly. I've done the odd stint for her, that's all.' He shrugged. 'Not ideal, but it's easy money.'

'What are they saying?' I asked. 'Can you tell me?'

'They just referred to an "incident".' He smiled. 'So, you going to tell me what the incident is?'

'It happened months ago,' I said. 'I had no idea who he was until I saw him outside school. He lied to me, back then. It was one night and he told me he was single.'

Glen was grinning now. 'I take it you're talking about Mr Walker? Janine's husband?'

I nodded.

'And you told her about it?'

'No. I just apologised.' I was shaky, had no idea why we were having this conversation. What was making me confide in him?

'Therefore, admitting your part,' he said, nodding, 'and then she did that.'

86

'She threw her phone at me.'

We stared at each other for a moment before he let out another loud laugh. 'Her face must have been a picture. Was he there? That rugby idiot husband of hers? You still seeing him?'

'No!' I checked the door, my voice had been louder than I intended. 'I didn't even like him. I was drunk. I didn't see him again until he was dropping his kids off the other morning and it was such a shock. He was gone by the time Janine worked it out. I feel awful about it, but now she's . . .'

I covered my face with my hands. I was hot, my heart beating. I knew my face was red, could feel the sweat on my brow.

'Was bound to happen sooner or later,' he said, 'because I'm guessing you're not the first person he's done this with.'

I looked up.

'You were probably just the first person to admit it to his wife.'

My throat was tight. I swallowed, shaking my head and then went to my computer. I brought up the spreadsheets I was working on for the upcoming residential, suddenly desperate to be busy, to have something else to focus my attention on.

'I shouldn't have told you any of that,' I said, not looking at him. 'There's an investigation pending and—'

'But if Janine is discussing it on Facebook,' he interrupted, 'then you can discuss it as well.'

I stopped for a second and looked at him.

'She shouldn't be discussing it on Facebook.'

'No,' he agreed. 'She shouldn't.'

We stared at each other a moment. It was mid-afternoon, the bell would be ringing for break at any second.

'Don't beat yourself up about it,' he said gently. 'She needed to know. He was playing away and you told her. You did the right thing.'

I felt my chest tighten, his kindness was too much. I was in danger of crying.

'I expect it'll all blow over,' I said, busying myself with the paperwork on my desk. 'What is it they say? Today's news is tomorrows' chip shop wrappers? Everyone will have forgotten about it this time next week.' I looked up and gave what I hoped was a bright smile.

'What?' I asked as I saw his face. 'You don't think they will?'

'I'm sorry you got hurt –' he smiled '– but I know her type. Everyone thinks she's this pillar of the community, but I know how relentless she can be with selling her tutoring, and I read how she responded on that Facebook post, so I'm guessing she's reacted a little bit more than what you're telling me.'

I swallowed, thinking of the letter that Ashley sent in. Someone came from her office, all suited up, didn't even come to my window, just went straight to John's door.

'You made a fool of her and she's retaliated. I don't think Janine is the type to forgive and forget.' He smiled suddenly and the air of naughtiness was back, the buzz between us. 'Not that you'd care about her forgiveness. You shone a light on her husband's fidelity, but she hurt you. Don't let her do anything else.'

His words lingered long after he'd left.

They were on repeat in my head. Like the earworm of a well-known song. She had everyone in her pocket, everyone on her side and my job was hanging in the balance because of her husband and his lies. I'd done nothing wrong, apart from apologise. And then there was Will and his phone call. His threat. And Sam, his needs being pushed aside because of Lisa and her cash-in-hand jobs over the summer.

Don't let her do anything else.

Hadn't it been what I was telling my son to do about Toby? Janine might be a lovely person outside of this situation, but wasn't she bullying me now? Wasn't trying to get me fired and gossiping about me on Facebook going a bit far?

After Glen had left I brought up the Facebook page. It was private – a closed group, invitation only. But there she was, and there it was. Top Marks, private tutoring. Janine Walker. I studied the profile picture. It was a head shot of her, big teeth smiling out, pen in hand, like she's just been caught teaching a student herself, and something inside me snapped.

I went hot at the thought of what they were all saying about me on there. After the way they'd treated me in the staffroom. I could only imagine what Glen Harrow had read about me. It was beyond embarrassing. I couldn't wait for this to blow over – like he'd said, my job was hanging in the balance. Shit, *my life* was hanging in the balance. It was just after afternoon break when I got the idea.

I took out the file.

Sally Walker. Orla Walker.

Home address, mobile and home telephone numbers. There he was, Rob Walker, and there she was, Janine Walker. Contact in case of emergency. It was confidential information, but I tapped the numbers into my phone.

I'm not sure what made me choose him instead of her. I suppose because it was his fault. He was the one who lied, who started this whole mess, and there was a part of me that believed Janine was a decent woman. That if we'd met under different circumstances, we might have even liked each other. If I'd been clever, I would've hidden my number before sending the text. But it didn't even occur to me and I didn't know how to do it. My text was only a few words.

I'm in contact with the police. They're advising I press charges.

I angled the phone around to the back of my head and took a photo of the large plaster I'd reapplied that morning.

Six months in prison for common assault. I have witnesses to the attack. Drop the complaint now or I will send her to jail.

My fingers trembled after I'd sent the message. I stared at my phone, unsure of what I'd just done.

'Shit, shit, shit,' I whispered as my heart beat rapidly.

My phone's screen went dark and I couldn't stop looking at it, staring at it, waiting for a response. Within an hour and a half, I had one, but it was the longest hour and a half I'd had in a while.

Just before the end of the school day, John came into my office. He smelt of the coffee I'd made him throughout the day.

'The complaint has been withdrawn,' he said, and took off his glasses. His face was bloated. It had been another warm day and the humidity of the school had made him swell. 'So. There is no longer a pending investigation, you are no longer in danger of suspension. Ashley Simmons is no longer acting as Janine's solicitor in regard to this whole ordeal.'

I was holding my breath.

'Janine Walker has retracted her complaint. So –' he thumped his side with his fist '– all accusations dropped.'

I let out a sigh of relief and he nodded, allowed his shoulders to relax, rubbed his eye as he did so.

'But,' he said, after a moment, 'this has been bloody hard work, Ruth.' He put on his glasses, straightened himself. 'And I'm not sure *I* can ignore what took place. You were on school property, in your role as school secretary. There won't be a full investigation, but I will have to do something.' He raised his eyebrows at me. 'Parents are concerned, staff are concerned, we'll discuss exactly what in the morning.'

'It won't happen again,' I said. 'I wasn't thinking and I explained why . . .'

He held up his hand to stop me. 'Ruth. It's been a long couple of days and I've phone calls to make. Go home.'

The phone in his office rang and he went to answer it. I took a moment. He'd probably give me a written warning, I assumed. That was to be expected. I understood that John had to look as if he were taking action. It would stay on my file for a few months and then everything would be forgotten. Will would never have to know that I almost lost my job again, the staff would go back to treating me civilly and Janine and her friends would go back to being women I didn't know or care about.

TEN

After school that day, we feasted on fast food. Double cheese burger, fries and large milkshake. A celebratory dinner of junk.

Sam was only slightly overweight but it was enough for the cruel to notice. As a result, I found I was ever watchful of what Sam ate, making sure that he had all the calories he needed, but without the sugar or fat. It was a constant battle, especially as I was often baking. I would try out a new recipe and have to keep it away from him, telling him it tasted bad, he couldn't lick the bowl, couldn't have anything I made. It felt as if I were punishing him, denying him one of the only pleasures he had. But not that night. That night was the first time in a long time that Sam had had a good day at school and all bets were off. That night, I didn't want to nag and deny him. He could eat whatever he liked. He actually let out a scream of delight when I went to the drive-through on the way home.

I passed him the ketchup, noting how his hair could do with a trim and debating whether I could do it again and avoid a trip to the hairdressers. He grinned happily at me, squirting a large dollop onto his plate and pushing a handful of fries in with his fingers.

If you were a stranger, you'd look at us and think everything was absolutely fine. Sam was happy, his body relaxed, munching on his burger and dipping his fries into the sauce. There was the background noise of his cartoons from the living room, and outside someone was mowing a lawn. It was most probably from the terrace to the side of us, a holiday let that had been host to never-ending groups of families over the summer, who were cheerful if the weather was nice and stroppy and sullen if it was not. It would now be let out to the walkers, the hikers who came with their walking poles and Ordnance Survey maps in term time, who were always up at the crack of dawn and returned when it was dark. They were the best kinds of neighbours.

Most of the terraces in our row were holiday lets. It was a sad fact, but as they backed onto open countryside and enabled tourists to explore the Lake District as well as South West Scotland, it was too good an opportunity for the owners to pass up. The only reason I'd been lucky enough to get one of the houses to rent long term was because the man who owned it had known my dad and had taken pity on me when he heard what Will had done. It was a little desolate, and it was a good twenty-minute drive to the school and away from my mother's, but it had a great kitchen, a cosy living room and was pretty much perfect for the two of us.

I'd had enough of the gossip and constant monitoring from when I lived on the estate, back when I was married. You couldn't do anything there without the whole neighbourhood knowing and asking you about it. I never wanted to live on an estate again.

'So,' I asked Sam, as he finished the last of the fries, 'how did it go today? Did it work, with the pen?'

Sam shook his head and grinned. 'Toby was off today. Stomach bug.'

I smiled back at him.

'But I still put Miss Gleason's pen in his tray,' he said, almost whispering, 'so that when he comes back into school, they can find it.'

I went to open my mouth, to tell him that perhaps it wasn't such a good idea after all, leaving the pen in there, and then I stopped myself. He was happy. The happiest I'd seen him in ages, and it was because he hadn't had to deal with the bullying. If a stupid pen with red feathers could make him feel like this for longer, then so be it. I nodded.

'So what else did you get up to?'

He shrugged. 'Stuff.'

'Maths? English? Science?' I prompted, and he shrugged again.

'Latin? Cookery? Brain surgery?'

He laughed, and I drank in every morsel of his smiling face.

'Fine art? Astronomy?'

'What's astronomy?'

'Space,' I told him, and he grinned.

'We did lots of that, that's all we did. Lessons on space.'

'You'd like that?'

He nodded again. 'I'd love that and then, when I'd learned all about it, I could take Toby Morley-Fenn up there and leave him. Floating around on his own in space. For ever.'

'Yeah,' I agreed, pinching the last of the fries off his plate. 'Toby Morley-Fenn. He deserves to be lost in space. Especially with such a stupid name!'

Sam giggled and then winced. He'd bit the inside of his cheek the other day and it was bothering him – he'd been up fretting over it in the early hours. I'd been groggy from the sleeping pill but had been awake enough to sit on the edge of his bed, stroking his hair until he fell back to sleep. I hadn't really had an unbroken night's sleep since the divorce. Sam was sensitive, he suffered when Will abandoned us, but at the time I was so lost in my own grief and anger I didn't realise it. He was four and everybody told me how resilient kids were, how they don't notice things and bounce right back. But not Sam. Once he learned that his dad loved another woman and he had to move out of his bedroom and into a smaller house, he got scared. And he'd been scared ever since.

'OK?'

He nodded, and I saw a shadow of concern pass over his face. The anxiety that plagued him bubbling underneath, threatening to surface, and I leaned forward, desperate to stop that from happening.

'How about,' I said, stroking his cheek, 'you play on the Xbox and I'll bring you some ice cream in and, after that, one of those muffins I made?'

His eyes lit up. What I was suggesting was forbidden. Fast food that included a milkshake and now ice cream and one of my muffins?

'Best day ever!' he announced and ran off into the living room.

I sat for a moment among the debris of our supper, absorbing the normality of the evening. It wasn't much to ask, I thought, burgers, ice cream and a normal day at school. A day where he could skip off into the lounge without loitering by the door, his face drawn and pinched. Where he didn't tell me how much he hated school. Where he didn't ask about what would happen if . . .? I gave a sigh and started clearing up the wrappers.

I'd deleted the 'SLAG' text. Deleted it as soon as I heard that the charges had been dropped. Unlike Janine I could forgive. Because it must have been Janine who sent it – who else would call me that? It was either her, or him, and I could let that go. I'd made them face the truth, I got that. I made them realise something and they were hurting, God knows I'd been there. When I found out Will was cheating I actually went around to the other woman's house. So a text? That was small potatoes, I could allow them that.

I still had my job, I could face the catcalls for a while. The silence in the staffroom, the teachers who worked for her being bitches, gossiping about me until it all blew over. For a second Glen Harrow's face reappeared in my mind and I had to sit down. I felt the urge to call him, to tell him that I'd stopped it, that the investigation he must have read about on Facebook had been dropped. I wondered, briefly, if she'd put a post up about it on her Top Marks page?

I've dropped the investigation as there was a chance I might end up in prison.

I smiled at the thought and then, as I was stuffing all the takeaway packaging into the waste bin, allowed myself to indulge in thoughts of him. Glen Harrow. I'd looked at his completed forms after he'd left. He lived over in Stanwix, had put down his sister as an emergency contact, so I guessed there was no wife or girlfriend, and he had worked on cruise ships for the past six years between teaching jobs. He was another face I'd never seen before, another person I would probably have bumped into at some time if I ever went out. And he was fascinating. He worked on cruise ships for long stretches of time, but had only put down 'entertainer' as a job description. What did he do? Kids' holiday clubs? Entertain the little ones while mum and dad sunbathed?

I found myself thinking of his eyes, how they looked when I'd told him what happened with Janine. He wasn't horrified or judgemental, he found it *funny*. We'd laughed about it. He'd asked me how I was, how I felt about it. God, he was nice. First nice man I'd considered since Will. But it could not happen. Nothing could happen, I told myself firmly. He might be nice and have taken pity on me, but that was it. I gave out a loud huff. What was I thinking anyway? The man had just learned that I was an easy lay, that I'd had a one-night stand with a married man. I was a single mother, no cash, not even a teacher, and in a spat with a parent. The chances of Glen Harrow being interested were zero. Nada. And I had Sam. He was my top priority. He was more than enough.

I heard the familiar sound of his game being set up and, after a moment, the mournful piano soundtrack that accompanied it. Why it was such a sad tune I'd no idea, and it still bewildered me how Sam could find joy in what appeared to be such a boring, futile game of putting imaginary bricks on top of one another, but he loved it. I gave a grateful sigh and took our plates to the sink.

There was a knock at the door and, thinking it was Becca, I answered without a thought of my appearance. I almost jumped back when I saw it was Will. Dressed in an expensive navy suit, his hair perfectly swept back from his face and still with a slight tan. Bastard.

'I thought it would be better if we spoke now, instead of Friday when I'm collecting Sam. Is he here?'

He was standing too close. He always stood too close, he knew I hated it. I needed quite a large area of personal space and he knew it put me on the back foot.

'In the living room –' I made an effort to stand my ground '– on his Xbox.'

Will nodded, then his eyes found the fast food milkshake on the kitchen counter and his face dropped in horror as if it were a bag of heroin.

'Really?' he asked. 'You're allowing him that now?'

'It's a milkshake, Will, calm down.'

'But we agreed.' Will shook his head, as if I was severely disappointing him and a ball of rage coursed through me. 'Sam needs to be on a diet, he needs—'

'Goodbye, Will.'

I went to close the door but he put his hand out, breathing hard through his nose.

'A quick word,' he said, 'that's all I want, then I'll be gone.'

I wrapped my cardigan around me tightly and looked at my bare feet.

'Please,' he said. 'It won't take long and I don't want Sam to know I'm here. I don't want to upset him. Could you step out for a moment? Please, Ruth.'

The stone pathway was cold on my feet. Despite it being another warm day, the heat was on the wane and there was a distinct chill in the air. I pulled the door closed behind me. Will was a good foot taller than me but he made no effort to give me space. He looked down at me and I crossed my arms, did my best to straighten my spine and ignore how my heart was thudding.

'You got my message?'

'If by message, you mean threat. Then yes, I got that, Will.'

He rolled his eyes in a dramatic, juvenile way and I wanted to slap him. To reach up and use my fingernails to scratch those eyes out.

'It wasn't a threat, Ruth,' he said levelly, 'and I wouldn't have to leave messages if you ever answered my calls.'

'I don't answer because I don't care what you've got to say.'

He took a moment, his jaw clenched, a muscle working at the side.

'Believe it or not, I didn't come here to argue,' he said, 'but when Rob called me, when he told me what you did . . . ' He shook his head. 'And there were others. Not parents at the school where you work, but friends of mine. They're members of the rugby club. They remember what you did, why you got your criminal record and, to be quite honest, your behaviour has surprised none of them.'

'I don't care what they—'

'Rob and Janine care,' Will interrupted, 'and it was very embarrassing to see them being told about you. When Rob said—'

'Yes, what did Rob say?' I cut in. 'Did he tell you that he lied to me? That I had no idea he was married, that he had children?'

Will sighed dramatically. 'I told him what you're like when I had a drink with them at the bar.'

'You're drinking with them now? You're best friends?'

'It's quite serious what you've done, Ruth.' He folded his arms. 'I'm not talking about the sex, or the affair, but the screaming of it in her face at the school gates. In front of the children.'

'That's not what happened!' I wanted to slap him, to punch him, to punch someone. 'I did not scream anything in her face or in front of any children.'

'You're screaming now.'

I paused for a moment. I was breathing hard.

'So you met with them, with Rob and Janine?'

He nodded.

'You're all mates now?'

'Rob's the chairman of the rugby club. They moved up near our end last year. He used to go to the club over by the hairdressers near the park, but that was closed down so he came to ours. We've known about each other for a while.' He puffed out his chest a little as he spoke. 'This is the first time he's called me, though.'

'Oh, I get it,' I said, 'you're using this, aren't you?'

'Using what?'

'You're using the fact that I slept with the chairman of that stupid little rugby club you attend so you can get some social standing.'

His face went slack a little and I knew I was right, could see it in the way he was weirdly proud to be talking about Rob and Janine as if they were friends of his.

'You're vile,' I said. 'I'll bet you couldn't wait to meet up, tell them all about me. Introduce them to all those friends of yours, all the ones who knew what you were doing while you were married to me. Bet you left that part out, didn't you? The part where you're the cheating bastard?'

'I'm not here to talk about that,' he said, cutting me off. 'I'm here to talk about Sam. As his father I—'

'Oh, you're his father now, are you?' It was no good, I couldn't contain myself. 'And were you being his father when you had that affair when he was four years old? Were you his father when you left us? When you wanted nothing to do with him for the next twelve months. When you said no to any visits, when you ignored him, were you his father then?'

'Ruth—'

'No, let me speak –' I was hissing out my words, making sure that Sam couldn't overhear '– because you forget, Will. You leave all these messages like you're the best dad in the world, you come here, making me feel awful for what happened with Rob, when it was you that was unfaithful. You left us. It was you who walked out on us, remember? You who left him, and wouldn't even see him, so don't come back saying all this. You've got no rights. Nothing at all. You left your son to go look after someone else's.'

'That was four years ago.'

'Four years is nothing.'

We stared at each other. My head was pounding, my heart skipping beats. I felt jittery, shaky; adrenalin and fury making me dizzy. I was always like this with Will. It came back like a hurricane, the rage, sweeping me up and leaving me breathless. I was amazed at the force of it, the power of how much I hated him. How I could ever have loved him, slept with him, let him touch me? I was married to him for eight years and the thought of that was shocking.

'It's been four years,' I spat out. 'The first year of which you weren't around. It's me and Sam, four years of me repairing the damage you did—'

'That's what I want to talk about.'

'How you damaged him?'

'His anxiety, Ruth. The whole thing with him, his mood swings, the not sleeping, the tantrums, his agoraphobia.'

'Sam is not agoraphobic.'

'He's struggling to go to school,' Will fired back. 'And when he's with me, all he wants to do is stay indoors and play on his games.'

'That's what eight-year-old boys do.'

'Not when they could be out playing football or rugby. I've got Sam onto training groups for both, enrolled him into the rugby club, he wouldn't even come to a match ...'

'Why would you do that?'

'To get him out of the house! To get him to act like a little boy should! You don't notice because you're mental as well. You're agoraphobic so it looks normal to you, but it's not normal. It's not healthy him living with you. He needs to be with me, to get out, have a childhood. He needs to be with his dad. And then, when I find out what you've been doing, sleeping around and screaming at people outside the school where you work, well I think it's best if he was away from that kind of situation.' He gave a big sigh, his shoulders dropping. 'Ruth, believe it or not, I did not come here to do this. I came here to talk—'

'I'm not doing this.' I went to the door, ready to go back inside. 'I'm not doing this again.'

'I'm getting social services involved,' he said, and I froze. 'I knew you'd be like this, so I talked to a solicitor. I've a good case, should I apply for custody.'

'Custody!' I almost screamed the word. 'You don't even have him, you only have—'

'I want him every other week, Ruth,' Will said. 'The full week, with me. Not just alternate weekends –' he sighed '– in light of what's happened. What you did to Janine, I just think it's best if he is with me more. I don't have the time or the money to take this to court, but I will if I have to. Think about it, you'll see it's the best decision for all of us. I've been in touch with the social, but they work at a snail's pace, and I've a strong case ...'

My pulse quickened. 'You can't do that.'

'I can,' Will said. 'We're both agreed Sam has issues. Problems.' Will's voice dropped. 'He's overweight, his anxiety is through the roof, he can't even go upstairs on his own when he comes to stay with me. He refuses to leave the house, won't go into the shopping centre, supermarket.' He let out a sigh. 'Ruth, he won't even get on a bus.'

'That's because he doesn't know anyone where you live. It's the other side of town.'

'He needs to get to know me better, know where I live, to know—'

'I don't want that woman near him!' I spat out. 'The agreement is he sleeps at your mother's. I only allowed alternate weekends because of your mother. Sam likes his grandparents. You can't just—'

'I can,' he said, 'and I am.' He paused. 'I'm getting married, did you know that?'

I went to open my mouth to argue but he spoke over me.

'And if you won't let me see him as I want, then I'll apply for full custody. If you refuse this now, then I'm going to go the whole way. I'm going to be the one who decides when *you're* allowed to see Sam.'

I took a shocked breath.

'You know I'll win the case,' he said. 'You're about to lose another job because of your behaviour. I know you're struggling for money, so with no reliable income . . . '

'I am not losing my job,' I told him, 'and my cake making business . . . '

He let out a laugh. 'Pipe dreams, Ruth. Do you think the court will take into account hobbies? They want to see real income, not pocket money. You would never take any money from me even though it was for Sam. You've a history of mental health problems—'

'We don't need your money,' I spat out.

'The court looks at what's in the best interest of the child. You're denying him things he should have. You make him live in poverty. You were assessed as having PND and anxiety, and now it's apparent you're passing on problems to our son. He's showing heightened anxiety, a reluctance to go—'

'I've booked us a holiday.'

Will stopped speaking. I nodded at him, taking pleasure that I'd managed to make him shut up.

'Disney. I've been saving up, my pocket money business, as you call it, is doing really well, and in the half term, this October, I'm taking us both to Disney.'

He frowned.

'So, tell me, Will, if I'm agoraphobic, if I'm on the poverty line, if I'm suffering and passing on these problems to Sam, who has also got heightened anxiety and agoraphobia, then how is that happening?' I stuck my chin out. 'Is that what you've based your case on? Is that what your outline is, what you plan on telling the social services? My financial situation and Sam's anxiety? Doesn't really stand up if we're jetting off to Paris for thrill-seeking rides on the fairground in four weeks, does it?'

Will's shoulders dropped. 'How are you managing to take him to Disney, he never said—'

'He doesn't know,' I said quickly. 'It's a surprise, early birthday present. But he's desperate to go, it's all he talks about if you'd ever listened to him. So please, before you call me names, before you tell me what a bad mother I am and go running to the social, make sure you get your facts straight first.'

He folded his arms. 'Bullshit.'

I scoffed. 'Goodbye, Will.' I went to the door, my legs unstable. 'I won't be dropping Sam off this weekend, he'll be staying here.'

'Ruth –' he put his hand on the door '– you can't just—'

'I can,' I said directly to him. 'Sam hates staying with you. He hates it. I only do it so your mother can see him. He likes Jean, it's you he hates.'

Will's jaw clenched. I could see his hands curling up into fists.

'Do it,' I said before I could stop myself. 'Ring social services, take me to court. See what happens, because you're not having Sam this weekend, or any other weekend.'

'But Ruth, that's not fair on Sam, on his routine.'

'Sam will be delighted he's not having to endure another Saturday night with you.'

'If you do this, Ruth,' Will clenched his teeth and took a deep breath in, 'if you do this now, you'll be giving me no other option than to—'

I shut the door and rested against it, my heart speeding. I'd just told Will that I had an extravagant trip to Disney planned. That me and Sam were travelling to Paris. Going on a plane. To a busy theme park with hundreds of others. Away from home. Away from Carlisle. In four weeks. I told him to take me to court. I more or less told him to apply for custody.

I had no money, was behind on the rent, had almost lost my job and, if I didn't pull off this holiday, was now in danger of losing my son. In danger of losing everything.

ELEVEN

'You said what?'

I went to the fridge and took out the wine.

'Disney,' I said, and offered her the bottle.

She hesitated for a fraction, then looked towards the stairs. She'd just come down from seeing Sam, who was up there in my bedroom watching television.

'He's fine,' I told her, 'you just said so.'

She smiled. 'He's more than fine, he's adorable.' She joined me at the kitchen table. 'We just had the most interesting conversation about star gazing and astronomy.'

'We talked about that over dinner.'

Becca nodded. 'He's so clever, gets it all from me.'

I raised my eyebrows.

'As his godmother –' she smiled as I handed her a glass '– my intelligence has obviously rubbed off.' I began to pour and she stopped me quickly. 'Just a tiny one,' she said, 'I've got a late spin class.'

'Spin class?' I looked over to the six cakes I had on the counter. 'So you won't be wanting a cake with that wine then?'

Becca stared at them a moment, all bright and shiny in their neon cases from where I'd been baking earlier. After Will had gone I'd done what I normally do to calm down, I'd baked. I'd done all of the fairy cakes for Sue's fiftieth birthday party, as well as a dozen for Gary and his charity event, only just finishing when Becca came to the door. I had six left over that I planned to eat that evening, but now, looking at the rainbow frosting, I wasn't sure I had the appetite.

Becca shook her head resolutely and patted her thighs. 'Better not. They have this big screen up at the gym showing a road through a forest that moves when you cycle, so it feels like you're really outside. And as it's in the evening, they put all these fairy lights on for atmosphere.'

I handed her half a glass of wine, picked up one of the cakes and started picking at the frosting. 'Here's an idea, why not just cycle outside?'

She took a quick sip. 'Because if I went outside, I wouldn't get to go to the gym, and if I didn't go to the gym, I wouldn't get to see the new instructor who does the late-night spin class and who is this close to asking me out.' She put her finger and thumb together so they were almost touching.

'I see,' I said, sitting down heavily.

I didn't ask Becca about him. She went through a steady stream of men, always exciting and brilliant until she'd been out with them a few times and declared them boring. I had tried to tell her that she might have commitment issues, but she refused to consider it, her argument being that as she was getting older, she didn't have the time to waste. She claimed she knew if they were going to be a good fit by the third date, but I'd yet to see anyone get to a fourth.

'So –' Becca took a small sip '– Disney.'

I nodded and we were both silent for a moment.

'He knows them,' I said, and she raised her eyebrows. 'Janine and Rob.'

'How? How is that even possible? Doesn't Will live over by Hammonds Pond, in Upperby?'

I nodded. 'Janine and Rob moved there early this year.' I leaned forward. 'Rob is the chairman of Will's rugby club.'

Becca looked horrified for a second, then started to giggle.

'It's really not funny,' I told her, 'it just keeps getting worse. Will didn't know them until it all came out about me and Rob. Rob phoned him.'

'*Rob phoned Will?*'

'Apparently –' I took a long drink '– after Janine left school, she went to Rob's work. To confront him. And Rob must've put two and two together and worked out I was Will's ex-wife. Actually –' I took a moment '– I think I told him all that at the Valentine's dinner.'

I shut my eyes as it hit me afresh, Rob knowing exactly who I was, exactly who Will was, when he told me all those lies. When he slept with me, the bastard knew it all.

'So he calls Will,' I went on, 'like it was all my fault. Like Will was somehow responsible for me telling Janine. And now they've all crawled out of the woodwork, all of Will's friends who hate me. All those who lied for him when he was married to me, all those idiots at the rugby club. All calling me names and telling Will he should get his son away from me.'

My throat got tight as I spoke. Since the outburst I'd been constantly trying to hide from Sam how upset I was. It was only now that I let the full extent of it show. 'At least that's what I think happened. He had all these reasons as to why Sam should go and live with him, it was horrendous. Just awful. He threatened to go to social services, to get a solicitor involved.'

'A solicitor?' Becca crinkled up her nose. 'Bastard. After everything he's put you through. Can he even do that? Won't social services see that he didn't want to see Sam at all when he first went?'

I shrugged. The truth of it was, I had no idea to what extent social services would get involved.

'He called me mental.' I closed my eyes, tears threatening. 'Said I was crazy again. It was just like when he left.'

'But plenty of mothers have post-natal depression.' Becca reached across and grabbed my hand. 'It doesn't make them bad mothers, or *mental*.' She shook her head. 'I can't believe he actually called you that.'

'I know.'

'And plenty of children suffer from anxiety, it doesn't mean that anyone's to blame.'

I took a sip of wine and nodded. Becca was my best friend, she'd been with me through it all, seen me at my lowest, and she was saying all the right things. But the truth of it was, she didn't know if I wasn't to blame for how Sam was, and neither did I.

Sam's anxiety and behaviour issues started when Will left us. Just as Sam was starting school and becoming independent, his father left. Sam developed separation anxiety, which went on to develop into other forms of anxiety, and I blamed Will, had always blamed Will, but now, after what Will had said, what if it was me?

What if my mental health had left a mark on him? I'd read in a magazine that you teach your children how to behave by your behaviour, but what if you can't control your behaviour? What if your husband leaves and depression and anxiety take over and it's all you can do to hold your child close and get through the day?

'Fucking bastard,' I said, and grabbed a piece of kitchen roll to wipe my eyes. 'Fucking Rob and Janine. I don't care if you think she's nice, Becca, this is something else. This is her not being nice at all.'

'You don't know it was them who told Will to do this,' she began.

'He said he was getting a solicitor involved.' I raised my eyes. 'A solicitor. That's the second time this week I've had threats from a solicitor and I can only think of one.'

'You think they got Ashley Simmons . . . ?'

'Oh I don't know . . . ' I pressed the tissue to my eyes. 'I don't know what's going on any more, only that Will is going to social services. I had to say something.' I screwed the tissue up into a tight ball. 'I had to prove everything he was saying was wrong, and it was the first thing that came to mind.'

'You could've said you'd got Sam in to see someone.'

I huffed. Our last visit to the GP, months and months ago, had resulted in a referral that we were still waiting on.

'Or that you were going to Cornwall for a few days or something, but Disney?' She shook her head. 'That involves getting Sam on a plane, or a train, getting *you* on a plane or train, then the journey, then organising theme park tickets and lining up and pushing through all the crowds, and the expense. Do you know how much it costs for a trip to Disney? Do you know how much it costs to go to Paris even?'

I looked up at her, my eyes heavy and shook my head. 'More than I have,' I said, and we were both quiet.

'I told him we were going in half term,' I said, and Becca reeled.

'You're a terrible liar.'

'I know.'

I took another gulp of wine. 'It'll strengthen his case,' I said, 'me lying to him. He'll file for custody and he'll get it because I can't afford to fight him. He'll take Sam away and force him to go out, to do rugby and football and do all those things he hates.' My voice had got higher and I was out of breath. I looked down and realised I'd been picking the skin around my thumbnail; it was bleeding. 'And Janine and Rob will be friends with him and they'll all agree how pathetic I am and that it's a good job Sammy's with them and not me.'

'Calm down,' Becca said, and reaching across the table she put her hand on mine. 'It's Will. Stupid, lazy Will we're talking about here.'

I nodded.

'Remember who your enemy is,' she said. 'A man who makes decisions with what's in his pants and based on what a few people in the rugby club think. He's probably got this idea to get custody because he wants to impress someone. Probably Rob or Janine. And as soon as they realise what an arse he is, they'll forget him and he'll forget about applying for custody.'

My phone suddenly rang. It was the landline and made us both jump.

'Oh my God, it's him again,' I said, as the answer machine kicked in.

'Hello,' my voice sang out, 'you've reached Ruth's Custom Cakes, sorry I can't take your call, please leave a message and I'll get back to you.'

I stared at Becca. We heard the person at the other end of the line take a deep breath.

'Ruth?' It was a woman. 'It's Eve here, Ryan's mum. I was, well, when it all happened I came to you. Anyway, I need to see you, could do with having a chat.' She faltered for a moment, let out a small laugh. 'Sorry. Sorry I hate these answer machines. Anyway, my number is . . .'

I stared at Becca as Eve recited her number and ended the call. We were silent for a moment.

'Interesting,' Becca said. 'Are you going to call her back?'

I was exhausted. Shaky from too much wine and Will's visit.

'Janine sent me a text, you know,' I told her. 'It was either her or Rob, calling me a slag.'

'Oh Ruth . . .'

'I've deleted it,' I said, and took my wine to the sink, throwing it away before I gulped it down.

'Did she say anything else?'

I shook my head. 'Just that one word: "Slag". At least I think it was from her . . .'

'It was from her –' Becca nodded '– and that's why you sent that text to Rob?' She gave me a look as I nodded.

When I told her that I'd sent a text to Rob threatening to send Janine to jail, she went a bit mad at me. I'd not been that clever after all. It could easily have gone the other way. It looked like harassment, Becca said; they could've called my bluff, shown my message to John and the governors and used it as proof that my conduct in my role as school secretary wasn't professional.

'Well at least it made her drop the complaint,' I said, and Becca sighed.

'For now.' She looked at me pointedly. 'But the reason why

you left the car dealership was mentioned,' she said, and my heart thrummed.

'In the staff meeting?'

She nodded slowly.

'Will that ever stop following me around?' I felt tears brim against my eyes again. 'Who brought that up? It was a minor conviction, John had always said that was confidential, between him and the governors only. It was years ago.'

'A few of the parents mentioned it to John,' she said, 'and he felt, as head, it was his responsibility to tell the staff what you did now. So everyone was aware should things develop further.'

I winced.

'So don't send any more text messages, OK?' She sighed. 'Not to Janine, not to Rob, and don't talk about it to anyone. Don't even ring that Eve woman back. Let it all go. Let it all die down.'

I nodded.

'If Will is serious about getting social services involved, you don't want to appear . . . ' She paused, as if looking for the right word. 'Unstable. And being involved in an ongoing dispute with Janine and Rob won't look good, especially if he's now "friends" with them.'

She paused again.

'You might want to reconsider letting Will have Sam,' she said, before leaving, and put her hands up when I tried to argue against it.

'Think about it: if you deny all contact, he'll have no choice but to get social services involved. But if you come to some kind of agreement . . . '

She let her words hang when she saw my face.

'OK,' she said at the door. 'We've got four weeks before half term so let's use them. Keep your head down, don't get into any more trouble and we'll build a case so that, if Will does apply for custody, we'll be prepared.'

Four years earlier, when I found out about Will sleeping with another woman, I'd gone to her house and thrown a brick through her window.

At the time, we were living on an estate over in the south of Carlisle. When Sam was about two or three, I had started a part-time job at the car dealership two days a week. Will was doing well as an independent estate agent. Back then, he was still focusing on houses and residential property; he'd not yet started on the holiday lets, didn't need to. Sam had nursery on the days I worked, and I was toying with the idea of having another baby.

I remember walking past the five-bedroom detached houses over by the cathedral, with visions of me being a stay-at-home mum. I imagined days of park visits and messy play, of baking and pushing a pram with a newborn. I didn't want Sam to be an only child, ideally. I wanted three or four children. A big family, and I thought, as Sam was reaching an age where he was a little more independent, the time was right.

We started trying. In those first few months I was really hopeful. I'd conceived Sam without any trouble and naively thought it would happen a second time just as easily. I even went as far as to start getting stuff ready for this new child. I got Sam's old baby clothes down from the attic, accepted a nursing chair that a friend was giving away. But it didn't happen. It didn't happen at all, and after a few months it became the focus of everything. The waiting, the convincing myself I was pregnant for the two weeks after my ovulation date until I got my period, and the crushing despair when I realised it hadn't happened again.

Will said my PND was returning, that I was sending myself insane. I'd become fixated, obsessed, he said, and if I wasn't careful I'd alienate the child I did have. He told me I was pushing Sam away and I agreed. I wasn't blameless in the failure of our marriage, I know that. I know it was a difficult time, but what I can't forgive Will for is how he reacted. How he went on to treat me when I needed him most.

It was around this time that Will's business took a bit of a beating – a new development was given the go ahead in the area and it quickly monopolised the housing market. For a time it seemed everyone just wanted the new builds. All plans to expand our family were put on hold. Will said he was working non-stop, chasing up leads, trying to generate sales. He had to take a drop in earnings and, I realised later, took out credit in both our names to keep the business afloat.

He should have declared bankruptcy at this point. He should have told me what was happening with his business and we could have worked through it together. But he didn't. What he did was blame me. He continued to tell me I was 'insane', that I was ruining everything. I was bereft, grieving for the child I was scared I'd never have, and instead of having a husband I could turn to for support, he wasn't there. And when he was home he was distracted. I tried – I cooked surprise meals, bought him presents, arranged 'date nights' so we could have some time alone – but Will wasn't interested.

I was crying out for help. I needed him. I was aware that my anxiety was returning, I could spot the signs: I'd started going to bed in the afternoons, I didn't want to leave the house, was suffering panic attacks and I needed support. But instead of providing care, all Will could do was offer platitudes. He told me I should 'pull myself together' and 'try harder', which only served to make me worse.

When I asked him if he was seeing someone else, he declared me hysterical. When the bank called and I tried to make sense of our finances, he said I was behaving irrationally and was jealous over his success. Accusing me of being resentful of how well he was doing and stupid for trying to understand something that I was incapable of. He made it worse. He made it all worse and drove me to the edge.

When his friend let it slip what was really going on, when I searched his phone and saw all the calls and texts, when I confronted him with the evidence, what he did then was leave us. He admitted to his affair, which was with one of my colleagues, a manager at the car dealership, and it rendered me speechless. It was a woman who knew me, who I trusted. Who knew what I was going through. He declared he'd never loved me, was horrified at the idea of having any more children with me, told me I was crazy, and then went to live with his mistress and her eight-year-old daughter.

In a fit of rage and humiliation, I went to her house to confront her. And when she wouldn't open the door to me, I grabbed a loose brick from her front wall and threw it at her window. I can still remember the dramatic smash, the satisfaction as her window shattered.

What I didn't expect was for her to call the police. To have me charged with criminal damage and for people still to be talking about it years after the event.

Will was absent from our lives for a whole year. She came from money; her parents had several holiday lets and they bailed out Will by starting up a new business managing holiday homes. He happily ran to her and left us to drown in the debt he'd left behind. It was a clear case of picking sides, but he not only left me, he left Sam, his son. Without a second thought.

After she pressed charges I lost my job, and we soon lost the house too. Then followed what my mother likes to call 'the wilderness years'. Three years of sporadic work, hiding from my old colleagues, renting properties as far away from Will as I could, all while fighting anxiety and depression. And all while Will began to thrive. With the help of his new wealthy investors, his business took off and he expanded into letting commercial property. He lived in one of the bigger houses over in Stanwix with his new family, and when he finally offered to give us some money, I found I couldn't take it.

By then I wanted nothing from him, nothing at all. It was stupid, but I felt that by accepting money from him, I was giving him some control, and I couldn't do that. So I took nothing, I wanted nothing from him. And now, the anger I felt towards him was still as strong as when he first left, so strong I thought it might rip me open.

The next morning I felt slightly more optimistic. Sam had slept well, no night terrors, and no tantrums at having to get ready for school, and I felt better as a result of undisturbed sleep. I'd thought about what Becca had said of Will's motivation in all of this. He didn't want his son back, he wanted to impress Rob and Janine, and she was right, that would all stop soon. His battle to have Sam would disappear as soon as Rob and Janine learned what an idiot he was, and that wouldn't take long.

And what else did he have anyway? He hadn't contributed financially since he left. Surely any sensible social worker would look at that and know that Will's case was ridiculous. What else? My bouts of depression were under control, and you couldn't take a child away from a parent for that, or for anxiety, or for being a homebody. It was a stupid suggestion. And surely it was better that a parent preferred to stay home instead of being out all the time? That only left the promised holiday that I couldn't yet deliver on, and we could come up with something between us, I was sure.

I couldn't take Sam to Disney, but I could take him away. Somewhere in the UK, quiet with a beach. It would counter Will's argument of me being an agoraphobic who refused to let her son get outside. And once I put my case forward about what Will was like when he left us, I was sure social services would be on my side. I planned to get online in the morning break and see what credit cards I could get. See if there were any more loans available I hadn't tried.

My mind was full of online banks and inflated APRs when I saw the envelope. Hand delivered. No address on the front, just my name in small black type. It was crumpled from where someone had shoved it through the letterbox, and there was a rip in the corner. Something bulky was inside. Checking Sam was still eating his breakfast in the other room, I opened it up carefully, and the smell made me recoil.

There was only one thing inside. It was a cupcake. Battered and squashed, old and dried out, but it was one of mine. I recognised the case – I sourced them online, they were bright colours, neon, my trade mark. I pulled the cake out and dropped it on the floor as I did.

It was my cake, but someone had replaced the filling. The sugar topping was still on, but instead of the buttercream centre, someone had replaced it with excrement.

TWELVE

Back to school is a shopping season. I had no idea of this, I thought retailers were just being really helpful by putting all the school stuff at the front of the store, but it's an actual shopping season, like Christmas and Easter. And those promotions, adverts and online campaigns begin well before the school year, all persuading parents what their children need to 'get a good start'. It affects around eight million households and something like £1.4 billion is spent in the UK getting our children ready for the start of term.

I read one article that estimated, on average, it costs £200 to get everything needed for one child. Two hundred pounds. Seems a lot, doesn't it? An exaggerated amount, but when you break it down to everything you really need to start a school year, such as the uniform, shoes, book bag, PE kit (including indoor and outdoor sports), lunch box, water bottle, stationery ... the list goes on and, suddenly, getting it all for £200 seems realistic if not a little hopeful. Because nothing lasts. In our house, we seem to have nothing that can be reused from the previous year.

Sam needs new things constantly, he's always losing his PE kit or school jumper, always growing out of his trousers and shoes, always leaving his water bottle somewhere. It's relentless, and that morning, as I searched online for credit card companies that I'd not yet applied to, I was more than feeling the pinch.

I had two large boxes of Tupperware filled with cakes to drop off. I was pretty sure that Sue would pay cash. I had planned to put that money towards the electric bill but now it would have to wait. I wanted that money for a deposit; I was going to book a holiday. Use the money to secure something and try and get a loan for the rest.

It was mid-morning and I was jumpy and fidgety. Since opening the parcel with the foul cupcake inside, I'd been constantly on edge. I could forgive Janine and Rob a one-word text, but actually taking one of my cakes, filling it with excrement and then posting it through my door? That was a bit much.

I wasn't sure how to deal with it. I thought about going to the police, but that wasn't ideal with my history and the fact that Will was now threatening to go to social services. And then I thought about telling John, but I didn't want to cause any more disruption where my job was concerned, so I did nothing. It was a cupcake, I told myself as I went about my tasks, not a bomb, not a horse's head, but a cupcake.

When I found out about Will sleeping with another woman I'd thrown a brick through her window. A cupcake was not a brick. It was weird and creepy, but it wasn't a brick and that's what made me keep a sense of reasoning about it.

It was odd, sitting on this side of the fence. Being the 'other woman', as Janine thought of me, even though I wasn't. But at least when I did throw that brick I was certain of my facts. I knew without doubt that Will was having an affair with her and how long it had been going on. I did research. I did not jump to conclusions as Janine had. By the time I was picking up the brick from her front wall and aiming it at her window, I knew exactly when the affair had started, what her part in it was and how much of a fool I'd been made of. I knew it wasn't a one-night stand, and I knew she was well aware Will was married and had a small child.

Janine didn't know the truth, but I'd been in her shoes, I knew what it was to find out you're being lied to. I'd been where she was, felt how she was feeling. I had compassion, and her anger was only to be expected. I just had to wait for it to exhaust itself, which it would. I figured, on balance, a text and a cupcake could be ignored.

'Sue.' I found her at the back of the kitchen. Most of the children had eaten and were now in the playground, leaving the dinner staff to clean up. I placed the two Tupperware boxes on the counter. 'Rainbow frosting, neon cases and a fiftieth decoration on each one!'

I looked up, expecting a surprised smile on her face. I was a day earlier than I'd said. I was already pulling off one of the lids, ready to show her the cakes, the way I'd painstakingly written 'Happy 50th!' in pink icing. Instead, she carried on wiping down the sink, busying herself with putting utensils away.

'Sue?'

I saw her shoulders drop.

'You're early with those.' She threw the cloth in the sink. 'I was going to come and see you. After clearing up here.' She looked at the Tupperware boxes. 'About them. They're only due tomorrow.'

I nodded. 'Just a day early, they'll still be fresh for Friday night. Just be sure you keep them in these boxes and you might want to refrigerate—'

'I don't need them any more,' she said, and looked at the floor. 'I was going to tell you. I'm cancelling the order.'

I felt my mouth drop open.

'Truth of it is,' she said, 'I had a call last night, about you being inspected by the health and safety.'

'What?' I shook my head. 'But I've already passed, my kitchen is—'

'And then there's the rugby club.'

'The rugby club?' I asked slowly. 'What's the rugby club got to do with it?'

'That's where I'm having the party,' she said, 'and they rang me last night. Sorry, Ruth, really I am, but we need that venue. It's the only one that's available and I've paid the deposit. I can't lose that just because of your cakes.'

'Sue –' I shook my head '– I'm not following, what's the rugby club got to do with my cakes?'

'It was them who called,' she sighed. 'Said that due to you being inspected, and changes in their policy, people aren't allowed to bring food onto the premises any more.'

'But do the rugby club do catering? I thought you needed cake? You said—'

'Changed now, apparently. Immediate effect. You're only allowed to bring in food from agreed suppliers.'

'And let me guess,' I said, 'I'm not an agreed supplier.'

She shook her head. 'As it's such short notice, they're giving me a cake. One from Simply Delicious. Do you know it, it's the big one on the corner? They're doing me a two tier one, pink icing.'

I was stunned into silence for a moment.

'I didn't make the rules,' she said, 'and I'm really sorry, but it's too late to change now. All the invites have gone out, I'll not get anywhere else and so —' she shrugged '— I don't need any of your cakes. Sorry, Ruth, I really wanted to help with your business, but you can see I don't have any choice. Here —' she delved into her pocket and pulled out a £20 note '— I expect that should cover the cost of the baking materials. I'm really sorry.'

I looked at the note in my hands. That wouldn't do as a deposit on any holiday. That would barely cover the cost of ingredients.

'Who called you?' I asked. 'You said it was someone from the rugby club. Is it the one down in Stanwix? That small one by the River Eden? Is it the one where . . .'

'It was him that phoned me,' she said, and her cheeks went red. 'The one you've been having that affair with.'

I breathed in sharply. 'I haven't been having an affair—'

'I don't want to know,' she held up her hand, stopping me from going on. 'I don't go in for gossip like the rest of them, but he's the chairman of the place, Ruth —' she shrugged '— and his wife, that Janine, she was the one on the PTA that made all that fuss last year about the school dinners. I can't deal with her again, it was a nightmare. She's not someone you want to get on the wrong side of.'

I took the Tupperware boxes, trembling. It was a personal attack, of that much I was sure. How they knew that I was providing the cakes for that party I had no idea, but they had, and they'd just cost me over £150. I had one hundred cupcakes, all personalised with a fiftieth birthday message, that needed eating within two days. I could freeze them, but they were no good unless I redid all the decorating. Took off all the personalised pink icing that had taken an age and replaced it with something else.

Once inside my office, I looked at the boxes.

I picked up my phone, then put it back down. What was I going to do, call her? Call Rob and ask them to stop? Ask them if they changed the food policy at the rugby club so I'd lose this order? Ask if they'd posted things through my letterbox? Sent texts? They'd deny it – I had no proof it was them – and then what?

I heard Becca's voice in my head, warning me that it could all go very wrong if I contacted them again. They could accuse me of harassment, and there might be another letter from Ashley about my professional behaviour. If they went to the police, my criminal record would be brought up. And what would social services make of it all if they got involved?

I went to the filing cabinet and got out the Walkers' file. There it was, Janine Walker's emergency contact number. I stared at it for a moment, ran my thumb over her writing. And then, despite the voices in my head telling me not to, I picked up my phone. I needed to let her know that I was on her side, that I wasn't the villain in all this.

I hesitated, my fingers hovering over my keypad, unsure what to send. How to explain it all, how to let her know my side of the story? If she understood that then all this would stop. Becca had said she was nice; she'd said she was a nice woman. John had said she made donations to the school, she was that type of person, caring and thoughtful. She was head of the PTA, bringing in gifts for the teachers. Surely she'd relent if I got in touch and told her the truth? Offered her an explanation?

I decided on a simple text. Something I would've liked to have got when I found out about Will.

> Janine, I've already said how sorry I am. But I feel it's all got a little out of control with you throwing your phone at me and my threat to go to the police, and now other things that are happening, so I thought I'd reach out to see if we can meet? Please believe me when I say that I did not know Rob was your husband when I met him. I did not know he was married. He told me he was single. He told me he'd recently broken up with his girlfriend. He lied to me. He lied to you. He's still lying to you now. I'm so sorry, Janine. Can we meet up so I can explain everything to you? Ruth x

I debated a long time over that kiss at the end. Over the words I'd used. I read over the message and argued through the consequences in my head for an age, but this wasn't a cupcake through my letterbox or a nasty message. This was them taking away my business. Taking money from me that was meant to pay for a holiday for Sam. This was something I had to stop. I hit send and then put my phone away, the cakes still on my desk.

Now useless. I could give them to Gary, make a huge donation to the charity event, but would he want them as they were clearly for a fiftieth celebration? Probably not, and then, as I sat there trying to calm down after the text I'd just sent, I had a better idea.

I picked up the Tupperware boxes and went into the staffroom. The lunch hour was almost over, but not quite yet. The room was filled with smells of coffee and food and there was a slight hush as I walked in. I couldn't see exactly who was staring at me as the boxes obscured my view. I went straight over to the coffee table in the centre.

The staffroom was silent, everyone watching me negotiate two large Tupperware boxes onto the table.

'Well!' I said brightly to them all, as I put the boxes down. 'It seems I made a few too many cakes for Sue's party. Sue from the dinner staff? I don't know if anyone's going to her party? It's tomorrow night, at the rugby club, and I know we've already done the collection and card, but I thought it would be nice if we celebrated in here as well.'

I peeled off the lids to the boxes. My cakes were in rows, lined up, bright pink, neon cases. They looked amazing. I took one out, held it up to the room.

'So, please, everyone, help yourself! These cakes are on me! Take home as many as you like.'

I didn't wait to see the reaction – I left as my legs were shaking. I went back to my office, collapsed in the chair and put the cupcake on my desk in front of me. Food always went down well in the staffroom, and hadn't Becca said that Janine was always sending treats in? So my cupcakes should go down a storm. It was a peace offering. I'd explain it all to Janine, treat the staff to free cakes and everything could go back to normal.

I figured that by the end of the day, the atmosphere would be over. Whatever was being said on Facebook wouldn't have such an impact and I would have an even footing. Perhaps even

Lisa, Sam's teacher, once she'd had a few of my cakes, might be easier to deal with. I reasoned that by leaving those cakes in the staffroom I was reminding everyone how nice I was.

At the end of the school day, I went to collect my boxes. I purposely went just after the final ring of the bell, the time when all staff were busy sending the children home.

I faltered when I walked in. I'd expected a few cakes to be left, there were a hundred after all, but not one had been taken. My boxes were exactly as I had left them. Full. My cakes, all in rows, and not one had been removed.

THIRTEEN

'Got into any more trouble lately?'

I jumped.

'Relax!' he laughed. 'I'm just getting a coffee.'

'But . . . ?'

'Oh the TAs can deal with letting the kids out of school. It's year five, they're not toddlers, they don't need me there to wave them off.'

He came over and stood next to me, my cakes on the coffee table in front of us.

'They look amazing,' he said.

I nodded, not trusting myself to speak.

'If I wasn't diabetic, I'd have wolfed the lot down.'

'You're diabetic?'

He nodded. 'But I don't think the rest of them are, so why's no one eating your cakes?'

I shook my head. Didn't answer.

'Teachers refusing free cake?' he said after a moment. 'This isn't like any other school I've worked at before. Hang on –' he went forward and looked at the other side of the Tupperware box, then back at me '– I think this might be the reason.'

I went forward to see what he was looking at.

'What?' I said as I saw it. 'That wasn't there when I put the cakes on the coffee table.'

We both stared at the small heap of rubbish that was piled high on the worktop right beside my boxes of cakes. Two filthy dishcloths, a stack of used teabags, spilling brown liquid onto the desk and over the side of my Tupperware box, and a small mound of other items of rubbish that were usually saved for the recycling and compost bin. Including empty yogurt pots and a banana skin that was touching the icing of several cupcakes. There were also all kinds of condiments – tomato sauce, salt, vinegar, salad cream – all far too close to the cakes. It looked like a small rubbish tip.

'And then there's that.' He pointed over to the counter top by the side of the microwave. The space that was usually reserved for condiments and recycling had been cleared and replaced with a large platter of what looked like cookies. There were only a few left.

I slowly walked over to them and noted how someone had put out napkins and side plates and gritted my teeth. Had I timed it so badly that my offering had arrived at the same time as someone else's? Or was it her? Had Janine managed to sabotage this as well?

'She stopped this order from going ahead.' I waved at the cakes. 'Her husband, Rob, the one I . . .'

I let my words trail off and Glen nodded.

'He's chairman of the rugby club, and these were meant to be for a party there, but he changed the policy, so the order was cancelled. And I thought by bringing them in here, that everyone would see them as a peace offering and it might . . .'

I shook my head; my eyes were brimming with tears.

'And it's the same stupid rugby club that my ex-husband goes to –' I wiped my face '– so now they've got him on board as well. After years of only being marginally bothered about being with his son, he's now threatening to apply for full custody.'

We were silent a moment, staring at the uneaten cakes. I felt his arm go around my shoulders and had to squeeze my eyes shut so as not to cry.

'Here.' He led me over to a seat and I went to protest. 'It'll be ages before anyone comes in,' he said. 'The place is deserted for a good half hour at this time and we can't let them see you crying over uneaten cake.'

I watched as he put the lids back on the Tupperware boxes, as he moved them and put them on the counter by the door.

'They're a right bunch of vipers, aren't they?' he asked, sitting down beside me. 'I thought this kind of stuff only went on in the playground.'

I gave a small smile. 'Janine's dropped the charges against me at least,' I told him. 'No more investigation, so my job's safe if nothing else.'

He nodded. 'I know.'

I paused for a moment. 'Facebook?'

He didn't reply and began to busy himself with making coffee.

'Am I still being discussed on there?'

He wrinkled up his nose. 'Not openly. The thread about the "incident" has been deleted, but –' he shrugged '– I don't know what she's saying to them all in private messages. Someone put a post up about how understanding and forgiving she was, so I guessed that something had gone on.'

We were silent for a moment. I took out my phone to see if she'd replied to my text. It had a small tick underneath it and the word 'Read' letting me know she'd seen it and read it, but had chosen not to reply.

'And as I'm now teaching year five –' Glen went on, handing me a hot cup of tea '– I'm her daughter's teacher, so I've seen a bit of her already at drop off and pick up.'

I looked up at him, and he made a gesture with his hands to express why he was in the staffroom and not seeing his class out, and I let out a small smile.

'I take it you don't get to talk with the teachers here much?' he asked, coming over to me. 'Can't tell them your side of things?'

'I'm talked to, not with,' I told him. 'This school is old fashioned, as in, I let them know about the children they teach, pass on messages, tell them who's absent and why, who's going to what after-school club, send down letters, make sure everything runs smoothly . . .'

'But no one has a real conversation with you?'

I thought for a moment then shook my head. 'There's this weird hierarchy going on,' I said, 'like if you're not teaching staff, then you're not . . . ' I shrugged. 'And I got this job quick. They were desperate for someone and I know Becca here, the year two teacher. She's my best mate so she put a good word in and John hired me without consulting –' I shrugged '– the PTA or whoever . . . '

'Does the head need to consult the PTA over who is school secretary?'

'I'm not sure. Only I know that a few people had a bit of

a problem with me taking this position.' I felt myself flush a little. 'In my last proper job –' I paused '– let's just say it didn't end well there, and a few people got wind of why I left and thought I wasn't right to work in the school.' I took a big breath. 'But I was proving them wrong. I'm really, really good at this job. I do everything right, keep it all ticking over and now … this.' I shook my head. 'I thought I was making friends. I'm a few months off being made permanent, and Sam, that's my son, he's having a few difficulties and I thought …'

I looked away – it was all too much to explain. I was exhausted suddenly. I pointed to the whiteboard on the wall with its hectic timetable drawn on.

'And everyone here is so busy, even when I do come down to the staffroom, it's unlikely that the same people will always be in here. Even Becca – I hardly see her in the day. So it's hard to make proper friends. Especially when I'm at the other end of the school.'

We both looked at the whiteboard, the schedule of the teachers, the bargaining of break duty, of PPA time. 'See that?' I said. 'That's how busy they all are. No one in this school has time for coffee, apart from John, the head, and it's only because I make it for him.'

Glen got up and walked towards the schedule. He studied it for a moment, the pen hanging by string at the side, the cloth balanced on the top. He ran his finger under the names, the underlined headings, the stars and exclamation points, the strict instructions, the times and pleas.

'Miss Gleason,' he said, finding her name, 'she's the one that teaches your son, isn't she?'

I nodded and joined him in front of the whiteboard. Lisa was down as having an hour of planning, preparation and assessment time the next morning, her name written in large red capitals, and underneath in brackets why she was having it and who was covering her class, which seemed was something to do with a music lesson.

'Yep,' I said with a sigh, 'she's Sam's teacher.'

'What do you think of her?'

I turned to him, confused by the question.

'Is she any good?' he asked, and I let out a surprised laugh.

'You're asking if I think Lisa's a good teacher?'

He nodded, and I took a moment. It was an unwritten rule that you never discussed a teacher's abilities. Unlike my job, which seemed to be under constant scrutiny, no one praised or criticised anyone's teaching.

'Well, I think she's ...'

He raised his eyebrows and I smiled. I was about to say 'fine', the habitual reply, and then I hesitated. The truth of it was, she wasn't a very good teacher. She ignored Sam's needs, and because I'd threatened her cash that she got over the holidays she was now ignoring me.

'Thought so,' he said, and took the cloth from the top of the board and wiped her name clean off the board. I let out a shocked gasp.

'You can't do that!' I began, but he'd already done it and was looking at me with an amused smile.

'Miss Gleason,' he said, picking up the pen that was hanging at the side of the board and taking off the top, 'I learned at the staff meeting is not a very good teacher.'

I looked at him, my mouth hanging open in shock.

'A staff meeting, I think, should concentrate on the children and the education they're getting. I've been to some tedious ones –' he looked at me and smiled '– one where all we discussed was whose job it was to replace the toilet rolls in the staff loo, but the one here? That was something else.'

'You were at the staff meeting?' I asked, a flush building from the base of my neck.

He nodded and started to write something on the white-board, in capital letters. 'Never been to one quite like it.'

I swallowed, my throat tight. 'But that was before you started, that was Tuesday night . . .'

He turned and looked at me. 'I got the call from the agency on Tuesday afternoon,' he said slowly. 'So I rang up, thought I'd introduce myself. You'd left early, so I spoke to John, who invited me to attend the staff meeting. He said something was going on in the school that I should be made aware of before starting to teach here.'

I was red. 'And you came in on Wednesday to have a look at me? To see what all the fuss was about?'

'I came in the next day to see my class –' he smiled '– and to see you. To see what all the fuss was about.'

I thought back to our first meeting, the way he'd asked what had happened, made me tell him.

'You knew!' I said. 'You asked me what the incident was, while all the time you knew exactly what had happened. Why did you . . . ?'

'I like to make my own mind up,' he said, turning back to the board. 'I was told a lot of things at that staff meeting, saw a lot of stuff on Facebook. But I like to work things out for myself.'

I was silent for a moment, trying to work out what he might have heard about me. What impression he had of me before actually meeting me, and then, him taking the time to come and meet me for himself. To not listen to the gossip and lies, but to meet me on his own terms.

'A situation like yours does funny things,' he said. 'I've seen it before. Something happens and it shines a light on people. It shows them for who they are, and, unfortunately, a lot of the women who teach here are being shown in a bad light.' He started to write slowly on the whiteboard, and I let out a little shriek, putting my hand over his to stop him.

'Really,' I said, 'you can't mess with that. If anyone finds out you'll lose your job.'

He gave a slight shrug of his shoulders as if he didn't care.

'The agency won't have you on their books,' I went on, trying to convey how serious it was. 'If they find out you've messed with this, you'll be lucky to get another teaching job.'

He smiled. 'I doubt it,' he said, 'but it's nice how much you care and, anyway, I'm only teaching until I start my real job again in a few months. In case you hadn't realised, teaching really isn't my vocation.'

He paused a moment then went on writing, and I didn't know what to do. I was afraid of what he was doing, while also being totally fascinated. No one I had ever met was like him, comfortable in breaking the rules and actually doing it with a sense of glee.

'See, I think you were brave,' he went on, 'and if I were head, I'd tell them all that we look after our own. Stand united. But Miss Gleason here, the woman who teaches your son, who works alongside you, she believes that because of what you did, you should lose your job.'

I took a slight gasp. Becca hadn't told me that. 'A few moaners' had been her words. She didn't say that Lisa wanted me fired.

'Lose my job?' I said quietly. 'Lisa actually said that?'

'And we both know why that is, don't we?'

135

I stared at him.

'I don't think it's anything to do with how competent you are, and I don't think that by being shocked and apologising you were acting unprofessionally. I think that when a parent attacked you and you didn't retaliate, or press charges, you were totally in charge of your conduct. So why all the gossip, why would she want to get you out of the picture?'

I was staring at him dumbfounded. He was so casual about it all, as if he were telling me something trivial, while at the same time doing something so reckless. I glanced towards the closed door, afraid that someone might come in and catch us.

'She actually said that?' I asked, my heart jumping in my chest. 'Lisa said she wanted me fired?'

He nodded slowly. 'She did. In front of everyone. In front of me, even, the new supply. She was very vocal about it. Very vocal about your son.'

'About Sam?' My voice was high suddenly, loud. I checked the door again. I hadn't meant to raise my voice, but then, I didn't think Sam was being discussed in the staff meeting.

He looked at me, pausing his writing on the board. 'Isn't she still a newly qualified teacher, Miss Gleason?'

I nodded.

'She's a lot to learn. And she's only got a contract here for a year, hasn't she? I learned yesterday that she's filling in on someone's leave? So she'll be looking for a full-time contract come next summer?'

I slowly nodded again. Lisa had been taken on to replace Pauline, who was off due to illness for a year and would be making a slow return back to teaching next spring. If it all went to plan, and Pauline did return full time, then Lisa would be out of a job at the start of the next school year.

'So if she gets rid of you,' he went on, 'then Janine will be her best friend, and not only will she get cash jobs in the holidays, but as Janine is chair of the PTA she'll help her out here as well. Perhaps, as Janine has contacts with most of the local schools because of her tutoring business, she'll be able to fix her up with a full-time position somewhere.' He looked at me. 'It's all wrong. The PTA lets anyone who wants to take part become chair, but it shouldn't work like that. Someone who privately employs the staff here shouldn't be allowed to be at the head of the PTA, year after year, with all of her friends as vice chair and treasurer and so on. It's a conflict of interest. She personally benefits from having that position, like she's running the school along with John. In my opinion, it shouldn't be allowed.'

I watched as he wrote Maggie's name in place of Lisa's. Maggie, the reception teacher, was now due to have PPA the next morning instead of Lisa. I felt my stomach spin at what he'd done, felt giddy with the sight of it, and I looked towards the door, convinced that we were about to be caught. That John or another teacher would walk in on us and see immediately what Glen had done.

'There,' he said. 'Lisa will look at this and think Maggie's done it, but Maggie, you see –' he pointed to another part of the board '– is doing the morning playground duty and has already asked if anyone can take over.' He pointed to her written plea underneath and then crossed it out as if it no longer applied and wrote Lisa's name. 'So when Maggie sees this, and then Lisa, fifteen minutes will have been lost in confusion. And now, if we do this –' he went to another part of the board where John had asked for volunteers to attend the residential and I gasped as he wrote Lisa's name underneath '– she'll also have that to deal with, because how do you un-volunteer?'

I let out a shocked surprised laugh as he replaced the cap, still glancing every second or two at the door, adrenalin running through my body. Then I looked at the board, knowing that Lisa would be expecting an hour off in the morning, but it had now been taken from her. She'd confront Maggie, who'd deny it, but who would now be expecting her to do the playground duty, and then Maggie would look at the board and wonder if she was in fact owed some PPA time, and it would cause chaos. It felt silly and mischievous and completely wrong. The board was sacred and we were messing with it. It felt deliciously naughty and I was surprised at how good I felt compared to when I first entered the staffroom.

'And I think we'll take this,' he said, taking the coffee and teabags out of the cupboard, and my hand went to my mouth. 'In my book they don't deserve a hot drink, they'll have to make do with –' he lifted out the herbal teabags someone had left at the back '– fennel.'

I let out a laugh.

'They can all accuse each other of nicking the coffee, all go without their daily dose of caffeine.'

'You can't take those!' I began, and he turned to me.

'You'd rather I replace it? Do what, exchange the sugar for salt? The coffee for gravy granules? I'm not that organised, sorry, but I do think it'll have more effect if we just pinch it.' He put the jar of coffee and the box of Tetley in one of my Tupperware boxes. I stared at them, knowing I should take them out and put them back, that I should wipe away the destruction that he'd caused on the whiteboard, put it all back to normal, but I did nothing.

'It's not much,' he said with a smile. 'A few names changed on the board, and if anyone guessed it was me I could easily explain it away by saying I'm new – didn't know how it all worked and I'd misunderstood a conversation I'd had with Maggie. I can see how shocked you are but, honestly Ruth, it's really not that big a deal.' He looked at me. 'But it *is* enough to cause a bit of disruption and that's all you need. Because in here –' he gestured to the staffroom '– they're only focused on themselves.' He tapped the whiteboard. 'This board. And their own superiority. And they're mean. Not eating any of your cakes, that's mean.'

I paused, looking at what he'd done to the whiteboard, the empty cupboard, then, after a moment, at him.

'Why?' I said quietly. 'Why are you doing this? It's got nothing to do with you and if they find out that it was you who . . . '

'Because I don't like bullying,' he said, and smiled. 'It's that simple. And your son, Sam, Lisa said he's being bullied as well?'

I nodded.

'Well, I can't do much about that, but I can at least mess up a timetable and cause a bit of trouble in here.'

'But,' I began.

'What?' he asked. 'Don't you agree that it's out of order what she did? To talk about you and your son like that was wrong, but what was worse was that no one picked her up on it.'

'Well, it's just a bit . . . ' I looked at his writing on the board, thought about the disruption it would cause, how they'd all be irritated without a morning coffee and how no one would be able to directly blame us. It felt devious somehow. Although I agreed with everything he said, it felt wrong to do something so sneaky. 'It's a bit passive aggressive, isn't it?'

'I didn't put you down for the confrontation type.'

'I'm not,' I said, 'but this seems . . . '

'Fun?' he asked, and I laughed.

'No one grabs a snake by the neck,' he said. 'That's how you get bit. No, the way to deal with snakes is beat them with a long stick. Well this is our stick,' he said with a laugh, 'and that –' he pointed to his writing and the drinks cupboard '– is a tiny jab.'

I opened my mouth to ask how often he did this kind of thing, when there was a noise from further down the corridor.

'Trust me,' he said, 'this will be far more effective than you going in to John, or filing a complaint, or whatever you're meant to do in these situations. You'll get far more enjoyment out of this.' He grinned, offering his arm like an old-fashioned gentleman. 'Shall we?'

I looked at the board. Lisa's morning was going to be ruined and it felt wonderful. Stupid and silly and juvenile, but as he picked up the full Tupperware boxes, full of my cakes, there was a lightness in my chest that hadn't been there before.

'Yes,' I said, taking his arm and left the room with him.

FOURTEEN

My mother rang complaining of a rapid heartbeat at seven thirty the next morning. We needed to be on the road at seven forty-five, but I'd foolishly answered on the landline and was stuck talking through her symptoms, which sounded, to me, like trapped wind.

'It's OK now,' she was telling me as I tried to get her off the line, 'but it might start up again at any moment. At *any moment.*'

We left, eventually, at eight fifteen, after instructing her to monitor it and, if it came back, ring the NHS helpline. I made promises to call and see her later and dived out to hit all the rush hour traffic. The result was that we arrived at school at eight forty-five. The same time as some of the parents.

It was inevitable really. I couldn't expect that I'd be able to avoid her for ever, but that morning it was like she was looking for me. Searching and waiting for me. She hadn't replied to my text and the silence from her had filled me with anxiety, knowing that she'd read my message but hadn't answered. I would've preferred another threatening text, a one-word answer, anything but the radio silence that made my mind go on overdrive.

I swung my car into the private car park for staff, rushing Sam to get his book bag, get his lunch box together and *come on!* And there she was. Loitering around the gates, the only exit from the car park to the school and she was there. As if she had all the time in the world, chatting with a group, Ashley among them, car keys dangling from her hand. They had no business being near the staff car park – the playground where her children should have been was on the other side of the building. A completely different entrance, and yet, there they were.

'Mum?'

I realised that I was sitting, frozen, in my car, staring at Janine and the group of women around her.

'Mum, shall we go? I thought we were late?'

I looked at Sam, his face expectant.

'Yes, we are late,' I told him, and opened my car door.

I busied myself with my son so I didn't have to look up, but I could feel their gaze on me. Could feel them staring.

'Mum, you're hurting.'

I released my grip on his hand and straightened my back as I walked towards them. My plan was to keep my head down and get past them as quick as I could. No more drama, Becca had warned, no more outbursts, John had told me, and I intended to keep to it. I would just walk past and say nothing. But when I got closer to them, Janine's voice suddenly got louder.

'Terrible hygiene standards,' I heard her say. 'She makes all these grotty little cakes in the kitchen of a rented property and health and safety need to be informed. Thank God Rob was able to change the policy in time or who knows what would've—'

'Are you talking about me?'

I couldn't help myself. What she was saying was clearly for my benefit; she was waiting for me to walk past so she could insult me indirectly.

Janine turned to me. 'I have nothing to say to you,' she said coldly.

'But the cakes,' I went on, 'the cakes you're talking about. The order you stopped, the cake you pushed through my door the other day, the one with ...' Sam's hand was in mine and I stopped myself just in time. 'And the text,' I said, 'I got that, and you've made your point, but you have to stop.'

I heard a laugh and saw it was Ashley, folding her arms dramatically and looking at the other women as if what I was saying was unbelievable.

I turned back to Janine. 'I've said I'm sorry. And I am, so sorry. I sent you a message explaining everything. I know you read it and I meant every word of it. I didn't know. I had the same thing happen to me, you see.' I leaned forward to her, lowering my voice to a whisper, aware that Sam was within earshot. 'My husband was having an affair, a proper affair that went on for months, so it's not something I would ever do. I would *never* be the other woman.' I looked at the group behind her, the rapt faces all listening in to my attempt at an explanation. 'And what happened wasn't an affair, it was a one-time thing and I didn't know he was married.' I took a moment. 'If you want to meet up, chat about this over coffee, you'll see that I've done nothing wrong here.'

Her eyes went dark. '*Nothing wrong?*' she hissed, and I felt Sam's fingers tighten around mine.

'That night, when you . . .' her eyes glanced at Sam. 'When you did that awful thing, did you know my husband was on medication?'

I stared blankly at her.

'That's right,' she went on, 'he was out of his mind on painkillers for his back. He foolishly mixed his medication with alcohol and had no idea what he was doing. Couldn't be responsible for his actions because he was drugged. And then you –' she stabbed her finger in front of me, not quite touching '– take him up to your hotel room and . . .' she shook her head, crinkled her nose. I heard one of the other women mutter something under her breath, which sounded very much like 'bitch'.

'You're shameless,' Janine announced, and there were nodding heads all round. 'So don't stand there saying you've done *nothing wrong*. Sending me messages about how you are being lied to. You took advantage of a man who wasn't in his right mind. He's disgusted with himself. Absolutely disgusted with himself at the thought of . . .' she put a hand up to her throat, in mock horror, 'that he did that . . . with you . . .'

I looked down at Sam, who was staring up at Janine with a horrified expression.

'It's all right,' I told him, 'it's fine.'

He looked at me but his face didn't change, his eyes were still wide.

'I've apologised,' I told her, trying to keep my voice calm for Sam's benefit, 'and that's not what happened, it was actually your husband, it was Rob who . . .'

She leaned in close. 'We've both had to get tested,' she hissed in my ear. 'I have never been so embarrassed at the doctor's surgery.'

I looked at her, puzzled. 'Tested for . . .'

'I don't know what people like you have got,' she said, and I felt as though she'd slapped me, like her words were something physical, 'what you could have given him that night. Rob couldn't even remember,' she said. 'He didn't even remember you until you had your outburst the other morning, in front of my children.'

'Your children were in school—'

'And we've spoken to your ex-husband. We know all about your criminal record, we know exactly what kind of person you—'

The school bell sliced through her words. She turned at the sound, they all did, moving slightly to gather their children and I pushed past them. I was shaking, unsteady on my feet as I pushed past the group of them, and as I did so, I noticed that Ashley was smiling. She was grinning broadly, a delighted expression on her face, and it shook me. It was so at odds with the situation that it was Ashley's smile that scared me the most as I took Sam to his class and played catch-up with my job.

It was the afternoon before I got in to see John. He was eating a tuna salad sandwich and his office was full of the pungent smell.

'Come in, come in,' he said, and a small bit of tomato landed on the desk in front of him.

The upcoming residential break, the one Glen had put Lisa's name down for, was proving to be a disaster. Year five were going to a youth hostel up in Scotland for a few days of canoeing, rock climbing and orienteering in the highlands as part of their 'learning through adventure', but the youth hostel had upped its prices, claiming that the transportation company they used had increased theirs and thus they were passing on the bill to us. It was totally unexpected, and had come after we had collected most of the funds from the parents.

I'd been in conversations with them since their announcement, which, apparently, was in their terms. It was a very tiny clause that briefly mentioned the price might increase due to 'surcharges'. Only I could find no evidence of this in any of the documentation they'd sent to us at the time of booking, and neither could John. It didn't help our case, but it was something.

Along with upping the price, the company that organised the orienteering had now declared they didn't have enough adults to fill the quota of children/adult ratio, hence John trying to rope in more teachers from the school to go with no extra pay. As a result, his face was puce, the sweat marks under his arms large.

'So, no joy?'

I shook my head and sat down, passing him the emails that I'd printed off earlier.

'They sent these on after we complained. The only small print I could find was a clause that declares they have the right to increase fees due to surcharges such as transportation, but would give appropriate notice period for us to cancel and be refunded.'

'A notice period isn't what we need!' hissed John, taking the paper from me, 'and neither is a refund! We need it at the same bloody price.' He put the papers down and shook his head. 'Year five are all set for this trip. I'll ring this afternoon.' He paused a moment. 'I'll threaten legal action!' he announced, and I took in a deep breath.

'You could do that,' I said, 'but it might be better if you said a journalist was covering the story instead.'

His eyebrows shot up and I smiled.

The thought had occurred to me when I'd got to my office after the outburst with Janine that morning. I'd sat at my desk, my face burning with humiliation, and tried to think of what more I could do. How I could salvage the situation. I thought of what she'd said in front of all those women, how she'd been to the doctors to get 'tested', and I wanted the floor to swallow me up.

What had she been saying about me on Facebook? And what would everyone think of me? The parents of the other children in Sam's class, would they know? I'd hidden my face in my hands and, as was often happening lately, my mind had wandered to Glen. About the whiteboard that he'd messed with and his words of 'not grabbing a snake by the neck, but hitting it with a long stick instead'.

And then, as I'd tried to get on with my work, I'd seen the email from the holiday company outlining why they were right in hiking up their prices. It was totally unfair, I'd done all the paperwork, done everything correctly, got the money out of the parents, which had been weeks in the planning. We'd sent the deposit in time, paid the remainder, and now, to find out that they needed more money from us, four weeks before it was due to happen, was totally out of order.

If the transportation company that they used had increased their prices, then surely it was up to them, not us, to foot that bill? We'd called them, emailed them, but they were standing their ground. It was obvious that, as a bigger company, they could afford to lose us. One residential from a primary school was something they didn't seem bothered about and it infuriated me.

I'd thought of Lisa, how the rota that Glen had messed with

would be causing chaos, how they'd all be looking for some coffee, and how Glen was helping me because he didn't like bullies, and realised the holiday company were doing exactly that: bullying us. I'd thought of Glen's words, about his analogy of how to fight a snake and had the idea.

'If you call, threatening legal action,' I told John, 'then I'm sure it will get a response, but perhaps not in the timescale we need it to. They would probably pass you over and wait for you to take advice . . . ' I trailed off. John was staring at me, his eyebrows still raised. 'But,' I went on, 'if you rang this afternoon and told them that a journalist from the *Telegraph* was covering the story, you'd get a much quicker response.'

'The *Telegraph*?' John put down the remains of his sandwich and sat back. 'But I've never spoken to anyone from the *Telegraph* in my life!'

'But they don't know that,' I said, 'and it sounds so plausible. School children unable to go on educational trip because of a greedy holiday company sounds like something they'd cover. It would worry them, and that's all you want to do. Worry them.'

John looked stunned for a moment, then huffed. 'Worth a try I suppose.'

'And if it doesn't work you can try legal action.'

He narrowed his eyes at me, then smiled.

'I like your thinking,' he said, and gave his head a tap, 'sneaky but smart. Good idea, Ruth.' A small balloon of pleasure rose in my chest at his words.

He nodded, picked up his handset and looked at me. It was my cue to leave, but I stayed sitting. He replaced the handset.

'I need to talk to you about something else,' I began, and he shook his head.

'If you mean the internal investigation with Janine Walker

then you'll have to wait.' He took the wrapper from his sandwich and screwed it into a tight ball. 'I've just been told of two pupils who are applying for additional support that we don't have the funds for, another teacher wanting early retirement and three council meetings that they expect me to attend. Could you look at my calendar for next week? There's some training I was meant to be going on but that will have to be cancelled. And I've the holiday company to call now and lie to about speaking to someone from the *Telegraph*.' He took a moment. 'Perhaps I will speak to someone at the *Telegraph*! Like you say, it makes a bloody good story.'

He threw the ball at the bin – it missed and lay on the carpet at the side.

'So, in a nutshell,' he went on, 'I don't have the time or the resources to investigate a dispute between my school secretary and some parent who threw her phone at her this week.' He swallowed and surveyed me. 'As far as I'm concerned an internal investigation can wait. Did you get hold of your union rep? Tell them it's on hold, no rush.'

I nodded. I wanted to talk to him about the staff meeting, about what was said, about how Glen had told me that Lisa, my son's teacher, wanted me fired. I wanted to tell him about me being discussed on Facebook and how Janine had insulted me just that morning, in front of my son, but I paused, not sure how to phrase the whole thing. However I tried to word it, it made me sound like one of the children. Whining about gossip and people waiting to ambush me at the school gates. I felt ashamed and didn't know how to protest my innocence in the whole thing.

'This morning,' I began, 'Janine and a group of women ... well they said some things ... '

'I don't have time to be involved in tittle-tattle,' John warned. 'I'm not interested in gossip.'

'It's just that, I'm scared she's starting rumours about me. Saying things to other parents and teaching staff . . . '

'I understand that you left some cakes in the staffroom?' He gave a nod. 'Very good of you, to smooth things over like that. I'm glad it's all back to normal.'

'But I'm not sure it is. I've tried. I've really tried to apologise, but everyone here seems to be . . . '

'Give it time, Ruth.' He went back to his phone, eager to get on with his work, and I realised I'd already lost his attention. 'There's bound to be the odd remark here and there, but after half term it'll all be forgotten and, if it isn't, come see me then and we'll revisit the situation.'

I said nothing about no one eating my cakes, nothing about how they'd all ignored me. Nothing about how they made me feel. John began to dial and I left him to his phone calls. What could he do about it anyway? Another staff meeting where he ticked off the staff for talking about me. How would that help? That wouldn't win me any friends. And if he got Janine in, had a word about her insulting me at the school gates, how would she retaliate? File another complaint about my professional conduct? Get her friends to lie about what they saw? I thought of Ashley's smile and a flush of shame rushed up into my chest. Those women were awful, judgemental and sanctimonious.

My office was quiet. It was that golden time just before the end of school. Most teachers would now have their class sitting on the carpet in front of them, telling them a story to wind down before home time. I'd had another message from Eve, the woman who'd witnessed the incident that started this all off, asking me to call her. It was about something to do with Janine, something else she'd probably done, and I realised, like John, I didn't have time for any of it. I didn't want it to carry on. I didn't want to feel this way. I couldn't wait until after half term, I needed it to stop now. I needed my cake business to be bringing in money. I needed to concentrate on Will and his threat to take Sam. I had to work out a way to stop Sam from being bullied. I didn't have time for Janine and Rob to persecute me. I didn't have time to fight them. I needed to stop it, to put an end to it all and quickly. I needed to do it for Sam.

Don't grab a snake by the neck.

After a quick search, I had the number. It was effortless, perfect. HMRC fraud hotline. And I couldn't believe I was actually going to do it, but then I'd hear Janine's words in my head, the way Ashley had grinned at me and, before I knew what I was doing, I'd dialled the number. The phone call took minutes, a few details was all that was needed. Totally anonymous. I told them I suspected tax evasion, the cash-in-hand jobs that were being undertaken by her tutoring company. I had her name, address, Facebook page – it was easy and simple and done very quickly. They thanked me. They promised immediate action. I replaced the handset with shaking hands. A giddy high feeling working its way up through my stomach. I was in awe at how simple and effective the whole thing had been. It had taken minutes, that was all, minutes. A simple accusation and Janine and her Top Marks tutoring business were now under investigation by HMRC for tax evasion. They'd want receipts, invoices, records and accounts. Janine's life was about to get a whole lot messier. I almost phoned them back to say I'd got it wrong, to say that I wanted to take the accusation back. I ran a small business, I lived in fear of HMRC, so I could well imagine how she'd feel knowing she was under investigation. But then I heard her voice again, heard John tell me to give till after half term, and it gave me the impetus to make a second phone call.

One to the local paper.

'I'd like to remain anonymous,' I told them, 'but I've a story about a local businesswoman. The head of the PTA at St Ambrose and St Stephen's primary school who also runs Top Marks Tutoring.' I took a deep breath. 'She's under investigation for tax evasion,' I told them. 'She's been fiddling her books, paying local teachers cash in hand and not declaring her earnings, and now there is a huge investigation into her business.' I was breathless, shocked almost at the words coming out of my mouth. 'I just think your readers deserve to know that if any of them are using her tutoring company, they should know they're being scammed. The money they're paying her is going straight into her pocket and not back into the community.'

They were eager for more details. I told them that she had links with all the local schools. I made her sound bigger than she was, as if she was running some huge tax evasion scheme and half the teachers in Carlisle were on board. I told them what the person at HMRC had told me, gave them the contact number I had just rung.

'Have you any proof?' the journalist asked after taking down the details. 'Anyone who works for Top Marks? A teacher perhaps?'

'Lisa Gleason,' I told them. 'She's a teacher at the school and works for Janine in the holidays, and I doubt she's declared any of her earnings.'

I ended the call and could almost see the headline: 'HMRC launch campaign into local tax-evading teachers'. Perhaps accompanied by a picture of a distressed Janine, the master-mind behind the fraud. I waited for a feeling of relief to wash over me, but my anxiety was still sky high and then I realised it would only be over when the investigation started. When they got the phone call, when their attention was taken away from me and onto something much more important. Thankfully, that was about to happen.

'Janine Walker,' I said softly. 'Lisa Gleason. Your lives are about to get a whole lot worse.'

FIFTEEN

21 JUNE

I've been moved.

They brought me here as I'm a category A prisoner, I should never have been in Westmorland so long as I'm classed as highly dangerous to the public. Me. Highly dangerous. It's ludicrous. It would be funny if I wasn't so afraid. The other people here are real criminals, sex offenders, firearms offences. People who have committed real crime and I'm not like them, I did nothing wrong.

I realise it will be harder for you to visit me here. It will be a longer journey for you, but I still expect you to come. I know you. I know you have a conscience, you may think that you can bottle what we did up, but you won't be able to for much longer.

I saw this in the library the other day and thought of you. It's a simple test, a series of questions to determine whether you have

154

a personality disorder. I know it's not medically certified but if you answered these questions and then looked at the outcome, I'm hoping it will give you an insight into what everyone else sees in you when you let them get close enough.

Try it.

Answer them honestly, especially question 16: Have you ever hurt someone intentionally? I did a little experiment and did the test as if I was you. I answered the questions as I think you would've answered them and then looked at the results. Do you want to know what they said?

They said you had a narcissistic personality disorder.

You believe you are special, different and more deserving. You resent other people's success. You take advantage and put your needs above others. Sound familiar? Like something you might have heard or said before?

I wonder if you treat everyone like this, children as well as adults. That would explain a lot wouldn't it, if you treated children with this level of narcissism?

But, as I said, the test is not conclusive.

It didn't ask the question if you were capable of murder.

It didn't ask if you would leave someone rotting in a prison cell when you knew they weren't guilty.

I think the results would come back very different then, they would most probably declare you psychotic.

Forgive me, I'm tired. I'm not sleeping well. They had us up in the night doing a physical, some sort of new regime they have here and I'm not adapting. I can feel myself fading, giving in. If I die in here then you'll be responsible for two deaths, not one.

Answer me this question: Do you ever feel guilty about what happened?

SIXTEEN

'You look happy, what's going on?'

We were sat outside enjoying the late September sunshine. Everyone was calling it an Indian summer. The hot weather had continued into the weekend and, that Saturday afternoon, I held my face up to the sun and enjoyed the sensation of it on my face.

I looked over the field at the back of my mother's house, trying to work out where her boundary ended. It was at least half an acre. At one time it was used as a paddock and the remains of outbuildings were over by the far wall. Stone buildings that were decrepit and falling down, that should really be removed as they were dangerous, but they added to the character of the place. So long as Sam or the dog didn't go near them, they were fine.

I turned to where I could hear him, over by the field that led on to the farmer's land. There was no real separation from what was meant to be my mother's garden and the farmer's field that was adjacent. Several times we'd asked for the fencing to be increased, as Mum would often find sheep grazing a little too close to the house, and there was a small fence but it was ineffective. But as my mother didn't have a gardener and the only person that occasionally went out there to play was Sam, we didn't see the urgency.

'He's fine,' my mother said, as I leaned forward in an effort to see Sam. 'Really, let the boy run about. What harm can he come to out here?'

I sat back, then after a moment, turned my face up to the sky.

'No more rapid heartbeat then?' I asked her, and she made a huffing sound.

'Was probably just a bit of trapped wind, like you said.'

I smiled. 'Good,' I said lazily. 'I brought you some peppermint tablets, I'll put them in the medical cupboard with everything else you've got there.'

We were silent for a moment.

'So why so happy?' my mother asked, and I turned to her.

'Does something have to be going on for me to be happy?'

I smiled. I was feeling something close to happy and I was milking the feeling for everything I could. I hadn't enjoyed being like this in an age. After making the phone call to HMRC and the local paper, I'd been relishing the outcome. The headlines and the downfall of Janine's tutoring business. Because I figured once everyone got wind that she was being investigated, they'd be reluctant to work for her. I didn't know for sure, but I was pretty certain that most teachers wouldn't have declared their earnings from Top Marks. Becca had said it was all cash in hand, and as they all had full-time contracts at school, it would be easy for them to take the money and not declare any of it. The thought of her being without tutors, HMRC breathing down her neck, made me smile.

Even Sam had noticed my change in mood for the better, telling me when I collected him from after-school club that my face was all 'shiny'. But he was happier as well, Toby had been absent from school again, and as a result Sam had been OK.

'You're up to something,' my mother said, adjusting her glasses, 'I can tell. Is it to do with you not letting Will have Sammy this weekend?'

And just like that, any happiness I felt evaporated. It only took the mention of his name for the anxiety to start nipping. I'd still not found anywhere for us to go at half term. The prices of even a caravan were extortionate in the school holidays. No credit card companies had agreed the loan I was asking for, so at this rate it was going to be a tent on a piece of land somewhere, because at the moment I couldn't even afford the campsite fees.

'He came to the house.'

My mother took in a sharp breath. 'What for? Jean never said he'd been around to your house. She said nothing of that!'

I took off my sunglasses and stared at my mother.

'I saw her in M&S,' my mother said quickly. 'I didn't go looking for her, we just bumped into each other in footwear.' A pained expression came over her face. 'She was ever so upset. Told me that you'd cancelled the visit, and she was so looking forward to seeing Sammy. She said she'd got his favourite food in, double cheeseburger and chocolate cake, and then Will says you've changed your mind. That she can't have him.'

I liked Jean, Will's mother, had always got on with her. She'd been more of a friend than a mother-in-law, but when Will left, although she was upset, although she cried with me over his actions, called him names and swore at him, he was still her son and that's where her loyalty lay.

'He came to the door,' I said, 'shouting all kinds of things, accusing me of being a bad mother, and then –' I took a steadying breath '– he said he's going to get the social involved. He's going to take me to court and try for full custody of Sam.'

My mother's eyes went wide, her mouth dropped open.

'Will, have full custody of our Sammy?'

She looked out to where Sam was playing in the field.

'But he didn't even want him! When he left he never saw him!'

I was nodding.

'Jean doesn't know any of this!' she said. 'I've a mind to call her, to ring her up with what that waste of space of a son—'

'Jean won't do anything,' I said, 'and she probably doesn't know about it. It didn't sound like she did, it sounded like it was all Will.'

'So that's why you didn't let him have Sam this weekend?' my mother asked. 'Why you stopped him from going?'

I nodded.

'And Will, just turning up out of the blue like that?'

I hesitated, unsure whether to tell my mother about Janine. About Rob calling Will.

'He just turned up,' I said, deciding against telling her everything. 'I've no idea where this has all come from.'

'Probably that new woman he's with.'

I turned to her suddenly.

She held up her hands. 'I didn't tell you because I didn't want to upset you, but he's not with the one he left you for. Jean says he's with someone else now, someone young.'

I took a moment.

'I don't care who he's with,' I said, and then remembered that he'd told me he was getting married. That he was starting a new family that he wanted Sam to be a part of.

'Has she got children?' I asked my mother. 'This new woman of his? Do you know who she is?'

My mother shook her head. 'Jean only told me that he's a new woman and it's quite serious.'

So that was it. Will was with someone new. Someone serious. Someone he probably wanted to appear like a good father to. He was so transparent at times it was sickening.

We were quiet for a moment.

'If I was like Jean,' my mother said quietly, 'if Will got full custody, and I was depending on him to let me . . .'

'I know,' I said, and leaned over to squeeze her hand. 'I know. And I'm hoping it won't come to that. I've told Will I'm taking Sam on holiday, this half term.'

My mother stared at me.

'Will was accusing me of having no money, of being scared to go out.'

'But you haven't got any money,' my mother said, 'and you don't like going out. You hate going anywhere crowded.'

I bristled slightly. 'I'm taking Sam on holiday to prove to Will that it's not true. That Sam isn't suffering.'

'Sam isn't suffering!'

I turned to my mother. 'You're not following,' I said. 'Will's trying to incriminate my ability to care for Sam. He's going to claim to the social that I'm denying Sam things because I've no money and because I don't like going out. Me taking Sam on holiday is to prove that isn't the case.' I put my sunglasses back on. 'I just have to figure out how I'm going to do that.'

We were quiet, listening to the dog bark and Sam's shouts.

'That was a bit of a daft thing to say,' my mother said after a while, and I nodded.

'I kind of told Will I was taking Sam to Disney.'

'Disney!'

I couldn't look at my mother's face. I knew exactly what her expression would be. Wide eyes, wide mouth.

'I'm not asking for money,' I said. 'I just, well, that's what's going on. That's why I said Will couldn't have Sam.'

We were silent again.

'Sammy wouldn't like Disney anyway.'

'I know.'

'Too many crowds and you'd never get him on the plane.'

'I know, but that was kind of the point as to why I told Will I was taking him. To prove that Sam's not like that any more.'

'But he is,' said my mother, and we were both quiet. 'He has panic attacks if he has to go into a crowd.'

'And so do I,' I said, and my mother reached out her hand to me.

We sat holding hands as the air got colder around us. A flock of geese flew by overhead and we both looked up to watch them.

'You know I'd do anything for you and Sammy,' she said. 'Anything at all. Your brother living in Canada is useless – you and Sam are all I've got. If Will took him, and I could only see him like Jean does, well . . . '

I turned to face my mother, shivering a little in the chill. It was time we went inside, but neither of us moved.

'I just have to figure out how to handle it.' I paused a moment. 'And I've a bit of an idea. I did something the other day,' I said, as Sam darted around the side of the house, the dog chasing after him. 'There's this new teacher at school, Glen—'

'Aha!' my mother suddenly cut in. 'I knew there was a reason you looked happy. What's he like? Good looking?'

'Mum –' I shook my head '– he did something, something

in the staffroom and it made me realise that I've been handling this whole situation with Will wrong. All these years, I've just been reacting to what he throws at me, but I need to think smarter than that.'

My mother stared at me, waiting for me to explain.

'Sort of like, he picks up a knife to fight me with, so I pick up a knife to defend myself, where really, I should be picking up a gun.'

She narrowed her eyes. 'Love, I'm not sure what you're getting at.'

'Like that,' I said, pointing to the field that Sam was running towards. 'We really need to get the farmer to partition it off. If we ever come to sell this place.'

'We're never selling,' my mother said quickly. 'That was why I put you on the mortgage. We're never selling this place, it's being kept in the family, it'll be Sammy's one day—'

'Well, for your own peace of mind then,' I interrupted her, 'to get rid of the sheep. We've tried asking the farmer, we've tried reporting him to the council, but we shouldn't be fighting him like that if we want to get results. Instead we should . . .' I thought for a moment. 'We should take one of his sheep.'

My mother frowned.

'OK, we're not actually going to take a sheep, but he won't build a fence if we ask him to do it; we need to force him to do it.'

My mother looked off for a moment. Sam was running up the field slowly. He came to a stop, resting his hands on his knees while he caught his breath, the dog running around him, barking loudly.

'So, you mean,' she began, 'if instead of taking Sam on a holiday to prove what a great mother you are to Will, you prove what a bad father he is instead?'

'Exactly!' I said, and felt a rush in my chest. 'That's exactly what I need to do. I shouldn't be reacting to him, flapping about, trying to sort out a holiday to prove something to Will because of what he accuses me of. I should be focusing on what Will is doing wrong.' I closed my eyes, the idea of it just forming. 'I need to find out what Will's vulnerable sheep is and attack that.'

I opened my eyes and my mother nodded. 'Guerrilla warfare, isn't that what they call it? Attacking small to exhaust the enemy and weaken them until they can't fight any more? It was on the history channel, I'm sure of it. But in order to do that,' she said, 'you need to let Will have Sam, don't you? So you can prove he's a bad father?'

I sat back, thinking. She was right. The only thing I had against Will at the moment was that he didn't want to see Sam for a year when he first left us, but now he did.

'You can't show social services how bad a father Will is if he never has Sam and —' she put her hand on my arm '— if you do let Jean have Sammy again, then Will might drop the whole thing anyway. You know what he's like. Will never sticks with anything, but not letting Jean have Sam, well, that might push him to actually go to the social.'

I went to tell her how I wasn't sure if I could let Sam go to Will after what he'd said to me. How I needed to meet this new woman of Will's before I could let Sam be with her, how I couldn't trust anything because I was sure that Ashley was helping Will, that she'd offered her services as a solicitor, when there was a shrill scream from Sam. We both looked to the field where we'd just seen him, but he was no longer there, the field empty, and all we could hear was the strangled cry of Sam and the dog's consistent bark.

The garden chair fell back as I sprinted around the side of the house.

'Sam?'

No reply apart from his crying, which seemed to be echoing from all around.

'Sam, where are you?'

'He's here!' I heard my mother shout from the side of the house. 'Over here!'

I ran towards them, around the back of the house, my feet struggling with the clumps of earth, the weeds, the uneven tread. What had I been thinking, letting Sam run loose out here? It was a minefield. My heart thumped in my chest as I went towards them.

'What is it? What's happened?' Sam was lying on the floor, massaging his ankle, his face white, his eyes wide. He pointed to the patch of grass in front of him and I immediately saw the problem.

'You said this was safe!' I almost screamed. 'You said it was safe last time I asked. You said the wood was stable!'

We looked over at the board that had rotted away and caused Sam to trip. It was over a disused well that had been at the bottom of what was my mother's garden. My father had found it when he started to create a vegetable patch that he never finished. The stone flags that adorned the opening of the well were visible through the decaying wood and I gripped Sam tightly. We should have contacted someone immediately, got them to fill it in, but my father had romantic ideas of bringing it back to life. He talked of building it back up, of making it some kind of wishing well, which of course never happened, and the result was a hole in the ground, surrounded by flags of stone, with a plank of wood over it.

Last summer the dog had nearly fallen down it, and we'd got a company out who'd quoted a small fortune to fill it with concrete. In the end, we decided to go with a 'man and van' advert who promised us he'd board it up so that it would be safe. That was a year ago, and now the weather had taken its toll on the wood. Along with the outbuildings and the ridiculously overgrown garden the whole place was dangerous. I was furious with myself and my mother for thinking we could sit out in it and relax.

'It is! It was!' My mother bent forward and examined the wood covered in moss and plants. 'It's rotted,' she announced, 'needs doing again is all.'

I looked at Sam, his face ashen, tears rolling freely down his cheeks and held him close. I examined his ankle, moved it around.

'It's just a bruise,' my mother was saying, 'he just tripped, it's not broken.'

'He could've fallen in!' I swept Sam up. His crying had abated a little, but he was obviously in shock. He was shivering, putting his arms around me as I helped him stand. His mouth a large open circle. 'Why didn't you tell me it had got like this? Do I have to check everything?'

'I didn't know!' She came forward to comfort Sam, but I pulled him away from her, wrapping him in my arms and protecting him from her touch.

'Ruth!'

'He could've been killed.'

'Hardly, it's still boarded. It's just the edge.'

'Can you stand, Sam?' I turned to him, his face full of horror. He was almost as tall as me, almost up to my shoulders, and it was easy to forget that he was only eight. Only a little boy and so vulnerable. I hugged him tightly, kissing the top of his head.

'I'll get some ice,' said my mother. 'C'mon, Sammy . . .'

'No,' I snapped and stroked Sam's head. 'I'm taking him home.'

My mother's face fell. I wanted to tell her that it was OK, that it wasn't her fault, but it was. She should have had this sorted or, at the very least, warned me of it and stopped Sam from playing there. For the first time I couldn't find the words to console her.

Sam whimpered as we hobbled towards the car. I was silent, my mother following on behind, the dog yapping at our feet. We were both shivering. If it was the cold in the air, or what had just happened to blame I didn't know. All I knew was that Sam would not be playing outside at my mother's again. My mother talked incessantly the whole time about how she didn't know, about how she thought it was safe, but I couldn't answer her. I was too full of rage to be rational, with everything that was going on. I just wanted to get my boy away from there and keep him safe.

Sam quietened after we got in the car and then closed his eyes. I reached over and stroked his hair as I drove. It was beginning to get dark, the twilight hour and the fields rushed by at the sides of us as we sped along the A road towards Carlisle.

'Have a little sleep, honey,' I told him. 'It'll do you good, and when we get home I'll make you a hot chocolate.'

He smiled before turning his head towards the window, as I joined the traffic leading into the city. I'd call her when I arrived home. Apologise. Tell her not to let the dog out of the back any more, not to go there herself until I got it fixed. I'd call someone tomorrow and then felt the drag of disappointment as I thought about how much the whole thing would cost. My mother didn't have money to spend on that and neither did I, but it needed to be done. Perhaps we could leave it till next summer, just get some fresh boards to cover it over until then and avoid the area?

The traffic slowed as we came to the roundabout and my mind wandered back over what I'd been telling my mother about Will.

What could I use to make him look like a bad father? In what situation was he open to attack? I suddenly realised I knew nothing about his life. I didn't want to know how his relationship was going, or how his company was doing now he was no longer with the woman whose family had helped set it up. I dropped Sam off at his mother's and left him at the door. The only time I spoke to Will was via text message. I'd long ago stopped talking to him. It was mostly just one-word texts about how Sam was doing, and people had stopped telling me about him when I cut them off as soon as his name was mentioned. To me, when Will betrayed us, he was gone from our lives. I saw my mistake now.

I pulled up to my house with a new agenda. I needed to know everything about him. His work, who he was with, everything. If he played rugby still, or was just involved in the training, what pubs he drank in, who he socialised with. I needed to know it all. Because if I'd learned anything from this past week, it was that everyone had a weak spot. I looked across to Sam who had fallen asleep in the car, the curve of his cheek reminding me of when he was much younger, when I could carry him to his bedroom if he fell asleep in the car. How he'd nuzzle into the side of my neck, and the way he smelt of milk and sleepiness. It pulled at me, the fierce love, and I knew without any doubt I'd do anything to keep him with me. Anything.

'Hey, sweetie,' I said, gently trying to wake him. 'We're home.' I looked up and noticed a red Fiat. There must've been new tourists in one of the properties, but what made me stare was that there was someone inside the car. I leaned forward, peering through the windscreen to be certain I was seeing a figure and not some luggage or a coat thrown over the seat. I saw a movement of the head and jerked back. There was someone in that car. And they were watching me.

'Sam,' I said, my tone no longer cajoling. 'Sam, wake up. Time to wake up now.'

He rubbed his eyes. 'Mum?'

'C'mon, sweetie, we need to get in. Now.'

I opened the door, keeping my eyes on the red Fiat. I almost expected whoever it was to get out, as if they'd been waiting for us, but they didn't move. It was unnerving. For a moment I wondered if they were perhaps locked out of a property and were sat inside the car waiting for the owner to open up for them. Perhaps I was being paranoid, but then they switched on the engine. They began pressing down on the accelerator, making it scream.

'Hurry it up, honey,' I told Sam, as the red Fiat continued to roar in the dark. 'Quickly now,' I helped him out, trying to get to our front door as fast as possible.

The car remained stationary. They hadn't switched on the headlights and I could only see the outline of whoever was in the house. The tang of the fumes filled the air, the sound was deafening and in my haste to get inside, I dropped my key so I bent down, scrabbling about on the pavement.

'Shit!' I heard myself hiss as I found them and opened the

door. I looked back at the stationary car, its engine still scream-ing. The dark shadowy figure seemed to be staring right at me, hands wrapped around the steering wheel.

'Mum?' Sam asked.

Suddenly the car jumped into action, accelerating down the street towards us at speed.

'Get inside, Sam,' I instructed. 'Get inside now!'

Still in complete darkness, it screeched past us, turning our corner and leaving us on the deserted street.

I stared after it, and looked to the terrace at either side of us. Both appeared to be empty, which was usual for this time of year. It was the lull between the end of the summer holidays and just before the autumn hikers.

'Mummy?' Sam asked, and I walked inside, nodding, trying to put a smile on my face. Trying to appear calm.

'Everything's fine,' I told him and that's when I stood on it. Another envelope. It had been pushed through the door and I'd squashed whatever was inside with my foot. Felt it compress under the sole of my shoe, something soft and formless. Panic rose as I guessed what it was. My name was typed on the front of the envelope in bold letters and I instinctively checked the back of my shoe, even though the envelope was still intact.

'What's this?'

'Don't touch that!' I shouted, but it was too late, Sam had already picked it up and was tearing it open.

He pulled the contents out and we both jumped back as he dropped it to the floor with a scream.

One of my neon cupcake cases, filled with excrement. Flattened by my foot with excrement leaking out. I put my hand to my nose as the stench of it hit us.

'Wash your hands,' I ordered Sam.

'But why—'

'Now!'

He looked at me for a moment before trudging to the kitchen and I stared at the cupcake a moment before opening the door and kicking it outside.

'Was that one of your cakes?' Sam shouted from the kitchen. 'Had someone put—'

'It was a joke,' I said quickly, and slid the extra bolt across that we never normally used. 'Just a silly joke.'

Sam stared at me as I checked the windows throughout the house and made sure the back door was locked. My heart thrummed as I tried to stay calm, but there was no getting away from it. Someone had left another of my cupcakes filled with faecal matter for my son to find. They were sending me a very definite message. They were trying to scare me. And it was working.

SEVENTEEN

Carlisle farmers' market is set in the pedestrian area, right in the middle of the city centre. Rows of brightly coloured stalls sell local produce, and it's extremely popular. There's all the usual stuff – crafts, plants, meats and various food stalls – and it's held just one weekend a month from April to December. I had managed to convince Poppy, of Poppy's Jams, to sell a few of my cakes on her stall. It was still early days. I'd only had the agreement with her for two months so far, and that Sunday morning I was late. Really late. So not only did it mean that I had to brave the crowds of people and try not to have an anxiety attack while getting to Poppy's Jams, it meant that I might lose my spot with her.

Last night I'd called the police, and after an hour of tense waiting a couple of tired officers had appeared at my door. They'd searched the property and informed me that there was no forced entry, no criminal damage and nothing had been stolen.

'I know that,' I'd told them, 'but someone posted this through my door.' I'd pointed to the envelope that they had since examined. 'Someone pushed a cupcake filled with –' I'd checked Sam wasn't in the room '– shit through my door. And there was a red Fiat, a car that drove off when we got home.'

They'd shared a look.

'It was either my ex-husband,' I'd gone on, 'who's trying to get custody of my son, or this woman from school, Janine Walker, who hates me because of a misunderstanding with her husband. Or possibly one of her friends, Ashley Simmons, or, thinking about it, it might actually be her husband, Rob Walker he—'

The police officer had held up his hand to stop me. 'You seem to have a lot of enemies, a variety of people who could be responsible for –' he'd checked his notes '– posting a cupcake through your door?'

'A defiled cupcake,' I'd corrected, 'and yes, it could be any one of a number of people. Janine is very popular at the school where I work. She has this whole clique who'd do anything for her.'

They'd shared another look.

'We can log this,' he'd told me, 'but as there's no direct threat and it could be any one of a number of people, the best thing to do is monitor it and, if anything else happens, call us.'

'That's it?' My voice had been high. 'But someone did this intentionally, they meant to scare me.'

'Try not to worry,' he'd said as they went to leave. 'Whoever it was didn't do much damage, and it's on record now, and we usually find that things like this –' he'd waved his hand in the general direction of my living room, as if referring to my life '– behaviour of this manner, is usually down to a small disagreement that tends to blow over.'

They'd left offering me no reassurance whatsoever and so

I'd spent the entire night with Sam and me barricaded in my bedroom and a kitchen knife under my pillow. I'd finally fallen asleep around dawn which meant I'd stupidly slept in.

In the morning, realising how late I was, I'd dropped Sam off at my mother's with a hurried apology and rushed to the market, but was now in danger of losing my spot with Poppy.

'Sorry, sorry,' I muttered as I heaved my boxes towards the stall. 'I couldn't get my car into the pedestrian bit as I'm so late and I've had to park where the punters do and –' I put the boxes down on the table '– these weigh a tonne!'

I smiled what I hoped was a bright smile at Poppy and didn't convey just how hard I found it to tackle the busy streets. Normally I would've been here as the stallholders set up, arranging my cakes with Poppy, leaving before the first customer arrived and when the streets were bare and calm.

She didn't return the smile. 'She said you'd do this,' Poppy said. 'I've been ringing and ringing and you didn't answer.'

'I called you earlier,' I said, pulling my phone out of my pocket. It was out of battery. 'I left a message and when I didn't hear back I thought it was OK, but my phone's dead and . . .' I took a moment. 'Sorry, who said what?'

'There was a woman here, told me that you're being inspected by the health and safety and that's why you weren't going to show up.'

I stared back, stunned.

'She saw the empty cake stands and told me that you've had three orders cancelled this week, due to your inspection.'

'I've had one order cancelled and it was nothing to do with my hygiene. I've all my certificates, you know I've passed everything.'

Poppy was shaking her head. 'And then to turn up here, two

hours late ... What if I'd not had enough stock? I'd have had half a stall empty. Ruth, it's not on.'

'Poppy!' I walked around to the side of her. 'Did you hear my message? I had to call the police last night because of an incident, and then I had to drop Sam off at my mother's because Will isn't having him this weekend. That's why I'm so late, and I'm not being inspected by the health and safety. I would tell you otherwise, that's just a rumour someone started.'

She looked at me for a moment.

'The police?'

I nodded. 'Someone had been to our house while we were out and—'

She raised her hand up to stop me from continuing.

'Thing is,' she said, 'I just don't need the hassle. It's always something with you, Ruth, and I'm just trying to sell a few pots of jam here.'

'Please,' I said, and looked at my full boxes, 'this was a one off. It won't happen again. Promise.'

'OK,' she said after a moment. 'Set up quick. I'll ring you later to tell you what's sold. But keep your phone *on and charged*.'

I left with a sick feeling in my stomach. It had taken a while to get a spot with Poppy. If I lost that then people would hear and the rumour that Janine had started would gain pace.

I was about to get back in my car and go to my mother's to collect Sam, when I felt a hand on my shoulder.

'Ruth?'

It was Eve, an unsure smile playing on her lips.

'I was hoping to find you here. I just came from your cake stall. I could really do with talking to you. I think you need to hear what I've got to say.'

*

174

We went to a local café – overpriced coffee and cakes that weren't a patch on mine, but it had an upstairs and a booth. Somewhere we could hide. Somewhere away from the Sunday crowds of people that horded into Carlisle when the farmers' market was on. If I tried hard enough, I could imagine I was sitting somewhere empty.

'We're moving schools,' Eve said, as she emptied a sachet of sugar into her flat white. 'This is our last term.'

'Oh,' I said, 'sorry to hear that.' I looked towards the door.

'We're leaving because of *Janine*,' she said, and my heart skipped a beat. 'Janine and Rob. That's the reason we're having to take Ryan and Zara out of school.'

I put my spoon down.

'I wasn't going to say anything,' she went on, her voice hushed. 'I know she's dropped the complaint against you but then, then I heard her telling someone about your cakes. About how your cakes weren't safe because of health and safety issues, and I knew she was at it again and I thought it was only fair to warn you.'

'Warn me?'

'She's done it to me,' Eve said. 'Well, not to me but to Zara. To both of us.'

'Eve,' I said carefully, 'can you start from the beginning and tell me everything?'

She took a slow sip of her drink.

'We used to be good friends,' Eve began. 'We met like everyone does, first day of reception welcome meeting. You see them there, don't you? All the other mothers, and you figure out pretty quick who you can get on with and who you can't. Well I got on with Janine – our girls were friends, which kind of pushed us together and Janine, well, you know her. She's charming.'

Eve gave a shrug as if Janine's charm were common knowledge. 'We've met up in the holidays, taken the girls out on day trips. Been to all the parties and school productions together. I've had Sally, her daughter, over to mine countless times and Zara, my girl, has been over to hers, sleepovers, all that. I helped her set up her tutoring business, a group of us delivering leaflets door to door for a month . . .' She shook her head. 'Janine makes it her business to be friends with everyone, she's the life and soul. Anyway –' she took a deep breath '– last year, I saw Rob.' She looked up at me. 'I was in Manchester, Christmas markets with my mother, and I saw Rob with –' she faltered '– someone else.'

I stayed silent, waiting for her to go on.

'They were definitely together, no mistake. He was kissing her. I saw him, saw him with his arms round her neck. I didn't do anything at the time, didn't know what to do, and when I got back I spoke with Shaun, my husband, about it, and we decided the best thing to do was to tell Janine. That if I was a good friend, which I like to think I am, I would tell her. So I did. As a friend would.' She took another small sip of her drink. 'You know that thing they say, "Don't shoot the messenger"? Well, Janine shot me. She didn't believe me, of course she didn't. And then she accused me of fancying Rob, as if I'd be after him. So –' she shrugged again '– I left it. None of my business and all that. I just thought she deserved to know. But then, Zara came home the next day and says that Sally, Janine's daughter, has fallen out with her and she doesn't know why.' Eve's mouth twitched, became a hard line. 'Girls fall out all the time, of course they do, but then, suddenly, all the other girls in Zara's class fall out with her as well. She isn't invited to parties any more, misses out on sleepovers. And suddenly, she's not eating.'

Eve took hold of my hand. 'She's not eating any more because they're all calling her fat. She leaves ballet and gym class because she says no one is talking to her in those groups, that everyone hates her, and I watched my beautiful little girl fall to pieces.'

I sat for a moment, stunned at what I was hearing. Eve had tears in her eyes. 'This all happened over the course of last year,' she said. 'It's been going on for months.'

'But that's bullying,' I said after a while. 'Did you speak to—'

'We spoke to everyone in that school,' she cut in quickly. 'Everyone. But her class teacher, she was always off on sick leave, and those teaching assistants were next to useless. Mr Cartwright would have a word with the class, but what can he do? What can you do when it's the whole class? When Janine's girl, Sally, is the leader, telling everyone to hate my little girl.'

'But,' I began, 'would Janine's daughter really do that? I mean, I know Janine can be spiteful but—'

'No one would sit with her at lunch, or play with her in the playground. There would be parties and meetups and sleepovers that she wasn't invited to, but Sally made sure she knew all about them. Janine made sure I knew exactly what Zara wasn't being invited to. No one talked to her any more, they called her names, put her PE kit down the toilet.' Eve shook her head.

'And John, Mr Cartwright, he didn't . . . ?'

'He did what he could. He talked to the class, got pupils out, but it never stopped. It was as if everyone had just decided to make my little girl's life hell all of a sudden.'

We were both quiet.

'And Janine ostracised me, repeated what Sally was doing to Zara. I used to think I had friends in that school, that we

177

weren't just thrown together because our children happened to be in the same class. I considered those women friends, so it hurt when they all suddenly stopped including me.' She shook her head. 'But that I could handle; what I couldn't accept was what was happening to my daughter.'

I stayed silent. Unsure what to say. My situation with Toby bullying Sam wasn't that dissimilar, but I knew it was only Toby and a few others. I knew Sam still had boys he thought were OK in his class. Ryan, Eve's son, being one of them.

'He doesn't work, you know,' Eve said after a while. 'Rob. Janine's husband. He doesn't work.'

An image of him at the school gates flashed in my mind, his suit, his large white Land Rover.

'He pretends,' Eve said. 'If you ask him or Janine, he's doing something in stocks and shares – wearing flash suits, driving about in that big car. But the truth of it is, he hasn't had a proper job in over three years. Used to be a director at some place that went out of business and hasn't worked since. Shaun, that's my husband, he knows people who used to work with Rob. And he sees him, over at Costa, reading the paper in his suit, whiling away the hours. Pretending like he's got a job.'

I remembered him at the Valentine's dinner, the way he told me he was a sales rep working in Edinburgh. The way he blamed his job for never getting a chance to meet anyone new since his break-up.

'Then at weekends,' Eve went on, 'he's at the rugby club. He's there two, three evenings in the week. He doesn't have to be there, but he doesn't want to stay home with her, but because he hasn't got a job, he can't leave. So he busies himself at the rugby club, uses it as an excuse to go out all weekend, meets his other women, and Janine gets to boast that her husband is

178

this big man in business and head of the rugby club, when in fact, it's something very different.'

I paused for a moment, suddenly feeling something close to sympathy for Janine. I checked myself, as it was so at odds with how I'd been feeling all night with the kitchen knife under my pillow.

'You see,' Eve went on, 'I think Janine is aware I know this about Rob. She knows that Shaun works with people who know Rob, knows people at the rugby club. That was all right so long as I pretended I didn't know, didn't say that her husband is a right prick. But once I came out with it, like you did the other day, once I told her that I'd seen him playing away with someone in Manchester, she didn't like that at all.' Eve gave a small smile. 'And I could handle that. It would've been OK if it was just me she ignored, that she stopped being nice to me. Just me that none of the other mothers would talk to at the school gates, who lost a whole group of friends I'd had since my daughter was five. I wouldn't have been bothered about any of that if it had just been me.

'I sent her a message, when it all started, begging her not to get the girls involved. When Sally had a party and Zara wasn't invited, I asked Janine not to do that. Not to take it out on Zara and that was my mistake.'

I looked expectantly at Eve.

'I'd shown her my weak spot,' she explained, 'my daughter. From then on, it was all about Zara.'

My heart thrummed as I thought of Will, his threats to go to social services. The 'solicitor' that was helping him.

'And now,' Eve was finishing her drink, 'we're moving. Zara can't wait to leave and, to be honest, neither can I. I'm sick to death of Janine and the rest of them. So, when I saw what they were doing to you, what rumours she was starting, and I saw that a crowd of them had gathered at the car park, well –' she shook her head '– I thought you should know what you're dealing with.'

I sat for a moment in stunned silence.

'Is she dangerous?' I asked. 'Because I think she's been sending me weird things and someone was outside my house last night.'

'She wouldn't do anything like that,' Eve said, and then paused. 'I've known Janine for a long time,' she said, 'and she can be really nice. There was a time when she was the one I'd phone if I needed help with anything. But ... ' she trailed off and was quiet for a while. 'And there's this.'

She brought up her handbag and took out a piece of A4 paper. It was a photocopy of a newspaper. The *Cheltenham Standard*.

'Teacher arrested for affair with fifteen-year-old boy' the headline declared.

I looked back up to Eve in confusion.

'Janine's employing her,' she said, pointing to the picture, 'this woman. She had an affair with one of her students while she was teaching. Well, an alleged affair. She didn't actually go to prison in the end, but she was struck off. Couldn't get a job. So she moved here, to Carlisle, and is now one of the most prominent teachers for Top Marks.'

I picked up the photocopy and looked at it.

'I was going to use it,' Eve said, and a flush went to her cheeks, 'when things were really bad with Zara, when she wasn't eating. I knew that this teacher was working for Janine and I was going to –' she shook her head '– I don't know, blackmail Janine or something but –' she shrugged, sat upright '– Zara wanted to change schools. To start afresh and so –'

she slid the paper over to me. 'So, I thought you might find it useful.'

I took the paper.

'Why?' I said. 'Why does Janine do it? Why stay with him, if she knows he's being unfaithful? Why do all this to us?'

Eve gave a long sigh. 'You know when you're a kid, and you have this image of the adult you'll become? I don't think Janine has ever let her image go. I think it's that simple. She's just being who she thinks she should be, and –' Eve shook her head, a look of pity crossing over her features '– her image doesn't involve being a single parent to those girls.'

EIGHTEEN

Lisa wasn't waiting for me. I'd done as she asked and made an appointment outside of school hours like all the other parents, but when I went I found her classroom locked. It had been a slow week, most of which I'd spent hiding in my office. There had been no announcement of Janine's investigation by HMRC, no journalists or headlines in the local paper and, to be honest, I was a little disappointed. I knew things didn't move at lightning speed, but I expected something. A rumour in the staffroom about Janine's tutoring company at least. But Becca reported nothing.

Since the cupcake incident in the house, I'd taken to sleeping how we did that night, the bedroom door barricaded and the kitchen knife under my pillow. Sam in bed beside me. This was no time to be pedantic about him sleeping alone. I'd had no more texts, no more special deliveries of vile cupcakes, but it didn't stop me from feeling unsafe. I hadn't heard anything more from the police, but after learning what Janine did to

Eve, how relentless she was, I found I was jumpy at everything. Everywhere had become a frightening place. I was waiting for her to do something next and it was driving me mad.

It was a good five minutes before Lisa arrived.

'Right,' she said, finally appearing along the corridor, 'let's get inside. I've had a terrible week, someone messed up the board so I'm all mixed up with my planning and, to make matters worse, I've been put down to volunteer with the residential trip.' She fiddled with the keys. 'I tried to tell John that it's impossible for me to go that week, I have a friend's wedding, but he insists my name is on the list.' I suppressed a smile as she opened the door. 'And now I have to lock up the classroom because we have a thief. Has Sam told you?' She nodded. 'Stickers were moved and my marking pen, my special red pen with a feather on top, has been stolen.'

'Stolen?' I asked, and glanced towards the children's drawers at the back of the classroom. Toby was still off school, which meant the pen was still in his drawer, as yet unfound.

'I know it's only a little thing –' she went to her desk '– but my mum bought it for me when I passed my teacher training so it's quite sentimental. It wouldn't be important to anyone else, which makes me think it's a child.'

She stared at me, waiting for a response.

'I'm taking it very seriously,' she said, when I didn't say anything. 'I've asked them all but, so far, no one's admitted it, so I'm not giving out any stickers until the thief comes forward.'

'No stickers for any of them?' I asked, and Lisa sat down, smoothing her skirt along her knees.

'They all love the gold stickers,' she said, 'so I'm confident that the culprit will come forward soon. Until then, everyone suffers because of their selfish actions.'

I had, up to this point, still wanted to make amends with Lisa. She was Sam's class teacher after all, and I needed her onside. Despite her wanting to fire me, and how she treated me in the staffroom, I'd reasoned she was still the best person to help Sam. If I made a friend of her, she would stop the bullying, so that's what I'd fully intended to do.

She'd got the wrong impression of me and I was going to take the opportunity of meeting her after school to try and change her mind. But as she sat there, showing me the pad of gold stars hidden in her drawer, knowing that they were coveted by a class full of eight-year-old children, I decided that being her friend was going to be impossible. I hated her.

Who does that? I found myself thinking, as she locked the stars away with a smug smile, and showed me the reward chart, which had a big red cross over the top of it. Who abuses their power over a group of children? Punishing everyone for a stupid pen going missing? She was a class teacher, not the chief of police. And it was a daft pen, not the crown jewels.

'No chaperone?' I asked, noting that we were alone, and Lisa flushed a little.

'Well, I trust you aren't going to attack me?' She gave a small laugh. 'I overreacted a bit,' she said, 'last week, when Janine told me what happened. I might have . . . ' She shook her head. 'But you need to realise that Janine is a really good friend to me. She's a really good friend to the *school*. Everyone loves her and, to be honest, I'm still shocked by it all, Ruth.' An alarming expression came over her face. 'What you did with her husband. And how you told her, in front of her children like that. And with your employment history I just think . . . ' She trailed off, shaking her head, and I could tell she'd discussed this many times before. Her words were well practised, too quick to come out. 'I know you're expecting forgiveness,' she went on, 'those cakes of yours in the staffroom . . .'

'I'm here to talk about Sam,' I said forcefully, 'not gossip. And those cakes weren't left for forgiveness.' It sounded petty but I couldn't stop myself. 'I left them there for Sue. For her fiftieth. So, can we crack on?'

She raised an eyebrow and crossed her legs. I noticed she was wearing heels and a shorter skirt than she should have; it didn't suit her. Her legs were bare, even though it was September, and they were gooseflesh. She signalled for me to take a seat. The chairs were small, made for the children and I looked at them, then perched on the edge of the desk so I was at eye level with her.

'Sam Clarkson,' she said, taking out a folder. 'Sam, Sam, Sam,' she repeated his name, as if trying to remember who he was, and I gritted my teeth.

'Here we are,' she said, pulling out a sheet of paper. 'So, he's up to speed on his literacy, although he's still writing certain letters backwards, that's one of his targets, and in regards to numeracy—'

'Bullying,' I interrupted, and she looked up. 'My son is eight years old,' I went on. 'I'm not really concerned with his academic levels at this point, but what I am concerned about, *extremely concerned* about, is Toby Morley-Fenn. He's making Sam's life a misery and I want to know what you're going to do about it.'

She blinked a few times, as if taken aback by my words, and it felt good. A flicker of something close to enjoyment passed through me.

'I'm aware of the situation between Toby and Sam,' she said carefully. 'We've had several little chats about it, the three of us, and I think we've come to an understanding of sorts . . .'

'Little chats won't cut it,' I said, and her eyes went wide at my words. 'Do you know what they're doing now? They're spitting in his food, Lisa. Spitting. In my son's sandwiches at lunchtime.'

She had the decency to look shocked. 'This is the first I've heard of it.' She looked down at her files as if an answer was there. 'And you're sure? Because I can't imagine that this is going on in my classroom.'

'Sam told me about it.'

Lisa shook her head. 'No other children have mentioned this to me at all.' She closed her file and shifted on her chair. 'I'll talk to Sam in the morning.'

'It's not Sam, it's Toby!'

My outburst surprised us both. In previous conversations I'd always gone for a soft approach.

'Sam is really suffering,' I said again. 'His anxiety is top pitch. He's worried about coming into school because of Toby. Worried about how he'll be with him, what he'll do, and as his class teacher isn't it your responsibility to make sure he doesn't feel that way?'

'I've spoken to Toby,' Lisa said, 'and have explained how his behaviour affects others. The problem is, Toby, in his own way, is trying to be friends with Sam.'

This threw me. 'Friends?'

'He thinks what he's doing to Sam is just gentle teasing, that he's just poking fun, although I agree that spitting is . . . ' She shook her head. 'When I've spoken to Toby about his actions he genuinely can't understand why Sam gets so upset about it. He feels Sam may be rather sensitive.'

It took me a moment. I had to remind myself about what Toby was writing on Sam's books, what he was calling him, and then I realised: Toby was also an eight-year-old boy. He might be a clever eight-year-old boy, but he didn't have the wherewithal to put this argument forward. This was coming straight from Lisa.

'You think Sam is overreacting? To Toby, to bullying—'

'Bullying is a strong word to use.'

'But he is bullying him. Writing "Fatty" on a small whiteboard and holding it above Sam's head to make the other children laugh is bullying behaviour, spitting in his sandwiches at lunch is bullying behaviour, constantly calling him names and picking on him is bullying behaviour . . .'

'We did speak about the whiteboard incident and that was a one off. Toby is well aware of how his actions then were too much, but as for the spitting in Sam's food, I'll look into this, but no lunchtime assistant has ever—'

'Sam won't tell them because he's frightened. He's scared to do anything in case Toby reacts badly.'

'Sam is rather scared of a lot of things, isn't he?' Lisa said, and I stared at her. 'I spoke to Julie, his last teacher. She told me of the things she had to do with him, about the special treatment he got, and I'm afraid I can't offer the same here. Year four is when the children need to start bucking up and getting serious about their work. I'm afraid that by pandering to Sam's fears last year, you've only held him back.'

'*I've* held him back?'

She nodded. 'Not you directly, but I think that a bit of tough love may be in order.' She smiled, and I was shocked into silence.

I couldn't quite believe what Lisa was putting forward. I'd expected to talk about how we could make things better for Sam, how we could ensure that he would feel safe in the classroom, not force him into it because of the notion of 'tough love'.

'I think you're wrong,' I said, and her smile became resigned.

'Why don't we try it this way for a couple of weeks?' she said. 'I'm the class teacher and I've seen this behaviour before. Honestly, believe me, Ruth, what I'm suggesting will work. It will be hard in the short term, but once Sam gets used to how things are in year four it will be better for him. He just needs to get used to our routine. I'll keep him and Toby away from each other and—'

'Where have you seen this before?' I challenged her. 'Not to be rude, Lisa, but you've only just left teacher training. This is your NQT year. Shouldn't you be going to your mentor to deal with a situation like this? Or speaking to someone with a little more experience?'

Her face hardened. 'I've had years of experience with children,' she said carefully, 'particularly children like Sam.'

'Children *like Sam*? What is that supposed to mean?'

'It means that I know what I'm doing. I've seen boys like him before, I've seen how they behave, in school, and I know—'

'Is this because of Janine?' I suddenly asked, and she stopped. 'How you were talking about forgiving me before? You told me that you're a good friend of hers, that she's been very supportive. I understand that you work for her in the school holidays, that you have a bit of tutoring going on outside of school. Is that the experience that you're referring to? Your private tutoring work?'

Lisa blinked rapidly. 'I wouldn't call it work. I just help out when Janine's stuck, give her a bit of a hand.'

'I heard it was more than that,' I said. 'I heard you've been

working for her all through the summer and you've been getting a nice little income from it.'

'It has no effect on my job here if that's what you're implying.'

'So John's aware of it?'

'John's aware that some of us do personal tutoring in the
holidays, yes. It doesn't impact on our roles within the school
and it's—'

'Is he aware that it's illegal?'

She shut her mouth then opened it again, flapping like a fish.

'It's not illegal.' She gave a laugh. 'Janine, unlike you, has
morals, she wouldn't do—'

'You get paid cash, that right? Nothing declared. You don't
pay any tax.'

'I think . . .'

'Janine is under investigation with HMRC and a journalist
is interested in the story.'

The look on her face was priceless.

'I'm surprised they've not been in touch with you.'

Her face went pale.

'Oh, they have? They've spoken to you?'

'I assumed that was a sales call,' she said. 'His message said
he was from the paper, and I thought he was trying to sell me
a subscription.'

I shook my head. 'Janine's under investigation and, what's
more, I've heard she's been employing people who shouldn't
be working with children.'

'What?' Lisa sat forward. 'What are you talking about?'

'I really hope that doesn't come out,' I went on, unable to
stop myself, 'because if you're associated with Top Marks, and
it becomes known that Janine has been employing tutors who
haven't had their proper checks done and sending them out

189

to children . . . ' I shook my head. 'It won't look good for you, will it, Lisa?'

She stared at me, stunned.

'I've a contact at HMRC,' I told her. 'They've been in touch as the school name came up and they need a little more information.'

'Information from you?'

'I am school secretary,' I told her, standing up. 'Who do you think is responsible for all the admin, the human resources element in the school? I may not have "personal assistant" in my job title, but it's what I do. I am John's personal assistant. I know everything that goes on in this school.' I was on a roll now, I couldn't seem to stop the words from spilling out. Lisa was flustered, agitated and I was enjoying it. 'John asked me to get a list together of the teachers who do the tutoring, to help the council and HMRC, and if the police eventually become involved . . . '

Her face blanched. 'Have you . . . ?

'Not yet, I'll start the list next week,' I said brightly. 'And I honestly don't know what names I'll pull together. I suppose it depends on lots of different factors.'

She stared at me a moment.

'If you fail your NQT year,' I said slowly, 'what happens then? As I understand it, it's not something you can retake, is it? You lose it all. Bit harsh, isn't it? I wonder what you'd have to do to fail?'

She stared at me. For the longest time we were silent, the clock on the back wall the only sound. My heart was beating, a great thump echoing through my body, and I was sweating but I held her gaze.

'I'll talk to Sam,' I said. 'I'm glad we've spoken about it. As you say, you are the class teacher and you know what to do for the best. I'll check up on him every night and see how his day at school was. I'm sure you're right, I'm sure he just needs a bit of,' I paused, 'tough love.'

I left her with her mouth open, staring after me. I managed to get into the hall before I had to take a moment. I was shaking, my body was starting to shiver slightly. I couldn't believe what I'd just done. How I'd behaved. Where did that come from? Me getting a list together for the council and HMRC? It must've been the photocopy Eve gave me – I thought I wouldn't use it, but once Lisa started talking like that about Sam it flew out of me. I couldn't keep the words in. I gave a surprised laugh; it was like a bubble in my chest, there was a soaring sensation filling my upper body.

It felt alien. I wasn't sure of the emotion. Happiness? Pride? Self-respect? I had no idea what it was, but it felt excellent. It left me jittery and giddy, like I wanted to jump or run. I wanted to do it again. I had to stop myself from marching back into the classroom and repeating myself just so I could see the look on Lisa's face. So my heart would thump and the soaring feeling would stay. And I wanted to call Glen, I wanted to see him, tell him. Admit to him what I'd done, tell him about my chat with Eve, tell him what I'd said to Lisa. So silly to be thinking of discussing it with him, of all people.

I smoothed down my shirt, tucked my hair behind my ears and, after a few deep breaths, went to collect Sam. I imagined Lisa would now be texting Janine, who must have, by now, received notification regarding her tax investigation. She would be forced to admit it and Lisa would naturally panic and, hopefully, also ask her about the woman who shouldn't be working for her. Perhaps I would never have to use the newspaper photocopy Eve had given me. Perhaps this would be enough. The problem was, it felt so good to finally be able to fight back properly.

I had something, something solid on her and Rob. I imagined photocopying the newspaper article and pinning it up all around school, for all the parents to see. For all the teachers who worked for her to gawp at and happily watch the devastation as it happened. But that would be going too far, wouldn't it?

Despite Janine attacking me and sending me threatening messages, she was a woman to be pitied. She was someone whose husband was unfaithful and yet she couldn't leave him. And if what Eve had told me about Rob being unemployed was correct, then Top Marks was the only family income. I couldn't do that to them, it would destroy them completely. Those poor two daughters, they would go through hell. I couldn't do that to them, could I?

NINETEEN

That Friday I was filled with dread. I had followed my mother's and Becca's advice and, via text messages with Jean, I'd agreed that I'd drop off Sam at her house that evening, and Will could have him on the Saturday night as usual. I was doing it in the hope that Will would reconsider applying for custody. It was the sensible thing to do. If I went ahead and stopped all contact and visits with Will, then it was a sure-fire way to make him go ahead with the custody appeal. But by allowing him to have Sam for the weekend again, I was showing that I was rational. I was proving that I could be diplomatic, that we could continue as normal. That I could be trusted, and there was no need to alter our arrangement, but it went against every instinct I had. What my heart was telling me was something very different. It told me to get Sam and to lock the doors. To stay hidden, keep my son close and stay safe.

It was the end of the school day. Another day of hiding in my office, staying out of the way of the teachers, having as little to do with the parents as possible and making sure there was no more drama. The small window at my office that had always been open was now always closed. I'd taken to depending on the bell if anyone needed me and, surprisingly, it was working wonders.

Now when parents came into the office, when faced with a closed window and blinds almost drawn, they were reluctant to ring the bell for attention. Odd, isn't it? But I'd hear them come in, and hear them shuffle around for a moment or two. They'd come up to the window, perhaps take a copy of the current letter for the class their child was in, and then I'd hear them leave.

I'd thought that by presenting myself as always on hand, always open, that I was being helpful and assisting. Now, I saw my mistake. I was being helpful, but I was also actively encouraging them to depend on me.

By presenting a closed front, instead of having a barrage of confused parents, as I had thought, there was just a lot less hassle all round. The parents were now reading the letters we sent home, they were checking the website, they weren't piling up outside my office asking me everything. It was a lot more peaceful and John had noticed. I was in his good books.

The journalist idea I'd had with the travel company had played out excellently. They'd not only promised to honour the lower price we'd originally agreed, but they'd also thrown in a free picnic lunch for all the children. He was delighted, said he wished more people would use their initiative like I had. There had been no more mention of the internal investigation, and no mention of Janine Walker. I'd not seen her or Ashley, her solicitor friend, since. I'd not heard anything else about the whole encounter and, according to Becca, fewer people were now talking about it overall. Another staff meeting had concentrated entirely on the upcoming trip and my name wasn't mentioned once. And in another turn of events, Lisa had moved Sam to the front of the class to sit right beside her. Toby had returned to school, the pen had been found in his drawer, he was branded the thief and, for once, it looked like things were on the up.

But I'd received another delivery. This time a letter.

Hand delivered to the school office. Why couldn't she just give up?

It had been pushed under my door, so when I went in that morning, I stepped on the white envelope. It was A4, my name typed on the front.

Four sentences.

YOU THINK YOU'RE CLEVER BUT YOU ARE STUPID
LEAVE THIS JOB
LEAVE THIS SCHOOL
LEAVE CARLISLE OR YOU'LL REGRET IT

I was beginning to think she was deranged. Eve had warned me that she went all out on her daughter, and that was on a child. I hadn't seen the red Fiat again and I'd convinced myself that I was being paranoid over that, but this letter disturbed me. The whole 'get out of Carlisle' thing was worrying.

'Tell the police,' Becca said that lunchtime when I showed her.

I bit into my tuna sandwich and shook my head. 'They were a bit useless when they came to the house.' I looked up at her. 'I think they knew my history. They must have looked me up when they took my call and had already made their decision before they arrived. They told me I had a lot of enemies and they couldn't do anything as I didn't know who was behind it, as I've only got suspicion.' I put the letter away. 'At least it's not been smeared with something.'

Becca wrinkled her nose. 'Gross. Perhaps it's not Janine. Perhaps it's one of her gang, one of the other alpha mothers thinking they're doing her a favour. Have any of them said anything to you?'

I frowned. Shook my head. They scowled at me, that's what the mothers did now. They turned their noses up, gave me the daggers. That's how I knew they were friends of Janine. But would their loyalty make them do this? Didn't seem likely.

'You don't think it's someone from in here, do you?' Becca suddenly asked. 'One of the teachers, or dinner staff, or cleaners?'

I stared at her.

'OK.' She shook her head. 'That was a daft suggestion, but I'm just going through all the possibilities. Who else would want you out of Carlisle?' She paused. 'Will? You don't think it's Will, do you?'

I took a moment then shook my head again. 'I thought it might be him but if Will wanted me to leave Carlisle, he knows I'd take Sam with me, so ...'

'Could you?'

I stared up at Becca.

'I mean, you can't, can you? Take Sam?'

'Why not? I'm only in Carlisle because my father got ill, and now my mum's on her own, but if she wasn't here, then –' I shrugged '– I could go anywhere. As far away from Will as possible.'

'But,' Becca laughed, 'is that legal?'

I nodded. 'I think I can take Sam anywhere so long as it's in the UK. I could move to South Devon tomorrow and Will wouldn't be able to do anything about it.'

Becca looked horrified. 'You can't do that! What about me? You can't leave me!'

I laughed. 'I can't leave my mother,' I said, and then after a moment, 'and you. Who else would bring me never-ending stories of her love life?'

She grinned. 'And who else would bring you lunch and make sure you were looking after yourself?'

We were silent for a moment.

'I am worried though,' I said. 'I thought it had all stopped.' I was about to explain to Becca about my call to HMRC, my veiled threat to Lisa, but realised she knew none of it. 'Thought it had all blown over,' I went on, 'but now this?' I checked the office door was shut. 'At work?' I whispered. 'What if John had seen it?'

Screams and shouts from the playground filtered though. The smells from the dining hall, the sausage and mash that had been made for school dinners, the fatty smell of the oil that had been used was strong and I threw the remainder of my sandwich in the bin.

'I think you should go back to the police,' she pressed. 'In case it is her. It's like she's stalking you. Got fixated. You need to report it if nothing else.'

I thought for a moment. 'Ask them to go around and have a word?'

Becca nodded.

'I might give the police a ring, log it if nothing else. But then, if they do contact her, she could tell John and you know what he said? No more drama. What will he think if he finds out I've been getting letters at school? In my job? And what if she told Will? Told him I was receiving threatening letters and packages? I know he'd use that as another reason for Sam to go live with him.'

We sat for a moment, both wondering what the best thing to do was.

'I need to think about it,' I said. 'I don't want to make it worse.'

Becca didn't agree. She thought I should call the police there and then. I said I'd think about it and she left, reminding me that I lived in a remote area, out of the city, in a street that was all holiday lets and occupied by tourists who couldn't be relied upon. No neighbours watching out for us, no family or friends close by. Her words hung over me all afternoon. Whoever was behind it all was being stupid and ridiculous but they were really starting to get to me.

'Hey you.' My stomach dipped. I'd been avoiding him all week, thinking about him constantly and purposely staying away from him. 'Are you in hiding?' He pointed to the drawn blinds, the closed window. 'Is there something you're not telling me? You're in police protection or something? You never come out of here, do you?'

I smiled, picked up my bag. John had already left and I needed to collect Sam from the after-school club, feed him and get him ready for the weekend with Jean and Will. I felt low and sick at the thought of it.

'I've been busy,' I told him. 'Was it important or can it wait till Monday?'

He grinned. I was standing, bag on my shoulder, jacket in hand. My computer was switched off and my finger was on the light switch. I couldn't have given a clearer message if I tried, but he leaned against my desk as if we had all the time in the world. He smiled again and I felt the familiar swirl of attraction.

'Where you running off to?'

'I need to go.'

'It's not even five.'

'I need to collect Sam.'

'I taught him today.'

I raised my eyebrows and he laughed.

'Lisa mixed up her PPA cover again,' he said. 'She put it down wrong on the board, thought Sheila was taking her class when I'd already swapped with her.'

I found myself laughing along with him. 'You switched names again? So you could take Lisa's class?'

He came forward. 'I didn't switch anything. I took Lisa's class, that's all.'

I could smell him, his aftershave and the laundry powder he used. I could see the stubble on his chin, the way his dimples formed when he smiled, the way his eyes danced.

'You never told me if it worked,' he said. 'What we did at our last meeting.'

I opened my mouth, then rethought my words before I replied. 'It was ...' I said, thinking back to the last time I was alone with him. The way he'd altered the whiteboard in the staffroom, and everything that had happened since, 'very effective. I learned a lot from you that day.'

I felt myself get hot under his stare and readjusted my bag, tried to find something else to concentrate on. 'I applied your advice to a few things and, well –' I looked up at him and felt an excited dip in the base of my stomach '– thank you.'

He nodded and I found I had a smile on my lips that I couldn't get rid of. There was a buzzing in my chest and a giggle at the forefront of my words. There was a lightness in the air that hadn't been there until he'd arrived. It was maddening the effect he had on me, his ability to change everything in an instant, and I was excited and frustrated with myself at the same time. I didn't have time to feel like I did around him.

'He's a great kid,' he said after a while, and I couldn't look away. He'd taught Sam that afternoon. He'd met my son.

'He is,' I agreed. 'Sam's amazing.'

'And I'm glad he's getting the treatment he deserves, Miss Gleason realising that he needs special attention.'

My heart was thrumming; he was holding my gaze a beat too long.

'You want to go somewhere?' he asked.

'What?'

'Now. Let me show you something.'

I glanced at the clock on the wall. 'I've got to collect Sam. He's in the after-school club and then I need to get him ready, he's staying at his gran's tonight so . . .'

'Half an hour,' he said, smiling. 'I've had this idea. And you've been cooped up in here all week, let me take you out. Both of you. Half an hour.'

He drove a campervan, an old green VW. I let out a shocked laugh when I saw it.

'Cool!' Sam said, running up to the back. 'Do you sleep in here, is that what you do? Do you go camping all weekend?'

He opened it up to reveal an immaculate interior, a small sink, a two-seater settee, on top of which was a guitar.

200

'Here,' he said as Sam jumped up, 'you sit there, your mum and me up front.'

'Where are we going?' I stayed still, in the car park, looking back at my lonely car. It was already getting a little dark, the sky taking on that purple-blue undertone. 'I need to be back in . . .'

'Relax,' Glen said, as he shut Sam in. 'Half an hour. That's all. Let me show you something. I had the idea when I was teaching Sam today. Just half an hour.'

We didn't really speak in the van. He put some music on, a slow folk band I'd never heard of before, and drove us confidently out of the city and towards Grinsdale and the River Eden.

'Sam's not,' I began as we went past the college, 'I mean, both of us, we don't really do crowds, we're not good with . . .'

'Shh,' Glen said and pulled up in a car park at the side of a field. 'You OK with a five-minute walk?'

I nodded.

We got out and walked towards the river and I suddenly realised how remote we were. Sam's hand was tight in my own, and for a moment I wondered what I was thinking, getting into a van with him, taking my son. He was a teacher at the school, but I barely knew him, he was a stranger. I'd been a fool.

'Up there,' Glen said, and I saw a tree beside the river, and in the river, a man, fly fishing.

'It's the end of the season,' Glen said to me, 'probably won't catch anything, but Andy's got the gear and –' he shrugged '– I thought Sam would like to see it. We were talking about it in lessons today and Sam said how he always wanted to try it because of some computer game he played.'

I looked down at Sam. He was staring at the river, mesmerised.

'He kind of came alive in class, it was the most he'd spoken all lesson, and I knew Andy would be here so . . .'

I looked at the river, the light playing on its surface behind the silhouette of the man as he launched his fishing line. This was something I'd seen Sam do on his Xbox. This was how they got food in the game he played. Sam would cheer if he caught a fish, shout me in to see.

Glen bent down to Sam. 'There's no one else here,' he said softly, 'and we won't be long, but would you like to have a try? See how it's done?'

Sam nodded shyly, his face bright and shining, and my throat got tight at the look on his face. It was so rare to see Sam enthused by something, something that wasn't on a screen or in a packet ready to be eaten.

'That is cool,' he said quietly and inched forward.

Glen looked at me, to check it was OK, and I nodded.

'I thought you might like this,' Glen said, as we started to walk towards the river. 'I knew it'd be something you'd want to have a go at.' And as they set off, Sam did something that I've never seen him do before, and it stopped me in my tracks.

Glen was talking to him about the fish, about how they have to be thrown back into the river, about the fishing season and, as he spoke, Sam lifted his hand and slotted it into Glen's. It was the first time I'd ever seen him hold a hand that wasn't mine, my mother's or Becca's. It was the first time I'd seen him hold a man's hand.

They walked in front of me, holding hands, talking of computer games and fishing like it was the most natural thing in the world, and I felt something soften inside of me. I could feel it melt, could feel my eyes water as it did. I went to the other side of Sam, took his other hand in mine, so he was between us, and I felt, for the first time in about a hundred years, safe.

TWENTY

I'd planned a weekend of binge-watching boxsets, baking and trying out a few new recipes. It was what I did when Sam wasn't with me. I'd decided to try and go to a car boot on Sunday, which meant I'd be kept busy baking for most of the day, but I found myself unsure of what to do. I was like this when Sam was with Will – restless and jittery. And it was even worse that weekend as I'd given him a phone. It was a cheap thing, only had £10 credit on it and only had the ability to send and receive calls and texts. And take pictures. That's why I got it.

I wanted Sam to record what he did with Will. I made up a reason as to why Sam was having it. I told him it was so he could practise for when it was our turn to have the class bear and we would have to take pictures of what the bear did at the weekend. It was a stretch, but Sam was delighted at getting a phone so he listened eagerly when I gave him a stuffed toy and told him to take pictures of what he did, especially anything that Will asked him to do.

My plan was to show what a bad father Will was, and I could only do that if Sam provided me with evidence. I knew that his time with Will was stressful. He often forced Sam into situations that he wasn't happy with, such as going into the city or the supermarket, and I thought if Sam took a few pictures and then explained in his own words why it was something he was being forced into, it would be a start.

'Take pictures of everything,' I told Sam as I gave him the phone. 'Take a picture of everything your dad makes you do, especially if it's something that this little fella doesn't like doing.' I held up the stuffed toy. 'OK?'

'Like the cinema?'

I nodded. 'Like the cinema, and the shopping centre, and the supermarket, all those places.'

I'd shown him how to use the camera on the phone. It was easy, simple enough.

'And you can call me,' I told him, showing him how to make a call, 'anytime. Even if it's the middle of the night, and you want to come home, call me and I'll come and get you immediately. There's only one number in there and it's mine. OK?'

He'd given a small nod and then thrown his arms around my neck. 'I love you, Mum.'

I had to squeeze my eyes tight so the tears wouldn't spill over.

'Love you,' I told him, 'very much, and here –' I handed him the magazine I'd bought earlier '– to take with you.'

His eyes sparkled again, his smile back on his face.

To be honest, when we left Glen, as we drove home before the packing and the introduction of the mobile phone, we were both in a little state of wonder and surprise. My mind was full of Glen, at how insightful he'd been to show that to Sam. At how he'd gained Sam's trust so completely, at him being able to introduce Sam to new things, to show him where his interests lay, to know him, really know who he was after meeting him so briefly. It was a marvel, made my head spin, and it had done the same to Sam. It showed him a slice of a different world.

He talked non-stop of fishing after we left Glen. Of going fishing, of joining a fishing club, how much fishing rods cost, where the best places to fish were, so much so that on the way home I'd stopped by a newsagents and bought him a magazine about it. His eyes had been shining, his head full of the idea of himself as a fisherman.

It was unbelievable, invigorating. I'd never seen Sam so excited about something outside of himself before. And I couldn't stop thinking about Glen, about his smile, about the way he looked at me, how he made me feel. The whole thing was mind-blowing to be honest. It was only a small thing, to show a shy boy like Sam the hobby of fishing, but it was massive to us. We both knew it, *I* knew it, and I couldn't stop thinking about him. What kind of man is so intuitive like that?

I dropped Sam off at Jean's that Friday night, as planned. She hugged me at the door.

'Thanks, love,' she whispered in my ear, before bending and kissing Sam. 'I missed you. What's that?' Sam held up his new phone. 'Oh fancy. Aren't you the little man with your own phone?'

'I know Will is with someone new now,' I told Jean, 'someone I've not yet met, so I'd really appreciate it if he stayed over at your house on the Saturday night as well as tonight.'

She nodded. 'Of course, of course. Whatever you want, Ruth. We're just delighted to have him.' But I may as well have been talking to the wall. We both knew that once Will got involved, Jean had no say in what happened to Sam.

I left him happy, telling his grandparents about his impromptu fishing trip. Showing them his magazine, telling them how he held the rod, what he'd done. It was strange to be leaving him without the usual clinginess, without Sam looking at me pleading with his eyes. He was too distracted to be concerned over a night away from me, his head full of fishing and a new mobile phone.

I was feeling a little bemused, pleased that Sam had found something but the whole thing was bittersweet. I think it was because I wanted to have him home that night of all nights. I wanted to be the one to see and hear his excitement over the possibility of this new hobby of his, not Jean, or his granddad, or Will, who wouldn't be interested. I wanted to share in his excitement and enthusiasm, something I'd not seen in him for so long.

I went straight back to the newsagents and bought him another magazine, toying with the idea of buying him a rod, or researching into any clubs he might want to join.

That evening, I left Sam with Jean believing they would be doing the usual, spending the night watching game shows, then being taken to Will's house on the Saturday morning and watching whatever sports Will had on throughout the day. But unbeknown to me, or Sam, Will, in his wisdom, had arranged for Sam to attend a training session at the rugby club that Saturday morning. At *that* rugby club.

It was such an idiotic thing to do, and the possibility of Will arranging something like that never even entered my head. But then, it was so obvious. Of course, Will wanted to show Sam off to his new friends, to Janine and Rob and everyone else who was advising him that he should take full custody. He wanted their nod of approval. Christ, I even think Rob might have been holding the training session. What mixed-up person does that? Arranges for their son to be trained by the man that their ex-wife had a one-night stand with? It was beyond unbelievable but so typical of Will.

The first I heard about it was a call, late on the Saturday afternoon, from Will. They were at A & E and, panicked, I asked why, and then the whole horrendous tale came out.

Will had bought Sam a new kit. It was too tight because Will didn't know Sam's size, so that was the first thing, I believe, that set Sam off in full tantrum mode and drove Will to anger. And then he made him go to the rugby club in this ill-fitting kit, looking and feeling awful. When they got there, he practically had to drag Sam out of the car.

I don't entirely know what Will was thinking, but when he forced Sam to walk on that pitch, in front of a group of sniggering boys he didn't know, in front of a coach who already had preconceived ideas and judgements, it was one of the cruellest things he'd ever done as a father.

Sam was already crying at this point I understand, begging his dad not to make him do it, but Will had insisted. On the drive to the rugby club, I learned that Sam had been constantly crying, shaking, pleading with his father not to have to do it, but Will hadn't listened. He got to the rugby club and looked at Sam, who by this point must have been terrified and hysterical, and instead of having any compassion or understanding for his son, instead of telling him that no, he didn't have to go on the pitch, he dragged Sam out of the car and forced him to do it. He marched him onto the pitch, and with all the other boys watching, he called him 'soft' and told him to 'toughen up'.

The outcome being that after five minutes on that pitch, five minutes into the session, Sam had a full-on panic attack and was taken to A & E.

By the time I got to the hospital Sam had calmed down. He was trembling, his body still tense and his face covered in red blotches. When he saw me he seemed to collapse a little, his body loosening as if he'd been holding it together until I arrived. I ran to him, wrapped my arms around him. I looked at the cheap jogging suit he was wearing, the trainers, the belt used for training tight around his stomach, two Velcro tags dangling from it, and felt burning hate for Will.

'What have you done?' I hissed at him, as I hugged Sam tightly. 'What have you done to him?'

Will was nursing a plastic cup of something, his face pale. He began to explain but I didn't want to hear it, I needed to see the doctor. It was all very well Will saying that Sam had been looked over and was fine, but I didn't believe a word he said. I needed to talk to a medical professional.

'I couldn't work the phone, Mum,' was all Sam said. 'I took pictures, but I couldn't call you. I couldn't find out where your number was.'

My heart pulled, ached at those words.

'I couldn't remember how to call you.'

I eventually spoke to the doctor who'd checked him over and was told the usual: nothing physically wrong, high anxiety, panic attack, see your GP, try counselling. He tried to give me a recommendation, a leaflet, a letter: I refused them all.

I'd heard it all before with Sam, been there, done that. The furthest I ever got was a session with a CBT counsellor who seemed intent on giving lengthy lectures in each session and asking Sam a series of questions that he was unable to answer. After three visits with this particular therapist we were given some printouts and that was it. A waste of time and, not that anyone had suggested it yet, but I was not putting my eight-year-old son on medication. The GP had referred us to another therapist, but we were still waiting for the appointment and I wasn't holding out any hope.

We dealt with his anxiety in our own way. We knew his triggers and it was something I was used to, but I'd not seen Sam in such a state in a while. Still, I was reassured there was nothing physically wrong with Sam. He wasn't injured, he wasn't ill. He'd had a panic attack.

Once I was reassured it was something I could handle, I went to deal with Will, out of earshot of Sam.

'*How could you?*' I hissed. We were in the waiting room, an audience of bored, ill people watching our drama. 'How could you do this to him?' I demanded, bordering on tears I was so angry. 'You're meant to be his father, you're meant to look after him.'

'I've never seen him like that ...' Will stuttered and Sam, who'd been over by the vending machine, came to me then, clutching at me, his large body curling into mine like he was a toddler again. I put my arms around him, held him tightly.

'I should never have let you go,' I told him. 'I'm sorry, I'm so sorry.' I kissed his hot forehead, held him tight, comforted him as best I could.

'He just went berserk,' Will was saying. 'It was only a game of rugby,' he said pathetically, 'it was only a game. And he wouldn't let go of that bloody phone you bought him; he's been taking pictures all weekend. He nearly bit me when I tried to take it out of his hand.'

I took a deep breath.

'You're not doing this again,' I told Will. 'I let you have him this weekend because I was being kind, because I thought we could come to some agreement, but nope. Not happening. You're not having Sam again.'

Will looked up suddenly and frowned. 'What?'

'You heard,' I said, and went to lead Sam away. 'Come on, sweetheart,' I told him, 'let's go home.'

'Wait.' Will grabbed my arm. The people in the waiting room hushed, watching us. 'It was a mistake,' Will said, 'a silly mistake. I didn't know he was going to react like that. You need to be very careful what you're saying. I've already called the social, and my solicitor . . .'

'Ashley Simmons by any chance?'

His face went pale.

'You're so predictable, you're pathetic,' I told him. 'They're playing you, Will. They couldn't give a toss about you. They're only helping you with this because they want to get back at me. They don't care about Sam, they only care about hurting me because of what I said to Janine.'

His face slackened momentarily.

'She's sending me texts – did you know that?' I told him. 'Weird packages, letters. She's deranged, I even felt a bit sorry for her but now . . .' I shook my head then leaned in close to him, so Sam couldn't hear.

'So fuck off,' I hissed. 'Go back to your demented new friends and do your worst.'

His face had flushed and a woman sitting at the desk picked up a phone. I assumed she was calling a security guard of some sort.

'We're leaving,' I said loudly to her. 'I'm taking my son home. To where he's safe.'

Will stared at me a moment. The people in the waiting room stared at him and he shifted his weight under their scrutiny. Puffed out his chest a little.

'That lad's got real problems,' Will said to the room at large. 'He made a fool of me out there on the pitch, did he tell you that? Did he tell you what really happened out there? Everyone thought he was having a heart attack. We dialled 999 but no, it's not an emergency. There's no need for everyone to run around, no need for the ambulance or anything, because it's just because he's panicking. Panicking over catching the ball and running about a bit? What kind of soft lad is he?'

I was on my way to the door but I went rigid. I looked at Sam, his face streaked with tears.

'It's OK,' I told him, and then I turned back to Will.

'He's my son,' I shouted, 'and the only problem he's got is a father like you.'

Sam whimpered at the side of me, and Will began to jog forward to him, talking to him as he came closer.

'Hey, buddy,' he said, putting on a show for the people watching, 'don't you listen to what your mother says. You'll be coming to live with me soon, promise. Then all of this can stop, we'll get you right. Don't you worry, I'll be coming for you soon.'

I felt Sam begin to tremble, pushing his head away from Will and into the crook of my arm.

'Over my dead body,' I hissed at Will, before walking away, holding Sam's hand tightly, whispering words of reassurance as best I could as we went through the door.

'See what a mess you've made of him?' Will shouted after

212

us. 'You've ruined him, Ruth. He needs his dad. It's going to take him living with me to sort this out.'

Sam was shuddering, as if Will's words had physically hit him. I heard a woman laugh loudly, I don't know if it was at us, or something else, but suddenly everything was overwhelming. We started to jog, then sprint through the car park towards my car. We got in without speaking and I drove us home in silence.

Those had been the last words Sam had heard from Will and, since then, he'd been a mess. Terrified. So frightened that he might have to go and live with Will and be expected to attend rugby and whatever else Will deemed would 'fix' Sam and his anxiety. I threw the sports clothes and trainers that Will had made Sam wear in the bin and dressed him in his pyjamas. I hugged him, held him close, let him eat whatever he liked and declared the rest of the weekend as 'duvet days'. Which in our house meant not getting out of our pyjamas, bringing down the duvets off our beds, snuggling under them on the sofa and watching movie after movie or playing game after game. Whatever Sam wanted to do.

As Sam was distracted, I checked over the pictures he'd taken on his mobile phone and it broke my heart. They were mostly blurry and out of focus – it was only a cheap thing – but I got the gist of it. Platefuls of food had been taken, then there were pictures of the car interior, and then lots of Will's home with the soft toy at the forefront. I'm ashamed to admit I found these fascinating. Having never been inside Will's house, only knowing the address, I devoured these photographs. Studying his choice of decor, wondering if he'd picked out that rug or if it was his new girlfriend? Did she pick out that sofa? That huge flat-screen TV?

'Hey,' I said to Sam as he was playing his game, 'this picture you took.' I showed him the phone: on the screen was a photograph of the hallway. The walls were decorated with pictures and, at the end, the soft toy in front of a pair of ankle boots.

'Whose are those?'

Sam glanced at the image. 'Don't know.'

I stared at the boots. 'Do they belong to your dad's new girlfriend?'

Sam shrugged. They were just a pair of boots, lined up against the wall, by what I was assuming was Will's bedroom, but they bothered me. There was something familiar about the tassels at the back, the small heel.

'Why did you take this picture, Sammy?' I asked. 'Was there something in that hall that you didn't like?'

He looked at the picture a moment. 'The smell,' he said. 'It was really smelly, just outside Dad's bedroom, like horrid perfume.'

'Perfume?'

He nodded. 'Only in Dad's bedroom, but it was all along the hallway when I first got there. It made me sneeze.'

'But she wasn't there?' I asked him. 'If you smelt her perfume, she must have been in the house?'

'She left before we got there,' he said. 'Dad said she didn't want to meet me.'

I checked the photo again and then switched off the phone, ruffled his head. What kind of man tells his son that his new girlfriend doesn't want to meet him? He was such a wanker.

'Don't worry,' I told him. She'll never be lucky enough to meet you, I thought, and you will never, ever have to smell her stinky perfume again.

TWENTY-ONE

The school run covers the times between seven-thirty and nine in the morning and between three and four-thirty in the afternoon. If you've ever been anywhere near a school at these times, you'll know how chaotic it is – how many kids there are running about and how many vehicles drive too fast and with too little care. It's estimated that every month, in the UK, over one thousand children are injured on the school run. Over a thousand. That's a lot of little bodies that are broken and bruised.

It's so dangerous, more dangerous than them eating sugar or putting on weight or being on the internet, and yet parents hear so little about it. Because who wants to accept that we're all potential killers? That as we drive our four-by-fours and park in stupid places so we can drop them off quicker, we're actually endangering the lives of our children?

It was a bugbear of John's and he had me typing out yet another letter alerting parents to the fact that the school run could be deadly. It would have no effect. I'd send out this letter, and a text to those parents who had supplied their mobile number to the school, and still cars would be parked on the double yellows, people would zoom off at speed and Rob, Janine's husband, would be one of them. Rob, witness to Sam's meltdown on the rugby pitch, what was he thinking when that happened? Did he remember our conversation that fateful night where I confided my concerns about Sam? Where I secretly confessed that I was unsure I was doing my best for him? Did he see Sam have a full-on panic attack and think of me at all, or was that too much to expect from someone like him? Will's new best friend? He must know what Janine was doing, the aggressive letters and texts she was sending to me. I'd called the police, told them about the letter and it had been logged. They said they could have a word, issue her with a police information notice, but that was all they could do until something happened where I could press charges. I'd heard nothing. I assumed they'd called around to her house, spoken to her, which meant Rob must be aware of it all, and I didn't know who was more deranged. Janine or Rob. Ashley or Will. People like them, they had no idea the damage they were causing.

I'd be doing the photocopying and be thinking about what it would feel like to go into Will's office and smash it up. Or I'd be inputting data and find myself imagining Rob and Janine in a terrible car crash, their white Land Rover twisted and smashed out of recognition. Or Ashley: I'd find myself daydreaming about her falling down stairs, breaking her neck, or severely ill, lying in a hospital bed, tubes and wires coming out of her. I surprised myself with how vicious my imagination could be. How hard I seemed to be becoming because of everything that was happening to me. I felt like a mother tiger, snarling at everything and everyone as she tried to protect her young.

When I discovered Will had been unfaithful, I had similar visions of him on a daily basis. Ones of him suffering, being made bankrupt and begging for my forgiveness, that kind of thing, but I never actually wanted him dead. Physically hurt yes, but not dead. However, since this whole episode with Rob and Janine, and how he'd got himself entwined in it all, how he'd taken advantage, I wanted him gone. I wanted them all gone out of our lives, and my imagination wouldn't stop presenting me with scenarios.

'Pie.' Becca placed the box in front of me. 'To cheer you up.'

I stopped typing and looked at the chicken and mushroom pie she'd brought.

'Because my guess is, with everything that's going on, with Will and his alliance with "the dream team" and Sam and his worrying, you've stopped looking after yourself, and you aren't eating.'

I looked up at her and smiled.

'That's why you're always in here at break and lunch, and I know you, Ruth, so –' she took my hands away from the keyboard '– stop. You're losing weight, I can tell. Have lunch, come to the staffroom—'

'I'm not going in the staffroom.'

'OK –' she held up her hands '– we'll eat in here, but stop working and take a rest.'

Becca had also brought me a chocolate eclair, a packet of salt and vinegar crisps and a pink bath bomb, 'to help you destress'.

I took out the pie and could've wept with how good it tasted and at her kindness.

'Lisa says Sam's a little better today,' Becca volunteered as we ate.

I nodded. 'I checked him just before the start of lunch. She's finally letting him eat in the classroom on his own, reading his comic, so –' I shrugged '– he's OK.'

A wry smile passed over Becca's face. 'How did you wangle that? Sam in there on his own. You know she's convinced her kids should all be in her routine, she's so anal.' She pulled a face. 'Typical NQT. But seriously, she's not easy on those kids, so are you two friends now? You been taking her out?'

I swallowed down my mouthful quickly less I choked on it. 'Hardly.' I looked up and smiled. 'I sort of, well, I kind of threatened her.'

'What?' Becca's response was priceless, and I let out a laugh. It felt so good to be finally speaking about it, because more than a week after me making those phone calls, nothing had really happened.

My great plan phoning HMRC and the local journalist hadn't played out as I expected. Lisa was being nice to Sam, so that was a win, but Janine's business didn't seem to be under threat and there were no scandalous headlines. There were rumours that she was under investigation, but I'd seen no evidence of the devastation I'd imagined, so I felt it was safe to share it with Becca.

I gave a small laugh. 'Not like that, I just told her, well, I told her that Janine was being investigated by HMRC. And that as she was tutoring for Janine, she could get mixed up in it.' I shrugged. 'I made out I was helping with the investigations, I might have implied that HMRC had contacted me to see if any teachers were involved . . .'

'Ruth!' Becca started to laugh. 'HMRC? Look at you.'

218

'I know,' I said, 'but I had to do something and, besides, it's almost true. She was doing it cash in hand, she could be investigated.'

'Yeah, funny that,' Becca said. 'I heard the rumours that Janine is being investigated. Good timing for you, isn't it?'

I looked up at Becca who was happily picking at her quiche. 'That's karma in action if ever I saw it,' she said and smiled.

'She deserves it,' I said after a moment. 'We all have to pay tax, so why shouldn't she?'

'I'm not saying she doesn't deserve it,' agreed Becca, 'just that it's happened at the right time.'

I kept my eyes down. It's not that I didn't want to admit it to Becca, it's just that something told me not to. And I didn't have it in me to explain it all to her, to say how I was responsible and go through the shocked and surprised chat. I'd only made a couple of phone calls after all and I had so much more I needed to talk with her about.

Since the episode at A & E I had received a barrage of threatening texts from Will. All detailing what an unfit mother I was and what action he was going to take. They had started since I refused to let him see Sam and were getting worse. The latest one had stated that I had 'no ability to understand the needs of Sam'. That I had a history and was 'emotionally abusing him'. They were so hurtful, I deleted most of them without reading them.

I'd also seen the red Fiat outside our house on two other occasions and, since I assumed the police had visited Janine and had a word, I was now wondering if it was something to do with Will. Perhaps someone he knew, someone he'd got to keep an eye on us. Make sure I wasn't doing a runner with Sam, which amused me because it meant he must've bought it when I said I was taking Sam to Disney. He obviously thought us capable of getting on a plane and jetting off somewhere and that was a small comfort.

'Any more orders for the cake business?' Becca asked after a moment, and I shook my head. 'They'll come back,' she said, 'once they realise it was all lies.'

I shrugged. I'd not had one order since Sue had cancelled hers, and the sales at the farmers' market on Sunday had been pitiful. Whether it was because of Janine's rumours, or because I was late arriving, I couldn't be sure, but one thing was certain, I wasn't going to be rich off it any time soon.

'And Will? He's ...'

'Being a complete dick as usual,' I told her.

'And any more texts or ...?'

'Yes, loads of mean texts from Will, which I've stopped reading. And my car wouldn't start the other day. For a horrible moment I thought someone had done something to it, but it turned out it was just the frost. And I'm opening the post wearing rubber gloves, sleeping with the kitchen knife under my pillow as the police have been useless, but apart from that, everything's fine.'

She smiled weakly and I threw the empty box into the bin. 'Thanks for lunch, that was really thoughtful.'

'No worries, any time.' She took a moment. 'Want me to come around later, bring a bottle? You look like you could do with a break.'

I smiled, I could think of nothing better than an evening with Becca. Sipping wine and letting her entertain me with stories of her new boyfriend, the spin class instructor from her gym. It would be like going back in time, to a place where ex-husbands and crazed parents didn't exist. Becca's worries were still of what to wear on a night out, what was on in the sales and if some storyline in a soap opera she was watching had been resolved. My life was fast becoming the soap opera and it was depressing in the worst way possible.

'I'm not good company at the moment, with all this going on,' I told her, 'and besides, I want to keep it simple for Sam. Want to keep him near me.'

'Of course,' she said, nodding. 'How is he at home?'

I made a face; he'd started with the night terrors again since his horrendous weekend with Will. Screaming in the night, me having to gently wake him up and then him panicking over something he'd dreamed about but couldn't quite grasp. I didn't want to admit it, to her, just how bad he was. He was OK at school though, and that was something. Since I'd had the word with Lisa and everyone thought Toby was a thief, that at least was OK.

'I'm worried about you,' Becca said, opening the crisps and handing them to me. 'You should get your mother to babysit,' she offered. I laughed at the suggestion.

'Or get Sam to go stay with her? He'd be OK there, wouldn't he? At her house?'

I thought for a moment. Sam might be OK with that, but how would my mother cope if he had a night terror? If he woke them both screaming?

'Well surely she can come to yours for a few hours?'

I looked at her.

'Two hours!' she pressed. 'Not even late. You could go out from eight till ten, or even earlier, six till eight. Be back to put Sam to bed. But you need to get out,' Becca insisted, 'do something. I see the road you're headed on and it's not good.'

'I'm not depressed if that's what you're worried about,' I told her. 'I'm OK for the time being.'

She put her hand on my shoulder. 'Ruth, you're isolating yourself again. Just like when Will left, you're pushing everyone away, hiding. You didn't even get out to do that car boot you meant to at the weekend, did you?'

'That was impossible, Sam had been to A & E, you know what Will did to him . . .'

'I know, I know,' Becca said, 'but baking two hundred cupcakes and then throwing them in the bin because your freezer is already full is not good. Not good for you. You need to blow off some steam.'

'Whose blowing what?'

I felt myself flush. I'd not seen Glen since the fly fishing on Friday – it seemed like a lifetime ago. I'd meant to go and thank him, to tell him what an impact he'd had, how brilliant it'd been, but the events of the weekend had taken everything from me. In the two days that I'd been back at school, I'd hidden in my office. Frightened to venture out.

'You've been avoiding me,' he said, walking into the office, and I went hotter. I looked at Becca who gave a wide smile when she saw the colour of my face, and I shot her a look, begging her not to make anything out of it.

'I've been looking for you in the staffroom, to see what Sam thought of last Friday.' He turned to Becca. 'Did she tell you I took her and Sam out?'

Becca put on a shocked face. 'She did not! How did you manage that?'

He laughed. 'It wasn't that exciting. Just to see someone fish.'

'Fish?'

'It was lovely of you,' I told him. 'I meant to tell you, to find you and thank you. Sam thought it was wonderful, just brilliant. It was perfect.'

The room was quiet and I suddenly thought I'd said too much, been too gushing, but then he smiled, a wide smile and my stomach flipped.

'I was frightened I'd done the wrong thing – upset you,' he said. 'I've been waiting for an excuse to come find you.'

'And what's your excuse?' There was a playful tone to Becca's voice. She jumped down from the table she'd been perched on and folded her arms, a smile on her face. 'What are you up this end of the school for?'

'This,' he said and presented a file. 'The rest of the data forms – well, the ones we've had in so far.' I took the file off him.

'You could've sent a child up with that,' Becca argued. 'You didn't need to waste your lunch hour coming up here.'

'Who says I'm wasting anything?'

'Aha!' Becca said, suddenly delighted. 'You, sir, are the answer to my problems.'

'What problems?'

Becca turned and looked at me. I felt a familiar lurch of panic jump in my chest – I'd seen that look on her face before.

'Becca, no, listen, really, stop . . . '

'Ruth needs to get out,' she said to Glen, silencing all my protests. 'She's in desperate need to get out as she's having such a tough time at the moment, and you just volunteered to do it. And before you think of a reason why not,' Becca said to me, 'I'll come to yours and sit with Sam. I'll watch whatever he likes, play whatever game he wants. He knows me and he won't have to leave the house so you've no excuse.'

'Sam's not really—'

'I won't hear a word against it,' Becca said, standing up and turning to Glen. 'Ruth is my best friend in the whole world.

She's having a shit time of it and you seem like the perfect person to help her out. Can I count on you?'

He looked at me, smiled, and I felt something inside soften. He turned to Becca. 'You can count on me,' he said. 'I'll take her out tomorrow.' He turned and looked straight at me, a flutter building in my chest with the speed of it all.

'Looks like we've got a date,' he said, and Becca clapped her hands in delight.

TWENTY-TWO

'Got any kids?' I asked him.

We were driving out of Carlisle, after Glen had picked me up at six-thirty from home. I'd had to drink two glasses of wine just so I felt normal. I was wearing a black knitted dress, heels, and Becca had styled my hair, and I felt ridiculous. Before she arrived I was in jeans and a blouse, trying to get out of going, but she'd insisted. She'd poured me a large glass, marched me upstairs and given me a mini-makeover.

I felt like I was pretending to be someone else, dressed up like a dog's dinner while Glen was wearing jeans and a shirt. My hair, sprayed into a solid mass, prevented me from putting my head back, and I felt a bit like a nodding dog, all spruced up and full of nothing. Sitting in his campervan, listening to the gentle folk music on his radio, my heart jittering and skipping about in my chest.

I'd given Becca Glen's number, made her promise to text me every half hour, made her lock all the doors behind me, even the dead lock, even though she said I was being stupid. But it was the only way I could go, and now I couldn't stop checking my phone and was having a hard time feeling anything close to OK.

'Nope,' he said, as he navigated the roads leading towards Keswick, 'no kids and never been married. You're divorced I take it?'

I nodded. I didn't ask any more about it, not trusting myself to say anything else in case I turned into one of those crazy divorced women who quiz every single bloke they meet on their past affairs. We drove along the quiet streets and he asked me how long I'd been in Carlisle, which developed into a conversation about the places we'd visit if money and time were no object. I found myself laughing as he justified his choice of destinations. As he pulled up to a pub just on the outskirts of civilisation, I realised that even though the Will and Sam situation was never far from my mind, I had briefly let it slip into second place.

'You been here before?'

I looked up at the stonework and creeping ivy. 'I never knew this existed.'

He laughed. 'Good. And you call yourself a local?'

The pub was small, dimly lit, and had a comforting smell of hops and homecooked food. There was a roaring fire, and we got ourselves a table in the back room, shared with an older couple and their terrier, who was asleep at their feet.

'Can I ask you something straight out?' Glen asked, a smile playing on his lips. 'Before we get started? And I know it's none of my business, but ... Rob?'

'What about Rob?' I asked, my heart beginning to pound.

'Are you and him,' he dipped his head, 'y'know ...'

I nearly threw my drink over him and he laughed, held up his hands.

'I had to ask!' he said, 'I just wanted to know.'

'Why?' I asked, 'why bring him up now?'

'To make sure I had a shot.'

'A shot?'

'A shot at you,' he said, smiling straight at me, and a swoop of adrenalin went through my chest. I looked down, not able to match his gaze any longer, my cheeks going hot.

'Oh,' I said, 'well, in that case,' I looked up, 'I can confirm you have a shot. With me.'

'Glad to hear it,' he grinned, 'so, you're not interested in…'

'If you say Rob again…' I threatened and he laughed, 'absolutely not.' I went on, 'I can't stand the man. I'm appalled at what I did with him. I'm really ashamed about the whole thing.'

'Why on earth are you ashamed?' he asked, and to my horror, I felt tears prick at my eyes. I was overtired, out of my mind with worry over Will and Sam, and here I was about to explain myself to a stranger.

'You did nothing wrong,' he said and put his hand on mine. 'you have absolutely nothing to be ashamed about at all.'

I stared at our hands, his over mine, his warm fingers curled around my palm and felt a buzz. As if an electric current were transferring from his hand to mine.

'I like you,' I said quietly, 'but I should warn you, I'm a mess. My life's a mess. I'm about to enter a custody battle with my ex-husband over my son. I'm broke and that woman who threw her phone at me, Janine? Her best friend is the solicitor helping my ex-husband in said custody battle, and I think Janine has been sending me threatening notes and texts, and little packages containing my cupcakes stuffed with shit. It's either her, or someone else she knows. I've told the police about it but be warned, I come with baggage and then some.'

He wasn't smiling.

After a while, he said, 'You think Janine's been sending you threatening texts?'

I shrugged. 'I think it was her, and she's not sent anything since last week.' I took a sip of my drink. 'Nothing terrible, just silly things, but enough to make me uneasy.'

'I'm glad you came out with me,' he said, and I smiled weakly. 'I'm really glad to give you a night off from it all.'

I ran my hand through my hair. 'Me too,' I said, 'anyway, enough of all that. I want to know more about you, about why you're not looking to become permanent at the school. Tell me why your CV is full of supply work and what you do on the cruise ships.'

He smiled. 'I only do supply,' he said, 'so I can concentrate on my music, and that's what I do on the cruise ships.'

I looked at him, 'Your music?' I asked, 'you have a band?'

He nodded. 'But not like you think. I don't play in pubs or at weddings, I play on the ship.'

'Oh,' I smiled, 'I see.'

'It allows me to go all over the world and be paid for doing so,' he grinned, 'and I was only going to stay at this school until the end of term, but because of you, I've just found myself rearranging things so I can be here longer.'

I smiled at his words, there was a giddiness in my chest that hadn't been there before.

'But you're from Carlisle?' I asked. 'That's why you're here? To see family and make a bit of money until you go back on the ship?'

He shook his head, finished off his pint. 'I'm in Carlisle for different reasons and –' he raised his finger to stop me from asking anything further '– I'm about to ask you if you want another drink?'

By the time we got back to my house I was happily merry and full. Sam was asleep on the couch, his head resting on Becca's knee as she watched *News at Ten*, and there was a giddy feeling in my chest.

'You like him then?' Becca whispered, as I took off my shoes.

'I like him,' I confirmed, and I did. He'd made me laugh, properly laugh with his tales from tourists on the cruise where he worked. He'd been unjudgemental about my situation, and had explained to me in great detail why I shouldn't give a toss about what anyone else thought and that I should stop getting so het up about it all. He'd made me see my life through his eyes and I'd realised it wasn't too bad.

I went over and stroked Sam's head as Becca got her things together.

'Glen told me about this solicitor he knows who might be able to help.'

'Great!' Becca beamed. 'I knew it was a good idea getting you two together.'

I nodded. 'He told me Will can't take Sam away from me. I told him about his threats, about how he'd stop me seeing him altogether, and it's all nonsense.' I looked down at Sam, his beautiful sleeping face. 'I'm his mother and any court will see how much I love him.'

'Exactly,' said Becca, 'it's what I've been telling you all along. You're his mum. You're the one who was there when Will buggered off. At worst, you'll have to go back to how it was before, Will having alternate weekends.'

I nodded.

'But you can put new rules in place, like what Will can and can't do. The fact that Sam ended up in A & E the last time Will had him will speak volumes.'

I looked up at her and smiled. 'Thanks, Becca.' I went to hug her. 'Thanks for making me go. It was just what I needed.'

'My pleasure,' she beamed, 'any time. Make another date with him soon, before he thinks you've lost interest.'

I laughed and then put my hand over my mouth to stop the noise, checking Sam was still asleep. 'I might,' I told her.

'Do it,' she said, putting on her coat. 'He's the first nice man you've met in an age, he's good looking, got a good job . . .'

'He's not really a teacher,' I told her, 'he's a musician.'

She rolled her eyes and we laughed and said our goodbyes, a lightness to my mood that I'd not had in days. Not since I'd got back at Janine. I locked the door, went into the kitchen and got myself a glass of water. Looking out onto the back yard I noticed that the small table and chairs I had out there had been moved. Rearranged, as if they'd all been pushed to the side for something. I frowned, wondering why Becca had been moving my scrappy garden furniture about, maybe playing a game with Sam out there.

'Mum?'

I walked back into the lounge where Sam was sitting, his face puffy from sleep.

'Hey.' I went over to him, stroked his head.

'Becca said I could wait up.'

I nodded. 'Bed now though. Did you have a good time?'

He nodded. 'We had four chocolate bars.'

'Did you?' I silently cursed Becca in my mind but it was short lived; she'd done me a favour, looked after Sam while I had an evening off. If she needed to placate Sam by feeding him chocolate, then so be it.

'C'mon,' I told him. 'Bed. It's so late. You go up and brush your teeth and I'll ... ' I stopped at the look on his face. 'OK, wait there,' I said, switching off the light in the kitchen. 'We'll go up together.'

I grabbed the post that I'd not yet had a chance to open and we climbed the stairs together. This was part of Sam's anxiety – he was afraid of being upstairs alone in the house. I wasn't quite sure why, but I'd learned over the years not to question Sam's rules of what was frightening to him. It was best to go along with it; his fears usually passed, or migrated into something else, and it was preferable to the screams and tantrums I would be faced with if I did insist he do things differently.

'Get your toothbrush,' I told him, 'I'm right here.' I perched on the edge of the laundry basket and went through the letters as he brushed. I ignored most of them, bills, flyers, nonsense, and then one that looked official. Hand written to Ms Ruth Clarkson. I opened it and my heart started to gallop. It was from Hallege Solicitors & Co. A letter acting on behalf of Will, who it confirmed was now Ashley Simmons' client.

The letter stated that their client, Will, believed his son was at risk. Contact had been restricted illegally, and as a result of that and the concern over Sam's welfare, the letter proposed that it would be in Sam's best interest if he lived with his father. Will was filing for full custody.

I could hardly breathe. He'd done it. Ashley had done it for him.

The letter ended with them stating that there was no need for mediation, on the grounds that Will thought Sam was at risk. He stated that I was mentally abusing Sam, due to my own mental health history and current evidence of Sam's issues, and that I was denying Sam the help that he needed. Attached was a letter from a doctor, I guessed it was the one from A & E, advising that Sam see a therapist for his panic and anxiety attacks and that I had denied any help. I had to lean forward to breathe. I was having trouble getting in any air.

'Mummy?' Sam's voice was small. 'Is everything OK?'

The letter ended by stating that I should expect my court order shortly.

TWENTY-THREE

The next morning, we were up early. I'd hardly slept. I'd spent most of the night Googling custody cases on my phone. Where we lived there was hardly any connection, it was painfully slow, and the screen kept crashing and failing to connect. In five hours of trying to get online and then losing my connection I found there was a slight chance it could happen. What Ashley and Will were threatening could actually happen. Usually, before applying for a court order, you had to attend mediation, but this could be avoided in certain cases. Such as abuse. Which is what Ashley was trying to claim I was doing to Sam. It made me so angry I was virtually spitting with rage.

They'd applied for a court order, which meant I would have to go to a court hearing, and would have to justify myself. Argue my case in front of Will and Ashley, as to why I was the best person for Sam to be with, and then tell them why Will was such a prick. And it would have to be me, because I also found out that I couldn't afford a solicitor of my own.

I'd done what research I could, tried to see what legal aid I qualified for, but as I was down as 'joint owner' on my mother's dilapidated cottage, from what I could gather it meant I had 'disposable capital' and therefore didn't qualify. And when I looked at the cost of hiring a solicitor I reeled. I just didn't have the money. Which meant I was left with no other option than to represent myself. And the thought of me going into court to try and argue my case against Ashley made me feel physically sick.

'You bastard!'

I'd managed to wait until seven. I told myself I wouldn't call him, but by that time the need to share my rage was overwhelming. 'It's not possible, you know; they won't award you full custody. It doesn't work like that.'

'It does if you've got a fantastic solicitor,' Will snapped back, 'someone so convinced of your manic behaviour that she's working for virtually nothing. That's what they think of you, Ruth. And it's so nice to have people agree with me, to know I'm not the only one who thinks you're completely demented and shouldn't be in charge of a child.'

My breathing became shallow.

'Bitch,' I was struggling not to shout, 'how did you get her to do it?' I paused. 'Are you shagging her? Is that it?'

There was a moment's silence. I was gripping the phone so hard, I thought I might crush it.

'God, you're pathetic,' he said with a sigh. 'I can't wait to get Sam away from you. You're toxic.'

'I hate you so much,' I hissed. Sam was in the next room, getting himself ready to leave. 'I wish you would fuck off and die.'

There was more silence and then a soft laugh. 'Thanks, Ruth,' he said. 'Ashley did say that you'd get in touch, so I've been recording this conversation, and that threat you've just made? That's perfect. Don't call me again or I'll have you done for harassment. But you know all about that, don't you? I gather Janine and Rob had a good laugh with the police about you when they visited. They said you were accusing more people than they could shake a stick at. Which doesn't surprise me. As soon as Sam is out of your dramatic, pathetic life, the better.'

He ended the call before I got a chance to say anything else and I screamed. Threw my phone on the couch in frustration.

'Mummy?'

I took a deep breath. I'd just been recorded screaming and hissing death threats down the phone to Will. Nice one, Ruth, that will certainly make you appear like a calm, sane mother. The court will be sure to award you full custody based on that recorded message.

I put my hands over my face momentarily as I realised that Will also knew about the texts and packages I'd been receiving. He could now argue in his custody case that Sam was in a dangerous environment. And what had he said about the police? They had *laughed* about me when they visited Janine? Said I was accusing everyone I could think of? So much for them warning her off.

'Get your coat on, Sammy.' I leaned against the wall for support. 'We're leaving in a minute.'

My heart was hammering. The temptation to call Will back was strong, the urge to drive round to his fancy house with his new girlfriend and smash something hard into them both was powerful. How dare he, was all I could think, how dare he.

'Mum.' Sam was at the side of me now, by the window.

'Got your book bag?' I took a big lungful of air. 'Lunch

box?' I closed my eyes and counted. One, two, three, breathe in, one, two, three, breathe out. I had to calm down. Needed to calm down.

'But Mummy . . .'

'It's OK,' I told him and tried a smile, 'it's all OK. Everything is going to be fine. You all ready, sweetheart? C'mon, let's go.'

He shook his head and pointed to the window, his face pale, his eyes round. I followed his gaze. For a moment I was confused. My car was parked right in front of our house, but that wasn't my car, was it? And then, as the image registered, I realised it was, in fact, my car. I gave a shocked gasp and hurried outside towards it.

'Mummy, wait . . .'

In black spray paint, along the side of my car, someone had written the words, 'I hope it was worth it'. And all four tyres were flat. Slashed. Dramatically slashed, hacked at. Someone had really gone at them, as if wanting me to see how much they'd tried to rip my tyres open.

Sam was now at the side of me and I could hear him panting. 'You go inside, Sam.'

He was staring at the car and I mentally cursed myself for letting him see it.

'What does it mean, Mummy?' he asked. 'Was *what* worth it? What is it talking about?'

I looked along the desolate street. An older couple were in the house to the right of us, tourists who'd arrived a couple of days earlier, but the other side was empty until the next holiday makers came. It would slowly begin to get busier as half term approached, but this particular week was quiet.

'Get inside,' I told Sam. 'Quick. C'mon now, you get inside.'

'But Mum, who did that, and what does it *mean*?'

'Inside,' I told him, and he stared back at me, his eyes intense, a look of complete horror on his face.

'It was Toby, wasn't it?' he whispered.

'What? Sam, let's go inside, I'll call ...'

'He came here in the night and did this because I put Miss Gleason's pen in his drawer.' He turned back to the car. 'He said that he knew it was me. He said he'd get me. That's what it means –' he pointed to the graffiti '– that's what it's talking about. It means was Miss Gleason's pen worth it.'

My face must have looked shocked, surprised at how he'd come to this conclusion, and because I didn't immediately reassure and deny his suggestion, he started screaming. A loud terrified wail.

'It's not Toby,' I told him, but it was useless, he was gone. Lost in his own anxiety and panic. I grabbed his shoulders, bent down so my face was level with his. 'Sammy, listen to me, it's not Toby. This was someone who hates *me*, not you. It's my fault this happened, d'you hear me? It's all my fault.'

My hands were sweaty as I took him back inside. I tried to make soothing comments, to reassure him, but I was struggling. Once Sam got himself worked up he was hard to get through to. I got him inside and closed the door, locked it. My mind was scattering over things that I had to do, new problems that now needed to be addressed.

'He's going to kill me!' Sam was hysterical, the words getting caught in his throat. 'He said he had a knife and now he'll stab me. He'll slash me.'

I held him tight, rocked him until his sobbing eventually subsided.

'Look at me,' I told him when he was calmer, now regretting everything to do with that stupid pen. 'This was not Toby. No one is going to kill you, no one is going to stab you. This was a silly woman I think, someone that I know, and it was just a joke. A stupid prank that's gone wrong. I'm going to talk to her today and make sure she doesn't do it again.'

'Who is it?' His face was puffy, two bright red dots on his cheeks, the rest of his complexion white. I shook my head.

'No one for you to worry about. Just a silly, stupid woman who thinks by doing this she's being funny.' I tried a smile. 'Now, how about we take a day off?'

He was silent for a moment, then did something I'd not seen him do in years, not since he was a toddler and then again when Will first left us. He closed his eyes and started sucking his thumb.

'Sam,' I said, 'please don't do that.' I went to pull his thumb out of his mouth, but he jerked his hand away – he could be quite strong when he wanted to. 'You're a bit old for that now,' I told him. 'Only babies suck their thumb.'

He stared at me, his eyes defiant, tears still wet on his eyelashes.

'OK,' I said, and took him back into my embrace and stroked his hair. 'OK.'

Two hours later and my mother had arrived. I'd put a bed sheet over the car to hide the spray paint and Sam was playing on his Xbox and eating a family pack of crisps. He was still intermittently sucking his thumb, but I decided to let it go. He would stop, he just needed the comfort now and I couldn't blame him.

We were in the kitchen, my mother making tea and me pacing. I couldn't settle, couldn't stop my heart from hammering. I'd told John that Sam had the beginnings of a stomach bug, and as it had come on rapidly I'd no time to organise child care. He was sympathetic, but I got the clear undertone that I had twenty-four hours. I needed to be back in work the next day.

'You should be calling the police,' my mother said, 'not the garage. Have they got the wrong person?' She put the cups down on the table. 'What does it mean, "worth it"? Was what worth it? What've you been doing?'

I shook my head, and then, after a moment, passed the letter to her from Ashley Simmons. I watched her face blanch as she read it.

My mother looked at me. She put the letter down and took off her glasses, an appalled look on her face.

'I know who it is,' I told her, 'it's one of the mothers from school. She thinks I'm having an affair with her husband.'

She raised her eyebrows.

'I'm not!' I told her. 'Of course I'm not. It's all a misunderstanding that's got out of hand.'

She pulled out a chair, sitting heavily, shaking her head, rubbing her hand over her mouth as she had done when my father first got ill.

'Stop it!' I hissed. 'I'm not having an affair. This woman's just trying to prove something. She's a daft cow who thinks she can do anything, but I'll call the police. This is criminal damage. I can press charges.'

'An affair? Who with?'

'There is no affair!' I took a deep breath. 'It's all nonsense. I said something and she got the wrong idea and it's her friend who's sent that letter. She's working for Will and it's all just . . . '

'So you think it's a woman,' my mother began, 'some woman from school who you think did that to your car and she's

239

friends with –' she looked at the letter '– Ashley Simmons, who is now Will's solicitor?'

I nodded, and my mother put her hand over her mouth again, rubbing it back and forth. 'Oh Ruth.'

'It's a misunderstanding,' I said. 'It's all a misunderstanding.'

'Oh Ruth,' my mother said, 'what are you—'

'I'm putting a stop to it,' I interrupted her, and picked up the solicitor's letter. 'You don't need to worry. I'm putting a stop to all of it. It ends today.'

TWENTY-FOUR

Later that morning, I was feeling faint. I spent an age firstly explaining it all to my mother, and then on the phone with the police, again, filing an incident report. I told them everything, accused Janine, and they asked for witnesses. Evidence. When I said I had none and answered that I wasn't in any immediate danger, they advised it would be investigated. I was told to wait, given the number of Victim Support and was told to speak to the officers when they came to the house to view the damage, but it wasn't good enough. I was furious and couldn't sit still. Which led me to be somewhere I hadn't been in years: Carlisle city centre on a weekday.

People surrounded me, pushing past, arms filled with carrier bags. Mothers with prams, groups of students boisterously laughing and shouting, huge rucksacks on their backs, swallowing up space as they came towards me. Swarms of people moved in every direction. Too close and too loud. The sky was wide open, a flat expanse above me, and as I squirmed through the packed city below its vastness reminded me why the centre was horrendous.

The invasion of space was why I never ventured in – the sensory overload, the sheer volume of people. This was why I avoided crowded areas, and all the while, at the back of my mind, was a voice whispering about the very real fear of terrorist attacks. Replaying images of vans being driven through crowds just like this, of bombs hidden in the bins of pedestrian zones, of men with guns rapidly firing through the throng. I walked and checked my exits, my route to safety should I need it.

There was a strong smell of coffee and a biting wind that seemed to cut right though the pedestrian zone as if it were in a wind tunnel. Hallege Solicitors & Co. was just out of the centre, on a street alongside dentists and a vet. I'd had to catch a bus into the city, and as I walked from the bus station to her office I mentally prepared my speech. My palms sweated and I tried to keep calm.

I had a plan and it involved appealing to Ashley.

Will had said that she was convinced of my inability to look after my son. He said she thought the same as him, virtually working for free because of her beliefs, and I planned to prove her wrong.

I'd show her what Janine had done to my car. I'd a picture of it on my phone and was banking on the fact that she didn't know it had been done. Then I planned to tell her how Sam had found my car first, I'd tell her of his distress and, as one mother to another, hope that she would sympathise.

And then I'd tell her about Will, about what he was really like. His affair, the way he abandoned us, the way he forced Sam onto the rugby pitch at the weekend resulting in a panic attack at A & E. And finally, I'd explain what really happened with Rob. How he'd lied to me, got me drunk and initiated the whole thing. As Janine's friend, she must know what he was like. That he was sending Janine insane, making her do irrational and mad things. Sending me cupcakes and threatening letters. They weren't the actions of someone of sound mind.

As I made my way through the city streets, staring down at my feet on the cobblestones so I wouldn't have to acknowledge where I was, I almost convinced myself that she might actually want to represent me after we'd talked. She'd see I was a reasonable person, she'd see that Janine was deranged and she'd understand exactly what type of father Will was. But when I eventually got to her office, sweating and slightly panicked, I was told that Ashley wasn't in. She only worked three days a week, and Thursday wasn't one of them.

'But she sent me this letter,' I said, and held up the envelope for the receptionist to see, 'she sent me this very personal, very distressing letter. It's postmarked yesterday, so she knew I'd be receiving it today. And she advised my ex-husband of what to do today, when I called him, so she was pretty confident that I'd react to this letter.'

The receptionist smiled, gave a sympathetic shrug. 'Shall I see if anyone else can help? Although if it is one of Mrs Simmons' cases, you would have to speak with her, but let me just see if anyone is aware of it, Mrs . . . ?'

'Clarkson,' I said, 'Ruth Clarkson. It's about the custody of my son.'

She nodded and pointed to the row of chairs in front of her desk, a small waiting area, not dissimilar to a dentists.

A water cooler by the side of a small coffee table, certificates and posters decorating the wall. Leaflets advertising the services they offered. I felt tears prick my eyes. I walked over to the far wall, pretending to look at the framed photographs as I waited.

She wasn't in.

She'd arranged for me to receive that letter on a day when she knew she wouldn't be in the office. When she knew I wouldn't be able to contact her. I wiped my eyes. I wasn't sure if the tears were due to the anxiety I'd had to endure on my journey here, what felt like such a personal attack from Ashley – she must have guided Will on what to say and do – or the sheer rage I felt.

I stared blindly at the photographs of the staff. She looked to be a senior member, why would she be taking on such a case? Why help Will? What did it have to do with her? Why would she get so involved?

Below was a group of photographs of a fundraising event. 'Over five hundred raised!' The staff were in fancy dress, at some kind of day out. I stared at their faces, smiles and expressions of delight as they did what looked like an old-fashioned sports day. A sack race, running with eggs and spoons, tied together in a three-legged race, and wondered how people had fun like this. How such wild abandonment could be an undertaking in anyone's life when mine was filled with the complete opposite, and there she was. One of three people dressed up in hunting regalia. The old-fashioned type, bright red jackets, white breeches and what looked like a pantomime horse of sorts on the bottom half of the costume to make them appear as if they were riding. Other members of the team were cheering at the side of her; perhaps they were meant to be jockeys and not huntsmen? Perhaps this was the final race of the staff sports day?

Her face was pure delight under her helmet, a broad smile as she undertook whatever ridiculous task was being performed. I reached for my phone.

I managed to take six pictures before the receptionist came back.

'No, afraid no one can help with this one,' she said as she came back in. 'It's a particular case of Mrs Simmons. Shall I tell her you called in? Do you want to make an appointment for next week?'

I turned back to her. 'That fundraising event?' I asked. 'Looks like fun.'

Her face broke into a wide smile. 'Oh, we do it every year. It's amazing, the company donates the money and we get to run about like loons! It's great fun, great team building.'

I nodded. Great team building. Ashley was part of a team, a professional team. A team that victimised single mothers and took their sons from them. Did the rest of the company know what she was doing?

'Next Wednesday any good?' the receptionist was clicking at something on a computer screen. 'She's got a free slot in the afternoon.'

I shook my head.

'No.' I went to the door. 'I've realised it was a mistake. Mrs Simmons can't help me, she's acting on behalf of my husband. For free I think. Maybe you should tell the rest of your "team". Tell them that Mrs Simmons would rather work for free, for a complete *wanker*, than hear about the truth.' The receptionist turned quickly as I said that word. She shouted a name. 'She's victimising me,' I went on, 'discriminating against me.' I opened the door before whoever she'd called came over. 'Tell that to your team, that you're all working with a bigot.'

I went out into the street, the wind cold against my face. My tears had left my cheeks damp and the icy air bit into them. Walking towards the bus station I checked the pictures I'd taken. Two were useless but the other four were good. I found the clearest one and cropped it. Took out the pantomime horse, the cheering crowd to the side of her, so that all that was visible was Ashley's face underneath the riding cap and the red lapels of her riding jacket.

'Hello.' John was surprised to see me. 'Did you manage to get someone?'

I nodded. 'Only for this morning though I'm afraid,' I told him. 'I just came in to check emails, get a few notes on the residential, see what I can sort from home.'

He nodded. Working from home as a school secretary was laughable, but John bought it. Proved how little he knew about what I actually did, and how much I did. No one really knew the extent of my job, and as I waited for the computer to boot up, it hit home.

The registers had been left, piles of letters, notes and envelopes from the parents were stacked on my desk. Post-it Notes with tasks by other members of staff had been pinned to my computer, pinned to the telephone. As if I were personal secretary to each and every one of them. They had no idea just how much I did, how much they all depended on me. Normally I would've undertaken those jobs without thinking, but now I noticed there was no 'please' on any of them, no 'thank you'. I peeled one off that had been stuck to my computer screen.

Twenty copies of student packing list letter.

It was from Julie, the teaching assistant. I only knew because I recognised her handwriting. They didn't even bother to sign their name. I screwed it up into a tight little ball and threw it into the bin.

My office was quiet; it was late morning. I had half an hour before the lunch bell. Half an hour and I had to be out of there.

I wondered if I was really going to do it.

The idea came to me when I was waiting in her office. I suddenly realised that if Ashley was helping Will, someone she didn't know, in order to hurt me, then of course she'd be the kind of woman that would think it was acceptable to do that to my car. She would know all about Janine, what she did to Eve, what Janine's daughter had done to Zara, Eve's daughter.

Ashley would know all about Rob – she must – and despite knowing all of that, she wouldn't talk to me. She'd purposely chosen for me to get that letter on a day that she'd be out of her office. She knew exactly what she was doing. This persecution was no accident.

I brought up the files and went into the database. Ashley had a boy at the school, Max, and with very little effort I brought up everything I needed. The rest of it was easier than I thought. I had no idea it was so simple, but a quick search told me it was effortless to hide what computer you were on, you just needed to hide something called an IP address and within thirty seconds I was downloading the software needed. Another quick search and I had a whole list of animal activist groups. It took me a while to find the aggressive type of group I was looking for, one that wasn't too organised, that was more for thugs than anything else, but after a while I found one. Lots of rants, lots of aggression. Perfect. A very vocal and proactive forum.

I created a new Gmail account and signed up within a matter of minutes. I was now anonymous and untraceable.

I had no idea if it would work, no idea if it would cause any trouble.

Upload a picture? Yes. Add a message? Yes.

Hunts are for Cunts

I uploaded my picture.

And this one lives here:

And then I typed in her home address.

TWENTY-FIVE

3 AUGUST

I met with them yesterday. The officer said it would be therapeutic, but it wasn't. It was far from any kind of therapy. I honestly now don't know why I agreed to it. I think I hoped it might make me feel better, but it's made me feel so much worse. To see them. Crying. Holding on to one another, their child gone. Dead and looking at me with such pleading.

'We forgive you,' the mother said. 'We came here to tell you that we forgive you.'

How I wanted to scream at them that they were forgiving the wrong person! That they should be talking to you and not me, but instead I found myself crying with them. I seemed to soak up their emotions as if I'd lost a child myself, as if I could relate to their loss.

And, afterwards, back in my cell, it occurred to me that I have grief. I have loss that can be identified with theirs. I was a child once, an innocent. I ran about and laughed and screamed with joy, and that is gone from me now. All those memories, everything, tainted because of what you did. How can I even think of myself in those terms after what has happened? I used to think fondly of my childhood, look back and smile, but since being in here I've found myself searching through my memories for clues.

Secrets and foreshadowing of what was to come. I want to know what I did wrong, how I became involved in all this, because as much as you are to blame for what happened, it's me who is locked in here. I must look at the part I played in it all, I know I'm not completely innocent.

But when I met with them, it was the first time I realised that I've lost that child I once was. I've lost all those happy memories, so perhaps, as I shook my head with those poor parents and let tears drip from my eyes, I was crying for the child in me that has been lost.

I want to be able to tell you, like those brave parents told me, that I forgive you, but I can't. I've tried, I've really, really tried. I must need to be religious, or a better person, but I can't forgive you if you won't admit your crime. At least visit me. Come here and talk to me, about anything. We don't need to go over that. Let's talk like we used to. Before. Visit me and we'll talk about television shows, weather, current affairs. Come see me so I can start to forgive you. Come here so I can get over this hurt, this rage, because this silence from you is killing me.

TWENTY-SIX

The thing about working in a school is that you become institutionalised. You don't realise it's happened until you find yourself looking at the calendar and it suddenly dawns on you that you're living your life in accordance with term dates. It doesn't matter if you're a parent or not, in school you think about Christmas at the beginning of a school year, summer holidays are on your mind from Easter and the whole year is measured in six- and eight-week blocks. You are counting down continually to the next holiday.

It was two weeks before half term. After the car incident, we'd been visited by the police. They had taken statements, told us the damage to my car was being investigated, that they would keep us updated, but the upshot was unless they could arrest and charge someone, there was nothing more they could do.

I was given the numbers of Victim Support and the Citizens Advice and told to wait. Wait. While my life unravelled. I had a crime reference number and nothing else, apart from a large bill from the garage and a second visit from the police, this time accusing me of harassing Ashley Simmons.

'You visited her office,' they looked at their notes, 'we have witnesses that you were aggressive. Abusive.'

'I was hardly abusive.' I shook my head in disbelief. 'I was angry. I'd just found out that she's helping my ex-husband and her friend had done that to my car.'

The officer raised an eyebrow. 'We have your accusations on file regarding the damage to your car but, as yet, no evidence.'

'Evidence.' I let out a scoff. 'We both know who did it, but you're not doing anything.'

They paused a moment while they looked at their notes again.

'We're advising you keep away from Ashley Simmons and her place of work, also that of Janine Walker. We've had several complaints. Someone has been posting up private details on a public forum and it's currently under investigation. And Ashley Simmons has requested we talk to you about—'

'Oh, this is rich,' I'd interrupted, 'they're accusing *me* now? Telling *me* to stay away from *them*? They need to stay away from me!'

They'd looked at each other then and I'd seen something in that look, something that was dismissive. Something that said they thought I might be responsible for the damage to my car, that I was sending myself my own cakes filled with excrement, that I might be doing it all. That I was lying. And that's when I knew exactly what I was up against and I felt weak with it. Weak and frightened because I was trying, really trying. I was surprising myself with how hard I was becoming and doing alarming things in the hope that it would stop, and yet it still all seemed to be slipping away from me.

Sam didn't want to return to school because of everything that was going on. He was scared and I could understand that. It was a struggle for us both, but now my car was fixed, back from the garage and repaired, my mother had a doctor's appointment and couldn't look after him, and he needed to go to school. I really needed him in his lessons. I'd lied about why he was absent but now I needed him in. I needed us to return to our routine. If I wanted to keep him, to stop the madness that Will had started, then I had to fight back. I had to appear as if I was in control.

'Please,' I said gently, 'please, Sam, I have to get to work. You have to get to school.'

I was sat outside his bedroom door, Sam on the other side. He'd barricaded himself in, pushing his bed up against the door. He'd never done anything like this before and I was thrown a little. Usually he went into his room and hung onto the door handle to prevent me from entering, but now he'd realised he was strong enough to move his bed and that was much more effective. I took a deep breath, tried to swallow down my mounting panic.

'Sam,' I tried again, 'just let me in. I won't make you do anything you don't want to. I just want to talk.'

'Liar,' he said, but I was glad he was talking, even if he was calling me names. 'You'll make me go back and I won't. I'm not going. Toby's there and he's got a knife.'

'Toby's not got a knife, no one is allowed to take knives into school—'

'I'm not going. I'm staying here.'

'Open the door, sweetheart,' I said, 'please. Let's just talk about it. How about I get us both a chocolate biscuit?'

I waited for an answer, and when he didn't speak I tried again.

'I wasn't going to say, but I guess this is the right time to tell you –' I waited a moment, hoping he'd take the bait '– but there's a whole tub of chocolate fudge ice cream in the freezer. Come out and I'll go get the tub. I'll make you a deal: you come out and talk to me, just talk, and you can eat the ice cream for as long as we're talking.'

It was seven-thirty. I should be on my way, arriving at school in fifteen minutes, Sam going into the breakfast club. We would be late. But better late than never.

'A whole tub?'

I smiled. His voice was small, frightened.

'Untouched,' I told him. 'I got it for you. For a treat at the weekend, but I suppose I can let you have a bit now. Have we got a deal?'

He was quiet for a moment. 'Deal.'

We sat at the top of the stairs, two spoons, the tub of chocolate fudge ice cream between us.

'You know I have to go to work,' I told him, as we dug our spoons in and licked the ice cream. 'I have to work to get paid so that we can stay in this house.'

He nodded. 'I'm not saying that you don't have to go, just that I don't want to.'

'Sam, you know Nanna can't come today and you know I can't leave you on your own.'

We were both quiet, Sam digging his spoon in to get some more of the hard ice cream.

'I'm old enough.'

'You're eight.'

'I'm big enough,'

I nodded. 'You are, but that still doesn't make it right.'

He was silent a moment. Then, 'I could come with you. I could hide in your office, under the desk. No one would know I was there.'

I suppressed a smile. 'People would know,' I said gently, 'and besides, you'd be bored. It'd be much better for you in the classroom. You like some of what you do in there, I know you do. You like reading and drawing.'

Sam had gone quiet as I spoke, thoughtfully licking his spoon.

'And Ryan, you like Ryan and he'll be there.'

He stopped licking and waited a moment. 'The thing is, Mummy,' he said, 'is that I do like some things about school, but Toby spoils it all.' He looked up then and put his small hand up to stop me from speaking. I'd been about to tell him that I had a meeting with John about it that very morning, but he stopped me. 'I know you've tried, Mummy, I know you've spoken to Miss Gleason and Mr Cartwright, and when you do, Toby stops for a little bit, but then he starts again. Only the next time it's worse because he's blaming me for him being told off. And then he came here and did that to your car . . .'

'Sam –' I put my hand on his arm '– we've been over this. That wasn't Toby, it was a silly woman that I know.'

He shrugged, shook his head. 'I've just had enough,' he said in a small voice, and I nodded, put my arm around him, squeezed him.

'I know,' I said, and to my surprise, tears blotted my vision. They came upon me unexpectedly and I had to wipe them away with the heel of my hand before Sam saw. 'I know, we've both had enough.'

I held him for a moment longer, then let him get back to his ice cream. He'd calmed down; he always did when he was eating. The red puce on his cheeks had simmered to a light pink and his eyes, although red and watery, were no longer wide with fear.

I finally got Sam into school an hour later by agreeing with him.

He'd had enough. I'd had enough. We just wanted it to stop.

Poppy's face kept on coming back to me from that day at the market, when I'd tried to justify why I was late, me bubbling over, explaining all that was going on, all the *drama*, and what she'd said: *I'm just trying to sell a few pots of jam here.*

Same here! I wanted to shout that morning as I dropped Sam off in class and lied to Lisa about why we were late. Same here, I thought as I went into John's office, asked him if I could have a meeting with him as a parent and not as school secretary. We were just trying to get on with our lives, like Poppy. We didn't need all the drama. We weren't asking much. Bloody hell, we weren't asking for much at all, just the chance to go about our day without fear. That wasn't an awful lot, was it?

'Here's the thing,' John said, after I'd explained how Sam was feeling. 'Toby is waiting to be assessed, we think he's on the spectrum, but –' he raised his hands '– I'm no specialist! But I hear the signs are there. The parents know, they brought it to our attention. We're waiting to have him assessed.' He looked at me over his glasses. 'That, by the way, is completely confidential. I only tell you so you can see what position it puts us, as a school, in.'

'I'm not sure I understand,' I said. 'The fact that Toby may or may not be on the spectrum isn't why I asked to talk to you. I'm telling you about his bullying behaviour towards my son.'

'And that's on record,' said John, tapping the desk in front of him. 'But if it should be that Toby has a medical condition then you have to see that he is very vulnerable ...'

'Vulnerable?' My voice came out shrill. 'You're saying that Toby, the bully, is vulnerable?'

'I'm saying that it's not all black and white.' He breathed out heavily through his nose. 'I've spoken to Toby, to his parents, and yes, they do admit that there is a troubled relationship with Toby and Sam, but they were quite adamant that it wasn't all Toby ...'

'Hang on a minute ...'

'Toby can't express himself, he isn't as articulate as Sam, and Miss Gleason did say—'

'Miss Gleason has no idea,' I spat out, and he recoiled a little at the force of my words. 'Toby is making my son's life hell in this school. Sam is terrified of him. Toby has been telling him that he has a knife, that he's going to "slash" him –' John went to speak but I held my finger up '– and the school has done, *is doing*, nothing. And now you're telling me it's Sam's fault?'

'Ruth –' John's voice was an octave deeper than normal, it was the voice I heard him use on students when they were out of line '– we take every matter of bullying extremely seriously. There is something being done about it. Toby is awaiting assessment and Miss Gleason is monitoring the situation. We've spoken to Toby's parents about it, and now I'm speaking to you about it. Talk to Sam, see if he's not doing the same to Toby ...'

I opened my mouth but John sat forward, his expression stopping me.

'Sam is a big lad,' he told me, 'twice the size of the other boys in there. He's not as defenceless as he would have you think. I've spoken to him, seen him. I know he can handle himself.'

'John –' I was swallowing back the rage as I spoke, my words coming out strangled with the effort '– I'm his mother, I think I know more about my son than you, and I know he's terrified. There are days when he's even too terrified to come into school! He is not the bully here, he is the one being bullied! I'll take this to the governors if I have to. To the council, anyone who'll listen.' I stopped and swallowed; John's face was intense. 'I'm just at my wits' end here,' I told him. 'I need help. We need help.'

After a moment, John nodded solemnly. Stayed quiet. I squeezed my hands into fists, bit the inside of my cheek from saying anything further. I couldn't shout, scream or call him a liar. This man was my boss after all. After a moment he reached across the desk and gave my hand a quick squeeze.

'I understand,' he said finally. 'I understand your concerns, Ruth. It seems this might be a little more serious than I first thought. Leave it with me.' He closed the file. 'I'll call the boy's parents again, speak to Miss Gleason. See what the assessment throws out. See what can be done about keeping him away from Sam. We'll sort it. Don't you worry.'

I couldn't seem to calm down all afternoon; the vision of Sam's face was never far from my mind. It obscured everything. I had a stack of paperwork to do for the school trip, all the forms for each child needed to be signed off and all the emergency information on file and on the database, when I found myself looking at Sam's class timetable and seeing what Lisa was down as having them do.

John thought Toby was vulnerable! Vulnerable? He was evil.

Telling another child that he was going to slash them, what kind of vulnerable boy does that? And what was he doing now, while John and Lisa and the assessment team gave him a label that came with a stamp of sensitivity. While I was told to *wait*. What was Toby doing to my son while all this was going on? Through all the red tape, the form filling, the following of protocol and procedures, what threats was he whispering in the ear of my son?

It was coming up to afternoon break. Lisa had them down as doing PE. It was last lesson before playtime, which meant it would be a scramble of children getting changed quickly to get back outside and it would be chaos. Without any more thought, I left my office and headed down to the playground, a pile of letters in my hand as a kind of alibi.

The school was busy, there was singing of times tables coming from one of the classrooms as I passed, the shout of a teacher from the year six room and then I came to year five. Janine's daughter would be in there, Eve's daughter as well. How was she? Now that she was leaving school, that the bullies had won. Had it stopped? I paused for a moment and peeked through the oblong window on the door. Glen was pointing at something on the whiteboard and I took a moment to watch him. His face was animated, a mixture of pure delight and charm; he was enjoying himself I could tell. And from the look of the children, who all seem mesmerised, they were enjoying it just as much. I tried to spot the girls, to see who was tormenting who, but it was useless. They were a class of thirty children, watching Glen and writing in their books. Maybe if Glen had been teaching them earlier, the bullying wouldn't have happened, he wouldn't have let a whole class torment one child. He would've stopped it before it started. But then, looking at them now, you'd never know that one girl in that room was going through a living hell. And one girl was persecuting her. No one had any idea what really went on.

I went through to the infants, passing the dining hall and coat racks, the lower half of the school. I could hear the usual screams and shouts from nursery and reception. They were at the bottom of a long corridor and there was a smell of something coming from there, the sharp tang of glue or paint. A smell that whipped me back to my own childhood, my own time sitting in a classroom, my life dependent on the whims of a teacher. And for a second, I felt the hopelessness, the despair, the unjustness of a teacher and the power they held. It was luck of the draw as to who you got, who took control. You could have someone like Glen or someone like Lisa. It was pure chance. The person who dominated you, who, while you were in their company, had complete authority, and it was a toss-up as to who that person would be.

Something needed to be done.

And then I came to Sam's classroom – it was the first room at the top of that long corridor – and I went inside. Empty. The classroom led out directly onto the playground, it was the quickest way to get there, and as I walked through the piles of discarded uniforms I saw them.

I stopped for a moment at the door, looking out. It's a large area, backing onto fields, and they were at the far side. It appeared they'd been doing some kind of obstacle course, Lisa and the teaching assistant had them tidying up. A group of children were gathered in a line, their backs to me, in front of Lisa. They were passing items to each other and then depositing them into various tubs. A few others darted about collecting bean bags and cones and passing them to the start of the line. I figured I could just about pull it off.

I ran quickly, my heels sinking into the grass, my skirt tight around my thighs. My eyes on the children and Lisa as I went. They were all involved in their task as I got over to where the gardening area was, a few trees and a small shed that I ducked behind, just as the bell started to ring.

I stayed half hidden as children poured into the playing field. They screamed and ran about like dogs set free. I recognised a girl from year six; she came running forward with a group of others who all got to a spot near me, then immediately sat down in a circle and began chanting, playing some game. I waited. Hidden behind the shed. Sam's class would now all be frantically getting changed, they would all fly out with an unjust feeling. Half of their playtime missed because of a lesson.

And then I saw Sam, staying close to the building, alone, fearful and watching, and then, there he was. Toby with about four other boys. They immediately went over to Sam. I looked at the teaching assistant on duty, chatting to a group of year three girls, oblivious to what was going on, and cursed her. I saw Toby reach up and poke at Sam's shoulder, push him a little, and I watched as Sam just put his head down and took it. He let them push at him and my heart nearly broke in my chest. Seeing that gave me the momentum to do it.

'Hey,' I called to one of the passing year six girls, and she jumped. I was obviously well hidden. 'It's Miss Clarkson.' I came out slightly, so she could see me, and held up the pile of papers in my hands, as if to show her that I was on an errand. Her eyes flicked towards the teaching assistant. 'Could you get Toby Morley-Fenn? Toby from year four? They've just had PE and I think he's left some of his kit out here.'

She came closer to have a look.

'It's OK,' I told her, putting my hand out, 'you don't need to see what it is, you just need to tell him to come over here to collect it. Alone.'

She stared at me a moment and then her eyes went wide. 'Has he wet his pants?'

I stayed quiet.

'Did Toby wet himself in PE?' There was a gleeful note to her voice. 'Has he left his underpants there and that's why you need to see him on his own?'

I stared at her a moment and then began to nod, as if what she was saying were true. 'Let's not tell everyone,' I said softly. 'Just tell him to come over here, without anyone else seeing.' I gave her the smile of a co-conspirator.

She nodded, puffed out her chest a little. Pleased and flattered to be my accomplice. 'I'll get him right away,' she told me, not realising she'd just given me the perfect reason to see Toby alone, and sped off.

She was true to her word. Without any hassle, she got Toby by the arm and they were running across the playground towards me. She presented him with a beaming smile.

'Good girl,' I told her, 'now remember –' I put my finger to my lips and she nodded.

'It's all right, Toby,' she told him before leaving. 'I won't tell anyone and it used to happen to me when I was younger. Everyone's done it.'

He looked at her confused and she gave another smile at me. I smiled warmly back, nodded my approval once more, and she was gone.

'Hello Toby,' I said. He was small up close. Quite weedy in fact, skinny little arms and legs. A puff of red hair on top of his skull, skin so white I could see the blue of his veins beneath.

'Miss . . . ?'

'Don't worry,' I told him, 'you left something out here from your PE lesson, just here behind the fence . . . '

He came forward, unsure.

'Quickly,' I told him, 'I don't want you to get in trouble.'

He took a few more steps towards me, uncertainty etched on his face, and when he was close enough I gripped his arm and took him behind the shed, out of sight. He winced, his eyes large as I dragged him.

'Stay quiet,' I instructed, 'I only want to talk to you.' His mouth had formed a small 'o' and there was a bubble of spit caught at the side of it. It wobbled as he breathed hard.

'You know who I am?'

He stared at me, didn't say a word.

'I'm Sam's mother. Sam, the boy in your class, the one you call "big fat giant".'

His eyes were saucers. I wasn't sure he was listening.

'You leave Sam alone,' I warned him. 'Bullying is not very nice, didn't your parents ever tell you that? So don't go calling him fat, or spitting in his food, or saying that you've got a knife, or tell him you're going to "slash" him. This stops. It stops now, d'you hear me? You stay away from Sam, or you'll be seeing me again.'

I went to let go, but then gave a final squeeze on his arm, just so he knew I was serious. It was a small twig of a thing, I felt I could snap it. I watched as he winced under my grip and then I let go. He didn't move. He stared at me, his mouth and eyes still gaping, and then his hand went to his arm, to where I'd been gripping it.

'You can go now,' I said, staring at him, and he still didn't move. I went towards him again, my arm outstretched, this time to nudge him back to his friends, and he jumped away from me. Frightened of what I might do next. And then, to my horror, the front of his pants went dark. Toby Morley-Fenn had wet himself after all.

TWENTY-SEVEN

LEAVE NOW AND WE'LL LEAVE YOU ALONE.

We'll.

It implied that there was more than one of them.

It arrived just as we were driving to my mother's after school the next day. I heard the familiar notification as I was getting in the car.

'Is that Nanna?' Sam asked, and I shook my head.

'Probably from a friend,' I said, noticing how in a matter of weeks I was readily expecting threatening messages rather than texts from my mother about her hypochondria. And also noticing how it didn't seem to unnerve me, it had become the norm.

I read it between getting Sam out of the car and us walking towards my mother's house. I was feeling bad about the way I'd treated Toby. He was a bullying sadistic little kid, but he was a kid after all, and perhaps I went too far.

I scared him so much he'd literally wet himself. But then, he was a little shit that was making Sam's life a misery. Fifty years ago, maybe even less than that, it was accepted that adults, other than the child's parents, could and should keep them in line. My mother often told me about neighbours shouting at her if she'd been disobedient; it had been the norm. What's the saying? It takes a village to raise a child. If you looked at it from that perspective then I was only doing what was right, what was needed. He'd run off back into school after I'd spoken to him. I'd tried to help, offered to get some paper towels, to go back into school with him, say I'd found him hiding and handle the whole business about him wetting himself, so none of his classmates would see, but he ran away from me and I'd not heard a word about it since.

But more importantly, it had worked.

Sam told me that, very suddenly, Toby stopped speaking to him. Stopped everything. Wouldn't look at him. Didn't go near him. I told Sam it was down to me talking to Mr Cartwright. I said that must have done the trick, that Toby had been told and was staying away. The result was, nothing had happened and, for the first time, Sam was tentatively starting to believe that the bullying might be over. That's the sad thing about the whole situation: what I was doing was having an effect. Lisa was now helping Sam; she had allowed him special privileges since I'd spoken to her. Sam could choose where he sat, and whom he sat next to, could eat his lunch in the classroom alone if he didn't feel like going into the dining hall, and he was now getting gold stars. Lots of gold stars.

The thing with revenge, I found, is that it worked.

It also turned me into a bit of a stalker. I wasn't proud of anything I'd had to do, but since phoning HMRC and the newspaper about Janine, since posting Ashley's picture on the animal rights forum, I'd had to do some digging of my own to see if my actions had achieved anything, and to my delight they had started to yield results.

I'd set up a bogus Facebook account, easily done with a new Gmail address, and with some light stalking had learned that Janine's business was in trouble – real trouble. The rumours were correct. I'd tried to join her Top Marks page and got a message about her not taking on any more people at the moment due to 'admin issues'. A small triumph. I could only imagine the admin involved in an HMRC investigation, the invoices and receipts she would be frantically gathering, and it had obviously been enough to distract her from taking on any more clients. On top of that, I'd had two enquiries and one order for a two-tier anniversary cake. Her gossip was no longer working, my business was back on track while hers was stumbling.

And then there was Ashley. My post on the animal rights forum had quickly gathered momentum. It was taken down by the moderator after three hours, but three hours was enough. I'd read some of the responses, what they planned to do to her 'kind', and it was shocking. A bit sickening. I'd felt quite bad about putting the post up at all, but I'd had to remind myself what I was up against. What she was doing to me. Then the post came up from the police, informing that appropriate action would be taken against anyone who posted offensive content or threats.

She'd have been scared after all that. I know I would be. Ashley would've felt some of what I did. Some of the fear I felt every day. That's why the police told me to stay away from her. She was scared of who wrote the post about her and what the consequences of such a post would be. It wasn't much but it was enough, enough for me to feel slightly smug. And yet the texts kept coming.

We'll leave you alone.

Who else was involved that I'd not taken care of yet? The person who spray-painted my car, who sent these messages, who posted defiled cupcakes back to me. Who else could be behind this? There was only Rob and Will that I could now think of. But would Rob really be so petty as to do this because I'd told his wife about his philandering? It didn't seem believable, after his attitude when I'd confronted him, and then I had to check myself. I was being sexist. I could believe a woman capable of this, but not a man?

My mother was giving me a running commentary about how she was approaching people to fix the disused well, the upshot being that it was still dangerous, but now various people other than her were aware of it.

'I've told Roger, the man at the post office, and he's getting me a number of a man he knows, and I've telephoned someone from an advert in the paper,' she said, as she poured hot water into the teapot, 'so one of them must be able to help.'

When we'd arrived we'd all gone out to inspect it – my mother had cleared away the vegetation nearby and rotting planks – and we'd stared at the gaping hole.

'How deep does it go?' Sam asked. He was over by the wall, a fair distance away on our instruction.

'Deep,' I told him. 'Stay where you are, you don't need to come and look.'

I watched my mother, who was busy covering it with fresh planks of wood.

'It'll be blocked up properly soon,' she told me, 'don't worry, this is just so no animals get trapped down there.'

'We should sell up,' I told her as we went back to the house.

She stopped walking, shocked at my suggestion. 'It's the answer to everything,' I told her. 'We could leave, use the money, take Sam away from Will, start over somewhere, a fresh—'

'Never,' she whispered. 'Your father died in this house.' She told me as if I was unaware. 'I'd never leave him.'

I opened my mouth to argue that just because he died in the house didn't mean that he had taken up residence as some kind of ghost, but it was a waste of time. The house made my mother feel safe, it was her hideaway, filled with memories that comforted her, and I could understand that. It was an effort for me to leave my four walls, so how could I argue with her?

It had gone cold. In the past few days autumn had made its mark and it was crisp and biting. Wood smoke filled the air as tourists enjoyed the charm of a real fire, and my mother was the same, with the fire going constantly, and as I sat at her kitchen table I realised I was looking forward to the changing colour of the leaves and the other autumn activities that I did with Sam. Unlike summer, it's usually acceptable to start hibernation in autumn. It's almost expected to stay indoors and be cosy. It was one of my favourite seasons. And, to my surprise, it was the first time I'd thought about doing any of it with a man. Glen, it seemed, was appearing in a lot more of my daydreams. It could be because he'd dropped off a few magazines about fly fishing for Sam, or that I was seeing more of him in the school day, or that he texted me sweet messages, asking when he could next see me, but I often caught myself thinking about him.

I'd found myself idly imagining baking for him the other day. I had an image of me at the worktop, kneading bread while he watched. Such a domestic scene that when I woke up to myself I had a mini panic attack. That was not my life, I had to remind myself. My life was complicated and messy. It involved a malicious ex-husband and a pack of spiteful women. I'd threatened a small boy yesterday, caused him to wet himself, and although my motives were justified – everything I did was for Sam – I couldn't invite a man into it. I was a long way off from any of that nonsense. But that little daydream told me otherwise. It was just one more thing I was being robbed of.

'Just make sure Sam doesn't go outside when he's here,' I told my mother, as I checked my bogus Facebook account once more for any updates on Janine, Ashley or Will. 'And keep that dog away from it. How much are we looking at?'

She breathed in through her teeth, then winced and put a hand to her jaw. I didn't even ask.

'About a grand I think,' she said, and I felt pain, physical pain, at her words. Where on earth were we going to find that kind of money? The respraying of my car and new tyres still needed paying for. I had some money due to come in from the cake business but not nearly enough for that, and then there was the holiday. Two weeks and I should be taking Sam somewhere, proving how 'outdoorsy' I was to Will. I closed my eyes.

'We could leave it,' she went on, 'keep that bit of wood over it and keep Sam indoors. The dog never goes around there and it's cold out now. Winter will be here before you know it, so we could take the time to save up? Get it sorted next spring?'

I nodded slowly. 'We might have to,' I said. 'I'm going to need every penny I've got to fight Will.'

'About that,' my mother said slowly, and I looked up at her, while she kept her eyes down. 'He was here the other day.'

'Here?' My voice was high. 'Will was here? At this house?'

She flapped her hands. 'Calm down, shh.' She looked

towards the lounge door where Sam was eating biscuits and watching television. 'I didn't tell you earlier because I didn't want to worry you.'

'Mother –' my heart was knocking '– you should have told me immediately. What were you thinking?'

'He just wanted to talk –' she took a sip of tea, '– about Sam. Jean called me—'

'Fucking Jean.'

'Language!' My mother shot me a look. 'I was glad she called. This whole thing has got out of hand, getting solicitors involved and going to court. And all that with your car. The business with that woman at school. It's not right, Ruth, you've got too much on your plate right now, and we had a good talk. Me and Jean both think it's ridiculous it's come to this, and more importantly, it's no good for Sammy. What you two are doing to that poor boy.'

'Mother, you can't just . . . '

'Well I did,' she said. 'He's my grandson and I agree with Jean.'

I stood up to leave.

'And what's more,' she cut in, putting her hand on mine, 'is that we think we can stop it.'

I paused.

'Jean doesn't want this ridiculous custody battle any more than we do. And she told me that Will doesn't either.'

I opened my mouth to speak.

'He's scared, Ruth,' she cut in, 'scared he won't see his son again.'

I leaned forward. 'You know he put Sam in A & E?' I reminded her. 'Made him have the biggest panic attack he's ever had? You know he forced him onto a rugby pitch?'

'He explained all of that,' she said, 'and he's mortified about what happened. Absolutely mortified. He thought he was doing the right thing. That's why he came here, he knew he couldn't apologise to you, so he came here.'

I gritted my teeth. Will always had the ability to charm my mother. Even when it'd been at its worst, with Will's infidelity all but being published in the paper, one meeting with my mother and she'd go from calling him a bastard to telling me that he really was very sorry.

'He was worried about Sam not being in school the other day, so he came here to find out why.'

'You told him it was a stomach bug?' I asked. 'Please tell me you told him that?'

'What do you take me for?' She shook her head. 'Of course I told him that.' She took another careful sip of her tea.

'Mother?'

'I may have mentioned your car, the tyres. How that woman who is his solicitor has another agenda.'

I put my head in my hands.

'He asked why I went to your house, why Sammy didn't come here. I told him about the well and he said I was so nice to go traipsing across the city to my grandson. He said that you were taking advantage of me and so I told him that you weren't. That of course I'd go anywhere you asked, and that Sammy didn't like the bus and it was no trouble for me . . .'

I was shaking my head. 'So, basically, you told him that someone had vandalised my car and Sam couldn't come to you because there's a death trap of a well here? He played you.' I ran my hands through my hair. 'He was here checking up on the reason Sam wasn't in school and now he'll know that it was because of my car.'

'I told him what you told the school, that Sam had a tummy bug.'

I shrugged. I didn't even know if that would matter, if Will finding out the real reason for Sam's absence from school would help build his case. If Ashley was still helping him or dealing with the animal rights group that I'd set against her.

'Will won't do anything about that anyway,' my mother went on. 'He was quite shocked to find out that someone had done that to your car, he had no idea. Quite concerned, and he seemed quite reasonable. He explained that he just wants the best for Sam and I think that if you talked to him, properly, somewhere neutral. Jean and I could be there, act as facilitators, make sure it doesn't get out of hand. Jean's already offered ...'

I started to gather my things.

'Ruth.' She put her hand out to stop me. 'Ruth, really, this might be the answer. If you talk to Will, with me and Jean, work out a proper schedule that we all stick to, he'll drop all this going to court nonsense. I'm sure of it.'

'C'mon, Sammy,' I shouted, and went towards the door. I couldn't listen to any more of it.

'Ruth, please don't be like this,' my mother was pleading. 'I just want to do what's right, can't you see? This might work? Ruth ...'

'Will knows exactly what's going on,' I told her. 'He knows them all. The more I think about it, the more it seems like he's working with them on some level.' I handed her my phone. 'See that? *We'll leave you alone.* It's more than one of them. I thought it was just a few women from school, but now I think there's more. There has to be.'

She looked up at me. 'You're getting texts now? Threats? Why didn't you tell me?'

'It's got to be Will,' I told her. 'He might not have sent this, but he'll know who did.'

'I don't understand. Ruth, this text is worrying, someone saying they'll leave you alone if you go? What happens if you stay? Why would Will—'

'To get Sam! To prove that it's better if Sam lives with him rather than me!' I snatched the phone back from her, deleted the text.

'Ruth, I don't think Will would—'

'Of course he would.'

'But he wouldn't want to scare Sam. Sam's his son, he wouldn't let people write that on your car, send you nasty text messages ...'

'It's his son that he forced to go on a rugby pitch, his son that he made have a massive panic attack. He doesn't care about Sam!'

'Mummy?'

I hadn't realised we'd been shouting.

'Who's sending nasty texts to you?'

He was at the door, looking at both of us. I wiped a hand over my face. Took a deep breath.

'No one, sweetie,' I told him as calmly as I could. 'It's just part of that silly joke I told you about.'

'The person who wrote on your car?'

I nodded. 'But I'm sorting it.' I smiled. 'Nothing for you to worry about. They think they're being funny, but they're not. Go get your coat on, time for us to go.'

I turned back to my mother. 'Don't try to be friends with Will, not after this. Not after what he's threatened, not when he's a part of all this. He comes here and says a few nice words and suddenly you're forgiving him?'

'I'm just thinking of Sam, I just want him to be—'

But I was gone. Out the door. I left Sam saying goodbye.

'Ruth!' she shouted after us as we got in the car. 'I'm only thinking of Sam!'

TWENTY-EIGHT

The next evening, I was in the Swan and Duck, glass of red wine in hand, unsure of myself. There was a buzz to my emotions. I felt both reckless and empowered, guilty and remorseful. I wasn't sure what was going on with me, this feeling was new to me and I wasn't sure how to handle it. I was checking my phone constantly for any messages from Becca, who was at my house watching Sam, but also to check Facebook. To see if there was any progress on Janine, Ashley or Will. Not being friends with any of them, I was only privy to the stuff they shared publicly, but it was enough.

Photographs they were tagged in, places they'd checked in to. For instance, I knew, as I sat there sipping my drink, that Janine was feeling 'anxious' and had attached a GIF of a monkey sat hammering a keyboard. I imagined her trying desperately to fabricate invoices and ringing parents for receipts. The copied newspaper article was in my handbag, nestled in between the pages of my diary, and the thought of it gave me a strange sense of pleasure. I still had that. Hadn't decided how to use it yet.

A quick check on Ashley and there was nothing new. She'd more or less come off Facebook altogether in the past few days. Her last post was still up, a rant about how the human race was a despicable thing. I didn't know what she was referring to, but the comments gave me a clearer idea. It seemed someone had posted something pretty vicious through her letterbox, some kind of organic matter, and it made me smile. It felt like good karma after opening my cupcakes that had been filled with excrement.

And then there was Will. His posts were more or less useless, all to do with sport in some capacity or other. Comments about rugby scores, football players, boring, useless updates, but he was still worth keeping an eye on.

'Everything OK?'

I switched my phone off quickly and took the menu Glen was offering me.

He'd dressed up. On our last date he'd been wearing a checked shirt, open at the collar, and jeans. He was still wearing the jeans but this time he had on a crisp white shirt and a tweed waistcoat. It made me want to use the word 'dapper', and that in itself made me want to giggle.

'What?' He looked down at his waistcoat, checked it for marks. 'I put this on for you.'

I smiled warmly. 'I know.'

'Since you've been dressing up all . . .' He waved in my general direction. I looked down at the gold jumper dress I was wearing. It was new, bought a few hours earlier from the cash I'd got from one of my baking jobs. It had been money that was meant to go towards the repairs on my car; that invoice was still waiting to be paid, but I hadn't done that.

Once I'd collected Sam from the after-school club, I'd visited two shops. A dress for me and a new game for Sam. In half an hour I'd spent £150. Money we didn't have, but it felt so good. I'd felt the need to celebrate, to do something because it was all working. Sam was having uneventful days at school. Janine and Ashley were suffering. I knew I should be saving the money – paying off something or putting it towards taking Sam away at half term – but I was fed up with that attitude.

I'd past the retail park and, before I knew it, I was driving us in. Something I've never done, something I've gone out of my way to avoid, but the money was in my pocket, begging to be spent. It was quiet, five o'clock, the time when people are just leaving work and the shops are getting ready to close.

'Mum?' Sam had asked, confused. 'What are we doing here?'

I'd grinned. 'I think we both deserve a bit of a treat, don't you?'

Sam had looked at the shops in front of us.

'There's hardly anyone here,' I'd told him. 'If we're quick, we can get you that game you're after and me a new dress and be back in the car before you know it.'

'That new game?' he'd asked in a small voice. 'The game where you get to choose your own parachute and you said it was too expensive?'

I'd nodded, and the look on his face was priceless. A new game. Brand new. Sam never got new games.

'C'mon,' I'd told him excitedly, and within minutes the game was in his small hands. Gripped tight while we'd gone to the shop next door and straight to the party dresses. They were fresh in, and I'd picked out a gold coloured one. I'd almost laughed out loud with the foolishness of it as I paid. It had made me light-headed and woozy, a giddy sensation filling my chest, Sam's shocked and delighted face at the side of me.

I'd started to laugh and Sam had joined in. It was silly, I felt like we'd just robbed a bank, the adrenalin rush was intense, but it felt good. Sam hadn't had anything that wasn't from a second-hand website in years. I couldn't remember the last time I'd physically taken him into a shop and let him choose what he wanted. It had been exhilarating.

I smoothed down the metallic threads of my dress. It was outrageously flashy for me, not my usual style, probably meant for someone much younger than I was, but I loved it.

'Do you like it?'

'You look sensational,' Glen said, and took a sip of his pint. 'I've noticed you've been looking very sensational all the time lately, anyone would think you had a new man in your life.'

He smiled and I felt myself flush slightly. He was right, I had been dressing differently, wearing items that I usually put aside for 'going out' or 'best'. But I realised the other day that there was no reason why I shouldn't be wearing the nicer blouses or the shorter skirts instead of the supermarket clothes that were my normal working attire. It felt nice to be a bit more dressed up, and if it was for Glen, or because of how I was acting, I had no idea. I only knew that it felt better.

'So,' he took another sip of his pint, 'how is everything in the world of Ruth?'

I raised my eyebrows, pretended I didn't know what he was referring to.

'OK.' He gave a small laugh. 'I went on Facebook the other day, onto the Top Marks page and –' he paused, looked at me '– sorry, I know you're not interested in this. What shall we talk about instead? The weather?'

I gave him a small kick under the table and he winced dramatically.

'She's having a hard time of it, Janine Walker.' He took another drink. 'Feel quite sorry for her actually. She's under investigation by HMRC and, apparently, she's lost all of her invoices and receipts and is trying to get information out of all the parents so she can replicate them, which is a bit . . . ' He let his words trail off, took another drink. 'So, understandably a few of the parents are complaining and not playing nice, because they paid in cash and are adamant they were never given a receipt or invoice, so it looks like –' he made a slashing motion across his neck '– for Top Marks.'

I bit my lip.

'And I see that Sam is doing well? Lisa was practically gushing over him at the last staff meeting, which is a real turnaround.'

'Was she?' I felt a rush of pleasure and smiled. 'That's brilliant news, I'll have to thank her tomorrow. Let Sam know.'

'Karma,' he said. 'Sorts everything out in the end, doesn't it, Ruth?'

I looked up, and he was staring at me. I smiled but he didn't return it.

'What?' I asked after a moment, and then let out a laugh when he didn't answer. 'Glen, stop looking at me like that, you're scaring me.'

He held the stare and then, when I was just about to ask him to stop again, let out a loud laugh. He took another sip of his drink and sat back. 'All I'm saying is, what we did in the staffroom a couple of weeks ago? Messing around with the timetable? I think that was the catalyst for all of this, the thing that put it all into action.' He held up his hand. 'You can thank me later.'

'Well—' I began, then stopped myself.

For a moment I'd wanted to tell him, confess it all. See his face when I told him that I was responsible, that I'd phoned HMRC, that I threatened Lisa. Tell him what I'd done to Ashley and the animal rights group, but I didn't. Instead we ordered, got more drinks, and the conversation turned to teaching and, more importantly, why he wasn't doing it full time.

'But you're a good teacher,' I said. 'I've heard it from Becca and I saw you the other day. Peeked in your classroom as I was passing.'

'You've been spying on me?'

'I know you're good,' I told him, 'and you love it and the kids love you, so why all the "teaching's not for me" stuff? Your contract's up at half term and I notice you've not signed a new one. John would give you a full-time post eventually, you know he would, and I'm sure you could get any permanent job you applied for.'

'I love it because I'm *not* a teacher.' He took another drink. 'I used to be full time, I did it for three years before I heard myself in the staffroom talking about a nine-year-old as if he were an old man. Calling this poor lad who wasn't even ten a misery, complaining about his lack of enthusiasm, as if his personality was set.' He shook his head. 'Don't get me wrong, I know some of them are little sods, but at the end of the day, they're still just kids.'

I took a moment.

'You don't agree?'

'I think,' I said, thinking of Toby, 'that a lot of children get away with too much now. I think we'd all benefit if stricter rules were in place.'

He coughed on his drink. 'Bloody hell, Ruth, I didn't expect that from you. I thought you were all liberal and equal rights.'

'I am, but lately I think too much of that attitude can be destructive. It doesn't hurt to be stern once in a while. Y'know, like this thing with my ex-husband. The custody battle he's insistent on. My mother thinks it would be best to meet up with him, talk it out, but I've been there, done that, and if it didn't work then, then it's not going to work now. I'm going to fight him. All the way.' I took a sip of my wine. 'And I'm going to win.'

His face broke out into a broad grin. 'Very assertive,' he said, 'if you're sure that Sam will be better off without—'

'The last time my ex-husband had Sam, he ended up in A & E.'

Glen's eyes went wide and I waved my hand. 'Sam's fine,' I told him. 'He had a panic attack and Will didn't know how to deal with it, but it was enough to show me. Show me that Will's not fit to have him, even for the weekend. I'm going to take Sam away in half term, prove to social services that I'm not denying my son anything. That Sam's capable of travelling, that I am, that we're having a nice time thank you very much, and all of Will's allegations are fabrications. I just need to find somewhere that's free.'

I smiled broadly and took a gulp of the wine that I could already feel was going to my head, and Glen looked at me a moment, a smile playing on his lips.

'I've been thinking about that,' Glen said, 'the half term thing. I've delayed going on my next cruise, and my parents live in Anglesey, but they're going away that week. Their house is near the beach – nothing fancy, but it's by the coast. Sam could do some fishing. It's a bit soon, and you can say no. I mean, this is only our second date, but we could go there if you fancy? As soon as I'm back from the residential, travel down mid-week?'

I put down my glass and stared at him. 'Are you offering to take us on holiday?'

He let out a laugh. 'I suppose I am.'

I was stunned.

He held up his hands. 'Too much, too soon,' he said. 'Forget I ever mentioned it, I'm way ahead of myself—'

'No, no,' I stopped him from talking, and put my hand out. Tears had come to my eyes. 'It's perfect. You're perfect. We'd love to. Thank you.'

The whole evening was relaxed and soft. I had another glass of wine along with braised duck, and we shared a dessert of sorbet and berries, Glen eating the berries whilst I ate the sorbet, the plate between us, using a small fork that we shared. By the time I was sitting in Glen's van, being driven home, I was happily merry. Everything was coming together, it was all working out. As I listened to Glen relay stories of his time working on the cruise ships, I'd go so far as to say that, for a brief time, I was immensely happy. I couldn't wait to tell Becca, to tell my mother. I couldn't wait to tell Will.

'I'm going to have to pull over,' Glen said.

We'd been in his van about ten minutes. Glen had driven us to a quiet pub just on the outskirts of the city and the journey, although through a myriad of country lanes, was lovely. It was a dark night and I was enjoying the solitude it gave us. I was enjoying being so close to him. So alone with just the beam of the headlights marking our way home.

'Why?'

'Some idiot behind me.' His eyes glanced in the rear-view

mirror. 'They've been on my tail since we left the pub. Right up my arse. Thought they'd turn off, towards the motorway, but they've followed me all the way through to this back road. Probably lost tourists, but they've got their full beams in my eyes.'

I swivelled around in my seat, then shielded my eyes from the glare. 'They've forgotten they've still got them on. Pull over. Let them pass.'

'First chance I get.'

We drove for a while, waiting for a place where we could pull over and, eventually, we saw an opening. Glen flicked on his indicator and pulled aside. We waited, expecting the car to pass, but it also stopped. We were in a county lane, miles from anywhere in total darkness.

'What the . . . ?' Glen undid his seatbelt.

'Don't!' It was too late, Glen had the door open.

I'd started to shake slightly; all my mellow mood had evaporated and the fuzziness from the wine was gone. I was suddenly razor sharp. There was a chill breeze from Glen's open door. I undid my seatbelt and swivelled around in my seat to watch. Glen raised his arms to the stationary driver of the other vehicle, as if in a question.

'You all right, mate?' Glen shouted. 'You need help with something?'

It was every horror movie I'd ever watched: a lone dark lane, an unknown threatening presence. A car that a moment ago had just been another traveller and was now menacing. Glen was approaching them with his arms still raised.

'You OK in there?' I could hear him shout.

'Glen!' I opened my door and watched as he approached the stationary vehicle. The glare from its full beams blinding us. He took a few steps before the car suddenly jerked into action and roared forward. It came at us at great speed, and I screamed as Glen dived out of the way and it flew past.

'Glen? Glen?' I shouted. He stood up, looked after the car and then back at me.

We were both quiet, shocked into silence.

'Idiot,' he said after a moment.

'Are you OK? Did they hit you?'

'Fine, fine.' He got back into the van and motioned for me to do the same. 'Probably kids. Wish I'd got their number plate, I'd get straight on to the police.' He looked at me. 'And if I didn't have you in the van, I'd be speeding after them right now.'

I stared at him.

'Hey –' he leaned over, put his hand on mine '– it was just kids. Just being daft, playing silly buggers. You OK?'

I nodded. I was shaking, my heart thrumming. He switched on the engine and we started to drive along the lane again. It was only when we'd been on the road for a while that I realised I recognised the car. As it had sped away I saw it was a red Fiat. The same red Fiat that had been on my street.

TWENTY-NINE

Parents' evening, by most, is thought of as a waste of time. A few years ago, a toy company did a survey and the results hit the national news. The headlines surmised that most people they spoke to thought parents' evening was confusing. They felt too little time was given and too little information. More than half said they were unable to make parents' evening due to work commitments, and on the whole it was felt that an email update about their child's progress would be better than having to come into school and talk to their child's teacher. I couldn't agree more. Ten minutes wasn't anywhere near long enough. A weekly update would be much more effective, but the survey had no impact on our parents' evening, or in the way it was undertaken.

The autumn term parents' evening was going ahead as it always did, and as I compiled the letters needed for each class, I wondered how many of them would go straight in the bin. How many would be left in the child's bag, reply slip unanswered. How many parents actually cared?

I'd been to every one of Sam's parents' evenings, I'd written down questions for the teacher before I met with them. Made sure I asked about his progress, his targets, made notes when they'd answered. I'd taken home extra homework, I'd ordered books that complemented the curriculum; in short, I'd done everything that every teacher recommended. And where was Will on all of these parents' evenings? Where had he been when I'd asked for extra time, when the teacher told me I had to go, other parents were waiting? Would social services take that into consideration?

Last night, when I'd arrived home, I sent a message to Eve. It was the first time I'd contacted her since we met in the coffee shop, since she'd given me the newspaper article.

Hi, Eve. Do you know if Rob Walker has a red Fiat? R

She hadn't replied. I couldn't blame her, she was done with them. She'd got rid of Janine and Rob and now they were my problem. I think she expected me to use the newspaper clipping immediately, probably disappointed that I hadn't done anything. Looking at it now, I can see that by giving that information to me, she was issuing a revenge of her own, but using me as a pawn. Someone to deliver the blow that she couldn't. Everyone has their own agenda.

The residential began the following weekend and I had a stack of work to do for it. Two letters to compile with regards to a packing list and emergency contact, the accommodation and travel to confirm, the insurance policy to double check. There was also a coffee morning to arrange, recycling changes to organise with the council and the flu immunisation pro-gramme to finalise for the younger children. My day was busy, barely enough time to complete what I had to, but instead of doing any of that I used the computer to Google Rob Walker. Rob Walker and a red Fiat.

After fifteen minutes, it was clear that Rob Walker was a common name. That the Rob Walker I was looking for had no Facebook page, no LinkedIn, Instagram or Twitter account. It became clear that the only thing I did know about Janine's husband, about the man who I had slept with, was the information I had on the school database. I knew his home, his mobile number. I knew he had a white Land Rover from what I saw that fateful morning, but perhaps he was driving Janine's car. Perhaps Janine's car was a red Fiat? Because, I thought as I sipped coffee and searched the internet, who else could it be? By mid-morning, I had got no further and sent another message to Eve.

Does Rob know about newspaper article?

When there was still no reply after an hour, I wondered what I expected Eve to say. It was like I was waiting for her permission, but the fact was she'd handed the newspaper cutting to me. It was up to me what I did with it. Taking it out of the hiding place in my bag, I looked at it once more. It was a simple report, a quarter page, just outlining the facts. I took a picture of it, and then, as my last message to him had been so effective, sent him another.

Stop following me. Stop sending texts. Stop sending parcels. Stop it all, or this goes to the police and everyone will know that Top Marks is employing paedophiles.

Paedophile was a strong word, the boy in question was nearly sixteen, but in the eyes of the law he was still a child, so paedophile it was.

Once I'd pressed send, I had a moment of regret before a giddy feeling came over me. The thought of him getting the message, of him showing it to Janine.

'She sent *that*?' I could imagine her asking, her face going pale. 'She knows about that? We're ruined.'

'Not yet,' I felt like answering her, 'but watch what you do next.' I had a loaded gun. And now both Janine and Rob knew I was pointing it straight at them.

'What's that then?'

I'd been sloppy, Becca was in the room before I had a chance to put my phone down.

'We're still waiting for the parents' evening and flu immunisation forms. Did you get the dates sorted? I was going to send Tina down, but thought I'd leave the class with her and visit you myself, so what's this?'

Becca had the paper in her hands. I'd fumbled for it, dropped my phone as she wandered in and came straight over to my desk. Chatting banally as she picked up my loaded gun and read it over with a confused expression.

'This is three years old.' She looked up. 'What's going on? Is this something to do with the school? Does John know something . . .?'

I snatched the paper from her just as my phone alerted me to a text message. He'd answered.

Have no idea what you're talking about. Please stay away from me. Any more texts and I will go to the police.

'Liar.'

'Who's a liar?'

I looked up, I hadn't realised I'd spoken out loud. She walked forward, was looking at my desk.

'Ruth, what's going on? Have you even done the letters?'

I shook my head. 'I'll do them at lunch, you'll have them before the end of the day.'

'We need them now, to put in the book bags before home time. Ruth?'

I felt a tingle of panic creep up my spine. She was right. It was almost lunchtime; the teaching assistants would need the paperwork at the start of the afternoon in order to get them all handed out. I'd let the entire morning slip away from me without doing any of my work.

'I . . .'

But I had no way to explain, I was useless at lying.

'You haven't done them?'

I shook my head, just as there was a rap at the door. It was Teresa, year one teaching assistant.

'Just came in for the forms,' she said, and put her hand out. I stared at it. 'Parents' evening and the flu—'

'Computer's been playing up,' Becca cut in quickly. 'Ruth's been trying to fix it all morning, there's no letters. They won't be going out today.'

Teresa's brow crinkled. 'But if we don't send them home today, then we can't . . .'

'It's only a couple of bloody letters, Teresa,' Becca said, 'it won't matter if they go next week. Do us a favour and go put a notice up on the board in the staffroom? So Ruth isn't bombarded by a string of TAs this afternoon.'

Teresa took a moment then left.

'Bit harsh,' I said, and Becca raised her eyebrows.

'What was the alternative? Tell her you've not been doing your job all morning because of –' she looked to my phone '– what? What have you been doing?'

I gave a sigh, shook my head and then my phone vibrated in my hand. Another alert. Another message. It was from Eve.

Rob has left Janine.

'Shit,' I said and Becca took my phone from me.

She looked up. 'Who's this from?' she asked. 'And why are they telling you that Rob has left Janine? What've you been doing?'

After a moment's hesitation, I told her. I told her it all. It didn't take long; a few sentences. What I'd done, what I was about to do.

'But it's working,' I said, as her face began to register disapproval. 'Becca, it's working. I wouldn't have done any of it if I didn't have to, but Will is trying to take Sam away from me. I can't have this going on, not now. The graffiti on my car, the texts, the packages? I didn't start any of it. And Sam is having a better time at school, Janine is losing her business—'

'But the animal rights forum, Ruth? That's messed up.'

'But it's working!' I pleaded. 'I've not had any more letters from Ashley; for all I know she might not be in the office any more. She might have had to take time off because of—'

'Because of what you did?'

I took a second, then nodded.

'She might have had to take time away from work, fearing what'll happen to her, because you put up her home address on an animal rights group site labelling her as something she's not? Janine might have lost her business because you called up HMRC—'

'She was spreading rumours about my business!' I interrupted.

'The stuff going on in school,' she began. 'The person who's been messing with the board, the rotten food left in the staffroom, the stuff being stolen, it's not a kid, is it?'

I stayed silent, looked down at my phone.

'Jesus, Ruth!' She went to the door, made sure it was closed. 'If John gets wind of this you'll lose your job. If Will finds out—'

'He's not going to find out,' I snapped back. 'And once I've sent this –' I pointed to the newspaper cutting '– then Rob will stop following me. Janine's business will be over. They'll have no money coming in and that will be the end of it.'

'The end of what?' She shook her head. 'When will it stop, Ruth?'

'When they stop,' I snapped back. 'We were followed last night, by Rob. He might not be with Janine any more, but once her business has closed down he won't be able to freeload any more. He'll have to pay child maintenance, especially if she's not working, and he'll have to get a job. He won't be able to—'

'Listen to yourself!' Becca cut in. 'You sound like one of the children from my class. Bloody hell, Ruth, stop, now. No one's following you, it was probably some kids, just like Glen said. Rob's just left his wife; do you really think he's going to be concerned with spying on you?'

'He blames me for it, blames me for everything, of course it's him.'

'But the more you respond ...' Becca shook her head. 'It all makes sense now. They know it's you. Janine, Ashley, Rob.

Why do you think you're getting all these texts and people are slashing your tyres – they know it's you!'

I thought a moment.

'It's obvious, Ruth,' she said. 'If I've just worked it out, then they have. C'mon, you can't be that stupid?'

I looked up at her.

'You have an argument with someone and the next minute there's been a tip off to HMRC about your business? The angry ex-wife of a client visits your office and the next thing your address is on an animal rights forum?'

I looked away.

'The HMRC call was anonymous, anyone could've done it.'

'The animal rights post?'

'I don't even have a computer.'

'And Lisa, you think she won't have told Janine what you told her? That you've been in contact with HMRC?'

We were both silent for a moment.

'You're lucky the police haven't been knocking on your door.'

'They have,' I told her. 'Apparently, Ashley has told them I'm harassing her.'

She stared at me, her mouth gawping.

'But they're harassing *me*! That's what I told the police,' I explained, 'and they're doing it as another way to attack me, don't you see? They push me so much, they force me to do this stuff then accuse me of it, and Will can say I'm losing it again.'

Becca was staring at me, the shock plain on her face.

'It's all a plan,' I told her. 'I know you don't think it is, but it's the truth.' I picked up the photocopied newspaper article. 'This,' I told her, 'was given to me by Eve, because they did the same to her. Victimised her. She's having to move her daughter

293

out of school. That's what they did to her, and they're trying to do the same to me, but I won't. I'm stronger than that.'

'As a friend,' she said, 'I'm telling you to stop. Stop it all now.'

I took a deep breath.

'Ruth, whatever you're planning to do, don't. Stop it all—'

'Becca,' I cut in, 'I understand what you're saying, and I know you think you're right, but to be honest, I think you should shut up.'

She blinked rapidly at me.

'You haven't got kids,' I told her. 'You live alone. Only yourself to look after, and you've no idea what it's like. No idea what it is to love someone so much you'd do anything for them. Sam is *my life*,' I said, 'my life, and I'll do whatever it takes to keep him safe and with me.'

The lunch bell rang sharply. Becca needed to be back in her classroom, seeing her children out, doing the numerous things she had to do. She gave a slow nod.

'I see,' she said. 'You think because I'm not a mother, I can't possibly understand? Is that it?'

I nodded. 'I'm sorry, but you can't . . .'

She left while I was still talking, the copy of the newspaper cutting in my hand. Becca had left the room to be diplomatic. It wasn't her son that was in jeopardy. She wasn't in a fight with a sadistic ex-husband and some deranged women. She had no idea.

I went back to my phone, found the picture I'd taken of the newspaper cutting and attached it to an email from the bogus account I'd made up.

This woman currently works illegally for Top Marks. The private tutoring company presently under investigation with HMRC.

294

Becca didn't understand what it was like. She didn't understand that this was needed. Something huge was needed to stop them. And, so what if they knew it was me? I wanted them to know I was responsible, I wanted them to be afraid of what I'd do next.

'Bang!' I hit send.

There were no headlines in the local newspaper when I'd told them about Janine before, but I was pretty sure this would do the trick.

THIRTY

23 AUGUST

I'm surprised more people weren't killed.

When I remember what you did, what we did, I'm surprised that only one person died. The saying goes, revenge is sweet. Revenge is a dish best served cold, but those sayings are clichés. Overused phrases that lack original thought. Revenge isn't sweet, it's bitter. Revenge isn't best served cold, it's best not served at all. Like junk food, the idea of it feels good and the act itself can feel rewarding, but the long-term effects of revenge?

Look at me, locked in here. Look at you, demented out there.

Because I know you will be. Demented. You'll be distraught, the guilt will be killing you. And I realised this just the other day, when I was having a particularly bad time, I thought about how you'd be handling it and it was then that I realised. You aren't handling it, are you? That's why you stay away.

That's why you can't visit, you don't reply. You're in your own prison. Your own hell.

I'm sorry to admit that the thought brought me pleasure. Why is it I can only find release in your misery? So I made a decision. I know you won't reply to this letter. I know you have no intention of replying to any of my letters, but the law says I can send them – if not to you, I can certainly send them to him, and I will.

Only I won't be asking you to visit me any longer. My letters will not ask for forgiveness or beg you to come. They'll only serve one purpose, to remind you of what you did.

I will send you one letter a week for the rest of your life.

Is that my revenge? When in ten years, I'm writing out a similar letter as this to you? Perhaps. These letters will be the one permanent. You can count on me for that. And every time you see my writing on the envelope, every time you see your name, you'll remember.

I'll be the reminder of your murder. I won't let you forget, I'll commit to being trapped in my own cycle of revenge. I'll keep this wound open and fresh. I'll do it for you, for us.

I'll remind us both, every week, exactly what we are, and what we did.

THIRTY-ONE

'Ruth? I wouldn't be calling if it wasn't urgent, please.'

I paused. I still hadn't forgiven my mother, was still bristling a bit with her for lecturing me earlier, but the panic was clear in her voice and I gave a sigh.

'What is it this time?' I asked, and nodded to Sam to get in the car, resigning myself to the fact that I had to talk to her, she was my mother, there was no escape.

It had been a long week, a long term, and I really wanted to get straight home. Becca wasn't talking to me; she'd avoided me for the past week since I'd confessed and I felt bad about it. Uneasy. I could understand that she was a little surprised at what I'd done, but a small part of me was quite pissed off with her. She'd been through it all with me before, but now, when I was finally standing up for myself, where was she? This was the first time that she'd abandoned me. It was the first time I'd done anything assertive, and a part of me wondered if she had a problem with that. If Becca actually preferred me being the victim, someone who needed her help. Perhaps me having such a shit time of it made her feel better about her life and now, well, now I was taking control and it was obvious she didn't like it.

'If it's chest pains again,' I said, as I checked Sam was buckled in, 'then you should call the doctors. I can't help with that.'

'No, no,' my mother's voice was trembling, 'it's something else. I need you to come here, I don't want to say what it is over the phone.'

I straightened up. I could hear real fear in her voice.

'Mum? Is everything OK?'

'Just come here would you, Ruth? Please?'

'I'm on my way,' I told her, 'but you're scaring me a little, Mum. If you've got chest pains—'

'It's not me!' she suddenly said, 'it's something else and I really need you here.'

Twenty minutes later and I was pulling up in her drive, unsure what to expect. As we got out of the car, she was there, at the door.

'What's all this about?' I said, going up to her, Sam at my side. 'You've got me worried, is everything OK?'

'It's Trixie,' she said, and her eyes bubbled with tears. 'Won't come out of her basket.'

It was the bloody dog.

'Mother,' I walked past her, into the lounge where the fire was blazing, the dog's bed right in front of it. 'I drove like a lunatic to get here. I thought you were ill, I thought it was something serious.'

'This is serious!'

Sam immediately went to Trixie, stroking her head and

299

talking softly to her. She was panting, but didn't seem to be in pain.

'How long has she been like this?'

'Since last night, I thought it was something she'd eaten, but she wouldn't get up this morning and she's been like that all day.'

'Trixie!' Her eyes flickered at my voice. 'C'mon,' I asked her, 'c'mon, girl. Out you get, c'mon and play.'

She made a move to get up and then, after a few feeble steps, went back to her basket.

'Is she going to die?' Sam's voice was a whisper.

'I don't know,' I told him, 'but Trixie's pretty old.'

Sam's lip started to tremble.

'You should call the vet,' I told my mother. 'She doesn't seem to be in pain, but this could be anything. She might've just eaten something off.'

'The vet'll put her down.' My mother stuffed a wet tissue to her nose. 'She's fourteen, I know exactly what the vet will do.'

'Trixie's fourteen?'

My mother nodded and I looked at Sam. He wiped his face with the heel of his hand.

'Hey,' I told him, 'just because she's old doesn't mean she's going to die. She might just have a stomach ache. Or feel a bit tired.'

'I told your dad, but he didn't want a puppy. He wanted a dog where all the hard work was done, but now look. He's gone and left me and now the bloody dog is going as well!'

'Mum.' I glanced at Sam.

'Sorry,' she said, 'it's just, well, it's all got on top of me. What with you shouting at me the other day, and then Trixie getting ill.'

300

I went to say something but her body shook as a sob overtook her. Now was not the time to call her dramatic. I put my arms around her instead, her face pressed to my shoulder.

'Cup of tea?' I asked after a while, and I felt her nod.

'You stay with Trixie,' I instructed Sam. 'We're having a cup of tea and then I'll call the vet.'

'You won't!' my mother said, as we went into the kitchen. 'Last time he looked at her, he said she'd not got long and then charged me a hundred pounds just to be told that.'

I said nothing as I boiled the kettle. The dog needed a vet, but what if my mother was right? What if they put the dog down and then charged us for it? I didn't have the money for vet bills.

'She doesn't seem to be in any pain,' I said, more to myself than my mother. 'Not crying or whimpering. We could see how she is in the morning.'

We drank the tea in silence for a while, my mother occasionally dabbing at her eyes. There was an atmosphere and I wasn't sure how to dispel it, or if I wanted to. I sipped my tea and watched her over the rim of my cup.

'Becca called,' my mother said eventually, and I put my drink down.

'Becca called you?'

'She's worried –' she sniffed '– told me she thinks you might be suffering from—'

'I'm not suffering from anything,' I interrupted quickly. 'We had a disagreement. That's all. Becca's not happy with how I handled something and she's making a point.'

I took another drink, slightly bristling at Becca ringing my mother like I was a child. A pupil in her class.

'I can't believe she called you. When was this?'

'Yesterday.'

I watched as she put her tissue in the bin and went to get herself a fresh one. I kept quiet. Waited to see if she would say anything else. Eventually, after a while, she did.

'She told me.'

I gritted my teeth.

'Becca told me that, well, that you slept with one of the parents and might lose your job.'

'What?'

My mother nodded. 'Why couldn't you tell me? I would've understood. I can understand you're ashamed of what you did, him being a married man, but you said you didn't have an affair.'

'I'm not ashamed and it wasn't an affair. It was one night.'

'But Ruth, it explains everything.' She put her hand out. 'That's why all of this is happening to you, isn't it?'

I put my cup down carefully, frightened that if I started to shout at my mother, I might not be able to stop. I was aware of Sam in the next room, of the poorly dog.

'Becca had no right telling you that,' I said quietly. 'A lot of stuff has happened since that morning and it's almost finished now. I've put a stop to it.'

'But that's why Will is so upset,' my mother went on. 'I think, in his own way, he's jealous.'

I was too stunned to answer.

Jealous?

'Men are like that,' my mother went on. 'He might've been the one to have left, but he won't be able to stand the thought of you with someone else. It makes sense, don't you see? That's why he's lashing out. I think he probably still has feelings for you.'

What she was saying was so left field, I couldn't grasp it. It was like something from the 1940s, some kind of weird sexist attitude of 'men will be men'. I stood up, my chair scraping the floor.

'Ruth –' she put her hand out '– please sit down. Don't go again. I'm sorry. I need you, I'm upset about the dog. I'm upset about you going through all this with Will. I'm upset about what it's all doing to Sammy. And –' she gave a weak smile '– I've tried to fix it.'

I stared at her, still standing. She had that look on her face, the one where she thinks she's been clever. The kind of look she used to give me when she'd got some herbal remedy for my dad that somebody had sworn by. The kind of look I knew to be wary of.

'I've not slept, with the worry,' she went on. 'It was eating me up. I had to do something. I'm so worried about you, about Sammy. And after what Becca told me, well, it all made sense. So don't get mad, just give it a chance, that's all I'm asking. Just five minutes.'

'Mother,' my voice was low, 'what have you done?'

'Just five minutes,' she begged and her face quivered. 'After Becca called, I knew what I had to do. And he thought it was an excellent idea. He's been trying to contact you. He wants to talk, don't you see, Ruth? He wants to talk, to sort it all out.'

'You didn't?' I shook my head, stared at her a moment in shock. 'Tell me you didn't?'

She didn't answer, her lip quivered and fresh tears sprang to her eyes.

'And as Trixie is poorly today, well, I knew you'd come.' A tear rolled down her cheek that she quickly wiped away. 'It'll be fine. Trust me, Ruth. I've done the right thing.'

'For God's sake, Mother!' I shouted. 'When will you stop interfering?' I snatched up my bag. 'Sam, get your coat! We're leaving. Now.'

But it was too late, as I walked into the hallway, ready to sweep Sam up and shove him in the car, I saw he was standing at the window, his eyes wide, his face pale.

I looked out to what he was staring at and saw Will's silver BMW coming up the drive.

'Mum!' Sam looked at me, his eyes wide with terror.

I turned to my mother. 'What have you done?'

THIRTY-TWO

'He's not coming in.' I gripped Sam by the shoulders. He was shaking and then I realised it was probably me, I was probably the one who was shaking or maybe we both were. Trixie looked up from her basket and started to bark. A piercing little effort. She sensed our anxiety and was being vocal about it.

Will pulled up outside the house. He was dressed as if he'd come straight from the office – light navy suit, shiny shoes, official looking. He took out a file from the passenger seat and a familiar gut-wrenching feeling swept over me. A tight clench of anxiety and panic rising from the pit of my stomach. He looked up to the house, saw me and Sam staring at him through the window, and raised his hand in greeting.

I turned to my mother. 'This is not happening,' I said quickly. 'Sam, get your coat. Now.'

'Ruth –' her voice had a quiver to it '– Ruth, please, just give him a minute. Give him time to talk.'

'I can't believe you've done this,' I said, gathering up my

bag and my keys as I helped Sam on with his coat. 'I really can't believe you've invited him here, that you'd think I'd talk to him.'

The dog was yapping now, clearly not at death's door, and my mother bent over to her.

'Trixie, there's a good girl. Look, Sam! She's OK, she's not that ill after all.'

Sam was torn between celebrating the dog's sudden energy and being terrified of Will coming in. I grabbed his hand.

'We've got to go, honey,' I told him, and my mother took his other hand.

'Stay,' she told me. 'Really, Ruth. I spoke to him, after Becca called. He told me about what you did, with that woman's husband, and how it's all just got out of control. He told me that he just wants to talk, that he might drop the whole thing. Get rid of his solicitor. That woman.'

That stopped me for a moment. The thought of Ashley no longer helping Will. Maybe she'd got rid of him, after what I'd done to her, with all the threats from the animal activists. Maybe she'd got scared. Frightened of what I might do next, and told Will that she wouldn't take on his case after all.

My mood swung from panic to curiosity. There was a knock at the door and I stared at my mother, frozen momentarily.

'Mum?' Sam's voice was a whisper. 'Mummy?'

'We're leaving,' I said loudly, and then, to my mother, 'we're leaving right now.'

'Hello?' Will, not one for waiting outside, had let himself in. He stood like a giant barring the doorway, and for a moment we all stared at each other. Suspended in some ludicrous pose, the only sound the dog yapping repeatedly from her basket.

'We're not doing this,' I told him. 'My mother had no right to invite you here like I was going to talk to you. Sam, let's go.'

'Ruth –' Will held his hands aloft '– just give me a minute. That's all I'm asking for, a minute. Hey, buddy –' he bent down to Sam '– how're you? Feeling OK?'

I pushed Sam so he was behind me.

'We're not staying,' I told Will. 'We're not talking to you.' I could feel Sam shaking behind me, I could feel his terror.

'Your mother asked me to come here,' Will said, straightening up. 'We both think we can come to an agreement. This is the sensible thing to do, Ruth. This is the best thing for Sam.'

I turned to her. She stood by the couch, a mass of angst.

'Ruth, just calm down,' he said, and that was a phrase I thought I'd never hear from him again. It was a tactic he used back when we were married. He used to tell me to 'calm down', 'stop panicking' and 'chill out', making me believe that I was being hysterical when I wasn't. It had the effect of making me stop and check myself.

'Out of my way, Will,' I said in a low voice. 'We'll do all the talking in court.'

'This isn't good for Sam,' he said, and as I inched forward, he didn't move.

'Mummy?' Sam's voice was small, tiny.

'It's all right, son, your mum will calm down in a minute.'

I felt rage build inside. I was calm. I was totally calm. He was doing it again, making me check myself, doubt myself.

'Will,' I said, 'move. Now.'

'Ruth.' My mother touched my elbow and I shrugged her off; I'd deal with her later. 'Ruth, just give him five minutes, just to talk.'

I stepped forward and, as I did, Will moved towards us. Sam jumped back in a panic and, as he stumbled back, he went right into Trixie, who had crawled out of her basket. He stood on her front paw and her high-pitched howl cut through the room.

'Trixie!' Sam dropped to the floor as the dog whimpered.

'Take her in the kitchen,' my mother told Sam. 'Take her in there while your mum and dad talk for a minute.'

'Mother . . .' I warned, but Sam was cradling the dog, looking at me, his face close to Trixie.

'I stood on her paw, I can't leave her,' he began, his eyes wide with panic, and I let out a deep sigh. I shook my head. 'Let's take her in the kitchen,' I told him. 'It's all right. It was an accident. Calm down.'

I turned to Will. 'Looks like you've got your five minutes.'

Trixie was fine. It was a combination of the shock of Sam hurting her paw combined with the excitement of the energy in the room. A moment later and she fell asleep on Sam's knee as he ate chocolate biscuits from the tin. I'd assured him that we'd be five minutes, no more.

'But what will you say to Dad?' Sam asked. 'Don't let him take me. Don't let him.'

I leaned forward and kissed his forehead. 'Not a chance,' I told him. 'Don't you worry. I told you, the only place you're going is home, with me.'

He gave me a smile, but still looked worried and as I gently closed the door on him I wondered what on earth I was doing. Why wasn't I just scooping up that boy (and dog if need be) and running away? Far away, anywhere.

My mother caught me before we went into the lounge, where Will was waiting. 'I'm glad you're doing this,' she whispered. 'You hate me for it, I know you do, but it'll work out. Just give it a chance.'

I glared at her, saying nothing. I was aware of Will sitting a few feet away listening to our every word.

'Ruth.' He was sitting in my father's armchair, the one by the window. We never used it, never went near it, and it jolted me a little to see his large frame in there. As he knew it would.

'Could I have a moment alone with your lovely daughter, please?'

I turned to my mother, then, after a moment, gave her a nod. 'Go sit with Sam,' I told her, 'make sure he's all right. Make sure the dog's all right. This won't take long.'

Will took a moment, waiting until my mother had left the room.

'Ruth, despite what you think, I'm doing this in the best interests of our son. Remember how you were before?' I immediately wanted to smash my fist into his face at the patronising tone of his voice. 'You imagined all sorts back then, you thought I was trying—'

'And I was right,' I said levelly, 'you *were* having an affair.'

'I was. Fair enough. But it wasn't what you imagined,' Will said. 'I wasn't telling everyone, broadcasting it, we weren't laughing about it with all of our friends. I was very upset about it. Your conspiracy theory of—'

'I don't need to hear all this again,' I snapped. 'We're not here to talk about what you did.'

Will went to his file. He opened it up and took out some papers, A4, printed.

'All things considered,' Will said, 'Sam should stay with me.' He glanced up. 'And I've got the reasons here as to why.' He looked at me steadily. 'Let me make it clear, I don't care what you've done. What you do with your life. I only care about Sam. My son. And if you're prepared to be reasonable, and just listen, you'll see it's the best thing for Sam.'

I gripped the edge of the sofa, my knuckles white.

'Sit down,' Will said. 'You need to hear this, Ruth, or I'll have to tell it all to the police and I really don't want to do that.'

'*Police?*' I spat out the word.

'I'm prepared to discuss when Sam should stay with you,' Will went on, 'but that would have to be after a period of about six months, then we'll see how you are. What state you're in, and I'll decide if you're fit for Sam to be with you again.'

I let out a laugh.

'I know what you've been doing,' he said, and I shook my head. 'I know all of it, Ruth, and like I said, I'd rather tell it to you now, and come to an agreement here, rather than have to go to the police.'

I sighed dramatically. 'This is pathetic,' I said. 'I'm leaving.'

'You slept with Janine's husband,' he began, 'boasted to her about it, humiliated her. You sent her husband a threatening text. You contacted HMRC and falsely reported Janine for tax evasion.' He looked up and smiled. 'Told you,' he said, 'I know it all, so sit down.' He went back to his paper. 'You called the local paper, tried to start a scandal over it. You then threatened Lisa, Sam's class teacher, as well as stealing from her.'

'Hardly stealing,' I said. 'It was a pen, and—' He held his hand up.

'After threatening his class teacher,' he spoke over me, 'and stealing from the school, you took our son out of school and kept him home for no good reason. You then targeted Ashley Simmons. You went into her place of work and shouted obscenities, then posted a picture of Ashley Simmons and published her name and address on an animal rights forum, claiming she was a "cunt who hunts".'

My heart started to knock against my ribs. *How did he know this? How did he know what I'd done?*

'You used your position as school secretary to gather information about her, confidential information. You also called the local newspaper again, claiming you had details about one of the tutors who works for Top Marks, Janine's company, alleging that she is a paedophile.'

He put the paper down and looked at me. 'False,' he said, 'complete fabrication and total slander.'

There was a pounding in my head now. I could feel it with every thump of my heart.

'That woman is not employed by Janine,' he told me. 'She employs someone with the same name, but it isn't her.' He gave a laugh. 'Do you really think Janine wouldn't do checks on everyone she employs? Do you think she's like you? Half arsed about everything?'

My thoughts skittered. They went to Eve, when she handed me the paper, to her texts. Was she lying? Is that why she hadn't been in contact since?

'She is employing her,' I said, 'the lady who—'

'Ruth,' his voice was low, 'you've already got a complaint against you for harassment.'

I gripped the couch. Looked at his neatly typed list.

'You lied about taking Sam to Disney,' he went on, 'you lie a lot to Sam. You told him the vandalism on your car wasn't anything to be afraid of, but it is, isn't it, Ruth? It is something to be afraid of—'

'I haven't—'

'Because you did that to your car, didn't you?'

311

I took a shocked gasp.

'Just like you've been pretending to get text messages and parcels through your letterbox. You're pretending to be harassed, pretending someone is stalking you when, really, you're the stalker. You're the one who is mentally unhinged.'

I was silent for a moment. Unable to comprehend what he was accusing me of.

'Is this you?' I spat out eventually. 'How do you know all this? Is it you who's doing it all?'

'Have you any idea what you've done to those poor women?'

'Those poor women?' I could hardly say the words. 'Have you any idea what they've been doing to me?'

'Janine and Ashley? You've stalked them in an effort to look like the victim.' He shook his head. 'Ruth, you could go to jail for this.'

'None of it is true!' I said and stood up. 'It's all lies. Someone is sending me messages, parcels, letters. Someone did do that to my car!'

'You've done it all on the school computer,' he said calmly, as if I was a child. 'They couldn't find the IP address of who posted that information on the animal rights group, but if they look on the school computer, they'll find the VPN software you downloaded, won't they? The software you had to download so you could post anonymously. It'll all be on there. They just need a reason to search the school computer.'

He held up his piece of paper and my heart picked up speed.

'You saw how Ashley helped me, how quick she was to defend her friend. What do you think she'll do to you when she knows you're responsible for her living in terror?'

I tried to swallow, but my throat was dry.

'You see, because of your history, you've made it really easy for people to hate you. So, I'm here to offer you something else. You can either go it alone, and I tell Ashley and Janine exactly what you've been up to, which will include the police confiscating the school computer. I should imagine it would be immediate dismissal, then Ashley would press charges, which would inevitably result in some kind of jail time. You would lose your house –' he ticked them off on his fingers as he said them '– your job, your money, your daft little cake business and your freedom.' He smiled. 'So Sam would come to me by default anyway, but it could take some time, or –' he took a deep breath '– you let Sam come to me now, and I keep quiet. Forget what I know while you wipe clean the school computer and have time to clear your tracks.' He shrugged. 'Either way, I'm getting our boy. I just thought I should offer you this chance first.'

I was silent. My heart thumping, the blood rushing in my ears. Outside a siren rang out and then disappeared in the distance.

'How do you know all that?' I asked quietly. 'It's you, isn't it? The red Fiat last night, the texts, the letter, the slashed tyres. All that has been you, hasn't it?'

'Are you becoming paranoid again, Ruth?' He faked concern. 'Conspiracy theories again? Should we make an appointment with the doctors, get you on some antidepressants? Maybe get you checked out by a psychiatrist? Get you sectioned this time?'

'I think you should leave now,' I said, and could hear the panic in my voice. 'Right now.'

Will took a moment. 'You're going to do this? After what I've just told you?'

I was silent. My heart was thrumming, my head pounding.

'I'm going to leave and go straight to Ashley, you know that. She'll have the police at your door within the hour.'

'Get out,' I said, and folded my arms tight to stop the shaking.

'I'll contact the social,' he said, standing up, 'tell them you're mentally ill, tell them about your stalking and inventing a stalker of your own.'

'GET OUT!'

He stood a moment, then shook his head.

'See you soon, Sam!' he shouted. 'Won't be long, buddy, you won't have to stay with the lunatic for much more.'

We watched him leave, his car screeching in reverse. My mother was pale. She'd come beside me as I was screaming at Will to get out of the house. We'd not spoken a word.

'Is it true?'

'You were listening?'

'Hard not to.'

We took a moment.

'He promised he was going to talk about an agreement for Sammy. He didn't say any of that.'

We stayed at the window. Will had left but we were frozen, looking out on the empty driveway.

'The animal rights forum?' she almost whispered. 'Ruth, did you put a woman's home address on there? Tell them to terrorise her?'

I stared out of the window.

'What did they do? Did they go to her house? Has she got children?'

I didn't answer.

'And that other woman, the one whose husband you slept with. You told the papers she was employing paedophiles? Ruined her business? Has she got children?'

'I did it for Sam,' I said, and heard her sigh at the side of me.

'Oh, Ruth,' she said, and I felt myself prickle. 'How could you stoop to—'

'I did it for Sam, OK? Those women, they were terrorising me, slashing my tyres, sending me texts, they were—'

'But didn't you just say that was Will? How do you know it was those women?'

'You don't understand,' I told her, 'they did things. They were—'

'But to do that to them, to ruin their homes, their businesses—'

'You don't understand.' I turned to her, rubbed my hands over my face. 'I had no choice. I had to do it for Sam.'

She stared at me and I looked away. I felt small, like I was child and had been found out.

'Ruth—'

'We'll talk about it later,' I snapped. 'Right now I need to get to the school before he does. Before he talks to Ashley. I'm going to ring Gary, the caretaker. He owes me a favour, I'll see if he can let me into school, then I'm going to clean up the computer of any evidence as best I can. Then I'm going to work out how Will knew all of that stuff and who told him.'

'I don't understand how you could do that to those poor women,' my mother went on, 'Ruth, what you did—'

'For Sam,' I said, grabbing my phone, 'I did it for Sam.' I went to the door. 'Tell him I've had to nip out, for some food. Tell him anything. I'll be an hour at most. Don't open the door, don't answer the phone and don't let Sam out of your sight.'

THIRTY-THREE

My hands were shaking slightly as I drove. It was silly, but I hadn't really done that much, had I? I'd used the school computer and confidential information when I should have been working. Yes, that was not allowed. I'd posted on a forum, but really, it wasn't a war crime, was it? It wasn't like Will was making out, like I'd committed some heinous deed that warranted me being sent to prison. Or how my mother made me feel. The way she looked at me.

You couldn't be sent to jail for posting some message online, could you? I thought about Ashley calling the police, her address on the forum, and I thought about my mother asking if she had children, and for a moment I remembered Sam's panicked face when he saw our car. His wide eyes, the way he'd cried. Did Ashley's children cry like that?

I'd made phone calls to HMRC, to the paper, about Janine's business. Rob had left her. There would be rumours that she employed paedophiles as tutors, not doing her criminal checks properly. I thought about her two daughters as I drove towards the school, how they'd be affected if her business went under, and my stomach churned.

Gary hadn't replied to my text and I needed to get to the computer before Will told Ashley and she contacted the police. I had no idea if what he said was right, if they would confiscate the school computer like I'd seen them do on the television crime dramas and go through it for evidence, but I couldn't take the chance. I'd break into school if I had to and steal it myself.

I put my phone on hands free and tried to ring Gary again as I drove. No answer. I was sweating. I tried another number. It was answered on the third ring.

'Becca?'

'Ruth,' her voice had a flatness to it and I remembered that we'd fallen out. That she'd called my mother and told her what I did. That we were still in the thick of an argument.

'Becca, listen, I really need your help.'

There was a pause.

'Please,' I said, navigating the traffic as I begged. 'I know we're not really speaking, but I need to get into school. Now.'

'It's Friday night,' she said with a sigh.

'I know, but I need to get in. I've left something in my office and I can't get hold of Gary. I've only got his home number, but have you got his mobile?'

She made a funny sound, like she was finding it hard to understand me. 'Why would I have Gary's mobile? Ruth, what's going on?'

'I just need to get something from my office!' There was a real urgency to my tone and Becca must have heard it.

'Well, hang on, doesn't the residential leave tonight? They'll be in, the school will be open.'

'Of course!' I flicked on my indicator, ready to take the main road that would lead me to the school.

'Ruth, are you all right?'

'I will be,' I told her. 'It's just Will, being an utter bastard. Come around later? I need to explain, to apologise and –' I paused '– I need your advice. I think I might be in trouble.'

'OK,' her voice softened, 'I can be at yours for about eight?'

'Perfect.'

It had started to rain, the kind of light shower that doesn't look menacing until you're outside and soaked in seconds. I was going through the city centre, the traffic painfully slow, and as I got to the quieter roads that led to the school, I could see cars parked everywhere. Parents lifting small cases out of cars and children dressed as if ready to climb up Mount Everest. A swarm of brightly coloured jackets and travel bags. It was perfect, a crowd of fussing parents, a mass of giddy children, all saying their goodbyes, all laughing and chattering. I could slip in and out without anyone noticing.

I went into the school just as Gary was starting to lock up.

'Won't be a second!' I said, running past him, 'I just left something in my office!'

'Two minutes,' he shouted after me, and I shut the door behind me and switched on the computer, my hands sweating. I had no real idea how to wipe a computer hard drive, or what needed doing. I'd taken no notice of how to uninstall the VPN software when I'd downloaded it, I didn't think I'd need to. I began by wiping all the history and cookies, then frantically did a search on how to uninstall the software. After a few minutes, I brought it up on the computer, right clicked and almost cheered when the option to uninstall the application appeared. I could've cried with relief.

As I was waiting for it to uninstall, my phone pinged. A notification. I snatched it up quickly, imagining it was my mother, calling about Sam.

You will lose everything. Stupid bitch.

Now I knew Will was behind the texts, it was obvious. He was so stupid. Trying to insinuate that these were a figment of my imagination yet sending me another as soon as he could. I growled at the phone.

Thank you for this text,

I wrote back.

It's proof that you are pathetic. Fuck off, Will.

I threw the phone on the desk. The computer was still doing what it had to and I stared at it, listening to the shouts from outside, while the panicky feeling built in my chest. Now that I'd thought of Ashley's children, of those two girls of Janine's, I couldn't get the thought of them out of my head. Along with my mother's face and her questions. Of all people, she should've been the one who understood, and yet she'd looked at me in such a way that I felt ashamed. I could hear someone crying outside, a child that didn't want to go.

There was movement behind the window, a shadow.

'Sorry,' I said, getting up, 'this part of the school's closed . . .'

I went to the door and stopped when I saw him.

'Thought it was you,' he smiled, a full grin that showed his dimples. 'You come to say goodbye? To see me off?'

I closed my eyes. I'd completely forgotten that as the year five teacher, Glen would obviously be going on the residential.

'I knew you'd forgotten,' he said, coming towards me. 'Can't say I'm not disappointed. I'm only back Tuesday evening, remember? So if you're not here for me, what are you here for? And where's Sam?' He walked into my office, brushing by me as he went. I could smell his aftershave, the faint polish from his hiking boots. 'Ruth?'

He was standing in front of the computer, the screen clearly showing the settings, the programs, the bar that detailed the progress of the software I was uninstalling.

'What you up to?'

I shook my head.

He folded his arms. 'The secretary, in her office at six on a Friday night, uninstalling software from the school computer.' He tilted his head. 'Have you been watching porn?'

Under normal circumstances I would've burst out laughing, I would've found it funny. I registered that he was making a joke, but there was no humour in me.

'Hey –' he came over to me '– what's wrong?'

I opened my mouth to tell him, about all the evidence that Will had. How someone close to me must have told him. And then a wave of nausea washed over me as I realised who it was. The hurt so raw that it almost took my breath away.

'It's you,' I said. 'You're the one who's been telling Will everything about me. Helping him build up his case so he can take Sam away.'

Glen was silent for a moment, and then: 'Ruth, what are you talking about?'

'Just admit it. Was it all lies? Everything you told me?'

'Will? Your ex-husband?' Glen shook his head. 'I don't even know him, wouldn't know what he looked like.'

'Is that why you got the job here?' I pressed. 'So you could find out things about me and report back to Will? It makes sense now, my life all began to unravel when you started working here. How do you know him? The rugby club, is that it? You and him good mates, are you? I'll bet you're even friends with Rob and Janine.'

'Ruth –' he came over and gripped me by the shoulders '– you're making no sense. I haven't been spying on you for anyone. I got the job because the agency told me there was a short-term vacancy at the school. What's going on?'

I took a deep breath. Searched his face. My stomach was a tight knot, my throat closed up and for a moment I wanted to lean on him. To crumble into his shoulder.

'I just saw Will,' I told him, 'and he knows everything I've been doing and he's going to use it to get Sam, to take Sam away from me. He's gone to Ashley now, that solicitor. Someone has been helping him, and I thought it might be you.'

'You think I might be a friend of Will's?' He frowned. 'I have never met Will, wouldn't know him if I fell over him.' He paused. 'And you think I came here so I could spy on you? Go to the trouble of getting a job, of getting to know you, of taking you out, all so I could report back to your ex-husband?'

I stared at him – hearing him say it, explain it like that, made me sound paranoid. Will's voice about my conspiracy theories loomed in my mind, the way he'd called me delusional, the way he'd threatened to get me sectioned.

'And why? Why would I do all that?' Glen asked. 'What would be in it for me? I'd have to be some friend to go to all that trouble.'

I shook my head, wiped my face. Everything was mixed

up. It had seemed very real a moment ago, and now I couldn't see anything clearly. I thought it was right to do what I did to Janine and Ashley, but now, after hearing Will state it like that, so matter of fact, after seeing my mother's face, I wasn't sure what was right any more.

'I'm sorry,' I said. 'I just know someone has been telling him what I've been doing.'

Glen was silent for a moment. 'And what is that? What've you been doing?'

I looked away. The computer screen was blank, the uninstall complete.

'I have to go,' I told him. 'I need to get Sam.'

'Ruth, will you tell me what's going on? What have you done? What does Will know?'

I grabbed my bag and jacket. I could hear the rumble of the coach engine outside, Gary's whistle as he came closer, I could hear him banging doors closed.

'Ruth –' Glen put his hand out, stopping me from leaving '– are you in trouble?'

I paused for a moment.

'I think so,' I whispered. 'I think I might be in a lot of trouble. I think I took that stick you gave me, to prod at them with, and somehow it changed into a shotgun.'

Glen's eyes went wide for a moment.

'I think I might have done some terrible things,' I said quietly. 'It went too far and I don't think I can undo them.'

'Mr Harrow?' It was the teaching assistant, peering around the door. 'We really need to leave. Oh! Hello, Ruth.'

I rushed past him, left him explaining what we were doing in my office, why the school computer was on, and as I got to my car tears were streaming down my face.

I'd lost my job. I figured that was pretty much certain, but I'd also lost the only man who I'd been interested in for years. The only man who understood me, who understood Sam, who I could've imagined a life with. Once he heard what I'd done, how I'd behaved, his face would take on the same expression that my mother's had. And that was something that I didn't want to see.

My phone pinged. A text notification. I grabbed it, even though I was driving, and stared at the message.

You daft cow. Don't you think we already have what we need from the computer? Your life is over.

THIRTY-FOUR

The traffic was terrible. It was rush hour. A Friday evening. Will had most likely informed Ashley or Janine, and what would they be doing now? Would the police be waiting for me by the time I got back to my mother's? By the time I collected Sam, would they be waiting for me at my house?

I stopped at the traffic lights. I felt shaky as adrenalin coursed through me. The message from Will said they already had everything off the school computer. Had they made a copy? Been in there before me? Was it possible that Janine could've gone into the office?

I broke out in a sweat as I realised that Janine would've been there, at the school. Waving her daughter off, and probably nipping in to the school office to get all the evidence they needed off the school computer. And there was CCTV. That would have just recorded me rushing into school, rushing into my office. Was that proof? Is that how they knew? And if the police didn't take action, what then?

I needed time. I needed to talk it out with my mother, with Becca. Explain it all to them, exactly what I did and why, and see how I could go forward, but one thing was sure: I wasn't staying at home. I'd collect Sam's things and we'd stay somewhere else. My mother's or, even better, one of the many bed and breakfasts in the city.

I drove blindly, only thinking how Will could have known. I'd been sloppy. Given it away somehow. He must have been spying on me since that morning outside the school gates when I first saw Rob, since it all happened. Keeping notes on everything he heard, making a complete picture of all of my actions. But I couldn't see how it was possible – no one knew everything. And then my mind swung to Glen, his horrified expression as he caught me wiping the school computer. How he'd asked what I'd done. What must he think of me?

I pulled up to my house, went to my door. Fumbling with the keys, mentally making a list of the things I needed to get together.

'Excuse me.'

She was nondescript. Navy blue jacket, black pants, walking boots. She held a purple umbrella and was studying a slip of paper.

I realised that she'd been wandering up and down the street, looking a little lost since I'd arrived. I'd noticed her when I pulled in.

'Sorry,' I told her, as I fiddled with my keys. 'I don't own any of the properties here. If it's a holiday let you're staying in, if you rented one from ...'

'I'm looking for Ruth, Ruth Clarkson? She's the secretary at the school down Maple Lane?'

I paused.

'Are you Ruth?' She looked at me expectantly.

'I really need to get in,' I said, and went back to my keys.

'You are Ruth?'

'Sorry,' I told her, 'not me, don't know her.'

'Your son, is he called Sam?'

I looked at her.

'You are Ruth,' she said, and stood a little straighter, sticking out her chest slightly as she took a deep breath, 'and your son, Sam, is in the same class as mine. I'm Nicole. Nicole Morley-Fenn, Toby's mum.'

'Oh.'

I felt my stomach slide away a little and went to open my door, but she put her hand out, preventing me from opening it fully.

'You spoke to him, in the playground the other week.'

I shook my head. The street was empty, dark.

'And now I've come here to speak to you.'

No tourists were in their lodgings, no one was leaving the house carrying maps and rucksacks. We were alone.

'I haven't got time for this,' I told her, 'you don't understand, I need to go. Right now.'

She made a surprised sound similar to a laugh. 'Did you hear me? Do you know who I am? I need to speak to you, about what you did to my son.'

'I didn't do anything,' I said, and could feel sweat begin to build at the back of my neck. She was small, but insistent and strong. There was no way to move her easily.

'I really need to get inside,' I told her. 'I'm in a hurry. If there's a problem, if it's to do with the school, then you need to come in after half term and speak to the headteacher, John. It's not something I can deal with now . . .'

326

'Wait until after half term?' Her voice was shrill and the sudden loudness of it shocked me.

'Wait until then to talk about how you got my boy by the arm? You were the reason he wet himself that day. He finally told me. After days of him suffering, he told me tonight. Told me what you did. And now you're asking me to wait until after half term? I don't want to wait until then for answers, I want answers now. From you about what you did.'

'I didn't do anything,' I said, 'and if you'll excuse me, I need to get inside my house.'

'Who does that?' she hissed, her face close to mine. 'Who threatens a little boy like that?'

I lifted my key, went to put it in the lock, but she batted it away. My keys fell on the pavement with a loud clatter. She stared at me, her eyes flashing anger, her cheeks flushed. I couldn't believe that she was here, shouting these words at me, now of all times. I checked down the empty street once more for signs of other people, anyone.

'I can't talk to you about this now!' I almost shouted, and her eyes went wide. Her mouth became a thin line and she gripped my wrist.

'Oh, you've got time,' she told me. 'You can't do that to my son and then tell me you haven't got time to talk about it. Tell me how busy you are.'

I went to pull away but she held me tight.

'You're the school secretary, aren't you? The one that's been sleeping around. How dare you do that to my son.'

She shook slightly as she spoke, and in the dim light of the street lamp I could see that she was furious.

'I'm sorry,' I began, 'but I really need to—'

'He's terrified,' she hissed. 'Bloody terrified of how you

grabbed him and how he wet himself. Do you know what that means to a boy like him? What damage you did?'

I tried to pull free again and then, when she still didn't release her grip, I shoved her away with my other hand.

'I'm sorry,' I said as I bent to collect my keys, 'but I really don't have time for this now. I've got to . . .' I felt a sharp pain in my right side and fell backwards.

She'd kicked me, and as I looked up I saw she was swinging her leg ready for another go. Her walking boot taking aim. The pain was hard, banging into my ribs. She bent down, her face close to mine.

'Toby is a gentle boy,' she said. 'He wouldn't hurt a fly and your son, he's huge. You think you can get away with it because you work in a school? Because Toby isn't clever? I'm going to the council. You shouldn't be working near kids, and I'm not waiting around for that fat bastard who calls himself the head to fire you. I'm going to the council on Monday to get you fired. But right now, I'm going to the police.'

She stepped back, staring at me. I was in the doorway, clutching my sides.

'I didn't believe it when Toby told me. I thought it was horrendous, couldn't believe someone could do that to an eight-year-old boy, and especially not the school secretary. He's having such a hard time, and now this? Now you do this to him? My husband wanted to come here, wanted to do this to you, but I told him not to.'

She swung her leg back for a final kick, but thought better of it.

'I told him we must have it wrong, that Toby must've got things mixed up, but now I see. You stand there, not wanting to talk to me, telling me you haven't got time to hear about how you terrorised my son. I thought you'd apologise. I was prepared to hear your side of it, give you a chance, let you say sorry, but this? You should be ashamed of yourself.'

As she walked away, I saw her take out her mobile phone.

My legs were shaking as I got up. I opened the door, wincing at the pain in my side and almost fell into my house. I shut the door, locked it, pulled across the dead bolt and took a moment, leaning against the wall.

I gave myself a minute, a minute of pure self-pity and crying into my hands. I let myself howl and shudder. I thought of Glen's face when he found out about this, me terrorising a little boy. I thought how my mother would look at me. This was the one thing that Will didn't know and now Toby's mother was on the way to the police herself.

A wave of shame washed over me. How could I argue my case? Tell them that it'd all been for Sam? I felt the pain in my side from where she'd kicked me, the heat on my face, and then shook my head. I didn't have time for self-pity now, I needed to get out, before the police or, even worse, Toby's parents, came back.

I knew one thing, I would never be able to face Glen again.

THIRTY-FIVE

By the time I arrived back at my mother's, I was something close to calm. It's funny, but when the worst happens and you think you'll fall into a zillion pieces, you don't. You accept it. Or at least, that's what I thought I was doing. A kind of defeated calm had settled over me.

I'd hurriedly got together a few things, a change of clothes for me and Sam, some of his toys and a few of my toiletries. I suddenly realised that I had a lot of enemies. Enemies with big boots that weren't afraid of kicking.

I planned to stay at my mother's that evening, and tomorrow I'd look at some other properties to rent. We'd get somewhere out of Carlisle, I was thinking. There was no use in Sam staying at school. I wasn't going to be there. I would home school him, we'd find somewhere closer to my mother's, somewhere over the border. Or, even better, I'd persuade my mother to sell up. We'd move, leave the area altogether.

As I drove to my mother's cottage I was finding a small

comfort in the image of me and Sam out in the sticks somewhere, him running about the fields. Telling myself that maybe
we'd get a dog of our own, a young one, he'd love that. I was
slowly building a new version of the future.

Becca would be angry about it all, but I'd get her to understand. She could never stay mad at me for long. I'd talk to her.
I'd ask her to meet me at my mother's that evening, rather than
home, and then over a glass of wine, before everything kicked
off, I'd tell her my plans. She'd been there for me when my
life fell apart last time; I just hoped she'd be there for me now.
That she'd forgive me. I might not be able to face Glen again,
but I couldn't lose Becca.

It would look bad on her, I knew that, considering that she
was the one to get me the job at the school. She knew all about
texts I was getting, the letters and packages, and offered her
usual sound advice. Why hadn't I listened? It was Becca who
told me not to retaliate, Becca who told me to go to the police
and keep a low profile, even when it was apparent that the
police weren't doing anything.

And when I told her what I'd done, it was Becca who said
I'd gone too far. She knew it all and yet had still agreed to meet
and hear my side and, I suddenly realised, with everything
that was going on over the last few weeks, I knew nothing
about her. Nothing about her new man. I didn't even know
his name. I'd been the worst kind of friend to her since all
this had started, and I shook my head at how self-involved
I'd been. Only a few short months ago I was interested in
everything about her. Even her shopping trips, asking to see
what she'd bought from town, oohing and ahhing over every
little purchase . . .

The air left my body as I thought back, remembering Becca

in my living room, arms full of shopping bags. As she pulled out new dresses, designer handbags and boots. New boots. Small heel, tassels at the back. The very same boots that Sam had photographed when he was at Will's house.

'No,' I whispered. 'That can't be possible?'

Becca's flat was in the city centre, close to where I was, and I swerved down a side street, going back on myself to get there. As I indicated left, I remembered her face after Janine had thrown her phone at me, when I told her about the text, how she'd told me to do nothing. When the first package had arrived, the second, the person in the red Fiat. Becca was the only one who knew it all.

I drove to her flat quickly, my palms sweating. I hardly ever went to Becca's as it was close to the centre. Too busy an area and too many people around. I swung into the car park and my foot hit the brake, hard. I swung forward. My mouth open in shock, my heart rattling in my chest.

In the space allotted to her flat was a BMW.

Will's BMW.

I let out a low moan.

'No,' I whispered as I got out. I didn't want to be right. I didn't want my paranoia to be correct this time, but the proof was right in front of me. I got out slowly and went over to it, peered in the driver's window. On the passenger seat was a jacket, navy blue, silk lining, same jacket that he'd been wearing when I saw him at my mother's.

I leaned against the car for support, the wind had been taken out of me. I was having trouble taking breath in, could feel a pounding in my head as my heart picked up its pace. Will and Becca. *Will and Becca*. No. Not possible. The world closed in around me, the sky bearing down as I pictured them together.

Four years ago, when I told Becca what Will had been doing, she was horrified. She was the one who sat up with me as I cried through the night, she was the one who was there after I'd been to his mistress's house and thrown a brick through her window. She was the one who'd helped me, who'd been loyal. Becca was mine.

'It's not what you think.' She was stood in the doorway, her face full of concern. 'Ruth, really. It's not what you think.'

I straightened and then, there he was, Will. Behind her, in her flat. Without his shoes, his socked feet on her carpet. I let out a wail.

'Ruth,' she said again, 'let me explain. This is not what it looks like.'

I walked in slowly. Becca's flat is a decent size, but all open plan. Perfect for one or two people, but any more in there and it suddenly seems small, and I felt claustrophobic as I stood in the centre of the room. My heart was knocking, my ribs aching from earlier. I felt light-headed, dizzy. They'd been drinking coffee, the smell of it in the air. Two cups on the table along with Will's file.

'You've been telling him,' I said, looking at it, 'you've been telling Will everything.'

She stared at me for a moment.

'Will was just leaving,' she said.

'No I wasn't,' he said, and looked at Becca. 'It's gone on long enough,' he said. 'It's not worked, so tell her. Just tell her.'

I turned to face Becca. She was staring at me, unblinking, her eyes watering.

I closed my eyes briefly; the thrumming of my heart was making my body shake. When I opened them, she was still staring at me. I marched past her.

'Ruth,' she called after me as I went out of the lounge and into her bedroom. She tried to grab me as I opened her drawers, opened her wardrobe.

'Ruth, please.'

I didn't listen. I made my way out of the bedroom and into the bathroom and I flung open the cabinet, the storage under the sink and then, knowing exactly where I should be looking, I went back into the bedroom. She was behind me, her hands grabbing me, her fingers clutching at me, and I opened the bedside drawer and there it was. Will's alarm. A small box-like digital alarm that he always took with him to every holiday, every weekend away, a 'back up' he called it, and there it was in Becca's bedside drawer.

I turned to her and she shook her head.

'I'm so sorry,' she whispered, and then screamed as I threw the clock at her. It shattered against the wall.

'You,' I said, 'all this time. You've been my friend and then telling him everything, spying on me *for him*. So he can have Sam.' I reeled as the whole thing suddenly became evident. 'You,' I said, 'you want Sam, is that it?'

She raised her arm, reaching out to me.

'Ruth, we all only want what's best for Sam,' she said, and I couldn't stand to hear any more. I looked from Becca to Will, unable to fully comprehend the two of them together. The way she'd just said 'we' when talking about my son.

'He just wanted to know about Sam,' Becca said. 'He came to me, months ago, when Sam was starting with the night terrors. He just wanted to know how bad Sam was. You wouldn't talk to him and so he came to me.'

I stared at her, unable to fully comprehend what I was hearing.

'We didn't mean for this to happen, for us to fall in love. Ruth, you know me, I hated myself for it, but Will loves Sam, I love Sam.' She took a moment and we stared at each other. 'Ruth, I love you. I didn't know how to tell you, we just wanted to—'

'Get rid of me?'

'Get Sam the help he needs. The help you need. The help you both need.'

'THE HELP WE NEED!' I screamed back at her. 'Becca, you are my oldest friend, you know that I'm all Sam needs.'

She shook her head, put her hands out as if to comfort me. 'I think Sam needs much more,' she said quietly. 'He's needed help for a long time. I've tried to tell you, but you won't listen. Ruth, he's bad. He's got severe anxiety, he's bullied at school, has panic attacks, night terrors, tantrums . . . you've refused to see any of it.'

I shook my head, backing away.

'You're his godmother,' I told her. 'You see him every week, he trusts you . . . '

'And I love him,' she pleaded. 'I just want him to have a chance at a normal life. To—'

'I trusted you,' I said, as the enormity of it began to focus in my mind. 'You made me go to that Valentine's dinner at your gym. You introduced me to Rob, you told me to go to his room that night. Did you know who he was? Were you seeing Will then?'

She glanced at Will.

'And you told me to let it all die down when Janine and Ashley started sending . . . ' I looked up. 'Becca, tell me it wasn't you. Tell me it wasn't you that's been sending the letters, the texts, the cupcakes . . . '

They exchanged a look and I gasped as if I'd been punched in the stomach.

'Becca?' I begged. 'Becca? You did that to me, sent me those things? You did that to my car, with him?'

My hand went to my throat. I was panting, the shock of it as real as if I'd been dumped in icy water.

'My car?' I whispered. 'You did that to my car?'

'We just wanted to frighten you a little,' Will said, 'just to prove that you weren't able to look after Sam. I said that doing that to your car was going a bit far but—'

'It wasn't planned,' Becca cut in. 'None of this was planned. I actually thought you sleeping with Rob might be a good thing, get you back out there. I didn't know you'd take it so bad, and then that morning, when Janine threw her phone at you –' she glanced at Will '– you were so upset about it and we just thought, if you got a bit more upset, you'd see sense. You'd see you can't look after Sam when you're under pressure. You're not fit, mentally. You'd see that you both need help. You'd hand Sam over and then, once he was away from you, we could get him the help he needed. And once you were alone, you'd see, see how bad you were.'

I stumbled backwards, unable to take it in.

'Only you didn't do that,' Will said, 'you got sneaky.' He looked at Becca. 'When she told me, when she said what you'd done, well –' he shook his head '– it proves how unhinged you are. You see that now, don't you, Ruth? That's why I came over to your mother's, why I wrote everything out for you to see in black and white. You're delusional.'

'We never meant for it to go so far, you have to believe that.' Becca was coming towards me, her hands outstretched. 'Why couldn't you have just admitted defeat? It's been so hard for you. Why did you have to do all of that?' She pointed to the file, to the list of what I'd done.

'BECAUSE OF SAM!' I shouted, and Becca gave a thin smile.

'It's over now,' she said. 'You see that? You've done too much. I knew it when you told me the other day, you've gone too far.' She glanced at Will. 'I took a copy of the school computer, pictures and files, evidence of what you'd done. You never cleared your history, so I have it all. We're going to call the police and it'll only be a matter of time. You might have that last text, but you've no proof of any others. The police will arrest you soon. If not today, then soon, and Sam will come to us.'

I watched in horror as Becca went over to Will and took hold of his hand. 'It's for the best, Ruth. There's no point in fighting it. You've got to think of Sam, think what's best for him. For your son. You've put him through so much. Think of Sam, Ruth, and what he'd want.'

THIRTY-SIX

I didn't have a plan as I drove to my mother's. They say that when you're in heightened anxiety, you have the 'fight or flight' instinct. To either stay and fight or run, and I was running. I couldn't bear to look at Becca's face any longer, to hear what she'd been doing. I turned over every text, every letter, every time she'd given me advice. It made no sense. It totally made sense. My best friend wanted to steal it all from me. She'd looked at the life I'd lost and wanted it for herself.

'It was Becca,' I told my mother as I got to her house. 'Becca is with Will, she's the one who's been telling him everything. She's the one who's given him all the evidence. And she's the one who's been sending me stuff, doing that to my car.'

'Becca?' My mother's face was confused.

'She's Will's new woman. It's her. She's been helping Will get Sam, it's all her. She wants what I had, what I lost. She's got Will and now she wants Sam.'

'What's Auntie Becca done?' Sam came out of the lounge, Trixie in his arms. He looked so innocent, so confused, my heart burst with love for him.

'Don't call her that,' I said quickly. 'She's not our friend any more, she's been lying to us.' His eyes went wide and I held him tightly. 'I thought Becca was a friend, but she's not. She's been lying to me so she can help your dad. She wants to take you away from me.'

I felt Sam take a gasp and squeezed him tighter.

'What did she do to you?' my mother asked, and I felt a sharp pain as she touched me. 'You're bleeding.'

I turned and looked at the scrape at the top of my left arm. It must've happened when Toby's mother kicked me to the ground. I heard Sam whimper.

'It's all right,' I told him. 'I'm fine, it's nothing.'

'Mummy?'

I felt a tear roll down my cheek. I wiped it away quickly but not before Sam had seen it.

'Mummy?' he asked again, his voice high.

'Your mum's fine.' My mother put her hands on my shoulders and steered me towards the kitchen. 'You go back in there with Trixie, she's the poorly one here. Let's all just calm down.'

Sam stayed in the hallway, frozen.

'Go on, Sam,' my mother said, 'while I get your mother a cup of tea and you can have a biscuit.'

He didn't move.

'Sam –' I smiled at him '– I'm fine, sweetheart, fine. I just need a cup of tea and a minute to think, OK? Then we should probably go, me and you. We'll get a bed and breakfast, a hotel for the night, a . . .'

'Cup of tea,' my mother said, 'and a plaster on that. You're

339

as white as a sheet, no fit state to drive. Sam, get in there and here –' she gave him a chocolate bar '– eat that.'

He slowly went back into the lounge, Trixie in his arms, her mournful eyes looking out on us.

'I haven't got time for this,' I told my mother. 'They were contacting the police as I left. I need a plan. I need to think!'

She was silent for a moment. 'I think it might be best to get the police here,' she said after a while. 'You can't run, Ruth. If you call them, give your side . . . ' she shrugged. 'What's the alternative? You go and stay in a hotel tonight and then what? Tomorrow you leave the country? Don't be ridiculous. Get the police, tell them what Becca and Will have been doing.'

I took a moment. She was right, but I couldn't think of what to say, how to put it. There were my logs, my incident report, but there was also my criminal record and Ashley's accusation of my harassment of her. I closed my eyes, thinking of Ashley, of Janine, of what I'd done to them when they hadn't been to blame at all.

I had no money to run off anywhere and, even if I did, how would that look to social services? Perhaps the only chance I had was to go to the police before they did, before Toby's parents did. If I went to them first, that might count for something.

I picked up my phone.

'Now?' my mother asked. 'You're doing it now?'

I nodded. I got through to the local police department after a few minutes.

'I'm being threatened,' I told them. 'I want it reporting. I've an incident report from when my car was vandalised and now I know who is responsible and I'm being threatened by them. It's Becca Kelly and Will Clarkson, they're the ones who've been sending me abusive texts, letters, following me in their car.' My voice faltered as I said it and thought about the night Glen was stopped. That must have been Becca, or was it Will? Shining the lights in our faces. 'They're threatening to take my son away from me.'

There was a pause.

'Are you in danger now?'

'No. I don't know. I'm not sure.'

'Where are you calling from?'

'My mother's, over by Hadrian's Wall.' I leaned forward. 'I could come by the station later,' I told him, 'make a statement, but I didn't know what the procedure was, I wanted to—'

A loud scream from the lounge stopped me.

'Sam?'

'They're here!' he shouted loudly. 'They're driving up the path!'

'Do you need assistance? Hello?'

I looked at my mother. 'Yes,' I told the police officer, 'send someone over. Now.'

Sam was hysterical. He ran into the kitchen, hugging Trixie who was yelping. He went to the back door, tried to run out, but I stopped him.

'Wait,' I said, 'calm down. We won't let them in and I've called the police.'

He stopped at that.

'The police are coming, no one is taking you anywhere. They'll go when I tell them that.'

'Ruth.' Will was suddenly in the kitchen, his bulky figure dominating the small space. 'We think it's best Sam come with us, in case you leave, in case you run . . .'

I looked behind him to where Becca was. 'He'll be safe

with us,' she told me. 'Let him come home while the police sort it out.'

She looked behind me, to where Sam was.

'Sam?' she said, her voice sickly smooth. 'It's Auntie Becca. You want to come home with me? I've got your favourite pizza and I thought we could watch that film you like, or we could get you a new computer game. Me, you and your dad?'

She was insane. It hit me then, as I watched her. I'd been thinking it was Janine, or Ashley, or Will, that they were the unhinged ones, but as I watched Becca, her eyes alight, trying to cajole Sam out from behind me, I realised it was her, she was insane. Acting like someone I'd never met as she tried to coax my son with promises of pizzas and games, with Will whom she'd called an utter wanker numerous times, Will, who she swore she hated and, now, she was with him? Getting married to him and trying to take my son? She was insane.

'You need to leave right now,' my mother shouted at Becca. 'The pair of you. This is my house and you need to get out.'

'Viv,' it was Will, walking towards us. 'Vivien, calm down, we all just want what's best for Sam . . .'

It was then that Sam darted past us all.

Without a sound he ran out from behind me, right through the house and out of the front door. Becca made a grab for him as he passed, shouting his name, but he was gone. He swung open the door so much that it banged against the wall then my son ran out into the night.

THIRTY-SEVEN

'Sam!' my voice echoed back to me. I could hear my mother's voice behind me shouting to him, could hear Will and Becca shouting. 'Sam, come here, it's not safe!'

I cursed the fact that we hadn't got the money to do the fence, to separate the land. Sam would be running, blindly running in the dark, probably over the farm land now, tripping over rocks, cutting his legs on thistles. There was nothing for miles and he was a frightened boy of eight.

'Please!' I shouted as loud as my lungs would let me. 'Sam, come back!'

I could see Will, using his phone as a torch, walking up the farm land, could hear his voice. I'd already told him it was useless, that there was no way Sam would come running back to him, but he'd refused to leave.

'Sam!' I heard Becca's voice. It sounded close, like she was near the house.

I walked to where it was coming from. If I had any hope of making Sam come back that night, I needed her gone.

'Go,' I said walking up to her. I had an old torch that my mother used, its light dim in the black night, but it was enough to see her stumbling about, her heels digging into the ground as she moved on the uneven terrain. 'You need to leave right now,' I said. 'My son is in danger and he won't come back to me while you're here, while Will's here, so you need to leave and take Will with you.'

She turned to me, her eyes wide. 'I need to make sure he's OK,' she said. 'I can't go with Sam out there, all alone.'

'You made him go out there,' I told her. 'You made him run. If you hadn't have come here my son would still be watching television and he'd be safe.'

She bristled then. 'Your son hasn't been safe for a long time.'

I opened my mouth in disbelief.

'You put on this act, Ruth, like you care about him, that he's your everything, but when it comes down to it, you only care about yourself. I've seen you. You forget, but I've seen everything. I saw you when you first had him, how you didn't love him.'

I let out a shocked gasp. 'I had post-natal depression.'

'Do you know how lucky you were? How lucky you are? And then you go and say you've got depression?' She flung her arm out to the dark world around us. 'There are people out there with real problems – people who are alone, who haven't got a mother like yours. Who haven't got a loving son, who have nobody. And yet, there you are, poor Ruth.'

I stumbled back, shocked by her words.

'Poor, poor Ruth. Lovely house and lovely baby and she's depressed, can't get out of bed. No wonder her husband has an affair and leaves her. And then, what does she do? Does she snap out of it? No, poor Ruth gets anxiety. Depression and anxiety, and loses her shit and wants everyone to rally around her but what about her lovely boy? What about Sam?'

As she was talking, she was walking towards me and, without realising, I was stumbling back, back into the garden behind the house. Her words were filled with venom, a spiteful rage. I was unable to do anything other than watch her face as she talked.

'I'll tell you what happens to Sam,' she said. 'He thinks that having anxiety and depression is the norm. He sees his mum not getting dressed or leaving the house for days and thinks it's perfectly fine, so he starts to do it, and what does his mum do? Does she help him? No. She encourages him. You enable him, Ruth. You're the worst kind of mother there is.'

'I didn't . . .' I couldn't get my words out. 'Sam is fragile, he needs care. He needs me . . .'

'And when he has problems at school, what do you do then, Ruth?' She was approaching me now, getting close. 'You had a little chat with the teacher about how he needs special atten- tion. You get her to *reward* his bad behaviour. Did it even occur to you that Sam has worked it out that the only way to get attention from you is when he's acting up?'

'No, Sam has a serious condition, the doctor—'

'Have you heard of those mothers who live through their children? Who make their children ill so they can get atten- tion? It's called Munchausen's by proxy, Ruth, and Will might not quite believe you're there, but I know it.'

I was at the side of the house now, the area where the ground is rough and uneven. I stumbled over a rock, felt something go underneath me and had to take a few quick steps to regain my balance.

'I knew you'd never give up the one thing that's giving you attention, but you need to think of Sam. That's why I sent you those messages, the letters, the texts. Your ridiculous cupcakes filled with dog shit. Will said it was too much, he didn't want to do it, but I knew it was the only way that it'd work. I know exactly what you're like, Ruth, how you only care about yourself. How selfish you are. You don't deserve Sam. You don't deserve a lovely boy like that, when I've got nothing. It's not fair. It's never been fair, and you don't realise it. That's why we followed you.' She laughed. 'I even got my neighbour's car! I persuaded Will to follow you about so you'd crack. I did all that so you'd stop, give Sam up. See what you're doing to him. See that you're not fit to be a mother. Sam will be so much better with me. He'll get healthy. See what it's like to be out in the world, have a better diet, start hobbies, do things. You need to give him up. You need to give him to me.'

She was close, too close. I could see her face in the dim light, her eyes wide and fierce.

'Never,' I said and pushed her away. 'Sam is never leaving me.'

'Oh, he is,' she said. 'I've finally got you now. Got enough to take Sam away, and enough to keep him away. I'll have the lot, everything you didn't appreciate. Your husband, your son, and we'll be a proper family. Only this time, I won't throw it all away like you did. I'll be the mother that Sam deserves.'

'You will never be Sam's mother!' I pushed her again, harder.

She shook her head, opened her mouth to argue, but my push had made her lose her balance. She did a kind of dance, where she sidestepped over the rough ground and then she went down. I lost sight of her, but I heard her.

346

Heard the bang as she went into the wood, and the crack, and as she screamed I realised where we were – the disused well.

I swung my torch round and saw where she'd fallen, the crack in the wood. I went forward. She was gripping the sides, sat awkwardly at the bottom. Her face was pale as she stared up at me, and I could see the whites of her eyes. I heard her whimper. Saw her hands scrape at the stone on either side of her.

'My leg,' she said. 'I think I've broken my leg.' She let out a wail. A high-pitched cry full of pain.

I looked around, desperately searching for something to lower in. When I couldn't see anything, I got to the ground.

'Here,' I leaned over, put my arm down trying to reach her, but it was useless. She was about a foot away from me. Reaching as high as she could, moaning and crying.

'I need a rope or something,' I told her. 'I need a better light. Hang on.'

'Wait!' she shouted as I scrambled to my feet. 'Don't leave me.'

'I'll be quick,' I told her. 'I just need to get a rope from the house. Or something. I think she's got an old washing line and then I can get you out.'

We stared at each other for a moment. She was panting, and in the semi-darkness I could see her fear, her pained expression. She winced. Let out a howl.

'Hurry!'

I ran inside my mother's house, my heart pounding. I went into the kitchen, pulling open drawers and cupboards, and as I searched the words she'd said before she'd fallen became fresh in my mind. Stinging like a slap.

I was a good mother, I hadn't caused Sam's behaviour. He was a fragile boy. My history of depression had nothing to do with how he was. I'd been so careful to keep it from him. To make my illness something separate. I'd never indulged his, I didn't think. Or had I?

I helplessly looked around, emptying drawers, and then I heard Will's shouts for Sam. They sounded close. I abandoned my search and made my way back to the front of the house, panting and gasping. I saw Will and ran up to him.

'It's Becca,' I told him and my mother, who'd now come back to the house. 'She's fallen down the well at the back. I can't reach to get her out.'

Will moved without speaking. The three of us ran, our lights breaking through the dark. We could hear her whimpering, making small sounds, as if in conversation before we got there.

'Becca?' Will shouted.

And then far off, Becca's reply. 'Don't come any closer!'

The terror in her voice stopped us. Will's light shone around, a pinprick of light breaking lines in the black, and then we saw him.

Sam was standing over the well, his clothes filthy, even in the dim light.

'Sam!' His name escaped me before I could say anything else and he looked up. He looked up straight at me and he smiled. And then I saw what he was holding. He'd managed to lift up one of the flags at the opening of the well, rotated it around and was now levering it up, his face a sheen of sweat. It scraped against the other stones as he moved it and, from below, I heard Becca's frightened cry. A terrified moan along with the grating of the stone as Sam gained purchase and began to tilt it forward.

'Sam?' I said, moving forward. 'Sam, honey, what are you doing?'

He looked up at me, his eyes alight.

I heard Becca say something, between sobs, a strangled, pleading sound.

'It's all right, Mummy,' Sam said, ignoring her, 'I know what to do.'

'Sam?'

'I understand now, Dad,' he said, as Will joined me at my side. 'I'm not going to be soft any more. I know what to do. I have to get rid of the bullies. I have to stand up for myself. Auntie Becca has been playing jokes on us that aren't funny. She's a bully. She did that to our car. She's not behaving nice. She wants to take me away. I know what to do, Mum showed me. You have to put them out of their misery.'

Something clicked at the words and I suddenly saw very clearly what my son was about to do. How he thought he was doing the right thing. The hare that he'd watched me kill at the side of the road, how he'd heard me talk about Toby, all the times I'd told him to stand up for himself, to be brave. Sam had been paying attention and was now doing what I'd been telling him to do in the worst possible way.

'NO!' I went forward as Sam began to lift the stone flag. 'Sam, no!'

He looked at me then, the flag raised in his hands, Becca whimpering, and for a moment time stood still. For a moment he was unsure.

'DROP IT!' Will shouted, and I turned to tell him not to say that, not to use those words, because Sam would take it literally. 'YOU DROP IT RIGHT NOW!'

I ran forward but it was too late.

Sam did exactly as Will told him, and dropped the flag.

I didn't stop running towards him. There was a moment's silence as the stone flag plummeted down the well, and then the sickening sound as it hit her. The dull thud-like sound as her skull shattered. And I grasped Sam in my arms.

THIRTY-EIGHT

The police arrived minutes after Sam had thrown the flag on top of Becca. I'd forgotten I'd called them, asked them to send someone over to have a word about her threatening behaviour, and now she was dead.

Will saw what had happened and began shaking, and it's then that I wonder at my actions. I was calm suddenly. Collected. I knew exactly what I had to do.

'Hello,' the officer shouted, her torch cutting though the light. 'Everyone OK back here?'

'No,' I screamed in answer, and there was real terror in my voice. 'Someone is dead. My ex-husband just killed my friend.'

Will looked up at me, and I stared back at him. Hadn't he done it? Sam had only done as he'd asked.

We never actually had the discussion where we decided that Will would confess to Sam's crime. I told the police what had happened, and Will began to weep silently at the side of me while my mother took Sam back to her house, and he didn't

351

argue the case. Because Will knew. He knew what he'd done and he knew he was to blame. You can't accuse an eight-year-old boy of murder, not when he's just doing as he's told.

He nodded as I told them that Becca had been sending me messages and letters. He wept while they searched her mobile phone, finding all the texts she'd written out. I explained that they'd arrived in an argument, that Will wasn't aware of Becca's behaviour, and after she fell down the well he'd gone to save her and inadvertently pushed a loose stone on top of her instead.

It was a terrible accident. It was manslaughter.

My mother agreed it was all very tragic, and when Will was sent to prison, we decided to sell up and go. She couldn't leave that house after my father died there, but after Becca had died there it was a different story.

Glen had put the idea in my mind, without even knowing. A cruise ship, a tour of the world that lasts for months. Away from the crowds on the open sea. It was the perfect solution. Time away, time to start afresh. It took a while to persuade Sam, who didn't want to go, but I told him it was for the best. There was no way I could go back to being the school secretary, back to the parents at the school gates, the teachers and their gossiping in the staffroom about what had happened. We needed to leave.

My mother sold her house quickly and, for now, we're all living on the ship. In six months we plan to go to Anglesey. Make a new life there with what money we have left over.

I wrote Glen a letter, apologising. Telling him that I'd like to see him again. That by the time we get back in the UK, perhaps we can start over. Perhaps. And I wrote four more letters, anonymous ones.

One to Ashley, one to Janine and one to Rob. Notes of heartfelt apology. And I am genuinely sorry for what I did to them, for the anxiety and fear I caused. For the turmoil I must have put their children in.

The last letter was to Toby Morley-Fenn. His mother never did go to the police, and after Becca died I never returned to the school. I wrote to him, telling him he was brave. I wrote words of what a great boy he was, how he was full of courage and strength. My letter was full of compliments because I couldn't make it full of anything else. I wanted to explain my reasons, to tell him why I did that to him at the back of the school, but I found it hard to write down. Hard to explain that, in trying to protect my son, I hurt so many others.

I never write to Will.

But he writes to me.

By law, I have to tell him where his son is, so he knows how to contact us, but I send nothing else. I don't reply to anything. I don't answer any of his questions or wonder how he is. I can't. My priority is Sam. It always has been and always will be. Writing to Will would jeopardise that, and it's a chance I can't take. If I talk about what happened I might break down and everything would fall to pieces.

He's in his prison and I'm in mine.

I do sometimes look at Sam and wonder if Becca was right. Did I encourage his behaviour? Was it my actions that made him think it was the right thing to do, dropping that stone on her head and killing her, and yes, I think it was. I have to take some of the blame. Even though I wasn't the one to tell him to do it, he got the idea from me.

Sam didn't mean to kill Becca – it's not like he's a murderer or anything. He just thought he was teaching her a lesson. Like

I'd taught Toby a lesson. He thought that's what you did with bullies, that's what you did with people who were in pain. I don't think he would've dropped that flag over the side of the well at all if Will hadn't shouted out to him. But it was my fault that he'd had the idea, and Will's fault that he carried it out.

We did that to him. As his parents. We provided the circumstances for our son to murder someone. We made him do it. We are to blame, not Sam.

Sam's the only one who's innocent in all of this. He's an eight-year-old boy, and I failed him. I've told him that he's not responsible for Becca's death. I've told him that she died of a heart attack in the well that night. I told him that Will had to go to jail for what he did to my car, and as an eight-year-old boy he believes me.

For now.

I've spared him that at least. My son doesn't know he's a killer, and I know it's what any parent would do. Everything I did, all my actions, are what any good parent would've done. I believe that. It might be wrong what I did, but I did it for all the right reasons.

And I can say that with certainty because it's what ties us together in this secret pact, the pact that all parents are in. The unspoken understanding of love.

The love we have for our kids, it cuts through all the bullshit and allows this kind of behaviour to take place.

We are all agreed that we'd do anything for our kids, and as you read this, if you have children, ask yourself what you would've done?

Let your innocent child be punished for the thoughts you put in his head? For him taking some words literally? For the mistakes you made while trying to protect them?

No.

Didn't think so.

We'd do anything for our kids. It's the unspoken rule. The secret pact, and I'm no different to any other mother. I'm no different to you.

ACKNOWLEDGEMENTS

There are so many people who have helped with this book and whom I would like to thank dearly. Firstly, to my family, to my mum and dad for buying me a typewriter back when I was a kid which sparked the ambition for me to write, and for their life-long belief in me even when the rejections were thick and fast. You showed me what it is to be a good parent and I can only hope I'm half as good.

To Stephen, thank you for listening to every thought I had about this book (and every other idea that didn't make it to the page), for your brilliant feedback, for chatting through issues, for your never-ending support and loving me the way you do. I take none of it for granted. To Aidan and Talia, you are the loves of my life and I'm so very lucky to have you both.

To Kirsty Brennan, Jill Pilkington and Heather Peake for reading the early versions and for the wonderful advice and pointers. And to the rest of my family, thank you for always turning out, for the hilarious and uplifting messages and for knowing that you are always there. Your support and friendship is invaluable.

Thanks also to Claire, Murt, Caz, Simon as well as Teresa and Gardi. Also, to my dear friend Paula Daly, thank you for the wine, the meals, the endless chats where we don't take a breath and for matching my giddiness in all things literary. I'd also like to thank Rachelle Upton for telling me a story of revenge over dinner one evening that was both horrifying and inspiring.

A massive thank you to my wonderful agent, Jane Gregory, and the rest of the team: Stephanie Glencross, Mary Jones and Laura Darpetti. I am very fortunate to have such a great team of people behind me. To my brilliant editor, Emma Beswetherick, your enthusiasm for this book has been wonderful and thanks also to the brilliant Hannah Wann, Charlotte Cole and the team at Piatkus.

Finally, I would like to say thanks to all of those that work in schools whom I have come across past and present. I'm pleased to say that I have never met anyone like the staff I've written about in this book and have never observed anything other than compassion and care. And a shout out to all the parents and carers who wait at the school gates, who do the after-school clubs and activities resulting in missed weekends and evenings, who taxi children around, who wait up, who worry and generally put their kids' wellbeing first – you have my admiration.

A Q&A WITH ZOE LEA

What inspired you to write *The Secretary*?

I'd had the idea of a woman performing anonymous acts of revenge in a small community for a while. There was something fascinating about a protagonist empowering herself by making anonymous phone calls, starting rumours and posting things online and then sitting back and watching it all blow up. That idea was batting around in my head, but I was struggling to find a place to set it. I think I was actually picking my daughter up from school when I thought a primary school would be the perfect setting.

Was any of the novel based on your own experience of the school run?

Definitely not! I have never experienced anything like what I wrote about in *The Secretary*, thank goodness!

Why do you think motherhood is such a popular topic in thrillers?

I suppose it's because it's so complex and there's an extraordinary amount to draw on. Everyone's experience of motherhood is different and yet surprisingly similar, so I think any story featuring it will be relatable for parents on some level, however small. It also comes with a huge catalogue of stereotypes and clichés, as well as a great amount of pressure – so challenging the labels associated with motherhood, whilst adding in the pressure of parenting, lends itself well to a narrative that is full of suspense.

What was the hardest part of writing the novel?

Working out the twists in the story. I knew the ending before I started writing, I just had to get Ruth up to that level. It was really enjoyable coming up with the cat-and-mouse game between her and Becca, but creating the flow of narrative so that, hopefully, the reader was kept guessing as to who was behind the sabotage was challenging.

Why did you choose to the set the story in Carlisle?

It's a place I know and love. It's where I went to university and it holds a lot of memories for me. It's also filled with history and I thought a border city was perfect for the setting of a woman on the edge.

What do you do in your spare time, when you're not writing?

I enjoy hiking and try to get a walk in with my family most weekends in the Lake District where we live. I also love reading and my other obsession is Instagram. I'm an avid booksta-grammer, and like to share my love of books and the fells. I'm over there as @zoeleawriter if anyone fancies coming to say hello!

To find out more about Zoe, visit her website www.zoelea.com or follow her on social media:

@zoeleawriter
/zoeleawriter
/zoeleawriter

To find out more about the Teen team, head here: www.teamteen.com or follow us on social media:

Newport Community
Learning & Libraries